The Spirits of Wintermist

Book One of the Circle of Union

Francis D. Homer

Order this book online at www.trafford.com
or email orders@trafford.com

Most Trafford titles are also available at major online book retailers.

Printed in the United States of America.

ISBN: 978-1-4669-6203-3 (sc)
ISBN: 978-1-4669-6204-0 (hc)
ISBN: 978-1-4669-6205-7 (e)

Library of Congress Control Number: 2012918425

Trafford rev. 10/02/2012

www.trafford.com

North America & international
toll-free: 1 888 232 4444 (USA & Canada)
phone: 250 383 6864 • fax: 812 355 4082

Dedicated to my wonderful wife Lillian and Rohan, the cat that saved my life.

Chapter One

Legend said the Thanatos Mountains were unclimbable.

It wasn't the chill of early spring that caused Corporal Gunther Dane to shiver. As he crossed the compound, he stopped, and his eyes roamed from the darkness of the valley to the brilliant white of sunlight on the snow-covered mountainsides. He tilted his head until he looked straight up, staring at peaks that were smudges against the dark, blue sky. Smudges no man had ever reached.

Gunther pulled his eyes from the mountain and looked toward the keep. He took a sip of his jada and watched the light breeze buffet the country's flag. The corporal paused a moment to salute his country.

The steady light of lamps spilled from the keep's windows while candlelight flickered from the barracks. From the stables drifted the voices of the groomsmen talking softly to the horses. On the palisade, he heard guards exchange quiet greetings with their relief. He took another sip of his drink then continued across the parade ground.

Reaching the wall, he climbed to the walkway and started his rounds. Little ever happened, but the men had to keep their senses trained on the pass. Vigilance was important. Inattentiveness was rewarded with death. During the Underdweller War, he watched the quiet countryside erupt into chaos in the time it took a candle to flicker.

"Good morning watch, Corporal."

Gunther turned, his hand automatically falling to the hilt of his dagger. His eyes took in the squat man behind him. No one that bulky should move so silently, yet he had often watched the dwarf move through the night and slip past the enemy.

"Halprin! You know better than to sneak up behind me."

The dwarf laughed as he combed his beard with stubby fingers. "Jumpy, Gunther?" The human jerked his head toward the mountain. Halprin smiled. "Aye, give me shivers they do. I be happy returned to North Wall."

"I thought dwarfs loved mountains?" a voice called from down the wall.

"Love Torscain Mountains, but not these. Not natural. Unnatural, with strange creatures."

"Oh ho, you believe the tales that they rose during a battle of the gods."

"Know not. I let gods handle own affair."

Gunther had rounds before he broke his fast, so he left Halprin to his discussion with the other soldier. He rubbed his chin as he recalled when he first met the dwarf during the Underdweller War. Neither were professional soldiers. He was a simple woodsman, and Halprin worked his clan's mines. It was a sense of duty that made both answer the Queen's call.

They were in a mixed regiment, humans and dwarves side by side. They had become partnered and fought many battles, saving each other countless times. They spent nights over mugs of grog, talking about their lives before the war and their plans for afterward. Neither gave a thought to staying with the army after hostilities ended.

Gunther had nightmares about the day they made the choice to serve a ten-year term. That day, they watched the funeral pyres in The Valley.

The Valley was the last major conflict of the war. It had been the costliest battle, more than five thousand of the queen's soldiers died preventing an attempted breakout of the Underdwellers. Gunther's company arrived the day after, but the evidence of the ferocious battle lay all around.

The sight of so many dead did not affect Gunther. In three years, he had seen horror many times. What shook him, made him spend hours reevaluating his feelings and beliefs, were the nine weaponsmasters escorting nine coffins.

Weaponsmasters are skilled in the use of multiple weapons, from small boot daggers to large siege engines. They were schooled in the art of combat and studied strategy. They performed many duties throughout the kingdom, from bodyguards for high-ranking nobles to commanding the local militia. Many dukes had a weaponsmaster in their household. A number of older weaponsmasters had their own salle, where they trained people in the art of combat.

The other duty of a weaponsmaster was to serve the Queen in time of conflict. When charged by a representative of the crown, they assumed command with full authority of the crown. They defended the land, planned campaigns, and led men in battle. Their authority surpassed that of dukes. They were second only to the Queen.

A duty they performed on rare occasions was to escort the fallen bodies of the royal family and certain nobles. This duty was the weaponsmaster's way of paying respect to one of honor. Even when there was a number of the nobility to be escorted, only one weaponsmaster acted as honor guard, never nine.

That day in The Valley, Gunther watched as the procession left. Within the nine simple pine boxes were common people, neither royal nor noble, just ordinary soldiers. They held the pass and kept their commander, a weaponsmaster, alive. The nine held the pass. It was the weaponsmasters' choice, their honor to escort the Heroes Nine home.

That night, Gunther and Halprin sat under a tree. Neither spoke, but both reached the same decision. Their duty, like The Heroes Nine, weaponsmasters, the dukes and queen, was to protect those who cannot protect themselves. Some had to forgo their lives to hold the rest safe. They enlisted for a ten-year term, at the end of which they would be given a small land grant.

Five years later, Gunther had two years left in his service to the queen. He still had to decide if he would stand down, take the small land grant, and live a peaceful life. The other choice was to continue and eventually have a comfortable retirement in a small village as an official of the queen.

For now, he had a duty here. The pass was lightening as the sun moved closer to topping the foothills. He drank the remainder of his cold jada and stepped up to the wall and looked north. Sunlight had moved to the base of the mountains, and Gunther could clearly see the only known pass through the Thanatos Range. That pass was the reason for the outpost and the North Wall, fifty miles south. Beyond the pass was the Northland.

Little was known about the land north of the mountains. In the last thirty years, the crown prohibited travel after losing many expeditions. When the king died, his daughter continued the prohibition. Since the Underdweller War, the Queen decided they needed to learn if the Northlands were a threat.

Halprin clambered onto a small ledge and laid his dwarvish thrower on the wood palisade. He adjusted his battle-ax and took a deep breath. "I feel the chill breeze of death blowin' from them mountains." He looked at his friend. "Aye, death be on the wind. Tell you, Gunther, from mountains come death."

"That's what you said at Tinkers Ford." Halprin always made dire predictions. He claimed the Grotto men sired great fighters with the ability to know danger. It was a gift that ran in the Goldlief clan.

"Right I was."

"Three weeks later, when we were four valleys away."

Halprin crossed his arms and hmphed. “Underdwellers follow their own time.”

“Or it was a counterattack from our own assault.”

“This different. We attacking nothing. That brings up, Captain sent out patrol, now two weeks overdue.”

“They may have found another pass.”

“This be only path. All know. Explored by humans and dwarf. No other pass, just misery in these accursed mountains.” He shook his thrower at the mountain. “Called Thanatos Mountains. Evil lurks in them.” Halprin frowned. “You say postin’, nice relaxin’ time, a reward. A few patrols, party at night, stand guard, at night party. Now stuck in middle of nowhere, no ale, no women, no ale!”

Gunther laughed. “You had plenty of that before we left the North Wall.”

“Never nuff celebratin’. Did I say no ale?”

“Think of the celebrating when we return. We only have a month left.”

Grumbling, Halprin turned and glared up the pass.

Accustomed to his friend’s contentious ways, Gunther just smiled and turned away. Hooking his mug to his belt, he rubbed his face and caught a whiff of bacon. His stomach rumbled a protest. As corporal, his duty was to ensure the night guards were relieved. With that done, he was ready to break his fast.

Halprin grabbed his arm. “Gunther, human eyes better at distance. Look!”

Gunther looked over his shoulder. “It’s called a mountain.”

“No, you floppin’ galwomp! Where the pass disappears.”

“Halprin, that’s fifteen miles away, you can’t see anything . . .” Gunther’s voice trailed off.

Flowing from the pass, a thin black line wrapped around the base of a mountain before it seeped into the valley. Sunlight was flashing from numerous reflective surfaces, otherwise, they would have missed it entirely. From this distance, it looked thin, but Gunther knew it had to be large. The corporal shook his head.

"I knew it. Death is coming."

"It may be nothing." He didn't sound convincing to himself.

"It be a glorious battle."

Gunther turned and looked into the courtyard. Spotting a bored-looking soldier, he sent him for the outpost's wizard. After a delay of several minutes, a man dressed in plain brown and green robes left the keep.

Wizard Amikin was a slender man with slicked-back dark hair. His beard was short, the preferred manner of the queen's soldiers. He had none of the wrinkles or the silver hair associated with magic users, the look that would come with age. Long dexterous fingers wrapped around the rungs, and he flowed up the ladder. As he stepped onto the walkway, the wizard's breath came out in a white mist that swirled around him.

"Wizard Amikin," Gunther said, bowing his head, "I need something at the base of the mountain identified."

Wizard Amikin squinted, then nodded. "This is no problem." His lips barely moved as he chanted, and from within his robe, he pulled a dirty rag and scrubbed the air. As the spell took effect, the air under the rag swirled and solidified. Within the area, the thin black line resolved into individual shapes.

Black-armored men marched four abreast, their features hidden by black helms. They carried lethal polearms, weapons topped with curved blades or triple-pronged tips. A new column marched into view, revealing fighters dressed in the same black material but armed with swords.

Mingling with the troops were men on a breed of horse never seen in the south. They moved back and forth, giving unheard commands emphasized with curt hand movements. Their black armor was of iron bands with gold or silver inlays that adorned the shoulder plates. The helms had scraps of cloth that streamed behind them.

Gunther sent for the captain of the outpost. Shortly, Captain Alphron stood beside him. Tall and thin, the captain held an air of the nobility. Even in the primitive conditions of the outpost, he managed to be immaculate. His uniform appeared freshly washed and pressed, the gold braid rope on his left shoulder looked new, instead of two months old. He smelled faintly of soap, and his face was smooth shaven.

Captain Alphron studied the view. It was showing large wagons drawn by strange creatures. The creatures were low to the ground, with large muscled legs that ended in claws. They had beaks for jaws and a hide of sickly gray leather. Despite their bulk, they moved with a fluid grace.

"How many?" Captain Alphron's right hand pulled on his chin, a nervous habit he had when uneasy or scared.

"Enough. See their bloody army from here," Halprin said.

Gunther shifted his view from the image to the pass. "Thousands."

"Damn. Damn. Damn!" The captain turned and looked at his little outpost. A small stone keep, a few wooden buildings, and a wooden wall. "We're only a hundred and twenty." In a hopeful voice, he said to no one, "Our wizard will stop them."

Gunther's mind drifted to the advice he received during the Underdweller War. A weaponsmaster lectured on stratagems, "Use your imagination, set it free. No matter how wild an idea, attempt it. It's the unexpected that wins battles."

Gunther studied the foothills around the outpost. The trees were respectable in size, but farther up where the trees ended, large boulders and rock outcropping dotted the landscape. Over the years, landslides had ripped large chunks from the mountain. Boulders, trees, earth, and small plants had cascaded down the slope, leaving great scars. The outpost sat in one of the scars. The debris had deposited across the stream, creating a dam and forming a small lake.

Gunther studied an outcropping five hundred paces away. Nature had eroded the mountain, and a segment hung in the air, waiting to be set free. Patrols avoided passing beneath the outcropping since it wasn't unusual for rocks to tumble down. If the wizard could release the large volume, it would travel down the mountain and roll across the valley floor.

"Can magic delay them?" the captain asked. "Long enough for reinforcements from the North Wall."

Wizard Amikin shook his head. "If they have wizards, they can undo my magic."

"What about throwing it at something else?" Gunther pointed at the outcropping. "Could you bring that down?"

Wizard Amikin stroked his bearded chin. "It looks ready to come down on its own."

Gunther quickly explained his plan, "We wait until they're almost on top of us, then Wizard Amikin brings the side of the mountain down."

Captain Alphron softly tapped his chin. "Yes, yes, it just may work. We can't fight thousands of troops, but we will slow them."

"Gunther said this be a boring assignment." Halprin's smile showed through his beard.

Captain Alphron looked at the simmering vision in front of him. The column of warriors was still filing past. "We should plan for retreat. Once they breech the slide, they will . . ."

Mage Jedrowler watched from the plane of Between. For a moment, the vision of the advancing army blossomed. Then the spirit was unable to maintain the mage here. The pull on the golden cord was too strong. Blackness exploded. A flash of searing white pain struck the soul of Jedrowler Kefzo, and the mage bit back a scream. He snapped from the astral plane hard, his noncorporeal form unable to acclimate to physical sensation. For a brief moment, he was unsure where he dwelled. Only the intervention of the Spirit kept him semioriented.

Jedrowler struggled briefly to hold his trance. As it stabilized, he directed a small part of his energies to heal the minor damage along his channels. Even a damage this minor would jeopardize the spell casting. He devoted his adult life to this spell, and he wasn't going to have it collapse from a minor detail.

Jedrowler had been setting the anchors when the Spirit led him north, past the North Wall to the outpost. This vision was strong and detailed, and he was sure the Spirit had shown him what is, not what will be. Mage Jedrowler knew the dangers that lurked within the range, and for generations, the outpost was the first line of defense. It had withstood countless attacks of Underdwellers, night creatures, barbarian tribes, and occasional mad wizards.

Nausea pushed at his shields and threatened to overwhelm him. Pushing the images aside, he concentrated on firming his trance. The trance was preparation for the spell he was to cast in thirty hours. An upcoming invasion was important, but the spell took priority. The spell would protect and heal the land, stop what he had just been shown.

Mage Jedrowler reviewed the last few hours spent in astral form. It had been a long night traveling the Dukedom of Mead, activating anchors he had prepared and placed over the years. They would hold the magic and keep the spell functioning long after he passed to the other side. When he finished with the anchors, he stood within the astral plane near the edge of Mead and watched the predawn activity. As he gazed over the valley spanning the North Wall, a Spirit came to him and insisted on dragging him north.

Jedrowler scolded himself. His mind had wandered, and he needed to concentrate on the present, not the past. He refocused, and layer upon layer of meditation formed. As his astral self centered on his physical form, he allowed his earthly awareness to enter. He slid from the astral plane to his body.

He smelled a hint of mountain laurel drifting on the wind and felt the rays of the morning sun upon his face. Under him, he felt the hard rock of the plateau. Keeping his eyes closed, he smiled and basked in the peacefulness around him.

His stomach gave a large grumble, the result of three days of fasting.

Mage Jedrowler slowly opened his eyes and witnessed the sun slide above the far distant mountains. Lake Mead stretched toward those distance mountains, its shoreline merging with the blueness of the mountains. Sunlight highlighted the fishing vessels as they left their home port, seeking the bounty of the waters.

At this end, the lake slipped into the gorge in a three-hundred-foot plunge to crash on the rocks below. The fall's mist filled the gorge and shrouded the Hellion River. Within the mist, the Spirits sang as they started their morning dance.

"Master" a young hand touched the mage's shoulder "it's time."

"Juice," Mage Jedrowler croaked. The young lad, dressed in a robin egg-colored students robe, handed the mage a flask. With a nod of thanks, Jedrowler took the flask, allowing the rim to touch his lips momentarily. Only a small amount dribbled into his mouth. He returned the flask, and the young lad quickly danced back a couple of steps.

"I have your room ready, Master."

"Please, help me to my feet, Anton." The mage slowly uncrossed his legs.

Anton approached from behind and slipped his hands under his master's shoulders. Jedrowler knew the student had his eyes squeezed shut. He heard the quickening of his breath and felt the tremor in his arm. The young lad quickly pulled him to his feet, then quickly retreated.

Jedrowler swayed at the edge of the plateau and turned his gaze from the far distant mountains of the east, to the near mountains of the south. Nestled at the base of the mountain, Duke Altrid's keep overlooked the southern pass to Gammount. Ages past, the keep guarded Mead from the barbarians of the south. Now it was symbolic since the barbarian people of Lashtar and Mead were one country.

A smile touched his face as he recalled his ninth season of life. The wizard at Gammount tested him and pronounced the presence of the mage's gift. His father brought him north to the city of Wintermist and the Mage School of Wintermist.

Before they went to the school, Jedrowler's father, a captain in the king's guard, paid respects to Duke Nardan, father to the present duke. While visiting Duke Nardan, his mage tested Jedrowler and was shocked at the strength of the glow surrounding the boy. "For centuries, there has not been personal magic this powerful!" He brought out a handkerchief and mopped his forehead and was heard muttering, "The ancient texts said a powerful mage would ride north and create a union."

That night, the young boy watched the city of Wintermist sparkle with the lights of countless homes. A half moon lit Lake Mead, and in the distance, the twin sentinels, the mountains on either side of the gorge, glowed. He breathed the fresh air of the mountains and the lake and heard crystalline voices dreaming in sleep.

With his head pillowed on his arm, the young boy fell asleep at the window.

The rising sun found Jedrowler, his father, and one of the duke's men moving through the early morning activity of Wintermist. They passed through the city streets and climbed the slope to the slate table surrounding the base of the twin sentinels. A roadway built of slabs of pudding stone and flanked by granite walls curved past the temple to Odian then across the gorge. It passed the mage school and through the gatehouse of Wintermist Wall. Small flecks of quarts imbedded in the conglomerate glittered from sunlight, making the road a diamond way.

Approaching Wintermist Bridge, Jedrowler heard crystalline voices.

"Da, who's singing?"

Before his Da could answer, the duke's man looked at the young boy and said, "What singing?"

"The crystal voices."

Surprised, the duke's man turned to the elder Kefzo. "Few hear the Spirits of the mist."

As the three crossed the bridge, Jedrowler looked over the low railing and within the swirling mist saw nebulous figures dancing. He slipped from his horse and drifted to the railing.

In the mist, he saw Spirits dance and sing the dawn song.

Welcome morning welcome light
Bring us a day filled with life
Allow the light to fill us all
Positive energy all around

Jedrowler sang with the Spirits, his voice uniting with theirs. As he sang, the Spirits rose and swirled around him dancing to the tempo. The falls became a hushed whisper, and the wind died to nothing. His soul rose with happiness and contentment. When the Spirits parted, their patriarch drifted to Jedrowler. As the Spirits sang the song of welcome, the large Spirit smiled and caressed the boy's face, then leaned forward and kissed his forehead.

Jedrowler had come home.

Anton watched his master inhale deeply. As he exhaled, he made sounds of contentment. "There's nothing like the early morning spring air and the dawn song to make one feel alive."

"I agree, Master, but please move away from the edge, you're still unsteady."

Anton felt the slight tremor of the ground and unconsciously took a step back. He knew the mountain was honeycombed with countless tunnels and was weak, despite the best works of the dwarves. He looked over his shoulder. Somewhere in the past, an unknown event provoked the mountain to shake off chunks. Where once a smooth face rose to the sky, now a cupped depression and a jagged, broken face overlooked Lake Mead.

"You should see this view," Jedrowler said.

"I see it just fine, Master." He looked at Jedrowler and swayed from the shaking. "The mountain moves."

Jedrowler turned and looked at his young assistant. "We have been working on controlling your fears for four years."

"There's nothing to control, Master. I have no fear of magic."

Jedrowler stepped from the edge and slowly circled the lad. Anton's left eye twitched, his breath increased and beads of sweat ran down his forehead.

The mage stopped in front of Anton and looked in his eyes. "Fear is the killer of confidence, the mother of indecision. For other users of magic, fear does not affect their use like it does a mage. A wizard's magic is outside, external. A mage pulls magic into them and uses their personal magic to tame it. If the Living Magic senses fear, it will turn on you, maybe kill you."

"I believe you, Master."

"You believe, but still you allow one great fear to control you." Jedrowler laid a hand on Anton's shoulder and gave it a light squeeze. "Magic is great within you. At twelve, you were already manipulating magic as a wizard. Your duke's wizard saw the power you have and taught you. Before sending you here, he named you wizard. If you wish to be a mage, you must learn what we taught you about fear and magic."

Anton looked down at his toes and mumbled, "A mage calls magic, shapes it with his personal magic."

"And?"

"Emotions get in the way and break the concentration." He looked up at his teacher. "Master, I have my emotions under control. I slip into the mage trance and leave emotions behind."

Jedrowler nodded. “As always, you’re skirting the issue.” Anton clasped his hands in front of him.

“Fear is a base emotion. Unrestrained, it drives the Living Magic away. The Living Magic feels your fear and thinks there’s danger.”

“I don’t have that fear all the time.”

“An unreasonable fear is always there. Casting a spell can trigger your fear. What makes mages all powerful is the fact we are in control of our emotions. You need to learn to control emotions.” He sighed, “In the five years you have been here, you haven’t done a leap.”

“It’s the bridge. I feel the way it shakes.”

Jedrowler held up his hand. “That’s your fear talking. The bridge is solid rock. The dwarves inspect it every year and pronounce it solid.” The mage indicated for them to start walking. “By hiding, you’re missing a beautiful sight. The Spirits have a lovely dance.”

“I watch the Spirits from the base of the falls.”

“That is nothing compared to being among the dancers.”

“I can’t,” Anton said quietly.

“Have faith.”

Around the plateau, mage students were casting spells while priests and priestesses moved around, blessing and cleansing the area. Around the plateau, workers had stacked supplies, laid out tools, and begun work. The first structure held seating for guests. Mage Jedrowler required people from all walks of life, so representatives of the guilds, dignitaries of noble houses, and even the queen’s representative would be present. Common folks randomly chosen by Mage Jedrowler would join the upper class. The people were the land, and this spell required the people of Mead.

Anton stopped at the stairs and looked at his teacher. “Aren’t you afraid my fear will ruin your spell?”

“This is an oxymoron. Fear drives the Living Magic away, but Ancient Magic is not driven away easily. It is actually drawn to fear. You will drive the Living Magic away, and the Ancient Magic will fill the void. We need its incredible strength.”

"It's almost impossible to control. Nacromages of old were powerful, but even they had a hard time with control."

"We know more about magic than they did. I will have it wrapped in the magic concentrated within the circle. The practitioners of the many disciplines will form their casting then I will bind it into one. Then the ten in the circle will be one."

"And I channel the power."

Mage Jedrowler nodded. He indicated for Anton to move along. Sunlight reached partway down the steps, then oil lamps gave a dim, flickering light. No mage lights bobbed in the breeze, and no runes, prevalent throughout the school, glowed. Before turning down the steps, Anton's eyes fell on the viewing stand. "A spell where the spectators are part of the casting."

"The ones in the circle have symbols of the land, and our guests are symbols of the people."

The lad nodded and continued down the stairs. "I can't figure out one part. I'm the channel, their link. Everything will flow through me."

"Anton, you have a strong sense of self. I know of no one who can keep from getting lost in the chaos of the binding. You'll bring control to Union."

"That's not bothering me." He looked at the mage. "Can I channel from my homeland?"

"It's doubtful."

"My commitment to my duke—"

"Let me handle your duke."

They reached the base of the stairs and stood in the convoluted hallway. The school was subject to the will of the living force, so mages had directed workers along the flow of magic.

Stairs tilted at strange angles or doubled around and turned into a vertical ascent. Doors sprouted at irregular intervals, and hallways flowed from straight, angled corridors into coiled tunnels that swayed in the current of magic. This construction allowed magic to flow smoothly or concentrate in workrooms.

Runes etched or painted on the walls filled the halls with light. The runes protected the school from the wayward magic students unwittingly released.

"Except for what I prescribed, no magic from the foot of the stairs and up," Jedrowler said.

In silence, they continued, each lost in his own thoughts. As they walked down a spiral staircase, Jedrowler spoke, "Anton, before we do the second half of the spell, you must lose this fear."

"I have tried. You don't know what it is like." Anton's voice raised an octave and cracked.

Jedrowler held Anton back, "You're not the first to have an unreasonable fear." He looked toward the ceiling, his eyes unfocused. "There once was a student who had a great fear of ants."

"Ants?"

"Ants. So bad he would freeze. He came close to having his powers blocked."

He spoke as they continued for his room. Along the way, they passed unfamiliar mages and wizards, servants and scholars. With the casting approaching, the school experienced a dramatic rise in visitors. This was the greatest use of magic, and everyone wanted to witness the symphony of power Mage Jedrowler would conduct.

"What did they do?"

"He knew he had to face his fear. As a first year student, he had not earned the privilege of a private room, so he asked his roommate for help. He asked for an ant brought to their room. The plan was for him to stare it down."

"That doesn't sound hard. A little ant can't hurt you."

"A little height can't hurt you either." A small grin played on Jedrowler's face. "The roommate cast a hold spell, keeping the ant on the bed and another. When the student returned from his lesson, the poor student found an ant the size of a wolf hound on his bed."

"By the gods, what did he do?"

"He let out a shriek heard throughout the school. mages, including the mage master, came running. The roommate explained to the senior mages, then they all waited hours while the student huddled in the corner, eyes wide, face white as the mists. He refused to run. Sometime later, he stammered to the thing. What he said is not important. What is important is he was facing his fear. After hours of being alone with the ant, he approached and reached out. He touched his fear.

"He started petting the ant like a dog then sat on the bed and put his arm over it. It took bravery, but he overcame his fear." They stopped at Jedrowler's door.

Anton smiled as he opened the door. "I never knew you were afraid of ants."

"Me?"

Anton chuckled. "You know the story too well. Who else would know?"

"The student's roommate."

"You?"

"Years later, I found out I did the right thing, but a dangerous thing. If it had not worked, it could have made things worse. A mind healer told me they desensitize a person by making their phobia an outlandish caricatures of real life. But they need to know the person and understand them." Jedrowler shrugged and indicated the room.

Sunlight, from the large bay window, greeted them. A crystalline note sounded as the breeze from the open window jounced the chandelier's crystals. Morning sunlight passed through the crystals, creating rainbows that chased each other around the small room. On the right-hand wall, the fireplace sent a wisp of smoke up the chimney. Two doors faced each other, one leading to his sleeping quarters and the other his workroom.

On the window ledge, elvish flowers turned their red blossoms to look outside. These flowers grew in the land of the elves, and they never withered. Elves gave them as a symbol of a never dying bond. Jedrowler received this batch from the elvish delegation that arrived the previous week.

Mage Jedrowler sat on the couch and faced the window while Anton brought a decanter of juice and placed it on the low table in front of the couch.

"You must rest, Master."

Mage Jedrowler nodded and lay down. As he wiggled his shoulders into the couch, he asked, "Is everyone here?"

"Mage Kytril had a late start from Gammount yesterday. He should be here at midday."

He hesitated a moment, then asked, "Master, I'm still not clear why you need a mage from the Western High Peaks School."

"For the Vlynies, the air elementals."

"Why bring a strange mage?"

"I don't have the mastery Mage Kytril does."

"That scholar comes with him, the one who caused a ruckus with Mage Umber two years ago."

"He comes on behalf of the Queen." Mage Jedrowler chuckled. "Hopefully, he'll be careful who he argues with."

"Isn't he some type of prophet?"

Mage Jedrowler nodded. "Ambrus Diamox, the reluctant prophet. He calls prophecies the ravings of a mind gone mad." He looked up at Anton. "Don't argue with him, or he'll leave you doubting your own existence."

Anton spread a blanket over the mage. "They should be in time for the midday meal."

Mage Jedrowler's stomach gave a loud rumble, and Anton regretted mentioning the meal. Mage Jedrowler looked at his midsection and sighed. "The price of creation."

"After the casting, the chef has a feast that will rival Duke Altrid's harvest celebration." Anton felt his mouth running, but couldn't stop it.

"Sea Kotter?"

"Mage Master Gardner has it coming from his homeland. The chef will bake it in cows butter and serve it with a lemon sauce."

A large rumble escaped Mage Jedrowler's stomach. He laughed. "I believe we should stop talking about food." Anton started turning away, and the Mage grabbed his right arm.

"Remember, at the feast, I want you seated to my right." Anton felt the love pour from his teacher's eyes, "Anton, I have faith. You will make my dream a reality."

Anton bowed his head as he softly said, "Thank you, Master."

Mage Jedrowler smiled as he tucked his hands under the blanket and sank his head into the pillow. As sleep quickly carried him into comfortable oblivion, Anton quietly slipped from the room.

Chapter Two

"It shall come to pass. A shaman shall unite the tribes of Terrapin Xon. Then Terrapin Xon shall command the combined might of the known world." King Rathveil's brown and green robes flowed in the cool breeze from the open window. He held the Sacred Scroll in his hands and looked at the man in shaman's robe.

"So say the Sacred Scrolls." Shaman Charara Kilar bowed his head.

King Rathveil turned and bowed his head to the rack holding nine other scrolls. As he rolled up the scroll, he smiled and said, "We are fulfilling prophecy."

"The priestesses of Norge disagree."

"Thirty years ago, the Czaran and her Voice were to be feared." King Rathveil stepped up to the scroll rack and replaced the Sacred Scroll of Prophecies. The design of King Rathveil's private study mirrored the ones in the shamans' wagons. There was a small desk and the rack of Sacred Scrolls on one wall. On the wall opposite the desk, a large map of Terrapin Xon, the nearby country of Norge; and along the southern edge, a red jagged drawing of the Thanatos Mountains. The only other item in the room was a mirror by the window.

"Thirty years ago, this was a few buildings and tents, a place for the tribes to gather. Now look at our city."

The wind carried the sounds of a living city through the open window. Cries of vendors echoed from the market, and the beat of hammers on metal and wood could be heard. Nearby, the growl of an annoyed wildebeast overrode the sound of children playing. Dogs barked in the distance, and the whine of a horse drifted from across the river.

Taking the two steps needed, King Rathveil looked out the window. To his right, the Thanatos Range reached to the heavens. Their snowcapped peaks and hidden glaciers fed the water of the Yau River, whose western bank Gareth sat on. During King Rathveil's rule, those banks grew with shops and warehouses. Barges, their decks loaded with marble or lumber from ancient forests, slipped up to docks. Food arrived from farms, and other goods came from new villages.

Across the river, the grasslands held the tents and wagons of the representatives of the wandering tribes. It was the end of the annual gathering, and they were preparing to return to their tribes and resume their travel around the Northland. Many people clung with the ways sent forth in the Sacred Scrolls, a practice King Rathveil encouraged as he believed in keeping traditions alive, remembering their heritage and their ancestor's sacrifice.

For thousands of years, the Sacred Scrolls commanded them to rebuild a land damaged by the war of the gods. The tribes followed routes laid out in the Sacred Scrolls, performing their duties like planting and tending trees and delicate grass. In the high hills and rolling plains, they planted crops to feed themselves and the wildlife. Slowly, Terrapin Xon moved from an empty wasteland to a garden of life.

As the scrolls commanded, each year, the nomadic tribes sent representatives to Spring Gather along the banks of the Yau at Gareth. They meet with the tribe that was leaving and the new tribe that would spend a year as the guardians of the mountains. The guardian tribe protected the land from evil that dwelled in the Thanatos Mountains. Only a few buildings stood in Gareth, one belonging to the Voice of the Czaran. The Czaran of Norge and her Voice were commanded by the scrolls to pass on the commands of the gods.

"Ten years ago, Norge was a concern." King Rathveil looked down on the city. "We were growing. Our city was forming, and our warriors were honing their skills. While we followed the scrolls and eliminated evil in the mountains, our people created new prosperities." He turned to the shaman. "Our new destiny is before us. Remember, Charara, we followed the Czaran's interpretation. We lived day to day, traveling the land in our wagons. Our tribes scattered, our people divided."

"Our gods gave us the scrolls."

"But interpreted by the priestesses of Norge, the Czaran claims divine insight." He clenched his fist, his arms shaking. "They have no interest in healing the land or serving the gods. The sisterhood only wants power over us."

"They have the Sacred Scrolls of Tantrinlonrum."

"Damn those scrolls. Only the Ten Sacred Scrolls matter!" King Rathveil's furious outburst caused Shaman Kilar to step back. He snatched a scroll from the rack. Holding it up he quoted from memory. "'The shaman shall grow powerful and shake from the people the guiding hand of the Tantrinlonrum.' The Scroll of Beginning, you know it well. It tells of our greatness, how Terrapin Xon ruled all."

"It talks of our fall because of the false god."

"What false god? The one the priestess says? Our scrolls state we were powerful because of the god we worshipped. It was our devotion to our forgotten god that we were chosen to heal the land. We were forced to worship the gods of Norge because they are jealous of the unknown one." King Rathveil pointed his finger at Shaman Kilar. "He waits for us to prove ourselves.

"It's time to become what we once were. Then our god will return and teach us his name." He turned to the scroll rack and talked softly. "The Czaran, she does not scare me. Our people are dedicated, and our Users of the Unseen Force are as powerful as hers."

"The Ten Sacred Scrolls and the Sacred Scrolls of Tantrinlonrum forbid the use of the Unseen Force."

King Rathveil put the scroll on the rack. "'Shaman, hold not to the use of the Unseen Force. Only that needed to teach and heal shall be used.' The other passage, 'No User of Unseen Forces shall dwell within the tribes.'" He stepped behind his desk. "Well, none do. Force Shapers live in the city, not among the tribes."

"We shamans use more of the Unseen Force than our fathers."

"An ability you don't mind. You're the most powerful shaman in Terrapin Xon."

"I never said I disagree with this path."

King Rathveil sat and looked at his shaman. Charara was his friend and confidante. When they met, Charara was an apprentice to the shaman of another tribe, and Rathveil had just become the shaman of his tribe. The old one had died of natural causes a few weeks previously. His tribe met Charara's as they traveled from their spring camp to their summer camp. Custom dictated they camp as one and join in a celebration.

Charara Kilar sat at a campfire and listened as a young Rathveil spoke of the tribe's destiny. As the skins of qwind decreased in volume, he saw the wisdom in the words. Before the night ended, he pledged to follow Rathveil into the future. Two years later, Rathveil set in motion the events to unite the tribes, and Charara encouraged his tribe to follow.

The only command of Rathveil he did not follow was the spirit walk in the Thanatos Mountains. Charara's spirit walk was deep in the land, along the border of the plains of the great cats. He traveled to the plains and spent his week among the tall grasses. There, he found his center. In that week, he grew from an apprentice to a shaman born to lead the people on the spiritual path to heal their souls and to keep the teachings of the Sacred Scrolls alive.

"I'm questioning why you don't eliminate Norge. You've had many confrontations with the Voice of the Czaran."

King Rathveil looked at the map. His eyes wandered to the Thanatos Mountains, where his first spirit walk found him. He had his spirit vision and walked the land of dreams while on the slopes of those mountains. On the paths of silver light, his spirit guide appeared and revealed his destiny.

"Over the years, you watched my dream take shape. We lay layer by layer. Each layer was made strong before moving to a new layer. We have powerful warriors and powerful force shapers, but lack knowledge. To fight Norge, we need powerful and knowledgeable Force Shapers. To the south is a land with more knowledge than the priestess of Norge. Their Unseen Force is different. That will be the next layer for our Force Shapers.

"You've told the council we invade because the land is richer with more resources."

"Another layer. We need dependable resources and that land is it." King Rathveil waved a hand at the map. "In the past, it was part of Terrapin Xon. The terrible war of the gods caused the Thanatos Range to rise and separate us. We must bring our brethren back. It is our duty."

King Rathveil's eyes sparked with an internal light. "The Spirit that walks with me revealed we will find allies at the Olim Pian Falls."

"Wintermist?"

Rathveil turned to Charara. "That's what the barbarians call it."

"In the ancient tongue of the priests of the forgotten god, *Olim Pian* means 'exalted immortal.'"

King Rathveil nodded. "The Forgotten God, the one all gods feared."

"The scrolls teach that the forgotten god was evil."

"He was not evil!" King Rathveil grabbed the Scroll of Beginnings. "The works of the vanquished one slowly fell to dust." He spit the words out, his face becoming red. "From this, evil came." He rolled the scroll up and clenched it in his fist. "The destruction of his creation released evil, evil he kept sealed away."

Charara chewed his lower lip. "The Voice of the Czaran says—"

"To the multiple hells with the Voice!" He slammed the scroll into the rack and spun toward his friend. "Our people have completed their work. They have healed the land and returned the wonders of the Forgotten God. It is time for our people's reward."

King Rathveil returned to his desk. "Remember, Kilar, the winner writes history, and the priestesses are on the side that won. They never tell the true story of the Forgotten God, how he gave his worshipers and the people of the world peace and love. His reward was to be hounded by the other gods."

"If there is no record, how will we know the truth?"

"The truth is in the scrolls. The Spirit that walks with me showed me, and I have found the rest. It is time to teach you the scrolls. Once Wintermist is ours, we will teach the people about the Forgotten God."

A crystal bell rang, and Charara walked to the mirror beside the window. He looked deep into the mirror then smiled.

"Warlord Thrawt has left the Thanatos Range."

"Good, good. First, Warlord Thrawt must take the barrier known as the North Wall. But first, there is a small encampment. A minor annoyance, but an opportunity for the younger warriors to experience battle. I believe Vella should show her skills as well." He stepped from behind his desk, crossed the room, and opened the door, guards on either side quickly stood straighter. In the hall, a man, dressed in multicolored robes, came to his feet.

"How may I be of service?"

"Gillmore, go to the Force Shapers. Have them open the portals, then call my council. The time has come to announce our retaking of what was once ours."

Chapter Three

Mage Master Gardner shifted in his chair. With his back to the wall and his desk facing the door, he watched the entrance and gazed out the grand window at the same time. His office was sparsely furnished, holding items related to his mercenary years and time serving the king. The only thing that was not his was the portraits of past Mage Masters.

Mage Master Gardner did not match the stereotypical mage image. Years serving military people created unbreakable habits. His beard was trimmed, his hair cut, and he did not wear the traditional robes of a mage. He wore pants and a billowing shirt. His belt held pouches containing small scrolls, components, and his power stone. A small dagger rested on his right hip.

He glanced at the angle of the sun. Mage Kytril's party should be arriving, but for now, he suffered Mage Aydrought's rant. The man was talking nonstop about Jedrowler and Anton, the dangers of a student in charge, and how there was no oversight. If it wasn't for the fact Aydrought sat on the Mage Council of Wintermist, he would have thrown him out long ago.

"Anton may be a good wizard, but he will be doing mage-level work."

The Mage Master sighed. "Supervised by Jedrowler. It's no different from how we teach students."

"It is! Besides the living magic, Anton must control the magic of other disciplines. The boy isn't ready to channel the magic of witches, druids, and the like."

"Aydrought, all magic is similar."

"Ancient Magic? Do you think a young Wizard can channel that power?"

Mage Master Gardner slapped his palms on the desk. "Anton is ready to prove himself a mage. I said it in the council chamber, and I say it now." He came to his feet. "Do you think I'm so incompetent I would allow a dangerous spell in the school without safeguards?" Mage Aydrought shrank back. "If you have a concern with me, bring it up with the council and find my replacement."

Mage Aydrought gave his head a slight shake. "No, Mage Master, I don't feel that way." His voice was softer, with a slight whine. "But it's all our responsibility to ensure the safety of the school."

Mage Master Gardner allowed his expression to soften. "I'm sorry, Lancar." He paused as he folded his hands. "You have to excuse me. It has been a stressful day."

"I understand, Sholem, but I too have concerns."

"I have noted your concerns. But understand the spell has started, and I do have mages watching the flux of magic." He loosened a theatrical sigh. "Now if you will excuse me, I have to get ready for Mage Kytril's arrival."

"Of course, Mage Master, I understand. Kytril is an arrogant pith." Mage Aydrought turned and hastened from the room.

Mage Master Gardner smiled. It always worked with Aydrought. Become forceful. Let him think you are about to blast him, then calm down and give him an out. As long as the man felt he had the upper hand or had you cowered, he would continue arguing.

Stepping from his desk, he walked to the window. Outside, people hurried along the lake road, and the sun glistened on the peaceful lake. He leaned on the sill and watched people hurry about their business. Not for the first time, he wished he was one of them. So little ability, so little power, and a blissful lack of great responsibilities. None had to decide the fate of many, only the fate of themselves and family.

Mage Master Gardner saw riders moving passed the Temple of Odium. He recognized the one in the lead. Only one person wore an outfit with a cloak of glittering Vlynies. He also recognized two other riders and knew those two would bring the curse of interesting times. The Mage Master groaned.

Mist dripped from Ambrus Diamox's large floppy hat. Leaning forward to relieve his sensitive parts, he breathed the sweet smell of Wintermist. His heart strummed to the beat of the falling water, and a smile danced on his lips. He never had a true home, and this place came close to feeling like one.

He groaned as his legs twitched. Horse riding was for enjoyment, not a marathon. The military can do their force rides, but he should be carried in style in a carriage. Next to him, his bodyguard, Duncan Pentock, urged his horse closer to the low railing of Wintermist Bridge. The young swordsman's chattering of praise reached the scholar's ears, along with a crystalline sound. Ambrus shook his head to clear his ears. He knew the falling water set up a resonance in a deposit of crystals. To hear crystalline music above the falls, it had to be a large deposit. That deposit may be the reason the falls have not eaten away into the lake.

Ambrus nudged his horse closer to the railing and looked into the mist-shrouded gorge. He searched for the famous Spirits of Wintermist. Over the years, he never felt the ethereal touch of the ghostly inhabitants and never had a specter float from the mist. All he saw were the air currents swirling the mist into mutable shapes.

Duncan turned his horse and gave a slight nod, then moved to the right and slightly behind the scholar. They hurried to catch up with their party.

Ambrus hired Duncan six weeks earlier after a caravan master no longer needed his service. Unknown to Duncan, the Queen had requested the caravan master to release him then instructed Ambrus to hire him and bring him to Wintermist. The Queen and her champion, Weaponsmaster Runic, had plans so the scholar, who couldn't stand Mage Kytril, tolerated the present situation.

Leaving the bridge, Ambrus stood in the stirrups. He was positive the mage chose to ride horseback just to annoy him.

Ambrus marveled at the creation of nature, man and dwarves. Wintermist Mage School was carved from the three-hundred-foot sentinel. Dwarvish stone workers created works of art rivaling any in country. At the base, stone workers had chiseled an arch thirty feet high. From the mountains of Mead, oak trees made the doors. The main doors were crafted in the shape of two great mages, the founders of the mage school. Gold rope, woven in the wood, glittered in the noon sunlight. Mages claimed magic decorated the lintel.

Human and dwarf stone workers worked the first one hundred feet smooth. Graceful curves flowed along the face, reflecting the flow of magic. Stone images of creatures, both mythical and real, hung from the mountainside. Above the plateau, artists worked to transform the mountain. Wintermist School was a pleasure to the eye. The man-made Wintermist Wall, jutting from the mountain into Lake Mead, was a black splotch on the beauty. Angular and dull, it was depressing to look at.

Ambrus knew within the school that stone workers took advantage of cracks and crevasses, creating living, working, and recreational spaces. The mages claimed magic carved many interior-twisting corridors to follow lines of magic. He did not argue, just nodded. If folks wanted to believe the mages of Wintermist used an unseen power, he wasn't going to disillusion them yet. He had studied magic users all his life, learning their secrets. At traveling shows, he caught the sleight of hand, the gimmickry props, and the misdirection. Mages were better disciplined. They never let their illusions slip.

He turned his attention to Duncan. The man's eyes examined the crowd, darting over every face. They stopped, and Ambrus noted the gray-haired man in simple brown leather. The bodyguard's hand slid from his sword hilt and rested on the pommel of his saddle. He sat straighter.

Ambrus met Weaponsmaster Xantrawler Baylore on his last visit to Wintermist. Well respected throughout the kingdom, his salle had turned out the best swordsmen, armsmasters, and weaponsmasters in the kingdom. When raiders destroyed it, he was ready to retire but accepted the challenge of security for Wintermist Mage School and the Wintermist Wall. Next to the weaponsmaster, but one step behind, was a man dressed in light leather, a short sword hung from his side.

"Duncan, how are you, lad?" a smiling Xantrawler said.

Duncan nodded. "Fine. I pray your life is boring."

Xantrawler laughed. "No curse of an interesting life since the destruction of my salle."

Ambrus watched a cloud pass over Duncan's face.

"I should have answered the summons."

"You could have done nothing. Besides, you were in no shape." Xantrawler shrugged. "What the gods take, the gods also give."

"Gods didn't take your salle and destroy the town, man and the Underdwellers did."

"I was ready for retirement. Too many young ones coming for training, and my old bones could take no more." He reached back and rubbed his neck. "And these old bones can't take looking up at you. Come on down so I can give you a proper welcome."

Duncan slid from his horse and in silence gripped the forearm of the weaponsmaster. Xantrawler slapped him on the shoulder. "This is a good retirement. Guarding mages keeps me occupied. They always manage to upset someone who then wants to kill them. Kind of like your charge here." Xantrawler bowed his head. "Good day, Master Diamox."

"Good day, weaponsmaster." Ambrus slid from his horse, suppressing a groan as his protesting legs took his weight. "I trust this day finds you well?"

"Well and busy. I have mages, priests, witches, druids, you name it. If they use magic, Mage Jedrowler invited them. Thankfully, the nobles are staying with Duke Altrid. If it wasn't for my second here, I could not have handled it all." He indicated the man next to him. "Captain Morse, our Queen's scholar, Ambrus Diamox. I believe you've heard of Duncan Pentock."

Captain Morse gave Ambrus a quick nod then grasped Duncan's arm. "It's a pleasure."

"Sounds like you have a small curse of an interesting life." Ambrus smiled.

"Well, it's a break in the mundane. It does keep my men on their toes."

"How many are under your command?" Duncan asked.

"Around three hundred. Besides retiring graybeards, I have good female fighters and young lads. The young ones think serving the queen is an easy way to earn a land grant."

"And all sore from riding practice." Captain Morse chuckled. "I've had them learning riding skills before the last of the snow was gone."

"I feel their pain," Ambrus muttered.

"We augment the local militia, and we need to get around fast." Xantrawler indicated the mountains, "They sprout creatures with a taste for human flesh. They need someone to lead that fight, and thanks to men like Duncan, I came highly qualified."

"I had nothing to do with it."

"Nonsense, you and others show what type of person I am."

"Maybe others, not me."

"Now, lad, don't be that way. You're the best I trained."

Duncan spat.

In the past six weeks, Ambrus had learned of Duncan's moods of brooding and self-recrimination.

Ambrus walked stiffly around the front of his horse. He put his hands on his back and stretched, feeling the vertebrae pop into place. "It sounds like you're enjoying yourself. Good food, entertainment from the mages, a major city, and a lovely view of the best sight in Lashtar. Can't think of anything more you could ask for."

Xantrawler caught the small nod the scholar made. "Well," he drew out the word as he smiled, "a free mug of grog is always good. What say you Duncan, want to taste what we have to offer?"

"I need to stay with Ambrus."

"Weaponsmaster Xantrawler likely has this place more secure than the palace of the queen. Besides, I'm off to a place that would bore you. Enjoy yourself and catch up on old times."

"One of my lads will take care of your stuff," Xantrawler said. He motioned for a young lad of around sixteen or seventeen seasons to approach. "Josh, take Master Diamox, and we . . . bodyguard Pentock's horses."

Duncan hesitated a moment, then handed the reins to the young boy, who stood openmouthed, staring.

"Josh has been with us three months," Captain Morse said. "During a break in the winter weather, he came up the pass with a squad of other recruits. For his age, he handles the short sword as well as his father used to." He looked at the boy. "Close your mouth, recruit, before you catch a spring fly and choke."

Xantrawler smiled as he turned and directed Duncan down the road, toward the Wall. As they moved away, Captain Morse commented, "Not what I expected."

"The Valley," Ambrus said. "The Queen thinks he's worth saving." To himself, he thought *that young man has taken more than his share of blame. Hopefully, his old master can help.*

He recalled meeting with the Queen and how she told him she hoped his old teacher, with the help of others, could heal Duncan.

Arrangements were made for the scholar to travel to Wintermist. Letters were sent to Mage Master Gardner, Weaponsmaster Xantrawler, and the priestess. Two weeks ago, the Queen's own healer had arrived at Wintermist.

"I have seen eyes like his. Death haunts that young man," a feminine voice said.

Ambrus turned to face a female mage dressed in a green robe with pink velvet trim. Her long raven hair was sprinkled with gray that enhanced her beauty. It flittered passed her face and carried the sweet smell of honeysuckle. Her long fingers were in constant motion. The serious look on her face melted into a smile of amusement. "I heard you wrangled an invitation from Mage Kytril."

"CynLisa, you know I never miss a chance to see great magic at work."

CynLisa was equal in height to Ambrus and looked him in the eyes. "Ambrus Diamox, you know you came to watch the gyrations of a bunch of superstition-believing barbarians." The smile lessened the challenge in her voice.

"I never called you barbarians." CynLisa's eyebrows rose. "I did say heathens or uncivilized a time or two."

Captain Morse interrupted, "A soldier knows when to retreat. If you'll excuse me." Nodding, he quickly left.

CynLisa laughed. "I believe we made the brave fighter nervous." Turning to the scholar, she said, "Ambrus, I've missed you. It has been what? Two years?"

"You know better than me. That steel trap of a mind can recall the date and time we last saw each other."

"Well, the date anyway, I don't worry about mundane stuff."

Ambrus looked toward the top of the mage school where a section of the mountain had been sheared off, creating the plateau where the ceremony was to be performed. "Are you actively involved in the casting?"

"A Cyn rarely participates."

"Always the recorder, never enjoying the pleasure life has to offer."

CynLisa sighed. Her life consisted of cataloging and filing facts, hours in the archives and the hall of memory seeking obscure information, time spent on the labor of making copies of scrolls by hand, as magic copying would destroy them. Hours in repetitive meetings, hours recording events, hours drifting with the wisdom of past Cyns.

"It's what I love. Just like you love being locked away for days in your laboratory."

"The pursuit of knowledge knows its own time."

"So join me for lunch? I can have something sent to my room." She watched Ambrus squirm. On his last visit, she had managed to back him into a corner where he almost admitted magic existed.

"CynLisa, there's nothing better than debating you, but I want to see some old friends."

"Ahh yes, those philosophers at . . . hmm what's the name. The Squishy Owl?"

"The Screeching Owl and I have seen you there."

"Well, have a good time, but be sure to make dinner."

Ambrus waved and waddled toward the wide circular stairwell that descended into the gorge. At the base of the gorge, a wide shelf followed the river to a dwarvish mining town at which point the river was navigable. Travelers and merchants used this route to access the western and southern portions of Lashtar. Over the years, dwellings and businesses were carved into the side of the gorge until another city grew, complete with shops, inns, and taverns. In the summer, these places were popular as the temperature was cooler. Foot traffic tended to be heavy at times.

CynLisa headed for the main doors of the mage school. Mage Kytril's party had already disappeared through them. As she stepped into the cavernous entrance, she shivered from the coolness. The short hallway led to an egg-shaped room where a combination of magic and artistic skills of humans and dwarves flowed into a dazzling display of beauty.

From multiple windows, light streamed to wraparound columns of granite that spiraled into the domed ceiling. Upon a web, strands of Living Magic wove, and motes of magic danced in an eternal dance of power. A second and third floor held small alcoves with statues of mages from the school's past. The second level balcony circled the room, and the banister was upswept oak wood that blended into the support columns. The columns were carved with graceful runes. Exits on the second floor led to the Mage Master's office and the council chambers. Beyond were the winding and twisting halls of the school, except one. That hallway was straight and true and used by nonmage guests.

Twin black onyx stairs arched from opposite sides to the ground level. Tapestries of the celestial night and the astral plane hung on the left and right side of the stairs, and between them, the flag of Lashtar and Duke Arden's banner danced in a nonexistent wind.

A single work of art dominated the center of the first floor. A fountain of multicolored water poured from the hands of a crystal mage. There was only one visible exit on the ground floor, and it led to the greeting room, a library, and the formal dining hall. CynLisa heard the sounds of Mage Kytril's party echoing from the greeting room. She knew nothing of note would take place. One of her students was present to record the informal occasion, so she slipped behind a statue of a forgotten mage and entered a concealed door.

This was one of the many servants' stairs that twisted through the school. Mages tended to use them to avoid the confusing corridors and crowds of other students and mages.

CynLisa climbed to the top floor, pausing occasionally to catch her breath. As she opened the door, she let out a groan of relief and vowed to spend less time sitting in the archives and more time exercising.

The cleaners had filled the hall with the smell of pine water, but fresh air from the open stairwell was slowly clearing it away. She stepped down the hallway and looked into a sparsely furnished room. Benches lined three walls, and wooden pegs held robes. A monk sat chanting while Anton folded sashes at a table in the center of the room.

"Good afternoon, CynLisa," he spoke in a monotone as he folded the last sash.

"How are things progressing?"

"Everything is on schedule." Anton laid down the last sash and nodded to Brother Theolopis. The monk stood and moved toward the table as the wizard exited the room.

As he closed the door, he said, "If you could slow down time, it would help. Master Jedrowler is preparing to go deep in a trance and is counting on me to make sure everything is ready." He shook his head. "Cleaners had the wrong solution, and I had to hunt up the head housekeeper.

"Someone left the incense out last night. Someone started using them, and the whole ritual had to be started over. In the meantime, the chef is screaming about the 'cook' from the duke's kitchen and complaining the flour is not high quality." He turned and looked down the hallway. "I have had three arguments in the last two hours. One person downright refused to follow my direction and tried pulling rank. I had Weaponsmaster Xantrawler's men escort him from the school."

CynLisa's eyes grew. "No!"

"He's banned till the spell is finished."

"It wasn't someone that lives at the school?"

"Yes. He can spend the next three days enjoying the local inns." Anton's voice rose, "I will not let anything interfere with Master Jedrowler's plans." In a quiet voice, he asked, "I did do the right thing, didn't I?"

CynLisa nodded, and Anton excused himself. She watched him enter a light trance in preparation for spell work.

Brother Theolopis came out, and Anton closed the door. Using her mage vision, CynLisa watched Anton draw living magic into him. She bit her lip to keep quiet and not distract the lad. This was mage work, and by rights, a mage should be supervising him. If the magic sensed his . . . She shook her head and refused to worry. The magic was minute, and there was little chance of it fleeing and the spell misfiring.

Around the lintel, Anton scribed runes. As the magic sank into the wood, their glowing image faded. Finishing the spell, he came out of his trance.

"One thing." A nervous smile played on his lips. "So much needs done in the proper order. I hope I'm not forgetting anything." He looked at the Cyn. "You know it's not normal magic?" He continued speaking as he walked to the plateau stairs, "In two hundred years, there hasn't been a spell like this." He was rambling, but the boy needed to get it out.

"Jedrowler has trust in you."

"He has no choice." He was not bragging. It was fact. "To control this magical energy, he needs cleansed, both body and mind. Right now, he is preparing for a deep trance, one he will be in until just before midnight, tomorrow night."

As they moved up the steps, she listened closely, not because she needed to learn about the spell. She listened to give Anton someone to confide in.

"Master Jedrowler says I'm the one," a small quiver crept into his voice. Stopping at the top of the stairs, he looked at the blue sky. "The spell requires someone levelheaded and competent, as well as strong with magic."

Using her Cyn's abilities, CynLisa recalled Anton's records. His innate abilities and the strength of his personal magic were above average. By all standards, Mage Master Gardner should have awarded the boy the mage title months ago, making him the youngest person named mage. His fear held him back and stopped him from advancing. Jedrowler's own notes reported there were times he needed to hold the living magic back as it tried to flee or corrupt a spell as magic tripped Anton's fear of heights and the boy froze.

Mage Aydrought had suggested Anton be sent to Healer's Hall in the capital, where the mind healers could help him. Both the Mage Master and Jedrowler vetoed this. They were worried the Queen Council of mages would order Anton's channels blocked.

"Anton, you will do well."

"Well isn't good enough. One mistake and the school will be gone. Master Jedrowler has set shields in place to make sure the energy stays contained. If it doesn't . . ." He took a deep breath. "The school, this end of the lake, and most of Wintermist are history."

"Wipe self-doubt from your mind. Hold on to your confidence."

"I will," he said softly. The boy walked onto the plateau.

Activities filled the plateau as craftsmen, laborers, and various users of magic moved about. Witches stood in covens. Druids swept the area with pine boughs, and on the eastern side of the plateau, near where the cup sloped up, a mage painstakingly drew a pentagram using multicolored sand. Each color represented a discipline of magic. It needed to meet the exact requirements of Mage Jedrowler, so the work was slow.

CynLisa watched Anton check with the Priestess of Odium, who was overseeing the dwarves' construction of a marble and granite altar. Nearby, an acolyte was washing a statue of Odium with holy water.

She studied the flow of magic. When Anton left the priestess's side and moved toward the rim, CynLisa watched magical lines of force—the Living Magic—flee from him. Yet some strands remained. They lacked the graceful flux normally seen in the ribbons of magic. These strands were angular, their movement sudden, like a striking snake. Ancient Magic, the magic Jedrowler claimed was important to the spell, gathered around Anton. He was the magnet for the younger, less-refined thread of magic. It was drawn to his fear. At the pentagram, the power within the lines pulled the Ancient Magic into the sand.

Jedrowler had prescribed a ritual for Anton to follow. Now CynLisa understood the purpose. The ritual would increase the concentration of Ancient Magic. This was why he had delayed teaching the young wizard to control his fear.

Anton turned from the pentagram with defiance in his eyes. "Magic doesn't scare me."

"Fear is the destroyer of confidence of control. A mage cannot allow fear to overpower them."

"I need to be fearless?"

"Only a fool is fearless."

Anton walked across the plateau. "When the spell is finished, I will sit down with Master Jedrowler."

CynLisa heard the slight tremor. No one else would have noticed, but a Cyn must notice the smallest detail. She pushed her windblown hair to one side. "Anton, I hope you and Jed know what you're doing."

Crystalline voices sang the song of relaxation.

Mage Jedrowler murmured, "Hello, my friends." Opening his eyes, he looked at the two spirits floating over him. His gaze lingered on the smaller of the two, and his eyes sparkled.

"Hello, young one," calling the smaller one young was relative, since it was two hundred years old. It let forth a childish, crystalline twitter

Jedrowler reached for the decanter of fruit juice and splashed a little in a goblet. He saluted the two Spirits then allowed a small amount to trickle into his mouth. Licking his lips, he let out a contented sigh, stood, and stretched.

"One little chore, then it's time." Crossing to the left-hand doorway, he entered his workroom. The workroom was small, but he made efficient use of the space in placing his paraphernalia to the lie of magic. The two work tables and large chests, shelves holding glass jars and pottery filled with components for spells, all set as magic dictated. Barrels with items not requiring magical attunement provided seats. Smaller tables against the walls were loaded with the tools of magical creation. Multiple shelves bowed with the weight of ancient texts. A twinkling tapestry depicting a woodland scene in late afternoon provided luminance. If one looked long enough, they could catch a glimpse of the stag that dwelled there.

Years earlier, the Mage Master tried to move Jedrowler to a new suite, one befitting a mage of his stature. Being satisfied where he was, Jedrowler refused. No other room took in the same vista of his beloved falls.

Mage Jedrowler stepped around a spinning wheel to reach the rolltop desk. As he ran his left hand along runes carved in the top of the desk, he pulled out the chair. Silently, the top rolled up, revealing scrolls, books, ink wells, quills, and unidentifiable items ready to spring out and drown him.

From a side slot, he pulled a leather-bound book and opened it to the last page. A few sentences composed of his neat, precise writing lay on the page. He picked up a quill and started to write:

In less than thirty-six hours, we commence with the first part of the spell. Despite the lack of food, I feel more alive than ever. Magic is gathering. I have touched the raw matter of old magic. I feel it flowing through my channels. Those in the past have been unable to hold it, to control it. Anton is different. Like a master, he has manipulated the small amount we have called. He is ready.

Jedrowler paused and chewed the tip of his quill. Ancient Magic, he felt it. He felt its intention and could almost hear its voice. Living Magic wanted to create, needed to create. Ancient Magic had that need magnified. Ancient Magic could and would take control. One needed to direct this control. If not, then one needed to . . . He shook his head. No time to start theorizing, they were committed. He scanned the last couple of sentence to pick up his line of thought.

The Spirits will guide me, for they were here when the land was young and magic was new. The mage lifted his quill, and a new page whorled into existence. *Anton is the key. On the pretext, I need him to ensure the magic was collecting properly. I instructed him to go to the pentagram every hour and spend ten minutes. His visit will chase Living Magic away, but his fear will draw Ancient Magic. Anton is the only one whose channels can withstand the influx of such energy. Not even I can handle this raw energy.*

His thoughts shifted, and he started a new paragraph. *He is foci. I pray I'm right, and he will resist the Legion effect. Anton is strong in self and will not be lost. It is the second part I have concern. The lad needs to control his fear. We have two weeks before the first half of the spell unravels. The two foci must join for . . .*

The young Spirit fluttered into the room, its crystalline voice sang the song of concern.

"What is it, young one?"

The Spirit swam around Jedrowler. The song of concern and worry filled the room. Its ethereal mouth moved in soundless motion, trying to form words the mage could understand. If it could speak, it would have been gibbering.

As Jedrowler stood, his desk rolled shut. The Spirit darted to the door and paused long enough to look over its shoulder.

"I'm coming. I'm coming."

Jedrowler hastened into the living quarters where the older Spirit turned from the window. It shot a warning glare at the younger one who emitted a crystalline coo.

Jedrowler noticed the flower's red petals were showing signs of wilting. "Is this what you're worried about?" He laughed. "Don't worry. They'll not die, not elvish flowers." He crossed to the window and allowed his fingers to glide over the red petals. Out the window, he noticed two soldiers walking toward Wintermist Bridge. The one he recognized, the other he knew by reputation. He watched Xantrawler turn and point back to Wintermist Wall.

"Or are you concerned about him?" the mage murmured as he reached out and caressed the misty form of a young face. "Don't worry. He's with a friend who can help."

The young Spirit let out the song of frustration. The older Spirit snapped a sharp whistle and began the song of relaxation, peace, and tranquility.

Jedrowler looked at the older Spirit and smiled. "You're right, it's time to begin. Come, join me my friends."

The midafternoon sun slid behind the mountain's peak, casting a shadow across the western shore and waters of Lake Mead. Xantrawler shivered slightly as the wind-driven mist wrapped around him. Pulling his cloak tighter, he stared back at Wintermist Wall.

Wintermist City was a hub of commerce. The southern pass saved weeks of travel for those journeying to northern or southern parts of the country. Without the pass, it would take weeks going around the mountain ranges. Other travelers entered the gorge and made their way downstream to the dwarvish village. There, river barges took them to parts of the kingdom and countries to the west. Daily, constant traffic of farmers, craftsmen, travelers, and merchants passed through the open portcullis.

After being settled, Wintermist became a prize sought by many. To protect his people, Duke Mead requested the nearby dwarvish community to construct Wintermist Wall. Built from the black lake rock, it stretched three hundred feet from the school to the lake. Three towers, almost as high as the plateau—150 feet—stood watch over the land. The western tower hugged the granite mountain, its battlements ten feet below the plateau. The square gatehouse topped one story over the wall and provided a gateway and living and working quarters. Barracks, stables, and a small armory clustered both sides of the road.

"And the tower in the lake was my idea." Xantrawler laughed. "I call it my coastal defense. When I arrived, the wall stopped at the tower on the shore, one any enemy could get around. Now they need to wade out a hundred feet."

He pointed to the western tower. "Where the wall connects to the school was a weak point that a recruit, fresh from the farm, could see. I would have thought Mage Master Gardner being an old mercenary mage would know better. Played hell before they allowed me to correct that weak point. I convinced them."

Duncan nodded. "I can imagine."

"Some of my better men snuck in from the other side. Got passed the guards and never tripped the magical alarms. They spent the night drinking Mage Master Gardner's dwarvish bourbon. Before morning, they used the mage master's own letterhead to order the mages breakfast sent to the lads in the barracks."

Xantrawler remembered the confrontation with Mage Master Gardner over the incident. He allowed the mage to rant, then slowly and calmly pointed out that if his men had been enemy agents, he and his fellow mages would be dead, not ranting. That day, the Mage Master and the Mage Council of Wintermist approved the upgrades to the wall.

"You've been busy the past four years."

Xantrawler laid his hands on his belt and stood straighter. "Duncan, I haven't felt this alive in years. I have raw recruits, not officers, but ordinary men and woman. Watching them succeed and watching them improve makes me feel good in here." He thumped his chest. "Oh, I'm proud of you and my other students, but this is different. They're ordinary people learning the martial arts. They're not some lord's son learning to swing a sword. They're no armsmasters or even weaponsmaster to be. They are people."

The two turned and continued walking toward Wintermist Bridge. "During the war, I watched common soldiers do things," Duncan said, "things many Queen's knights, and nobles were unable or unwilling to do. Many a knight ran from battle while the local militia farmers stood their ground."

"Nobles blah," Xantrawler pantomimed a spit. "Too many think peasants owe them. Most are not worth the clippings from the horse's hoofs."

A young lad of ten years danced across the road, dodging people, sliding by horses, and narrowly missing wagons. He zeroed in on the two warriors, coming to a stop, panting. He nodded to Xantrawler, then turned to Duncan.

"Sir Duncan, you're needed at the Screeching Owl."

Xantrawler let out a snort, "A tavern posing as a club for sages, scholars, and other busybodies."

"Diamox!" It was a curse, not a question. The lad nodded. "Damn scholar got into another fight. How do I get there?"

"I'll show you the way," Xantrawler said.

Duncan tossed the young boy a copper piece and followed Xantrawler.

The iron staircase wound into the gorge, then turned into a path that followed that switched back and forth, sometimes hanging over the gorge as a wooden bridge, other times burrowing into the cliff. The echo of Wintermist Falls rose and fell as they passed in and out of tunnels. A whole community thrived along the cliff. Duncan followed Xantrawler passed shops selling hats, cloaks, fresh meats, and charms. They sidestepped around people on their own missions. At one point, a Spirit floated past, concern on its face.

Xantrawler stopped at a solid oak door holding a chiseled relief of an owl, wings spread in full flight and its beak open. He pushed it open and stepped into the tavern. The room was small, with one other exit, a curtained doorway on the opposite wall. An empty bar held half-full glasses. Opposite the bar, stuffed chairs gathered around a fireplace. Tables and wooden chairs crowded the rest of the room. Men and women, of varying ages, were murmuring their thoughts or shouting opinions. In the center of the group was the still form of Ambrus Diamox. The sage's hands clawed the air, his legs jerked as his heels beat a tattoo on the floor. He was hissing, and drool slid from his mouth into his beard. His lips moved in silent speech.

Duncan pushed past the weaponsmaster and stepped down into the room.

"Will you, clucking hens, shut up and find a healer!" a young woman kneeling at Ambrus's head shouted.

Duncan shouldered patrons aside, their protests dying on their lips when they saw the size and build of the man. Kneeling, he placed a hand on the sage's forehead. Sweat poured from the scholar, his skin cool to the touch. "What happened?"

The young woman holding Ambrus's hand spoke, "Ambrus was talking and suddenly started shaking and drooling."

The woman was plain. Her hair, the color of a red sunset, was pulled back into a ponytail. She looked out of place among the finely dressed people. She wore a simple green circle skirt with matching bodice and a plain white chemise. Her hands showed she worked at manual labor. Xantrawler had seen her once, a couple of years earlier, delivering baked goods to his men at the Wall. Other times, he noticed her leaving the gorge at all hours of the day or night.

Duncan grabbed Ambrus's face and looked into the rolled up eyes. "Ambrus! Ambrus! Let go. Let it come. Don't fight it."

"He's about to prophesy?" a male voice said from the crowd.

"I've always wanted to hear a true prophet at work."

"Shut up!" The woman glared at the people. "He's trying to speak. And stand back, give him some air."

The sounds of shuffling feet stopped as Ambrus spoke.

"From the north, blackness seeps. The horseman comes at the becking of the north. He comes upon his black steed. He cannot be denied." Ambrus's eyes flew open. "He rides the land of the mist. He comes for he who leads! The mage that rules the ancient powers!" His head swirled, and Xantrawler found himself looking into the black eyes of the prophet. A chill ran down his spine. "Ignore me at your peril! The horseman will come for him! The wall will die in fire." He collapsed into Duncan's arms.

"What does that mean?" Xantrawler asked.

"I don't know," Duncan said. "I just listen to prophecies. I don't understand them."

"Sounds like an assassination attempt," the woman said. Both Duncan and Xantrawler looked at her. "Sorry, I'm Sasha Magnate, Ambrus's friend."

"You understand prophecies?" Xantrawler asked.

"What's to understand?" an older gentleman asked. "The horseman on the black steed is death."

"And the north summoned him." Sasha chewed her lower lip, her eyebrows closing in on each other. "He comes for the . . . no, for a leader."

"Not just any leader," a lady wearing a bad wig said, "he comes for the ruler of magic. Only one ruler of magic in the land of the mist."

"Mage Master Gardner!" Unconsciously, Xantrawler's hand fell to the hilt of his sword.

"It's not going to happen right now," Sasha said. Under her breath, she muttered about sword swingers and their thirst to carve up people. She glanced at the two men. "He saw the future. Gives you time to get ready with your sword things," she spoke slow, giving them time to absorb her words.

Xantrawler looked at Duncan. "Can you get Ambrus on your own? I need to . . ."

"I understand, go."

"I'll help with Ambrus," Sasha said.

As Xantrawler left, he called over his shoulder. "I'll have a student waiting at the main entrance of the mage school to show you to his room."

Sasha watched Duncan gently lay Ambrus on the bed. The scholar's face was drawn, his eyes held black circles and his hair hung limply to the side. She drew the bed spread over the scholar. "I'm surprised Ambrus is staying here. I would think he would want a room in the duke's guest quarters."

"He wants to be where the magic is, how else to learn their secrets?"

She tucked the end around his shoulders. "Does he always look this abused after a prophecy?" Duncan shrugged. "Still, he looks peaceful, like a child."

Duncan grunted and turned the wick in the bedside lamp down. "A child with a mean, stubborn streak."

Sasha brushed her hair from her eyes. "I know. I've watched him debate at the Screeching Owl. He never gives. I've debated him. I never won, but once came close to a draw." She forced her eyes from the swordsman's face. She scolded herself for staring. Still, she admitted. He did have an aura about him that she felt an attraction to.

"What is the Screeching Owl? Looked like a tavern."

Sasha snickered. "It's far from a tavern. It's an unofficial club where people discuss philosophies or debate their favorite theories. Our poor reluctant prophet has been the subject of many debates. I'm sure they're having one right now, which will get bigger when he returns."

"He won't be returning tonight. The last one had him out for eight hours and was mild compared to this one."

She looked up, and Duncan locked his blue eyes on her. She felt he was measuring her, deciding if she was worthy of his notice.

"I didn't take you for the scholarly type. You have the hands of a worker."

Sasha broke eye contact and subconsciously rubbed her hands on her skirt. "I'm a baker's helper. My dad owns a bakery in Wintermist. Bread, sweet cakes, and the like."

She glanced at Duncan's sword. The scabbard's—that was its name—frayed leather was reddish brown. The color reminded her of blood. She bit her lip and felt her shoulders tense. This was a man of violence, yet she recalled the gentle way he handled Diamox. She clearly remembered his face as they made their way through the passageways and upstairs. It was the look of genuine concern.

Sasha stepped from the bed and walked to the mirror. She had observed soldiers and sword swingers all her life, a rough, crude, and vulgar lot, except her uncle. But he was a captain in the queen's army, and officers were refined. Behind her reflection, she saw Duncan, his sword hung from his side, his stance that of a man ready for a fight. Yet his face reflected concern, caring.

Sasha needed to get her mind away from where it was headed.

"I have the basic education the Queen commands of her subjects. Our similarities end there." She forced her eyes to look at Ambrus. "I enjoy learning. You enjoy swinging your sword." Sasha winced. That was not how she wanted to say it. She fumbled for her next words. "Unfortunately, my parents didn't have the funds for University or the academy here in Wintermist." She sounded like she was whining. She hastily added, "But I have learned from books and hanging out at the Screeching Owl."

Duncan turned from the bed. "Is that how you met Ambrus?"

Sasha nodded. "Five years ago, he came into the Screeching Owl and found this scrawny girl listening to the debates. Someone brought up his prophecies, so he dragged me out of my little corner." She turned and faced him. "It was sink or swim as he started to debate me. I didn't know what to think. I had never seen someone try to disprove a power they have, especially one as important as his."

"Well, he thinks it's the result of something physically wrong in his brain." Duncan shook his head. "Don't mention healers. 'Damn healers and their mumble jumble of looking into the body with healer's sight.'"

Sasha laughed. She felt something about this man. Something she was unable to put into words. She started to say something but changed her mind and stayed on firmer ground. "He's so logical. He says if something can't be duplicated then it's fakery or trickery."

"That's why he's here. He wants to see Mage Jedrowler pull off this stunt. He was bragging to Mage Kytrill that he would catch the sleight of hand, catch Mage Jedrowler in the act. He's planning on poking his nose into everything between now and midnight tomorrow." Duncan stepped around the bed before looking at Ambrus. "Also, he thinks he overlooked something and his subconscious is working overtime. He's had a lot of visions relating to this area."

"And what about you, Sir Duncan? What does a sword swinger think?"

"Just Duncan." He started pacing. "I have been many places seen many things. I don't dismiss something just because I can't explain it."

"You don't need to explain something. Just duplicate the effect and achieve the same outcome. Magic is a good example. You or I can't duplicate it. So is it real?"

"We can't duplicate it because we're not able to manipulate the magical forces."

"Is there a magical force? Why can't we measure it? We only have the words of the mages." Sasha found this fun. This sword swinger was better than she thought when it came to debating. Of course, she hadn't thrown any tough maneuvers at him yet.

"Before you measure something, you need to understand what you are measuring," Duncan stopped and looked at the woman. "I thought you believed in magic." Sasha gave him a tight upturned smile. "Ahh, you've learned from Ambrus. I have seen him take the opposite view and have his opponent argue his case for him."

He was good, caught on to her maneuver fast. Her opinion of him went up, but he was still a sword swinger.

"Learning and increasing my knowledge interests me." Sasha cast her eyes toward the floor and quietly added, "It keeps my mind off the fact that no one has done a leap for me." She bit her lip. She was talking without thinking.

"A what?"

Sasha cleared her throat and looked up. "Jumping from Wintermist Bridge." She realized he was unfamiliar with the tradition. "To leap, you tie a rope around you. One end is attached to a large spool. You leap into the mist, and the spool unwinds as you fall. If you're in love, you leap in the spring with a rose in your mouth. You find yourself with the Spirits, and it's said to strengthen the relationship." She found Ambrus suddenly interesting.

"Sounds romantic."

Sasha laughed. "What would a sword swinger know about romance? I'm not talking about wenching."

Out of the corner of her eyes, she watched emotions play over Duncan's face. He turned from her and stepped to the window. Looking down on the courtyard at the people going and coming, he said, "Men who make a living with swords know about love. We love deeply, sometimes too deeply." He took a deep breath and turned, walking to the foot of the bed. "Who knows, you may find a sword swinger is just the man for you." She caught him looking at her out of the corner of his eye.

"Fat chance." She let the words slide from her mouth and in a practiced voice said, "I want a man to be my intellectual equal. What would I talk about with a sword swinger? The best way to carve your opponent for the holiday?" She looked at Duncan, daring him to look at her.

"We do more than carve up people."

"Yeah, I know. Drink whiskey, eat meat, and chase women."

He turned, and their eyes met. She locked hers with his, daring him to keep looking at her.

"Never said we didn't have interesting hobbies."

Ambrus started mumbling in his sleep.

"Listen. We're bothering Ambrus." She waited for Duncan to break eye contact, but the man was stubborn. When Ambrus moaned, she used it as an excuse to look away. "I need to get back to the bakery. Dad needs help with the evening chores." She paused for a moment. "Perhaps we can, er, well, get together sometime. You can educate me on the ways of the sword swinger."

"How about dinner tomorrow night?" Duncan asked.

Sasha felt her heart beat faster in fear she told herself. In a noncommittal voice, she said, "Sure, sure, pick me up at my dad's bakery. Ambrus can give you directions." Before she said any more and sound like a young airheaded child, she turned and left.

Chapter Four

Anton made a face and poked the condiment-filled salad. In a bowl, next to the salad plate, was an unidentified purple object.

He grew up on a farm, where meat was a staple. Salad was a poor substitute for a slab of beef, and the purple thing and its thick, almost-too-sweet sauce was no replacement for cured ham. He knew this was penance for fighting his mother over eating vegetables.

He shoveled a mouthful of leaves in his mouth and glanced at the sixteen people of the circle. They were indulging in the same course as they needed to cleanse their body for the deep trance required for casting. The druids enjoyed the meal, while the witches tolerated it. The mages and religious members accepted it as part of their profession.

Around the room, conversation flowed as mages and guests enjoyed the other meal prepared by the school's chef. Anton's mouth watered as the aroma drifted from the tables of the nobles and honored visitors. He could almost taste the roasted duck resting on a bed of fresh spring tubers, the oxtail soup, the grilled beef, and fresh bread and rolls. Duke Altrid had brought wine from his own cellar, and the servants made sure goblets stayed filled.

The members of the circle enjoyed water.

Mage Master Gardner sat at the apex of the arched head table. To his right sat Duke Altrid and Duchess Vallrin. To the duke's right were the Lord Marshal and a young lady. Anton heard she was from one of the cities' noble families. The Lady Gladaya was charming, if a little flighty. Rumor had it that her family hoped a union with the Lord Marshal would bring them prestige and influence in the duke's court.

The Queen's representative sat to the left of the Mage Master. Next to her was Anton's duke, Duke Bartow, who was pleased that one of his subjects was a key participant in an event of such magnitude. He talked with Anton at length about the homecoming celebration being planned. Duke Bartow felt after the casting the Mage Master would have no choice but to pronounce Anton a mage.

Weaponsmaster Xantrawler's increased security was evident. Two guards flanked Mage Master Gardner. Each door had two guards, and others were stationed around the room. The weaponsmaster was present, having his own seat on the right side of the table. He wore a formal outfit, and in place of his ceremonial sword, he wore a special sword said to be a gift from a dwarvish clan and endowed with magical properties.

Seating of nobles and dignitaries had given the steward fits. With the mages, druids, witches, priestesses, and priests to be seated, he needed to ensure no one was next to someone they would consider offensive or beneath their station. The poor man was wringing his hands because someone had seated the dwarvish clan leader next to the Lady Juliana, whose husband was the head of the Textile Guild. The dwarf was slurping loudly from his bowl of soup.

The banquet hall was situated deep within the school, and Jedrowler had requested it, feeling it was more intimate than the Grand Banquet hall. Servers came and went through the doors on either side of the fireplace. The temperature was constant year around, so the fireplace was more tradition than need. Cool air flowed from four vents, one on each wall.

Anton looked toward CynLisa sitting at the end of the left-hand arc. She had a small plate of food but had eaten little. When someone spoke to her, she responded. But mostly, she just observed. He saw her eyes were out of focus, indicating she was in her Cyn trance. He felt a twinge of sympathy, as she had little chance to enjoy special functions. All she saw and all she heard were being recorded.

Anton thought of his first time at the mage school. Everything was new and strange. His years of living with the duke had not prepared him for what he found. The school his duke maintained was nothing compared to Wintermist Mage School. Here, there were no large classrooms, just small instructional rooms shielded against mishaps. There were so few students that each was assigned a mage. The master worked with the student one on one, teaching them how to draw the Living Magic to them and into them.

Anton had classes in history, math, and writing conducted in a larger room with other students. In addition, they had instructions in using magic for self-defense taught by a combat mage. Senior students, like Anton, had lessons with the weaponsmaster. They were no experts, but he drilled them in using their magic to protect themselves.

From the first day, all students learned to do research, so they became familiar with the school's archives. This was where he first met CynLisa.

He had wandered into the archives, looking for a text Mage Fristin wanted him to learn. While searching the shelves, he managed to knock over a pile of scrolls. In the ensuing scramble to capture them, CynLisa walked in.

"What do you think you're doing?"

"I'm sorry . . . I reached for . . . my elbow hit the pile and . . ."

"And now you're making a total mess. These are sensitive scrolls, young man. They are magical in nature, and your mishandling could cause the magic to fade." She looked at him, her lips set in a firm line. "In the future, Anton Towner, you will come get me or one of my assistants."

"You know me!"

"I'm the Cyn. It is my business to know things."

From that first meeting, their relationship could only improve. Over the next five years, CynLisa taught Anton how to use the archives, how to access the delicate magic sensitive documents, and the use of the Room of Memories. Here, the combined knowledge of the Cyns of Wintermist Mage School resided.

He formed a deep abiding respect for her and felt sorrow. She had few friends and in all events was always on the outside looking in as it was important for a record to be made. Even now, she was committing everything around her to memory. Later, she would enter it in the school's archive book and the Room of Memories.

Anton's thoughts were interrupted as a servant removed his half-eaten salad and placed a bowl of spring berries, covered in a syrup made from their own juices, in front of him. He looked and noticed he was the only one with spring berries. He smiled and made a mental note to thank the chef.

As everyone was finishing their dessert, Mage Master Gardner rose and tapped his crystal goblet. All eyes turned to the head table.

"First, I must thank our chef for a fine meal." Years of speaking before large and small crowds had trained his voice, so it filled the hall without being overwhelming. "Yet this is a small sample of his skill. Our wonderful Chef Kelso has promised a feast after the spell casting to rival the duke's Harvest Festival." Mage Master Gardner smiled at the duke, who returned the smile with a small laugh.

"Normally, this type of festivity doesn't surround a spell casting, but Mage Jedrowler feels this is a cause for celebration. As you know, this spell will benefit not just the land of Mead, but will also one day cover all of Lashtar."

Mage Master Gardner turned to Anton. Suddenly, the blueberries were not as sweet, and the young wizard felt his stomach drop. His mouth went dry, and the tremors started. He felt like he did when he looked down from heights. Part of him welcomed the fear, a familiar, almost comfortable feeling in this stressful setting.

"Mage Jedrowler cannot be with us tonight," the Mage Master said. "So, Wizard Towner, shall brief us."

Anton slowly rose to his feet. He felt surrounded by the expectant faces that turned to him. All the faces were old. The men had creases around the eyes that disappeared into beards that went white years ago. Witches had streaks of gray in their hair. One had hands permanently bent into claws from arthritis. The Priestess of Odium had no hair, but her eyes whispered her age.

Only the Lord Marshal and his lady friend were young. The Lord Marshal was a couple of years older than Anton, young for a Lord Marshal. He had just started his tour of duty with the Queen's army last year, when his father died. By right of inheritance, the position passed to him. His lack of experience caused him to depend on his older officers and the duke's swordsmaster for advice. His arrogance and bullheadedness caused him to ignore a lot of that advice.

To have respect, one earned it through deeds and experience. The Lord Marshal had neither. Anton felt like him, little experience and the youngest person here. He hoped he wasn't coming across as arrogant. He had an important job and required the cooperation of these older and more experienced people.

"Th . . . hmm thanks for coming." He mentally took hold of himself. Calm down, he advised. "You know—tomorrow—I have last-minute instructions, not last-minute, but instructions that need followed at the last minute. Ahh actually, um, what I mean is Master Jedrowler . . ." Anton stopped and took a deep breath. He sounded like an idiot. He may not be a mage, but these people knew he was a powerful wizard. It was time to start acting like one.

Removing a parchment from inside his tunic, Anton looked at the blank paper. "Master Jedrowler needs the following things accomplished." His voice firmed, and the squeak left. "Presently, the Priestess of Odium is praying over the pentagram. When she is done, a representative of the witches' coven will perform their ritual of cleansing at midnight." He kept staring at the parchment, focusing on the white of the paper and allowing everything else to fade from his view. His breathing slowed, his heart eased and the smell of fear faded. His stomach returned to enjoying the blue berries. All hesitation left his voice.

"Come sunrise, the druids will conduct their morning ritual and at noon the ritual of birth. They will conduct this in and around the pentagram. Then the temple guards of Odium will seal the plateau.

"For your meditation, we have provided rooms on the top floor. You have received your instructions on when to meditate and when to enter your trance. Weaponsmaster Xantrawler will have men standing guard, so you will not be disturbed."

Anton took a deep breath. He looked up and found himself staring at the Cyn. For a moment, CynLisa's eyes came into focus, and she winked. It had been her idea to use a blank parchment to focus on instead of all the faces looking at him. He gave her a slight smile.

He turned to the audience and looked at the guests. They covered all levels, from the duke through merchants and farmers to a peasant. "All who will be watching this casting need to know your presence is highly important. It is important and necessary for those who do not manipulate magic to be present."

"Why?" one landholder asked.

"Master Jedrowler can explain better, and after the casting, I'm sure he will answer your questions. I can only give you a simple explanation of this magic. In ancient time, magic was often done in front of the group. The nonmagic people's presence helped with the manipulation as they became part of the magic flow due to the nature of magic. We'll be using that Ancient Magic."

"Magic will be flowing through us?" The Lady Valrine had a small estate up the coast, where she oversaw her late husband's winery. Her voice held only the smallest of quivers.

"Yes. Well, kind of. The Ancient Magic and Living Magic are in you always. Because of you, they will identify with the people and their connection to the land. Because of you, the magic will be easier to control, pliable. I'm sorry I can't give you a better explanation, but it's complex, and Master Jedrowler is the one who understands it all. If you don't want to be there or are afraid of the magic, you may watch from the ground."

"What do you mean by Ancient Magic?"

"Magic unchanged since creation, the magic of our ancestors." The room filled with babbling as the magic users commented.

One voice boomed over the rest, Mage Aydrought's. "Who will be channeling this Ancient Magic?"

Anton took a deep breath. The fingernails of his left hand dug into his palm as he turned to the mage. Aydrought sat on the Mage Council and knew the answer. All the counselors had the spell explained to them a year ago.

"The first part of the spell is set in motion by the sixteen who will stand in the circumference of the pentagram."

"Someone needs to channel the energy of those sixteen. Who is channeling that?"

"I will."

Even the fire stopped crackling as silence descended on the room.

"You can't," Mage Aydrought said. "You are a wizard. Wizards do not channel the Living Magic. They control it from without. If you could channel magic, you would be a mage."

"What is your fear?" Mage Kytrill asked in a soft voice. "My understanding is you knew this a year ago. Now, on the eve of the casting, it has become a problem?"

"He has trouble holding the Living Magic!"

"I understand he is nearly ready to be named a mage."

"That may be, but this spell is using Ancient Magic. Those who have tried using Ancient Magic found it hard to manipulate. That's why no one has used it for three hundred years. The boy will lose control, and the magic will explode."

Mage Aydrought stood and looked around the hall. "I don't want us to miss this opportunity. Anton must show a mage what needs to be done. I believe Mage Wandel can handle the power."

CynLisa's eyes focused for a moment. "Guards removed Mage Wandel from the school today."

"I don't believe. I consulted the Cyn!"

"I was stating a fact, so everyone would have them." She pulled out more information from her memory and slipped into her Cyn voice. "Let it be known by all within the sound of my voice, the Council of Mages three months ago voted to give Mage Jedrowler complete and total control of the school and its surroundings for ninety-six hours. The vote was unanimous."

"Mage Jedrowler, not student Anton!" Mage Aydrought pounded the table. A goblet of wine jumped and spilled its content on the Priest of Lenna.

"Wizard Towner. He's a first-level wizard. Give him the courtesy of acknowledging his achievements."

"He's a wizard, not a mage!"

"Aydrought, shut up." Mage Hassle sat at the opposite end of the arc. He always disagreed with Mage Aydrought on any issue. "One of two things will happen. He will do everything right and all will be good, or he messes up the magic and the school will be a couple of floors lower and you will be gone. Ahhh quiet at last."

There was sporadic laughter, and Mage Aydrought turned red.

"We . . . we can't have anyone else. There's no time," Anton said in a quiet voice.

Mage Master Gardner stood. "Enough! Unless one of you knows this spell better than Mage Jedrowler, this subject is closed."

No one said a word. "Good. I didn't think anyone would know a spell better than the mage who created it. Anton, please continue."

Taking a deep breath, Anton looked at CynLisa. She was his anchor, his one point of stability. She helped to keep the jitters at bay. "This is phase one. It will bind those within the pentagram to the land. They will feel the land and know what is happening. Phase two will take place in three days, and the land will be bonded to them. Once completed, they and the land will be one. They will be able to draw on each other's ability. The land will supply them with energy to combat invaders and sustain the circle. The circle can act as one entity."

"I have a question," a soft voice asked. Karaleon Magespinner from the elvish community looked at Anton. "If phase one should go wrong, is there a danger of phase two being triggered and causing damage?"

Anton shook his head. "Both phases are separate and different." He turned to the Mage Master, "That's all I have, Mage Master."

"Very well." He smiled at Anton before turning back to the assembly. "For those interested, bards are in the grand ballroom. Let us enjoy the night."

As people filed out, Anton remained standing, quietly acknowledging those who paused to speak to him. As the crowd slowly moved away, CynLisa approached the young lad.

Anton exchanged pleasantries with his duke, who in turn told him of news from home. When he noted the Cyn standing there, he nodded and left so she could talk with Anton about "mage stuff and saving the world."

"You did well, Anton." She smiled as she took his arm and led him from the room. "Now don't let self-doubt creep in. Jedrowler has taught you well. You know what needs to be done."

Anton nodded. "I do have some worries over the Ancient Magic." He held up his hands to forestall any protest. "Don't worry, my concern has nothing to do with channeling. It's having enough for what we need. Too little and the spell will fizzle away."

Chapter Five

Day Two

A false dawn glowed in the north as the enemy's campfires lit the night sky. Morning moved in late as clouds blanketed the valley. As morning light filtered through the clouds, the camp's light was slowly pushed aside. In the gray light, fog slowly rolled down the mountains. Mixed with the chill, a cold drizzle clung to the land and filled the valley.

Gunther Dane crouched behind a tree. Next to him, Halprin gently stroked his thrower. They had traded their light-duty leathers for battle chain. Their breath was coming out in a cloud of white as they shivered from the cold. Around them, other soldiers hid behind trees or brush. Farther up, archers crouched. Only a handful was left in the outpost, standing on the palisade. On top of the keep, Captain Alphron and Wizard Amikin watched the advancing enemy.

Around him, Gunther heard the soft clink of metal on metal, the scraping of a boot on gravel. From the outpost, the whine of a horse sounded through the light fog. Overlaying these sounds, he heard thousands of feet marching in step. He shifted uneasily, his hand resting lightly on the hilt of his sword. His heart started racing as the enemy drew closer.

The previous day, Halprin took the wizard up the mountain and showed him the best spot to strike the rocks. His years of working the mines of his people gave him an eye to the weak points of rock.

While Wizard Amikin was discovering the weakness in the mountain, the rest of the company was busy digging trenches along the path. Once dug, the trenches were concealed. It was hoped in the confusion many of the cavalry and wagons would run off the path and be disabled.

The warriors of the Northland came into view, marching to the soft beat of battle drums. Warriors in the front ranks held banners that fluttered in the morning breeze. Behind them, polemen held high their wicked-looking weapons. Triple-pointed ends, gleaming ax blades, and hooked ends, designed to pull a man from his mount, were carried by these men.

Next came strange creatures pulling wagons no horse or team of horses could pull. These were heavy wagons, but the creatures were moving forward with no apparent problems. Dull military colors covered them, except for three splashed in bright colors. Men dressed in robes of greens and browns rode on these wagons.

Mounted warriors rode up and down the line. Gentle reminders from their staffs kept the procession moving. Gunther watched two mounted warriors ride to the front to lead the horde toward the outpost. The polemen parted, allowing a column of men with ropes and ladders to come through. Archers broke ranks and started moving up the mountain. They had left the path short of where the trenches were. Across the stream, Gunther could see scouts move through the woods of the eastern range.

Twin bolts of wizard energy shot into the mountain. Silent explosions erupted from the overhang and threw dust and rock into the air. A third bolt, trailing tendrils of crackling energy, whipped across the sky and slammed into the overhang. Simultaneously, a white blue flailing ribbon of energy arched and flowed between the keep and the mountain. Magic crackled its fury, echoing along the mountain's top and rolling through the pass.

The foreign mages looked from the mountain to the keep, and the warriors shifted, their polearms dipped, and a general murmur grew. Horses skittered sideways, and the large creatures growled and snapped at each other.

A rider came charging from the rear, flanked by two men. Their elaborate decorations on their armor marked them as officers. The first officer yelled in a foreign tongue at the mages. Two of the mages leaped from their seat and linked hands.

On the keep, Wizard Amikin released the spell. As the energy tail flew, he unleashed two wizard bolts to chase the ribbons into the hole. Magic's full power plowed into the overhang, and explosions rocked the mountain. Debris boiled from the hole. Rocks and stone blew into the air to rain down on the enemy. The overhang shook, danced, and tore free. With a groan, the mountain sent its load into the pass.

Trees and boulders disappeared as a cloud of dust billowed across the mountainside. The last of the magical energy expended itself as the rapidly moving landslide settled in the valley. As the slide slid into the valley, the screams of the enemy reached the ears of the Lashtar soldiers. Dust billowed into the air, and a new scar scored the mountain.

The dust quickly settled in the damp morning air. Trapped beneath the rubble, the injured cries filled the air. Some enemy warriors stood, dazed and confused.

With his sword in hand, a battle cry issued from Gunther's lips. He left his cover and moved on the enemy. Next to him, Halprin fired his thrower, taking out a man who was reaching for his sword.

Soldiers, their battle cries shaking through the still air, charged the dazed warriors. On the mountain, archers sent volleys into the enemies midst. Other soldiers scrambled up the shifting mound of earth, climbing twenty feet above the valley floor.

Gunther finished the last warrior and followed the others up the slide. From the top, he looked down on chaos. Confusion ruled. The slide had pinned many enemy's warriors. Others lay upon the ground, lifeless. The strange draft animals dragged overturned wagons and trampled warriors that didn't move fast enough. Horses were down in the trenches, and wagons had tipped. Up and down the pass, men struggled to calm beasts. Officers yelled orders as they tried to control their own mounts.

Mages were nowhere in sight, their wagon empty. The creature harnessed to it stood motionless, looking around with aged eyes. The officer that had been there a moment before was off to one side, watching the confusion.

Gunther spared a glance up the enemy's back trail. Voices yelled in a strange language. He watched wagon drivers try to control their beast. Foot soldiers scrambled to the side in an attempt to avoid the large beasts. Some took to the stream, only to find it deeper than they assumed.

Gunther smiled and looked up. Overhead, a lone bird high in the sky circled.

The encounter had been short, with no loss of life on the defender's part. Shouts of victory roared across the rock slide, and Gunther felt his lower back slapped by Halprin, who shouted a dwarvish congratulation chant, wiped, then sheathed his sword. Thanking the gods, he looked toward the sky.

"Everyone down!" Gunther shouted. He grabbed Halprin and jumped from their perch and into a hole created by two rocks.

Plunging out of the sky, the bird transformed into a legend. A body of a lizard and the wings of a bat, the creature was as long as three wagons. It swooped over the slide, and fire shrieked from its mouth. Swinging its head, it spread flame. Men had no time to dodge, their bodies became encompassed in flame, and their mouths opened in a soundless scream. The dragon sent its flame traveling up the mountainside, roasting the archers.

Gunther watched the flaming form of a man disappear, falling onto the enemy's side.

"You don't exist!" Halprin screamed.

"That's a dragon."

"They only legends."

"You tell it, it's only a legend!"

The dragon flew into view, landing on the slide. Like a dog in grass, it kicked its rear legs, sending stones, boulders, and body parts flying toward the Lashtar soldiers. A burst of smoke puffed from its snout as it snapped its mouth open and flung its head back. The roar caused men to cover their ears.

Gunther watched a lone figure break from shelter and scramble down the slide. "Stay down!" he shouted. Halprin grabbed his arm, keeping him from running after the man.

The dragon leaped, one leg reached out and sunk talons in the man's shoulders. With a flap of its wings, it lifted the struggling, screaming man into the air. Bringing the body into its mouth, the creature took a bite, cutting the screams short. With a disgusted grunt that echoed from the mountains, it spit the remains out and dropped the body.

The dragon now gave its attention to the outpost and filled the compound with flame. Smoke billowed into the air as the stables went up. In a matter of seconds, flame wrapped the wall, the barracks and the storage buildings in yellow and orange. Men leapt from the wall, only to find themselves surrounded by a wall of flame.

As the dragon spiraled up, two wizard bolts shot from the keep. Screeching in pain, it curled into a ball and fell. It dropped only a short distance before it unfolded its wings and glided to the keep. The flame that shot forth was weaker, but sufficient to cover the top of the keep.

Gunther and Halprin watched in horror as the dragon destroyed the outpost. They saw the smoking body of the captain, his sword clenched in his hand, hanging over the parapet. Trying not to gag from the smell of burnt flesh, Gunther looked at his friend. Halprin's eyes reflected his horror.

They knew this was the beginning of a larger slaughter.

The North Wall was larger, but without advance warning, it would fall to the dragon and the might of the enemy force.

Warlord Thwart reined his horse in next to the dragon. As it held its left wing out to its handler, it whimpered. A scorched mark ran from the wing joint across the chest. The scales were intact, and no blood was visible. The handler felt around the injury before looking up at Warlord Thwart.

"Vella, okay, just bruising under scales."

The dragon looked at the damage, then whimpered louder.

Warlord Thwart nodded. "Give her an extra goat tonight, reward for a job well done."

Vella looked at Warlord Thwart and made a sound between a cat's purr and a serpent's hiss. The warlord snorted as he wheeled his horse around. "The meat can come from the Force Shaper's larder."

As his command slowly reorganized, Warlord Thwart moved among his warriors. Wagons were being uprighted, supplies reloaded, and men collected the dead. He watched as a force shaper held his robes up as he danced his way through the muddy ground.

"Where have you and your group been?"

The Force Shaper looked up. "As you would say, we did a strategic retreat."

Warlord Thwart swung down and in the same movement backhanded the man, sending him sprawling to the muddy ground. "You run away when my men are dying? You and your band are supposed to stop these southerners from using the Unseen Force."

The Force Shaper wiped a trickle of blood from the corner of his mouth. "We had to drop the field. It's a drain to keep it up."

"You all need to shape the Unseen Force?"

"No." The man was crawling backward on his elbows. "We need only one."

"Then I suggest you take turns." Warlord Thwart clenched his fist. "I want that field back up. And reopen the portal, we need replacements for the men you got killed." As he remounted, he looked at the force shaper. "And make me a path through this rubble." He didn't wait for a reply.

Reaching his officers, he said, "We got lucky. I want scouts not just on the mountains, but I want patrols on the road. They're to report every quarter sun." He leaned forward and patted his horse's neck. "These southerners are resourceful. I won't underestimate them again."

Chapter Six

As he walked into the common dining hall, Xantrawler rubbed his hand over his face. His night had been spent conferring with the school's assassin, prowling the corridors, checking for areas that would provide cover for an assassin, and posting his men in key areas. When his stomach started protesting, he didn't have the energy to walk to the barracks.

As he walked past the school's dining hall, the odor drew the weaponsmaster inside. Wintermist had no set time for meals. The nature of magical work set its own timetable. The school's chef tried to maintain the illusion of a civilized eating schedule, so breakfast was set out.

The dining hall was a large room with wooden tables and benches. To one side, a door led back into the kitchen area. A serving table stretched in front of the door. Chandeliers hung from the ceiling, the oil lamps filling the room with light. The chef had insisted on no mage lights, claiming they gave off a harsh light. He held to the belief that meals were a creation and deserved the proper setting. Students sat at one table, servants at another. In a corner, a couple of mages or wizards were carrying on an animated conversation. Xantrawler never learned the difference between a wizard's robes and a mage. A mage was more powerful, but both were useful. That was all the information he needed.

The weaponsmaster's footsteps echoed in the nearly empty chamber. Chef Kepler Drang stood behind the heavily laden table with his hands on his hips. A scowl covered his face as he looked around the room.

Picking up a bowl, Xantrawler reached for the fresh fruit. The chef turned and looked at him. "Have all you want, Weaponsmaster."

Xantrawler chuckled as he grabbed some biscuits. "You have outdone yourself this morning, Kepler. I could feed my entire company."

Chef Drang made a sour face "Send them. The gods created food for enjoyment, not to sit around and mold." His lip curled as his eyebrows joined. "No one told me our special guests would be off meditating, the students busy running errands, and the rest on special missions." He emphasized the word *special*.

"Well, the duke and his people stayed over, so they should be along."

Chef Drang snorted. "The duke's chef already made it clear that only he cooks the duke's meal. As for the rest, I don't serve breakfast for lunch. Nobles believe in getting up at the crack of noon."

Xantrawler smiled as he poured a dollop of honey over his porridge. People forgot he was of noble birth. His family was not typical. His father taught him nobles owed the commoner, not the other way around. His family worked the field at harvest and planting time, when disaster struck, they were there with the people. His father spent time at taverns, in the market, or in the town square. The people of his land knew him and stood loyal to him.

Growing up, Xantrawler thought that was the duty of all nobles. He learned differently at the age of ten when they fostered him to the royal court. He saw and experienced how people treated others that they presumed were beneath their station. As a page, he was invisible and saw nobles and royalty maneuvered for power, petty bickering, the use of lesser people, and the subtle and not-so-subtle attacks.

On trips home, he noticed the same dance on a smaller scale in his father's court. His father tolerated it, telling him learning the dance was necessary if they wanted to hold their position. He explained if they lost their land, the king could give it to a noble who was not as benevolent. In talking with the other pages, Xantrawler learned not all nobles and landholders treated their people as his family did.

His family suffered the way things were, but he could not. He applied himself to what he was good at. Weapons. Ten years, he stayed away from politics and learned his art under one of the king's weaponsmasters. When he turned twenty, he became a weaponsmaster

He was unable to escape the court.

Weaponsmasters are sworn to the crown, leaders in the royal's army. Xantrawler became the best and found himself at the royal court. Over time, he escaped, opening his own salle and teaching future swordsmasters, armsmasters, and weaponsmasters. Later, at the Queen's request, he taught her officers.

Now, he found himself getting involved in the duke's court. His simple retirement grew more complicated with each passing day.

Xantrawler took the steaming mug of jada the chef offered him. "They're part of the leisure class. They feel they deserve compensation for their contribution."

Chef Drang snorted. Laying down his ladle, he looked at the weaponsmaster. "None are worthy of sleeping till false dawn. If they contributed half as much as my kitchen staff, they may have the right to stay in their feather beds till the sun was up." He paused before changing the subject. "Speaking of dawn, control your men or feed them better. They were in my pantry and knocked over a basket of eggs and bag of flour."

"They're supposed to be in the living quarters or overseeing the plateau. I'll have a talk with them."

"Well, we'll find them soon enough. Took a sack of mushrooms some kids sold me. Hadn't had time to go through them but seen some types that aren't fit to eat. They also took herbs I was holding for the healers. You find some sick or dead guards, and you have your men."

"When I find them, I'll send them to you Chef. A month working in your kitchen should cure them of raiding the pantry."

As Xantrawler picked up his breakfast, Duncan entered and approached the serving table. He nodded to his friend.

"Good morning watch, Duncan."

The young swordsman gave his old teacher a slight grimace. "It would be if I hadn't been up half the night with Ambrus."

"Told you to ignore what he said and that I was wasting my time heeding his warning?"

Duncan shook his head. "Worse. He never fully came out of . . . well, wherever it is that he goes. Normally, he sleeps it off within a few hours. This time, he kept yelling in his sleep."

"What was he yelling?"

"Something about the gods and blackness from the Thanatos Range."

"Now that I could believe is his subconscious. Blackness has been associated with that range for years."

"He kept yelling about wraiths and rejoining a legion." He turned to the chef. "Now he is wide awake and famished. Do you have a tray I could use?"

Chef Drang slid a tray from under the table. He looked Duncan in the eyes. "I know you will return it, right? These mages forget to eat. When they do remember, they send a poor student, and that is the last I see of the tray."

Duncan nodded and took the tray.

Xantrawler rubbed his face, trying to bring life into his exhausted mind. "There are no wraiths here, and the only country using the designation legion for their fighting units is the Rolar Empire."

"Which need to go through the elvish land and Vervcracken to reach us. Doubt that will happen," Duncan said as he piled the tray with biscuits and took the small container of honey the chef handed him.

"How's Ambrus doing now?"

"Fine. Has his nose buried in a book." Duncan picked up a mug of jarda and took a long drink. Setting the mug down, he asked, "How did your night go?"

"Nothing unusual. I hate talking with assassins. So many ways to kill a person."

"You know them all. You taught me."

"I taught you to fight face-to-face, looking your opponent in the eyes. Assassins operate differently. Some of their methods are barbaric."

Duncan looked at Xantrawler's plate and motioned for him to eat. "You need your strength, forget about assassins."

Xantrawler looked down at his plate. Mentioning assassins brought back his conversation with Helena, and he suddenly found his appetite gone. He changed the subject. "After this is over, I need to talk with you."

"About what?"

"Returning to the service of the Queen."

Duncan's face set, his eyes turning to cold steel. "I vowed to never be in the Queen's service."

"Duncan, you are the best I ever trained. I am a weaponsmaster, but you are more . . ."

Duncan cut him off, "I am not! I'm a simple swordsman selling my sword. Right now, I'm the bodyguard of a scholar." He picked up the tray of food the chef had brought. "Who I need to get back to."

"Duncan, it's been five years."

"Good day, Weaponsmaster."

Xantrawler watched the young man leave. A heaviness settled in his chest, and he silently cursed the Underdwellers, cursed himself. He instilled loyalty in his pupils, loyalty to the realm, loyalty to their command, and responsibility to your men. It stuck to varying degrees.

With Duncan, it stuck the most.

General Brandon Klaydon nodded to the guards as he walked from the keep. Large enough to be called a castle, no commander of the North Wall would insult the dukes and lords and call it one.

The keep was home to General Klaydon, his officers, and the Queen's knights. It had an inner courtyard, holding a stable, a well and a small flower garden. Well-trimmed grass covered the ground, and soldiers in need of corrective action kept it in shape.

The courtyard opened onto the parade grounds. There were other parade grounds up and down the wall, but this was the principal one. The area held various buildings found on a military post: barracks, blacksmiths, stables, and supply. Knights, archers, foot soldiers, pikemen, and squires drilled or hurried about on various missions. The air was filled with sergeants shouting, feet marching in unison, fighters skirmishing, and the clinking of metal on metal as armorers worked steel. General Klaydon took a deep breath, smelling horse, sweat, wood smoke, and the earth.

General Klaydon approached a group of light horsemen whose faces were still smooth from adolescent. The men and three women wore riding leathers and short swords hung from their hips. A couple of handlers stood to one side, their pack mules loaded and waiting. They were led by a knight not much older.

Queen's Knight Marko Fensin saluted, and General Klaydon gave a grim smile.

They're so young, he thought. He reminded himself he was younger when he took command of his first company, when the Queen's grandfather was king. So many years. Now, officers were being given command sooner, as the army was recovering from the loses of the war. Too many good people had died and not enough to fill their spots.

"Are your men ready?"

"Yes, sir," Knight Fensin replied. His voice carried above the surrounding noise but belonged more to the courts than a battlefield. It was gentle with a soft lilt.

General Klaydon looked at Marko. "You've been with us a couple of weeks, so remember, this is not the rolling hills of your home."

"I have good men, General. They have run patrols in the pass and know the land. I know enough to listen to the veterans. That's why they're veterans. They know how to stay alive."

General Klaydon was pleased. Many times, a new knight was arrogant and ignored the advice of older, wiser soldiers. That type got their command killed.

"Well, let's hope there's no fighting." General Klaydon looked toward the Wall. The Thanatos Range dominated the sky on the other side, their size not diminished by distance.

"I pray too, General. I was a new squire during the Underdweller War. The knight I served lost his horse, killed right under him. He went down in a group of them. He lived, but lost his left eye and right arm."

The General turned from the Wall. "Underdwellers are the least of your worry. The Thanatos Range has other creatures, bands of barbarians and wild mages that wander the foothills. The gods only know what else."

"Do you think there are ten thousand warriors?"

General Klaydon laughed. "No. The message was quickly scribbled. The scribe was hurried, so he added an extra zero or two. A hundred, yes, maybe a thousand. Ten thousand screaming barbarians? No.

"You got your spurs six months ago, and you're young. You show the quality of a good leader, and this will be a good experience. Now, mount up."

Queen's Knight Fensin turned and swung into the saddle. "We should make the outpost by midafternoon tomorrow."

General Klaydon nodded. "Later this morning, I'll have one hundred men-at-arms leaving. They should arrive a day after you. They will be carrying orders relieving the men at the outpost and putting you in command. The present detachment can return. I know it's early so they can consider it a reward for keeping the screaming barbarians at bay."

A woman rode up on an old gray nag. In her early forties, her golden hair had turned dull and showed streaks of gray. Crow's feet surrounded two coal black eyes separated by a simple nose. Her mouth held smile wrinkles. Her hands were gnarled, with prominent knuckles, but were still agile. Her brown robe was patched with cloth shaped as green fronds, yellow flowers, red leafs, or a white moon. In the center of the robe was an embroidered pentagram. The robe was belted with a silver rope, and she wore only sandals. She reined her mount next to the light battle horse of Queen's Knight Fensin.

"General Klaydon." She nodded to the general then to the knight. "Good morning watch, Sir Fensin."

"Witch Cardura."

"Esprin," General Klaydon said, "why so formal?"

Esprin shook her head as she focused her eyes on the general, "I'm sorry, General, I was distracted. I sense magic, earth magic, old magic to the north. Now, nothing. Just blackness."

"A short-lived magical battle?"

"No, everything went black. I can't penetrate the blackness."

"Could be shamans blocking your senses?" Fensin asked.

Esprin looked at him. "This is something else." She paused a moment, weighing her words. "Amikin is there. He's not of the coven, but because of his mother, we are coven bound. I can't feel him."

"Dead?"

"No, I would have felt that. He was there one moment, and the next, he was gone."

"Well, keep your senses alert," General Klaydon said. Turning to Marko, he added, "Keep me informed. You have plenty of birds and the fastest messenger. May the gods watch over you."

Marko saluted and signed to his troops. The men mounted and headed for the gate.

The wall was more than one hundred feet high and wide enough for six horses to race side-by-side. Large watch towers, their top covered with catapults and ballistas, kept watch over the valley. The towers served as barracks for noncoms and special forces. A network of tunnels inside the wall and underground provided protected routes between the towers. Soldiers patrolled or stood watch, and artillery manned the tower. There was constant traffic in, out, and on the wall.

In the center of the valley stood the gatehouse. Larger than most keeps, it rose above the wall and provided the main route to the pass. Presently, the portcullis was raised, and the gates opened. A tunnel, 120 feet long, cut through the gatehouse. The walls were riddled with arrow slots, and murder holes hung overhead. The floor was wood, the stream from the Thanatos Mountains running underneath. Any invaders who made it into the gatehouse would have the floor collapse, finding themselves in the creek.

The general walked over to the command tower, a construct of stone, mortar, and wood and 120 feet tall. It stood apart from the Wall, but there was a constant flow of people in and out. In addition to providing protection from the north, the North Wall was the center of the royal government for the Central Northern Provence. The first two floors were devoted to the bureaucrats. When not overseeing the queen's business at the Wall, they spent time in Trader's Junction. For the most part, General Klaydon wished they would spend all their time there as a large part of his week was spent dealing with them.

Along the outside of the command tower, a stairway wound up to the top floor. From the command floor, General Klaydon oversaw the wall, the path north, and the roads leading from Trader's Junction. In the command room, he and his officers could watch the tactical situations if an attack ever took place. Officers would order countermeasures using flags that flew from the top of the tower. Only a few were flying presently. In addition, the head of the combat mages would be present, directing his magic users in the defense of the Wall.

Slowly, he climbed the stairs, stopping occasionally to catch his breath and mutter, "I'm too old for this."

Wendell Fythe, a knight who grew up in the area, was at the map table in the command room. He acknowledged the general's presence with a nod, then returned to his reading.

General Klaydon looked out the north window and watched Queen's Knight Fensin's party approach the edge of the clearing. The roadway wormed from the wall to the forest. For half a mile north, the valley had been cleared, creating a large killing zone. The creek was widened and filled, creating a quagmire. As it drew near the North Wall, the channel narrowed, and water flowed freely to disappear under the gatehouse.

General Klaydon leaned on the sill, his breath coming hard. He was ready to retire. Forty years of his life had been devoted to the service of the country. It was time to step aside and let the younger generation take charge. He knew in reality he was semiretired. The North Wall was a noncombat posting, a position given to those who served the crown loyally. It was a way for them to stay in the army, serve the queen, and still relax from the normal stress that filled a man-at-arms's life. It wasn't as quiet as Wintermist Wall, but the men stationed here expected little in the way of action. There were minor conflicts with the occasional bandits or creatures from the range.

But the Wall was the only thing standing between what lived in the north and Lashtar. Neither the foothills nor the Thanatos Mountains worried military commanders. It was the Northland. No one knew what lay north of the Thanatos Mountains. The previous king had curtailed exploration, and the activities of the northern tribes were unknown. Only recently had the Queen started sending forays into the mountains. Presently, a small party was exploring the pass. If there was a large force coming, the party was either captives or deceased.

He crossed to the south side of the tower. It was doubtful whatever was coming would breach the wall, but a determined group could go over the ridge and come in from another pass. If that happened, they could strike here. The town of Trader's Junction sat upon three trade routes. A center for commerce, it was a juicy prize for any invading army, rich plunder, and access to major routes. Its city walls would be useless against a force capable of breaking through the North Wall. The barbarians would be stopped. They needed to be stopped.

General Klaydon looked over his right shoulder. It was just theory, a game he played with himself, how to take the North Wall if he had the resources. He was a realist and held no delusion. What man can build, man can destroy.

His second in command straightened from the table and looked at the General. "Scouts along Smugglers pass report all quiet. Nothing amiss in any of the other passes. Even the Underdwellers are being quiet."

"I doubt the outpost's problem is related to the Underdwellers. It could be an incursion from the Northland."

"The northern barbarians?"

"You grew up here, Wendell, what's your thought? Who could organize the savages of the foothills and the Thanatos Range?"

Shaking his head, Colonel Fythe pointed at the top of the map. "We know little of the Thanatos Range beyond this point. We know less of the Northland, except that it contains groups of wandering nomads."

"Those reports are more than thirty years old. The king stopped expeditions after the third force of one hundred were lost."

"Could another country be using the Thanatos Range and the Northland to get to us?"

"This is the only pass directly into the Northland."

"That we know of."

General Klaydon picked up a copy of the translated report from the outpost. "Captain Alphron is not given to panic or exaggeration. A couple thousand warriors are hard to accept, let alone ten thousand."

"The pass is narrow where it comes out of the mountain that could cause a small force to look large."

"Does the enemy have mages?" A man dressed in gold and brown robes stepped into the command center. His beard was short—trimmed weekly by an aide the general supplied—his white hair was tied back in a knot, and his eyebrow was one continuous furry worm. "Wizard Amikin is good, but if they have mages, he would be outclassed."

"Mage Margella, good morning watch," General Klaydon said. "And I had a good morning watch too. Thank you for asking."

"Some things need to be said first, General. If you have a serious incursion, you should be prepared to deal with mages."

"The Northland has shamans," Colonel Fythe said. "Mages living in the foothills are brainsick."

Mage Margella leaned on the table. "I believe I heard the phrase *thirty-year-old reports*. A lot can happen in that time."

General Klaydon said, "If there is anything to worry about, Captain Alphron has enough sense to pull back."

"I warn you, gentlemen," Mage Margella said. "There is something in the north, something I can feel. It's old and evil."

General Klaydon nodded. "You may have something," he told the two of Witch Cardura's experience.

"Esprin is strong in her powers," Mage Margella said.

"There is a legend," Colonel Fythe added. "Something about a war thousands of years ago. An ancient evil was defeated, but will someday return."

"An evil locked away in the Northland?" the mage asked.

"In the Thanatos Mountains."

"Tales to scare children. We had them in my town."

"This one comes from the original people of the area. They lived here, protecting everyone from the north, like we are doing."

"You think this ancient evil now stalks the land?"

"We will find out, gentlemen, we will find out," General Klaydon said.

The gray clouds grew darker as they piled against the Thanatos Mountains. The clouds hid the peaks as they slithered down the crevice, working into the range and spread across the pass. Midmorning they opened up, dumping a cold rain on the outpost. Gunther Dane and Halprin Grotto watched the downpour sizzle and put the fire out.

The dragon had flown away earlier. On the north side of the slide, the enemy had regrouped, draft animals came under control, and officers got men in place. As the rain fell, the decorated wagon moved forward, carrying a half dozen men in robes.

Gunther and Halprin had seen enough. They slid down the rockslide.

Nothing moved. The outpost was a black skeletal remain. The hiss of rain hitting hot coals was the only sound. Smoldering timbers laid blacken where the wall once stood. The barracks and stable were heaps of ash and unburnt wood. The horses that didn't escape were burned, their stiffened legs sticking in the air. Man and animal trapped, the horror of the flames burned into their face. Black smoke poured from the windows of the keep.

"Where is honor in this!" Halprin said as he pushed a smoking charred log aside. Hitting the ground, it showered the dwarf with black water. "None!" He started on a string of curses Gunther found inventive even for his small friend.

The smell of burnt flesh filled Gunther's nose, causing his stomach to roil. Seeing a smoking body, he turned away as he started coughing and gagging. He never got used to seeing burnt and charred bodies. During the Underdweller War, he had smelled burnt flesh and watched men burn to death because of fire lizards. He looked up at the gray sky and wondered if the dragon could be a distant relation.

For a moment, his mind saw the battlefield during the Underdweller War. He watched a fire lizard flame an entire squad. Men became running pillars of flame. Another time at another place, the Underdwellers sent fire lizards into villages, and he saw whole families dead.

His mind saw the North Wall. The carnage around him repeated on a larger scale. He saw the dragon destroying the North Wall and the army of the north moving through Lashtar.

He threw off the vison and looked at his friend. "There's nothing here for us, Halprin. We need to leave."

Halprin spun, anger flashing in his eyes. "These our friends, our comrades! They deserve honor burial! Not leaving them for barbarians or for creatures of mountains. They deserve honorable rest!"

Gunther shook his head. "As much as we should, we don't have time. It would take days to get through that pile. The mages will be through before you know it. Our duty is to warn the North Wall."

"We can't leave them like this." Halprin stomped his foot as his hand swung out.

"Look around. This is the North Wall if we don't warn them. Do you think our comrades will have better luck against the dragon?"

"They have mages. Mages can take unholy thing down."

"They need to prepare, be ready. The general needs to know."

Halprin turned and started stomping around the courtyard. Clenching his thrower in one hand and the shaft of his ax in the other, he mumbled dwarvish curses. He kicked a plank aside and pushed over a timber leaning on the keep. His growls and sneers rang around the compound.

He stopped and swung on Gunther. "Something in keep."

Gunther jogged up to him. "There is nothing. Everyone is dead."

Halprin glared. "Tell you, I heard yelling inside . . . There, hear that?"

"You're just hearing the rocks cool."

"You not think dwarf knows sound of cooling rock? Stupid human."

Gunther heard it, a faint yelling and thumping. As they moved around the keep, the thumping became louder. They stopped at a door that used to lead to the stable. Behind it, they heard a voice yelling.

Gunther and Halprin put their shoulders to a beam that had crashed into the keep and slid down on the door. It now was braced at an angle, holding the door shut. Coughing on the smoke and wincing from the heat, they pushed until the beam broke free and crashed to the ground, splashing gray ash mud in the air. The impact knocked charred pieces lose, and flames briefly flared to life.

Gunther yanked the door open, and the body of Wizard Amikin rolled out. His robe was splattered with burn holes, his hair singed and hands reddened. Blisters covered what was visible of his arms. His trimmed beard was singed, his blacken face smeared with dried blood, and a gash stood out on his forehead. He lay on his back, the cool rain relieving some of the pain of the burns. With puffy bloodred eyes, he looked up at Gunther,

"Thank the gods," his voice was thick and hoarse from heat and smoke. He tried to stand but fell back. Gunther and Halprin helped him to his feet.

"See, dragon fry you," Halprin said.

Wizard Amikin shook his head, "I dived down the stairs. Still, his flame came at me. I just kept rolling. Then the entire room burst into flames. I got out and kept going deeper, but the place filled with smoke. I finally made it to the door, only to find it blocked."

Wizard Amikin looked at the remains of the outpost. "Where is everyone?"

"We're everyone," Gunther said. "The only survivors of the attack of that thing."

"By the gods! We had a hundred thirty men here!"

"Can you do some magic and get a message to the North Wall?"

Wizard Amikin looked down and shook his head. "Between the magic I used and my physical exhaustion, there's nothing I can do."

Gunther described what was on the other side of the rockslide. "We have to leave now. We'll use game trails on the eastern mountains. Halprin has hunted there and knows them."

"You go. I'm in no condition to travel. I would only slow you down."

"We not leave you for them!" Halprin said. "You come, even if I drag you."

"Don't argue with a dwarf. They're a stubborn lot."

The trio left what was left of the outpost and moved slowly into the mountains. Pausing long enough at the stream, they cleaned and bandaged Wizard Amikin's wounds. Halprin found a stout branch for the wizard to use as a walking stick.

An hour into their mission, Wizard Amikin stumbled and sat down hard. He shook his head and moaned. Around him, he watched magic jerk and flap. It changed into sharper lines, but less graceful in its dance. Shortly, a shrill whine filled the air. It reverberated through the valley and the air shimmered with power. One side of the rock slide shimmered, the rocks flowing and mixing into one mass. The mass soften further as it slowly drained into the earth.

A section of the rock slide had been carved away, leaving a clean smooth passage.

Wizard Amikin watched five mages slowly lower their arms, magical energy still glowing around their hands. A shudder ran through him as he realized the power the enemy controlled.

"I will make it. These devils can't make it into our country."

Chapter Seven

King Kandell Rathveil sipped his tea, luxuriating in the solitude of his private chamber. Each day, he took his noon meal here alone. When he first took rulership of his tribe, he started this tradition. He found the demands of a ruler overwhelming and learned that if he didn't have time away, even for a short time, he would become irritated with the smallest detail. Thirty minutes a day, a small half hour was all he asked of his people. He could be interrupted at breakfast, forced to take dinner with honored guests, have his sleep ruined, and time taken from his concubines, but this small span of time was his own.

Today, he was enjoying a lite lunch, sharp cheese and honey bread. He reclined in his chair, sipping a fine tea and reading, just for the joy of reading. King Rathveil delighted in the art of story spinners. He marveled at how they created tales, weaving common words that transported a person from their dreary lives. Story spinners took him from his troubles, made him forget the responsibility of his position.

Sighing, he sipped the last of his tea. To draw out the moment, he slowly lowered the cup to the saucer. Slowly, he placed his marker in the book and closed the covers. As if the two acts were connected, the chamber's door opened, and Warlord Thrawt entered.

The warlord, his armor covered with dust and the smell of sweat about him, marched up to King Rathveil. He knelt, head bowed. "Our army has taken the Lashtar outpost, sire. We now continue to what they call the North Wall."

"You just cleared the outpost?"

"Their mage brought the side of a mountain down. We lost two hundred men." He looked up at King Rathveil and smiled. "Vella took care of the Lishtarens."

"How did their mage do anything?" King Rathveil slammed his book on the table. The warlord's smile slid from his face. "My Force Shapers are supposed to have our Unseen Forces blanketing the area!"

"They claimed to need a rest."

King Rathveil stood and looked down at his warlord. "I lost many force shapers learning about the Southlands. They found our magic would neutralize the mages, and we could call it to us." He stepped away from the table. "Did they think these people were going to let us walk into their country? When you return, tell those Force Shapers to have the Unseen Forces flowing."

Warlord Thrawt stood. "My lord, that is already done."

King Rathveil nodded. "Never forget, General, the enemy whose land you are invading is the most dangerous."

"These southerners are resourceful. I'm afraid they will counterstrike and retake what we conquer."

"Oh, they will attack. The companies you leave behind will contend with that."

"A thousand is not enough. I need to spend a few days securing our position and have five thousand warriors sent through the portal. A few Force Shapers would help."

King Rathveil shook his head. Walking to the window, he pulled on his chin and stared at the mountains. The warlord faintly heard him muttering, "People will fight hard for their land, harder than for gold." He tapped his chin with his forefinger and hummed a bit.

"But there are those who can be bought. Yes, yes, I agree that would work."

With a shake of his head, King Rathveil brought himself out of his deep thought and turned to his warlord. "No, warlord, I can't give you the five thousand you want."

"But, sire . . ."

Rathveil held up his hand. "I can't spare five thousand troops. You may need them when you attack Wintermist. I do agree, you need Force Shapers, so I'll send three after you take the wall. In addition, I will send a message to our spies, have them recruit mercenaries."

Warlord Thwart bowed his head.

"Remember. You have Vella."

General Thrawt nodded. "Your pet was invaluable at the outpost."

King Rathveil smiled whenever he thought of his pet. The spirit walk was the time a shaman sought guidance. It was a yearly duty, and he did his spirit walk in the Thanatos Range. For a week, he sought peace and guidance, his time spent in contemplation and prayers. At night, he meditated; and during the day, he looked inward.

He entered the range during his first spirit walk. It was forbidden for a shaman to enter the Thanatos Mountains, and he had no intention of doing so. He had camped near the mountains one night, but when he awoke, he found himself on the slopes of one of the mountains. His heart raced as he saw where he was, and he was close to bolting back to his tribe. He would have if he had not recalled what he had been told. During a spirit walk, you never question where your feet took you.

It was the start of his dream.

On his first night, he had a vision. His spirit guide came to him, and he listened to whispered words of the past glories of Terrapin Xon. The Spirit promised the glory of days gone by could be recaptured. His nights were filled with the dream, and during the day, he had awake visions. He looked upon Terrapin Xon and saw the future.

The dream followed him and grew.

Each year, he returned to the Thanatos Range, and his spirit guide came to him. He learned to make the dream a reality. He took control of Gareth, brought a number of tribes under his control, and confronted the representative of Norge.

It was during one spirit walk that he came across a baby dragon. The creature took to him immediately, and the two bonded. He knew it was a sign from the gods, a reward for doing their will. He returned to Gareth with the dragon riding on his shoulder.

The dragon, who was called Vella, traveled everywhere with him, to his throne room, council meetings, on procession through the city, and when he visited new villages in the growing land. Soon, she was too big to be in the palace, so King Rathveil had special quarters built.

Vella showed a rudimentary intelligence and the ability to follow simple commands. As she got older, he used her in securing his rule of Terrapin Xon. With her size and her ability of flight, she terrorized tribes that had not conceded to his rule. She would swoop down and overturn wagons, chase livestock into the countryside, and disrupt the entire camp. The more the tribe resisted, the worse it became. Vella would flame tents and feed on the herds.

His enemies feared the creature, but his people loved her. Vella entertained the people during festivals and rescued people during storms and other emergencies.

"As a gift from the gods, she is special. Take good care of her and protect her. When this is over, she will be honored as the war hero she is."

King Rathveil walked to the table and picked up his tea cup. He saw it was empty and sat it back down. "Our spies at Wintermist have sent separate reports on a threat from the Force Shapers. I gave the order to eliminate the problem." Looking at his book, the golden page marker sticking out, he sighed. Mentally, he shook himself and shoved the chair in.

"Drive into Lashtar, take the land of Mead, Warlord. We need that land, especially Wintermist. I want the Spirits."

"You shall have Mead within half a moon."

"Good!" King Rathveil rolled his eyes toward the ceiling. "Now, I need to listen to petitioners' petty gripes and complaints. It was simpler when we were tribes."

"That is the price for greatness."

King Rathveil made no comment, just proceeded out the door and down the hallway, his guards falling in behind him.

Warlord Thwart sighed. He had voiced his concerns, but the king had ignored his protests. His supply lines were too long, too many untested men, a heavy reliance on the Force Shapers and Vella. He had not lost any of the siege equipment passing through the Thanatos Range, but there was a long way to go. Wagons wore out, and beasts became ill or lame. Illness could quickly spread among the men.

The king was a good man at unifying the people, creating a new world, but he had no concept of military actions. Warlord Thwart had tried to convince him the plan was too ambitious. It required the army to move too fast, to hold more ground than possible with limited men. It relied too much on luck and not enough on foresight and planning.

After taking the wall, they should stay and secure it from a counterstrike. His men should rest, have time for themselves. The plan allowed for no proper rear guard. Mercenaries were not the solution. They can always turn on their employer, then they would lose the wall and be trapped. At least, he now had Force Shapers at the wall.

He worried about the three prong attacks. One column would take the dwarvish mining community, another would travel the center of the land, and the last would secure the western borders. The lines would be spread out, unable to support each other.

He worried about the eastern column, the one attacking the Dwarvish community. Dwarves were ferocious fighters, and he respected them. They could never be part of his army or part of Terrapin Xon, as they bowed to no one but their own king. He had given the order to kill them all.

Warlord Thwart left for the portal room. He was a soldier. He did as commanded and carried out his orders. The king's invasion plan was flawed, but he could work with it. He was allowed the freedom to adjust the plan as he saw fit, and he saw fit to use his own plans.

King Rathveil stepped into his changing room, a room large enough to hold a wardrobe, chair, and a table with a mirror. His herald had laid out his full regalia and was removing the king's ornate medallion of office. King Rathveil scowled.

"I said make it simple and short today."

"I'm sorry, milord, but the Ambassador of Norge is demanding to see you."

Norge was the other country of the Northlands. Governed by priestesses, they kept the complete copies of the Sacred Scrolls. They interpreted the words and handed down the commands of the gods. They did until King Rathveil started to interpret them.

"I can refuse her." He smiled as his herald's eyes went wide. "Don't worry, Gilmore, I'll see her. It's time we had this little meeting. You remember your orders?"

The small man nodded. "Do you think it will be necessary?"

King Rathveil took the velvet robe and settled it on his shoulders. It was held in place with a heavy clasp in the shape of a dragon. From the top shelf, Herald Gilmore removed a heavy stone crown. It symbolized his connection with the land, the past, and the people roaming the land. To him, it was more impressive than a piece of metal.

Setting the crown on his head, he checked himself in the mirror and put on his royal face. Herald Gilmore opened a door opposite the one the king entered. At a nod from King Rathveil, he stepped through the curtains and thumped his staff.

King Rathveil ignored Gilmore's speech. He had heard it countless times. He spent these few seconds preparing. The rulers of Norge, stating their benevolent ways, showed leniency for his change of Terrapin Xon. In return, he made concessions.

This time, there would be no concessions. It was time for a new power in the Northlands.

"Ruler of all before you. All kneel in the presence of our ruler, King Kandell Rathveil."

The audience chamber was modeled on the traveling tents of the tribal chiefs for he never wanted the people to forget their heritage. Light entered through curtained windows high in the walls. Brown fabric, made from beasts of burden, hung from the ceiling and flowed in waves down the walls. Where the fabric did not cover, tapestry dangled. The floor was covered with rugs and large pillows were grouped around low tables or piled in the corner. The only large piece of furniture was the ivory-colored throne upon a pedestal of granite, which in turn rested upon a slab of blue stone.

King Rathveil stepped from behind the curtains and made his way to his throne

As the king made his way to the throne, he looked at his subjects. All knelt, except for a woman at the front of the chamber. Her lavender robes were made of material designed to appeared ready to fall from her body in a light breeze. Her dark hair rolled over her shoulder, hair ribbons woven within. Large golden hooped earrings sparkled in the light, and a silver broach glistened over her left breast. A bronze-colored rope wrapped around her hips.

She stood facing the throne, refusing to look at the king.

The man in King Rathveil enjoyed looking upon the ambassador. The ruler dreaded the sight of her.

Upon reaching the blue slab, he turned to his subjects and gave them a smile. He bowed slightly and slowly sat down. As his court sat, Herald Gilmore stepped forward, stood to the right of the blue stone slab, and pounded his staff three times.

"From the realm of the powerful and wise Czaran Jessablee, her royal voice and faithful servant, the just and knowing Keeper of the Scrolls of Tantrinlondrum, and the Giver of the Ten Sacred Scrolls, the Lady Yelanda Trantro."

Lady Yelanda stepped passed the herald onto the audience platform. Her lips were in a grim line, her face impassioned. She stared at King Rathveil, not curtsying or acknowledging his rank. King Rathveil nodded to the ambassador, giving her a chance to show proper respect and to follow proper protocol.

Lady Yelanda started talking. Her silvery voice carried to the far reaches of the chamber. "Your recent activities have alarmed us, Kandell Rathveil. We command you to stop and withdraw from the Southlands. Immediately!"

King Rathveil heard the gasp run around the room. The court held their collected breath as he leaned forward and in a low voice asked, "Who do you think you are, giving commands to me in my own chamber?"

"I am Yelanda Trantro, Keeper of the Sacred Scrolls and the Voice of the Czaran."

"I know your tittle. It doesn't give you the right to order me around as if I am a common worker."

"We interpret the scrolls and enforce them. What you have done and what you plan to do concerns and affects all of us. The consequences will lead to grave repercussions for the Northland."

"The Northland or Norge?" King Rathveil asked. He sat back and steepled his fingers under his chin. "It seems that Terrapin Xon achieving the greatness it deserves would have grave consequences for your country." He sat up straight in his chair. "We no longer bow to your commands."

"You have broken the covenant with the gods. It is written, in the Sacred Scrolls, that the tribes shall not unite, the tribes shall travel the land, and the tribes shall care for the land until the day Terrapin Xon is likened unto a garden."

"Terrapin Xon is a garden. As for the scrolls, our people carries out their commands. We've grown, learned in the last thirty years what the scrolls really say, not what you want us to think they say. We are interrupting them, not you. Remember, I was a shaman. I was taught the Ten Sacred Scrolls."

"Another break with the scrolls. The shaman shall not rule. The shaman shall guide the people along the spiritual path."

"It is also said a shaman shall unite the tribes and bring glory to Terrapin Xon!"

Lady Yelanda took a step forward, her eyes narrowed. "You dare to claim to be the holy one?"

"I make no claim. I only prepared the way for he who is to come."

"First, you corrupted Gareth. It was never to be a permanent place for anyone. You teach the use of the forbidden forces. You have taken an unclean creature of the range into your home. We have been patient. We have waited for the people to see the evil of your ways return to the traditions, the ways of the Sacred Scrolls."

King Rathveil slowly ran his fingers over the smooth white surface of the armrest. He grew weary of the constant challenges, the trading of quotes from the Sacred Scrolls. He should banish her. He chuckled, not now. He had plans for the Lady Yelanda. Later, he would shape her bones into a gift and send it as a peace offering to the Czaran.

Lady Yelanda misinterpreted the chuckle. "So you feel we jest. It is time you learn the full power of the priestess, what it means to feel our wrath.

"Woman!" Without shouting, King Rathveil let his voice echo from the walls. "That is the last time you will threaten me in my chamber. I will no longer tolerate it. Return to your quarters and pack. You and your entourage are to leave my kingdom immediately.

Tell the Czaran no one from Norge will be welcomed until she sends the proper apology and you receive punishment."

"So be it, Rathveil." Lady Yelanda began chanting.

Time twisted with multiple events. Energy pulsed, Lady Yelanda's power built rapidly. Power from her god filled her. The power snapped and screeched, her eyes taking on a golden glow and her god's light shining from inside.

King Rathveil's guards flowed from their hidden places, each intent on reaching the ambassador.

King Rathveil spoke his power word and a bluish green globe of energy encircled him.

Gilmore slammed his staff hard, on the blue stone, called out a nonsense word, and waited.

From the blue stone, sparkling ropes of energy spiraled around Lady Yelanda. Her golden energy swirled with the ropes. The power of her god danced with the ropes as they moved away from her and sank into the blue of the stone.

As the glow left Lady Yelanda's eyes, her muscles went slack. Before she could fall, four guards took her to the cold blue stone. Other guards surrounded their king, weapons drawn.

King Rathveil stood and brushed by his guards. He approached a wilted Lady Yelanda, her feet unable to support her as the guards hauled her up. Her hair combs and ribbons were scattered on the floor, her hair hanging in front of her face. As she weakly lifted her head, he saw blood flow freely from her nose and the corner of her mouth. The glow that always surrounds her was gone. She looked plain. King Rathveil found no desire for her. "Did you think I would be so foolish not to have protection?"

"You can't do this to me," Lady Yelanda's voice was weak, a slight roughness had developed. Her crystal voice had fled, and she sounded like an old crone. "I am the voice of the Czaran."

"You are an assassin. I shall send a letter to your Czaran and tell her of your act."

"You won't be able to hold me."

"I have plans for this treachery. I have a special cell, made of the same blue stone you are standing on. Your use of the Unseen Forces is over."

King Rathveil nodded to the guards. "Take her to her new quarters. I will speak with her in a day or two. Perhaps, by that time, she will be willing to cooperate."

As the Lady Yelanda was taken away, he spoke to the guard chief. "Your men acted quickly and efficiently, and I shall reward you. Tonight, come to the concubines' chambers."

The guard chief backed out, bowing and thanking his lord. King Rathveil turned to Herald Gilmore. "Cancel the rest of the afternoon and fetch the council members for an emergency session."

As the page hurried off, King Rathveil felt worries creep into his mind. The Czaran would respond. He was not sure if he could handle two fronts, not with the limited resources he had.

A voice whispered in his ear. When he took Wintermist, all kingdoms would bow to him.

Chapter Eight

"Really, Diamox, you don't need to accompany me," Duncan said for the fifth time.

The sun was low as the pair skirted through the crowd filling the streets of Wintermist. Farmers and craftsmen pushed their carts while other people made their way with bundles of goods. Horse-drawn carts pushed their way through, receiving glares or curses depending if the beast stepped on them. People were heading home, shopkeepers were closing their doors, and traveling bards strummed their way to the taverns. The city watch was walking in pairs or trios in anticipation of the night crowd. The air was thick with smoke from fire pits being doused, the smell of the street venders' food replaced with the smell of sweaty bodies, horse dung, and ripe fish.

"Don't be silly, Duncan. It's only proper for a young lady not to be seen unescorted in the company of a gentleman."

Diamox led them down a side alley that emerged on a less-traveled road near the lake.

"I know Sasha, and I can give you advice." He smiled at the young swordsman. "It's my pleasure to help a developing relationship."

"It's not a developing relationship. It's dinner so we can continue our conversation. I want to prove to her that swordsmen are not a bunch of uneducated barbarians." Duncan had left his sword in his room and was dressed in somber colors of dark blue and light gray.

"Not a proper discussion to have with a lady, too deep. I understand wanting to impress her with your civilized manners, but let me lead the conversation." Duncan let out a sigh of exasperation.

Turning the corner, Lake Mead came into view. The thoroughfares ran straight to the docks, buildings on either side forming an honor guard with their brightly colored trim and their signs swaying in the lake breeze. The land sloped to the water edge, the sound of water slapping the retaining wall reached their ears. Small fisher boats rode the still water, and birds flew lazy circles around the masts, their cries of hunger and anger swarmed in the air.

"Where do you plan on dining?"

"I thought I would ask her."

"No, no, no. Haven't you ever courted a lady?"

Duncan lowered his eyes and watched the cobblestones. "Never met a lady worth courting. There were a few in taverns and such."

"Wenching does not count. Sasha is a lady and should be treated as such. Her father expects it. Remember, he has high regard for officers of the military, and your type ranks with them." Ambrus indicated a small shop, its windows held pastries and bread. "This is it." He paused before entering the store. "I know where you can take Lady Sasha."

A small bell over the door announced their arrival. The shop was intimate. The display cases were laid out in a rectangle, most of their shelves empty at this late hour. The smell of confectionary filled the room, which held the warmth of baking. A large man with thick arms and a bald head came from the back, wiping his hands on a towel tucked into the strings of his flour-covered apron.

"Welcome. I don't have much left, but you're welcomed to whatever strikes your fancy." The man swung his arm to indicate the near-empty shelves. He had a contagious smile that made his customers feel like an old friend. "Half price on everything."

"Master Magnate, it is a pleasure," Diamox said. He removed his hat with a sweep of his arm and bowed. "May I introduce Sir Duncan of Pentock." He straightened, replacing his hat and adjusting the fur collar on his great coat. "He has come to call upon your lovely daughter, the Lady Sasha. With your permission, he would be honored for her to dine with him at the Lakeshore Parlor. I shall escort them to ensure proper decorum is followed and your daughter's honor is not soiled."

"Is that a dead animal around your neck?" Baker Magnate stepped forward and looked Diamox over. "Can't have a dead animal in my bakery." He stepped back. "Ahh, you must be that scholar fellow she talks about, Dye Pox."

"Diamox, yes, I am. But tonight, I am a simple escort for the youngsters."

Sasha's father held out a beefy hand to Duncan. "I'm Bran Magnate, and it's an honor to meet you, Lord Duncan."

Duncan took Bran's hand, giving it a firm shake. "It's a pleasure, sir, but I am no lord, just a simple man making a living."

"I know you, Duncan of Pentock. My entire family knows you. Well, Sasha doesn't. She thinks she is educated. Humph!" He smiled as he released Duncan's hand.

"I don't understand."

"Duncan Pentock, the hero of Briggins Ford. My brother was part of that battle. His detachment was under attack by the Underdwellers, and your company saved them, drove those nasties right back underground."

"We did what we had to do."

"You did more than that. He told me how you visited the wounded of both companies. Said you even got extra healers from the general. Many could have died from battle wounds if it wasn't for you."

"Well, I would prefer if Sasha didn't know who I am. Just think of me as a simple bodyguard watching over a crazy scholar." Duncan gave Ambrus a hard look.

"Let me get Sasha." Bran left, and they heard him climbing the stairs, calling her name.

"Well, that went well. You made a good first impression. Let's hope the rest is as smooth."

"Providing you don't make a fool of me. Diamox, this isn't the royal court. I know common folks, and they don't live by the same rules."

"Well, what would you have done? Walked in and said, 'Hay I'm here to take your daughter out, get her drunk, and boff her under the pier.'"

"That's what the last guy said," Sasha's voice held a hint of amusement. "Da tossed him out with the mealybugs." She entered the shop wearing a light green dress. She had no jewelry, but a simple white cloth encircled her neck. A closer look showed simple embroidery in an off-white thread.

"See. I did the right thing."

Sasha looked at Diamox. "Actually, Da is upstairs debating if he should go with us. Something about a crazy old man with a funny flat hat and a dead brown animal draped over his shoulders."

Ambrus brushed his hand through the fur-lined collar. "This is the latest fashion in court."

"And that's why I live in Wintermist."

"Shall we discuss fashion over dinner?" Duncan asked. He looked at Sasha. Her hair was not pulled back in a ponytail like when they first met. It fell around her neck, two combs holding it back so it cascaded over her shoulders and down her back. It had the fresh washed sheen that glowed in the light from the windows. He detected a hint of fragrance, a perfume smelling of the mountain flowers.

"Yes, dinner sounds good. I heard something about the Lakeshore Parlor. Diamox must be paying you too much if you can afford that place."

"I have nothing else to spend my money on. I may as well spend it on a pleasant evening with a lovely young lady." Duncan felt his cheeks flush and bit his tongue. That was the second time he had managed to put his mouth moving before his thoughts.

Sasha smiled and held out her arm.

Lakeshore Parlor sat on a pier and catered to nobles and the merchant class, people that enjoyed their luxuries. During warmer weather, meals were served on the roof and patios, providing a grand view of the lake and the twin sentinels. Starting in late spring, a dining boat took patrons on midafternoon cruises. Evening cruises were scheduled during full moons.

The main dining hall held tables constructed of maple, stained and waxed to a high polish. They were set with glass plates and crystal goblets crafted by master glass smiths from Glassand. The polished silverware came from the dwarvish mine of Mead. Runners on the tables were white, blue, green, and for high-ranking nobles, purple. Oak chairs encircled the tables. The floor's carpet was a thick red pile from the southern island of Gentrill. Noted for their colorful workmanship, it was said the people of Gentrill wove magic into all their work.

As the sun set, candles on each table provided the only illumination. The staff's outfits were subdued colors, helping them blend in with their surroundings. Waiters constantly circulated, ensuring goblets were full, empty plates were removed, and the guest's every desire was handled. Serving wenches brought food on covered silver trays, gold for the nobles.

Near one of the many fireplaces, bards played on a raised platform. Their songs ran from the romantic to ballads. Occasionally, a bard walked among the guests, singing love song to couples. On this night, they sang about heroes and their deeds.

Diamox had talked the maitre d' into giving them a table overlooking the lake. They watched Lake Mead and saw the mist from the falls. Birds flew graceful patterns, diving into the lake, settling on the piers, or flocking on the shore. As the twilight neared, merchant boats sailed in from the east and docked at the wharves.

Sasha was fiddling with the stem of her wine glass. Her mind was dwelling on why she accepted the swordsman's offer. She never acted so brash, and she wasn't interested in his type. She wanted a man with intelligence, refinement, and poise. She didn't want a man who solved problems at the end of a sword. She forced herself to stop thinking along those lines. This was a simple dinner, not unlike the dinners she had with Diamox or others from the Screeching Owl.

Looking at her dinner companions, she released her wine glass and picked up her spoon and took a bite of her casserole. Diamox had recommended it, made of beef, potatoes, and some type of green vegetable. She found it acceptable, even though the crust was a little overdone.

Diamox was enjoying a lake bass smothered in butter and herb sauce. Sasha looked at Duncan, eating a steak still red through the center. He dabbed his napkin on the corner of his mouth and commented about the chef's skill.

"Lake Shore serves the best lake bass in the kingdom," Diamox said.

"Mead is the only lake that has lake bass," she reminded him.

"They win by default."

She was surprised Duncan knew which fork to use for each course. He ordered wine compatible with their choices. She held her breath when he picked up the napkin, expecting him to tuck it in under his chin. She had picked on him for not drinking from the finger bowl.

Duncan knew etiquette, and she was impressed. She felt hope for the sword swinger, then she looked at his dinner. *Your meal shouldn't moo at you. One more reason*, her mind told her, *you should forget this man.*

Duncan was debating Ambrus.

"Look, you've traveled as much as I. You know there are things that can't be explained by this science."

"You are making a common mistake. If you can't explain it, it must be magic. If you can't see it, it is a powerful Unseen Force."

"I have watched mages do incredible things."

"Things that given time I could do. Well, time and the knowledge of their secrets."

"Magic is a force all around us. It lives because it is," Sasha said.

"I think. Therefore, I am? That argument has been disproved countless times."

"No, Diamox, magic is here because of all living things. It came into being when we did. We are part of it, and it is part of us. It changes as we change, matures as we mature." Taking a sip of her wine, her eyes glistened. It was always enjoyable debating the man. "You have to admit there may be a force your science doesn't know about. Something invisible that appears out of nothing."

"Like what?"

"Like lectricity," Duncan said. "It's invisible, but you can make it visible."

"Ahhh, you have been reading my books by Haraday. He is convinced it is magnetism, an invisible force. He has created lectricity using magnetism."

"So is it magic?" Sasha asked.

"No. Anyone can repeat his experiments, and they don't need years of selective training."

"Anyone?" Looking at Duncan, Sasha's gleam brightened. "Even sword swingers?"

Duncan raised an eyebrow. "I may have trouble not hacking the experiment apart when it doesn't work right."

Diamox winked at Sasha. "Be careful, my dear. Duncan has been with me and watched some of my debates. He's learning."

"Well, Sasha, do you believe sword swingers can pass in a civilized setting?"

Sasha nodded. "Oh yes, sir knight." She tossed her hair. "I now see you are a refined gentleman of the finest upbringing." She tilted her head and fluttered her eyes.

"Aha, my fair lady, I am pleased you recognized the refinement contained in this frame of mine." Duncan closed his eyes and half rolled them as he bit his cheek. He kept forgetting himself. Why he said what he did, he didn't know.

Before Sash could respond, Diamox let out a bark of a laugh. "I knew you two would make a perfect couple."

In unison, the young people turned and commanded Diamox to shut up.

"Of course," Sasha said, returning her attention to Duncan, "you don't have any weapons, no sword to cut your half-dead cow with."

Diamox laughed. "Duncan without a weapon? That's like a duck without feathers."

"Ah, he hides them well. See, Diamox, you have proven there is magic. The sword swinger has invisible weapons."

Duncan shook his head. "They are only invisible to the untrained. My dinner knife"—he held the utensil up—"I could easily defend us with this." He pointed out common objects. "Wine bottles and glasses can be broken. A smashed chair has a nice club."

Propping her elbows on the table, Sasha folded her hands, rested her chin on them, and looked at Duncan. "It appears there's more to sword swingers than hacking. Perhaps you could teach me to be one."

"You don't have the character. You could be trained to defend yourself, but you could never do this as a job. You care too much but not enough to suffer the pain. It's not a job. It's a lifestyle, a choice. We dream of peace and harmony. Reality is conflict, greed, hatred, and domination. Some want to fight for the sake of fighting. Others have no ethics or moral values. Then you have the Underdwellers, aggressive by nature.

"We who have chosen this path are realists. Common folks need protecting. You need swordsmasters, armsmasters, and weaponmasters, the ones who dedicate their lives to protecting others."

"What's the difference between the three masters?"

"Swordsmasters, well, are masters of the sword. They are skillful with any number of swords: long swords, short swords, bastard swords, more than I can name right now. Some learn the swords of the other races, the dwarvish rockmore and the elvish flay.

"Armsmasters are knowledgeable in weapons used for personal combat. They know the pike, the ax, the flail, and the mace. Bows and javelins, any type of arms used by a fighter.

"Weaponsmasters start young. They have the skill of swordsmasters and armsmasters. They learned weapons of war and battle tactics. Their leadership skills are developed, and some are taught the fine art of diplomacy. That's why weaponsmasters are in the Queen's service."

"But how could anyone dedicate themselves to a life of violence?"

"It's a calling." Duncan laid down his silverware and leaned forward. "Someone needs to protect those who can't protect themselves. Look at Diamox, a great fighter with words. But if someone should punch him in the nose, all he would know to do is lay there and bleed."

On stage, the bards switched. The new one pulled up a stool, snuggled his gittern on his lap and plucked the strings, speaking to the crowd as he brought his instrument into tune. In a deep bass voice, his words rippled over the crowd:

It was the end of the Underdweller War
The enemy was done
One last move they made
One last place they came, The Valley

Diamox nodded. "Without them, we would lose many great people of the world."

The Valley where many died that day
Many who gave their lives for you and me
The Valley where many heroes were made
None so great as the ones I now sing

"Brothers and sisters of the sword, a bond deeper than family, deeper than a lover." Duncan sat back in his chair and looked at Sasha. "When you share death, you share life. We care because we know there are things greater than us, things worth fighting for."

The Nine gave their lives
Not for you and I
Not for Queen and country
Their lives they gave for all
The Heroes Nine

The bards ran the entire complement of chords, part military, part religious, but overall a somber melody.

Sasha's face brightened. "Like the Heroes Nine!"

Duncan stiffened, his head cocked as if he was hearing the ballad for the first time. His eyes locked straight at the lake, losing focus. Slowly, he brought his napkin up and touched his lips. As he finished, he looked at Diamox. "If you will excuse me." He stood, tossing his napkin on his plate. "Sasha." He nodded.

The bard started the tale, recounting the deeds of the Heroes Nine. Duncan took the long way around, avoiding the bard. The entire way, his eyes focused straight ahead, looking neither left nor right.

"For a smart girl, you're one dumb woman."

"What did I say?"

"Listen to the song."

Around the wounded hero they lay
Nine great people who fought that day
As the healers lifted the hero
As they carried him from the field,
He shouted!
"Hold! My men you must save
Treat them first I can wait
Brave they are give them your all."
And it was told a great man cried that day.
He Shouted!
"Forget them not, remember their names
The Heroes Nine they saved the day"

Diamox watched comprehension flow through Sasha. Emotions chased each other around her face, through her eyes. He nodded as she looked at him.

"He's . . . he's Pentock!"

"I know. Please keep your voice down."

"But he's Duncan Pentock. *The* Duncan of Pentock!"

Diamox leaned back in his chair. "And that makes him different than when he was just *a* Duncan Pentock?"

"I thought he was dead." Sasha looked around the room, expecting to find herself at the ghost tavern. "No one has seen him since the war. Not for five years."

Diamox nodded. "Some wounds take a long time to heal."

"He seems well healed now."

"Some wounds you don't see."

"What do you mean?"

"Duncan is haunted by ghosts that consume his soul."

Sasha paused and listened as the bards worked through the instrumental of the song. She had heard the ballad many times. One could not escape it. Now she was hearing it in a different light. The

Valley was no longer a faceless entity fought in some far off part of the kingdom.

"The Heroes Nine?" She breathed it more than asked it.

"He ordered the massacre of every man and woman in the Valley."

"But he . . ."

"Had his own company."

"The songs, the ballads, they show he had no choice." She paused a moment. "The line in another ballad, 'The Queen's Lament.' '*She took no joy in the battle that day, her men the life they gave. To retreat was not their way, the kingdom's fall lead that way.*'" She took a breath. "I'm not a weaponsmaster. I know nothing about battle strategies. But I know if he had pulled his men out, the Underdwellers would have won."

"Others believe as you do." He took a sip of wine, then looked into the goblet as he swirled the contents. "Being my bodyguard is just a pretext. I took him in on behalf of the Queen. She needs him. His country needs him. There are things happening that people don't know about. There's the Rolar Empire and Vercracken, pirates and brigands, even internal matters. They threaten the country. The present champion is old, ready to retire. The Queen needs a strong and respected champion." He looked at Sasha. "Arraignments were made for me to join Mage Kytril to bring Duncan here. The Queen hopes talking with his old master will help him put to rest the ghosts of his past."

Sasha shuddered. "My uncle has told a few stories. I can't imagine the nightmare Duncan is having."

"You don't know swordsmen, do you?"

"I've never knew one like him. The rest seems so barbaric."

"Duncan learned from his father and Xantrawler that a leader is responsible for those he leads, for their welfare. He made the decision to stay and fight. Outnumbered, they all stayed and held the valley." Diamox gave a humorless grin. "You cannot imagine his demons. They need to be exercised before they consume him."

The bards finished the tale of the Heroes Nine with the chant of their names. As they went on to another song, Sasha commented, "Duncan needs a friend to talk to."

Diamox nodded. "Don't treat him any different and don't let him know you know who he is. And for the gods' sakes, don't let your father know. He's enjoying having one up on you." He gave her a grin, and she smiled back.

They started a new topic, and when Duncan returned, Sasha was going on about the casting that night. "I wish I could be there."

"I'm sure you will see much from down here," Diamox said. "Never knew a mage who could do a spell without a lot of flashing lights and noise."

"Ever the hardened skeptic. Someday you will be convinced magic is real. You will believe."

Duncan let out a snort. "Diamox believes in magic? That will be the day the Grand Mauler of the Goblins declares peace with the surface world and worships at the temple of Odium."

Chapter Nine

A cool breeze flowed with the moonlight as it descended the stairs. It carried the scent of incense, the smell assaulting his nose.

With the smell came the sound of people, restless and impatient. Jedrowler pulled up the hood of his robe, causing the moon to cast shadows across his face, hiding his features. No one could see the look in his eyes, the dance of a small child waiting to open a present. He slid his hands into the large sleeves of his simple robe and waited.

Magic was coming into sync as students beat animal hide drums. The rhythm matched magic's flow, causing it to dance. The primitive people used such beats to call magic. Under the stars, in the moonlight, magic was filling the plateau.

Anton descended the stairs. The wizard wore a white robe, cut like Jedrowler's. His eyes held the gleam of one in a light trance. He nodded, and together, they ascended the stairs. As they rose, the young wizard pulled his hood up so that when the two stepped onto the plateau, they look like two apparitions come to the gathering.

Xantrawler's men stood around the rim, the weaponsmaster next to Mage Master Gardner. Jedrowler saw, with normal sight and mage sight, Xantrawler's sword. It glowed with old magic, magic from the early times. For a moment, he wondered why he didn't include martial magic in the spell casting.

The drums grew louder. Jedrowler felt the magic change, and the power grow. The magic swirled and throbbed, almost visible to normal sight. From the falls, the crystal voices of the Spirits rang as they took up the music. The song of ancient bounced from the gorge.

As the pair approached the pentagram, the drums stopped, and silence descended. Jedrowler stepped up to the premarked spot inside the pentagram. Anton took his place in the center. All who were to participate stood outside the pentagram, their robes reflecting their various disciplines.

A chill spread across the mountain, and people's breath formed vapors.

Jedrowler lowered his hood. To his right, the Priestess of Odium, wearing her full vestment, waited.

Jedrowler brought his hands from his robe. With palms facing up, he raised his arms to the heavens. The full moon slid into position directly overhead as one day turned to another.

"Now, it begins."

Day Three

Magic added an unreal glow to the moonlight-filled plateau.

As he faced his mentor, Anton raised his arms and watched as magic came alive. The two users of magic started to chant. The magic swirled and danced to the sync. Anton slowly lowered his voice while Jedrowler increased his. The magic within the pentagram responded.

Jedrowler stood between two radiating lines of the pentagram. Around him, the air crackled like frosted leaves in autumn. His white hair became a halo. He brought his hands together, creating light motes that danced around his fingertips, flowed down his arms, and slowly engulfed his body. A white mist of light motes spun into existence around him.

Anton opened his robe.

Spreading his hands, Jedrowler spun the light motes into strands, weaving them to his will. The light strands flowed around the mage, reaching out to the magic within the circle. Inside the pentagram, the magic settled into a hypnotic rhythm.

Kneeling, Jedrowler raised his arms and waited.

The Priestess of Odium entered the pentagram and stepped behind Mage Jedrowler. Laying her hands on his shoulders, she started to pray. Her mantra harmonized with the mage and power built. From the heavens, a golden strand of light spun down and engulfed the priestess. Her body glowed with the touch of her god. Gold swarmed with silver as the strand wrapped around the mage.

As the magic reached its crest, Jedrowler lowered his hands, slapping them on the lines of the pentagram. The combined power of magic and religion flared in a silver golden flash. Light strands slid from his arms, the magic dancing to the outer ring. Racing around the ring, they spun power into the sands. When the circle of magic met, golden blue lightning etched lines of force into the pentagram. As they bounded down the spokes, the air hummed.

Anton waited, relaxed in body and mind. Magic came at him, leaping and bounding over itself. Colors exploded from the spokes as magic took on its true shape. He felt no fear as he willed the magic to flow into him to consume him. As the arcana power flowed through him, his nerves burned, but he held it within.

Four priests stepped into the outer circle. Spaced evenly around the pentagram, they recited the prayers of their faith. The Priestess of Odium removed her hands from Jedrowler, stepped back, and stood outside the circle. With her arms outstretched, she encompassed the circle and started her chant, a prayer, a spell, a promise. A spell of binding that bound only the willing.

Reaching down, the priests touched the sands of the circle. Power of the gods flashed golden ribbons. They mingled and fused with the pulsating magic. The ribbons spun around the circle, combining and arching to the center.

Anton took the energy. The priests' presence became a part of him. His eyes burned as they opened to the domain of the gods.

Four witches stepped into the circle, taking the positions of the four winds. Outside the circle, the rest of the coven waited, their arms upraised. The ones in the circle turned their faces toward the moon and gave thanks to the goddess. As the witches called upon the forces of the four winds and Mother Earth, the Priestess of Odium started her spell. A breeze stirred their hair as the witches sang the song of nature. The mountain replied, the lake responded, and the falls thrummed.

The witches bent down, and from their hands slid amber sunbeams and glistering dew. A translucent snake of power slithered, curving and squirming. The four snakes traveled the circle, combining and growing. Collectively, they spun power strands and shot them down the spokes. The remaining coven chanted, sending Earth Magic to their four sisters. Like the power of the priests, it combined and flowed into Anton.

Anton took the new power, and his senses exploded. He felt the goddess and felt the elements of nature. Mother Earth waited.

The druids' quiet grace was a contrast to the chanting of the Priestess of Odium. They summoned the boundless energy of living land, the entities of the forests and the fields. Opening themselves to the binding, they brought their hands together and bowed their heads. Their lips moved in silent communion. When they lifted their eyes and gazed toward the unseen forest, they parted their hands.

One hand held a branch from an oak tree of their forest, in the other a silver knife. They brought the knife blade down, slicing through the stems of the leaves to allow them to flutter to the sands of the pentagram.

The sands boiled as ribbons of power washed through the outer circle. The forms of magic twisted and braided together. A wave wrapped the magic in the circle, then raced down the spokes. The power met in the center and engulfed the young student. The Unseen Force convulsed, and Anton felt it as a cooling, refreshing chill. As the presence of the druids settled, he sensed the moist earth of the forest and the slow hum of life in trees. Somewhere, a cricket stirred, a frog clung to the edge of a pond, and a bird laid her eggs.

Jedrowler intoned the spell of calling, and four mages took their place outside the pentagram. They gathered the magic in their hands, and as one, they draped themselves with a shimmering multicolored cloak. With power swirling, they shouted their power word in unison and stepped into the circle.

The ground shook, the air reverberated, and the moon darkened. The Priestess of Odium finished her spell of binding, and Jedrowler grasped the power and cried out his command, molding the power.

For a brief moment, concern crossed the mage's mind as he watched young Anton's legs buckle. Pushing aside the fear, Jedrowler allowed calmness to return. He held the power and spun. Slowly, his feet tapped out the beat from the magic, and he danced over the lines of force. He flowed around the runes and danced past the people in the outer circle.

Anton stood, glowing with the combine essence.

The air sparkled as small motes of energy sparkled into existence. Mage Jedrowler stopped his spinning and dancing and nodded. Mage Kytril called these molts, and the Vlynies entered the circle, swirling and traveling along the lines of force.

The Vlynies followed the path, joining all in the circle and connecting all to Anton. The circle clasped hands, allowing their personal power to flow and travel the pathways to Anton. Outside the circle, the witches' coven brought forth their rope made of hay, braided around vines. One by one, they touched the ends of their neighbor's rope, and the parts became whole, became one. As the ropes fused, the circle of the pentagram was encircled. The priestess and priests now sent forth their blessings.

Within the center of the pentagram, Anton watched Ancient Magic weave its own strands. The strands flowed from person to person, from object to object. It climbed the pedestal, and Anton touched the raw untapped power. He channeled the magic into him. Little magic, but much power. It tried to turn, tried to take control. He clamped down, forcing it to obey. It was time. He sent it out.

One by one, Anton felt the circle surrendering. Their essence flowed as one.

Jedrowler cried out, "From ancient times, the circle has been Alpha and Omega, the beginning and the end."

The energy built, and colors swirled. The coven laid their circle of rope on the outer circle. The runes came alive, lifted from the sands, their power joining and flowing to Anton.

Anton slowly brought his arms up and commanded the energy to close, to form over the group. As the power came together, Jedrowler started his dance. As he moved among the power, he flowed out of his robe.

Power coursed through Anton. Energy flowed around him, through him.

Nature, spiritual, and mage energy coursed through his veins.

The life energy of all in the circle was part of him.

He felt souls ready to blend as one.

His lips formed ancient words and brought all into focus.

Every discipline of the separate entities was his.

With a simple command, the souls were his.

Power was his.

Power to control the earth and stars.

He became one, one with the power. One with all. The circle had come together.

He is a new being. He is an old being.

He is Legion.

Legion, many who are one. Legion is power. Legion is wise.

Legion shouted his power to the heavens.

In the north, he felt another him.

He felt the yearning, the urge, and the need.

He cried out for his ancient self. The part that lay sleeping.

He needed to go north to be whole.

Then no power could defeat Legion.

His land would be safe.

His land would be his.

The small part of Legion that used to be Anton knew the power of Legion was absolute. Power to create, to destroy. The power called for him to surrender, to allow all he now touched to fuse with him.

Legion could protect the land, protect the people. He could protect the Spirits. The people would see the might and mercy of Legion. The people would bow to their god.

The power was there.

But not the wisdom.

Anton's lips formed the last words of the spell of control. The temptation of Legion slowly faded as each member of the circle held on to that, which was them. They let their personal magic flow, but not themselves. The magical energy settled, lowering into the pentagram. Small tendons of silver energy spun out, encircling everyone and connecting everyone to Anton.

Anton felt the relief of the group. The lure of Legion had been powerful, and none would have resisted if Anton had led them on that path. They would have surrendered, willingly followed Legion to their downfall and the eventual ruin of the land.

"I knew you could do it," Jedrowler said as he stepped behind Anton. He placed his hands on Anton's temple and molded himself with the young lad. He allowed his personal energy to combine with the boy's. "Now, we finish the spell." Lifting his head, he shouted, "We call the land's channel to come forth and take all within the circle so they may bind with the land."

Jedrowler's lips moved, forming the words of the spell. But Anton's voice filled the air. His voice echoed from the mountains, reverberated across the lake, and penetrated the gorge.

From the falls, an answering cry sounded in the mind of all bound. It was the words of calling from the unseen channel.

From the base of the falls, misty forms with indescribable shapes came. Their essence flowed up the mountain, sliding into the circle joined with the pentagram.

Nebulous faces swam before Anton's eyes as the Spirits of Wintermist pulled him into them. He melded with the Spirits becoming part of them.

Water was everywhere. It fell from the sky, ran down the mountains, cascaded through rivers, and nourished the land. The waters of the land ended their journey at Lake Mead. Their travel took them over Wintermist Falls and through the Spirits.

Jedrowler continued chanting, his words pouring from Anton's mouth, "Accept us into your fold. Allow us to flow along the common ground we all cherish."

The power mantra spread from the Spirits, engulfing Anton and flowing to the sixteen within the circle.

Anton felt the land. He felt himself become part of Mead. With him, the rest came, not as many who were one, but as one who was many, as unity.

The Spirits guided Anton where he went. With him went the Vlynies, spreading out and becoming part of the land. He channeled to all in the circle, and they felt the land. Moonlight shimmered as they surveyed the land with new eyes. They felt the power of the land, felt the love of the Spirits.

Anton's eyes laid in the mountains to the east, and they peered from the rivers of the land. He felt the richness, felt the farmlands. He felt what was ill, felt the land coming alive with spring.

It was over.

The spell faded into the pentagram, the anchors of the land held the magic, and the people were joined. All experienced the weakness. Before they could collapse, students, who had been waiting, rushed to their side, supporting them. Jedrowler and Anton supported each other.

"We did it," Jedrowler said as they stepped down from the center.

Around them, the sands of the pentagram were fused part of the mountain. Where each participant had stood, their footprints glowed.

"This is where the future defenders will stand, binding with the land and the Spirits of Wintermist."

Chapter Ten

Nigel Tomamark twisted closer to the grate. This air shaft was narrow, but the grease on his leather outfit helped him slide through the tight confine.

Nigel had spent months studying the mage school, looking for a weakness. The maze of air ducts suited his needs, and he mapped them, then waited. In time, he would carry out the command.

Nigel had grown up knowing only the rule of King Rathveil. He was taught, by the learned ones of the twelve tribes, their history. The king did not want the people to forget the sacrifices their ancestors made, so the learned ones taught why the tribes wandered the land for so long.

In clear language, the Sacred Scrolls spoke of the will of the gods. The tribes had been chosen by the gods to heal the land after the Great Confrontation. The scrolls laid out the expectations of the gods, their duties to the land, and things to come. They praised the people of Terrapin Xon and talked of their destiny. It was promised that one day, Terrapin Xon would rise and command the united people of the world.

Passages that were vague and open to interpretation were explained by the priestess. Claiming the guidance of the gods, the Priestess of Norge enforced their version of the Sacred Scrolls. They advised the shamans and when required, used the Unseen Force. There were times when they sent their powerful army to punish a tribe. For thousands of years, Terrapin Xon was a slave to the Czaran.

King Rathveil changed that. As a shaman, he brought forth the true interpretation of the Sacred Scrolls. He revealed the true words of the gods, truth that had been kept from the people. They were not punishing, but preparing the people to fulfill their destiny.

He brought change, brought prosperity, and brought greatness. Nigel used to listen to his father talk of life before the change and through his father's words saw how King Rathveil had blessed the people. King Rathveil freed the tribes from their endless wanderings. No longer did the tribes scrounge in the wilderness. They had homes. They had freedom.

Nigel decided to pay homage to the one who was spoken of in the Scroll of Prophecies. When he was old enough, he presented himself to the local warlord and became a warrior for the king. His act brought honor to his family. From the first day, he worked and studied harder than any warrior

Nigel was taken from normal training and taught the use of a multitude of weapons, learned of poisons, and learned the art of stealth. Like the field cat, he moved through the low grass invisible until his prey was his. He became like the spider. He learned the skill of climbing shear surfaces, to spot the smallest fingerhold, and how to brace himself in corners and drop on his enemy.

Nigel was taught the language and ways of the people south of the Thanatos Mountains. Daily, he spoke the words of the people of Lashtar and learned the worship of their gods. He learned the dress of the south and learned what colors they felt belonged together. At the same time, he learned to eat their food and participate in their meal rituals. He dressed as they dressed, ate as they ate, and talked as they talked. He became one of them.

Once his instructors were satisfied, he went south to prepare the land for King Rathveil. The Sacred Scrolls had prophesied that one day, the King of Terrapin Xon would rule the Southland.

His time in Lashtar enforced his belief in King Rathveil. The people here were not bound by the Sacred Scrolls. They prospered, and the arts flourished. The users of the Unseen Forces made life easy for a large share of the population. It was just as King Rathveil promised Terrapin Xon could be.

King Rathveil had foreseen a conflict between Terrapin Xon and Norge. To win, they needed resources and an advantage over the priestess. The land of Mead and the city of Wintermist held a resource they needed.

Nigel reported faithfully, sending information about the mage school and the defenses around Wintermist and the land of Mead. Other spies infiltrated Wintermist, and he relayed their findings. Then three months ago, he learned of a spell that could stop King Rathveil. It did not bother him when orders came to eliminate the leader.

What was the death of one insignificant mage?

The aroma of food reached Nigel's nose, and his mouth started to water. He had not eaten in days, knowing any weight could prevent him from using the ducts. Checking the banquet hall, he saw tables heaped with food and drink, mages and nobles eating, drinking, and laughing. In one corner, a quartet of bards played. Jugglers wandered up and down the tables, while two acrobats put on a show.

Guards were covering the exit, discreetly watching the nobles and checking the food. Nigel spotted Weaponsmaster Baylore behind Mage Master Gardner. Two other men flanked the leader of the mages. At another table, a swordsman stood to one side of the annoying sage. Rumor held that the swordsman was as good as Weaponsmaster Baylore. It was not a worry. Neither could reach him, and none was looking at the air vent.

Nigel removed two items from inside his leather vest. One was a powerful small hand crossbow. The dart tipped with poison he made from supplies he found in the kitchen and cooked down in a side air vent.

The other item was a small glass globe. Inside the Unseen Forces swirled blue, green, and red. The magic of Terrapin Xon was stronger than the magic of the Southland and once released would eliminate the Unseen Forces of the mages of Wintermist.

Nigel picked up the crossbow and was moving the glass globe near the edge when Mage Master Gardner stood up.

Mage Master Gardner cleared his throat. "This morning, we celebrate a monumental occasion. Not only were the forces of magic employed, so were the disciplines of multiple schools of power."

Mage Master Gardner picked up his goblet. "Seventeen people are linked to the land. Tomorrow at sundown, Jedrowler shall link the land to them. A mutual beneficial relationship. The land will augment native abilities, and in return, the seventeen can give power to the land for healing."

He turned to Mage Jedrowler and raised his goblet. "To you, my dear friend, I salute you."

Gobbets of wine were raised, and cheers filled the room. Mage Jedrowler rose to acknowledge the acclaim. As the applause settled, he turned to Anton and bowed. "No man could have done such an extraordinary feat without extraordinary help." The mage signaled Anton to stand.

"I could never have done this without the help of my young assistant, Wizard Anton. He deserves as much credit as I."

In the air shaft, Nigel nudged the glass globe. It tumbled from the grate and smashed. As the magic was released, the hall faded into blankness, and the assassin squeezed the trigger.

As voices rose in alarm, Nigel slid up the air vent. His last view in the flickering light from the fireplace was Anton kneeling on the floor, reaching for the still body of Mage Jedrowler. A crossbow bolt stuck from the mage's left eye.

Outside, a crystalline howl rose from the falls.

The sun spread cheery light across the front of Wintermist Mage School. The falls' mists glistened in the sunlight. The roaring of the falls were subdued, and the Spirits of Wintermist, entities that had greeted the dawn since people first came to Wintermist, were absent. As people crossed Wintermist Bridge, they felt a chill run through them; and from deep within the falls, an occasional wail was heard.

Across the gorge, the Temple of Odium's doors remained closed. No morning prayers echoed from the balcony. The high priestess and her acolytes were deep in mourning meditation.

Atop Wintermist Wall, guards walked in pairs, weapons at the ready. At the gatehouse, the mourning crowd was stopped and searched.

Xantrawler Baylore slowly walked the halls of the mage school. His face drawn, his eyes shadowed. His shoulders slumped, his fists clenched. He spoke to Duncan and Diamox through clenched teeth.

"When we got to the air shaft, he was gone. The only thing we found was a hand crossbow."

"The Farchart Guild uses that type of weapon," Duncan said.

"Actually," Diamox said and paused. He tapped his teeth for a moment. "A number of tribes of the Underdwellers are proficient with that weapon. I believe some raider's groups as well."

Xantrawler glared. "There are no Underdwellers lurking in the air vents. This was an assassin. Helena is checking everyone. If anyone can spot an assassin, she can."

"If only we had some warning," Diamox said.

"We had one! Your prophecy."

"I'm not a prophet."

"You hit the future square between the eyes. You saw Jedrowler's."

"I saw no such thing."

"If you would accept your gift and learn to use it, this would never happen."

"I have no gift!" Diamox's was irritated. "The sooner people give up their superstitions, the better."

Xantrawler grabbed Diamox by the shoulder, spinning him around. "Listen, you overeducated repository of useless information, you have a talent. Learn to use it for the kingdom."

"As one of the keepers of knowledge and dispeller of superstitions, I serve the Queen in my own way."

Xantrawler's hand fell to the hilt of his sword. "You're afraid to face the unexplainable, afraid to admit there are things you don't know."

Duncan stepped between the two, lightly putting his hand on Xantrawler's sword arm. "Calm down, it's been a long night. We're emotionally and physically exhausted."

"I'm tired of self-righteous people who shirk their responsibilities."

"What are you suggesting, Weaponsmaster?" Xantrawler took a step, but Duncan pushed him back.

"That's enough! Both of you go to your rooms and get rest."

Xantrawler locked eyes with Diamox. "Next time, hope there is someone else to help you." He turned and headed down the hallway.

Diamox watched him go. "Thank you for your timely intervention. I know he didn't mean what he said. You know old warriors. They can be touchy."

"Don't say another word."

Chapter Eleven

Queen's Knight Marko Fensin reined in his horse as he brought his column to a halt.

The forest of hemlocks receded here, opening to the sky and allowing sunlight in. They were on a small rise at the bottom of which the road crossed a stream before swerving east and disappearing. Behind them, the road disappeared in the gloom beneath the branches.

It was this gloom and the closeness of the mountains within this pass that brought the force to an early halt the previous night. The days were getting longer, but night came early to the forest. The pass had narrowed, and the ridge towered over them, blocking the sun earlier than elsewhere. The hemlocks shunted most of the light away and darkness descended with no warning.

Marko had hoped to make this clearing before nightfall, where they could have campfires. Instead, his men spent a cold night camped along side of the road. Because of the age of the trees and lack of light, the lower branches were dry and brittle, making the trees and ground a tinderbox.

Four riders, dressed in the queen's colors, splashed through the stream and spurred their horses up the small rise. As they neared Queen's Knight Fensin, they slowed, and the lead rider saluted.

"Sir, Sergeant Danlowson from the outpost."

"Report, Sergeant."

"A large force of uncountable men-at-arms, mounted warriors, siege engines, and mages have exited the Thanatos Range."

"Uncountable?"

"Sir, I have the message from my captain right here." He pulled a scroll tube from his pouch and handed it to Queen's Knight Fensin.

After quickly reading it, Marko signaled Captain Richter Penmon to his side. Handing him the report, he waited.

Captain Penmon shook his head. "I've never known Captain Alphron to give an inaccurate report. If he says there are scores of fighters, I believe him."

"Do you think they can hold them?"

"A day, possibly two. This message says Wizard Amikan has a plan. But he wouldn't be a match for mages if they breakthrough."

"Begging your pardon, sir, but this morning, we saw the glow of their campfires. From the glow, I would say they are already passed the outpost."

Marko shifted in his saddle. What was heading his way? "Mages and siege engines," the knight said, answering his own unvoiced question. "Would the mages at the Wall be able to hold off a mage attack?"

Captain Penmon shrugged. "The ones trained in combat magic have studied the strategy and use of combat magic. The question is, how many mages do the enemy have?"

"No, the question is how much time can we give the Wall. We have twenty-five cavalry with Witch Cardura. There are one hundred men-at-arms coming."

"A witch is no match for mages."

"A witch uses different abilities. These mages may not have a defense against that."

"May I ask your plan, sir?"

Marko looked at the stream. It wasn't deep, but it was wide. The map showed it went around the rise and spread, creating a marsh right up to a sheer cliff on the western side. A marsh would be filled with razor grass, dead tree stumps, and mud pits.

The narrow ford was the only way through.

"There is no clear way to flank us. The marsh is impregnable, the valley unclimbable. There are game trails on the eastern range, but nothing wagons can use. If they try to push through the forest, they will be hindered by the dead lower branches and fallen logs."

The captain nodded. "The only way is up this road."

"We can erect barricades along the road, just inside the woods. Witch Cardura can set magical traps. Meanwhile, I will send these men to the wall." Marko smiled. "We won't stop them, but we can slow them. Give General Klaydon time to set up his defenses."

Mage Kytril walked the deserted banquet hall, the sound of his footsteps returning from the stone walls. Magic had resumed working, but only one lone mage light was lit. In the gloom, he could see the cold remains of the banquet sitting on the table, waiting for the celebration to continue. He smelled the dying smoke from the fireplace and tasted ashes in his mouth.

Mage Jedrowler had met with him numerous times at High Reaches School. His interest in the Vlynies and the time he spent learning of them impressed Mage Kytril. Before he left High Reaches School, he was capable of rudimentary commands of the elementals.

Moving toward the center of the room, Mage Kytril reached out with his mage sense. He felt for the type of magic used. As he reached out, he felt a presence in the room and snapped his shields up.

"I've tried to reach out myself," CynLisa said as she stepped from the shadows. She looked at Mage Kytril. The way his hands had instinctively moved, power flashing between his fingers. "Sorry, I didn't mean to frighten you."

Mage Kytril lowered his hands and gathered his robes. "You did not frighten me. I took precautions in case the culprit had returned to rid this place of any evidence. Have you found anything?"

CynLisa pointed beneath the air vent. "Broken glass reverberating with magic. I don't recognize the mage signature."

Mage Kytril walked over to the shards and knelt. Holding out his hands, he dipped his senses into the residue of magic. All devices created by users of magic held an impression of the caster. He didn't recognize this signature.

"The magic has the sharpness and primitiveness of Ancient Magic." Suddenly, he felt a presence merge with his mind. He grabbed his head and fell to his knees.

"Kytril!" CynLisa was at his side holding him, keeping him from collapsing.

"I'm okay." He held his hand up and squared his shoulders. "Something was within me, something that recoiled at the feeling of the magic."

"Something tried to possess you!"

Mage Kytril smiled. "No. Mage Anton is having the same headache. If I'm correct, a Spirit was looking in."

CynLisa nodded. "You're all connected through Anton. I thought this wouldn't be possible until the land was bound to you?"

"He is connected to us, and that makes us connected to the Spirits."

"Do they know this magic?"

"If they do, they are not saying or can't." He stood and looked toward the ceiling. "I'm okay. The headache is fading."

"Where did this magic come from? Not the west, Veracken has the same magic we do. The Rolar Empire is old, but their magic has been refined as ours. The elves of Failon Gree have little interest in outsiders."

"The countries to the east practice ritualistic magic, minor magic, no real power."

"Then where?"

"The Northland."

CynLisa shook her head. "I have access to reports on the Northland. They have shamans. That is part ritualistic, part spiritual, and part religious."

Mage Kytril lowered his head and looked at CynLisa. "We have not been in the Northland for thirty years. Things change."

"Not true, I have been to the Wall. I have seen our forces entering."

"Only the foothills and the range. The Queen won't allow anyone to venture to the Northland. I fear that may be a mistake."

"Why would the Northland want to kill Jedrowler?"

"If you were going to invade a country, would you want them to have the ability Jedrowler was casting? No, you would want it destroyed."

Mage Kytril looked back up at the air vent. "Jedrowler never made it a secret that he wanted to protect the land. Remember his visions? Then there was the prophecy that twice cursed Diamox made yesterday." He waved his hands, and his robe billowed. Slowly, he lifted from the floor. "They have a spy. Let us see who this spy is."

Mage Kytril floated to the grate. Reaching into his robes, he pulled out a sealed paper tube and tore the ends off.

"I call upon the Vlynies, the dwellers of the air. Come show me the signature of the one who hid here." Bringing the paper tube to his mouth, he blew.

Silver sparkles dusted the air shaft. A shape fluttered in the breeze then coalesced into a defined face. The head was tilted to one side, one eye squinting. It was frozen in time.

Mage Kytril felt the presence enter him. This time, there was no revulsion, no fear, just a sense of gratitude. Satisfied that the vision was etched in his mind, he allowed himself to descend.

As Mage Kytril touched the floor, CynLisa looked at him, the question on her lips.

"I know what the spy looks like, so does someone else." He walked to where Jedrowler had sat and picked up the chair. As he gently placed it in position, he raised his voice a bit. "Justice will be done."

Chapter Twelve

King Rathveil sat in his workroom, looking at a scrap of parchment containing one word, *done*. He leaned back and smiled.

A quick knock at the door proceeded Kilar. The tribal shaman was dressed in golden brown robes, and he walked with the aid of a staff, one foot dragging on the floor.

"My lord."

"Charara, old friend, please have a seat."

"Thank you, my lord, but I must decline. My old injury." He indicated his leg. "If I should sit, my leg would stiffen."

King Rathveil looked at his old friend, grief and worry crossing his face. "Have you talked with the healer?" Charara shook his head. "I worry about you. You push yourself too hard. I needed some things done, but I can ask others."

"No. It will be okay. Besides, if you start treating me like a cripple how soon before I become one? Enough on my leg. You chose me to be your chief shaman, your second in line. Command me so I may carry out your work, my duty."

King Rathveil nodded and handed him the note. "The Southland is ready. The last possible obstacle has been eliminated."

"That mage is eliminated, but there are others."

"They will be ineffective. They use, what I call, the new Unseen Forces. We have the knowledge of the old. By creating an area of old magic, the southern force shapers or mages won't be able to function. When we attack, we will use the Unseen Forces, and they will be powerless."

"I believe you. I just don't understand." Charara held up his hand. "No, don't, I will never understand, no matter how many times you explain. I'm a shaman. My use of the unseen powers comes from the gods. Now, you did not call me just to talk about what we already know."

King Rathveil reached into his desk and pulled out a parchment. "I need you to do two things. I want the five thousand troops at the capital to prepare to move out. Now that I hold the Lady Trantro, Norge is sure to retaliate."

Charara took the parchment and looked over the order. He nodded. "I hope you have not made a mistake. Acting against the Lady Trantro this early could be costly."

"She left me no choice. Besides, to grow, we need to break the yoke the Keepers of the Sacred Scrolls have on us. Look at the reports of the Southland. That life has been denied our people, denied because these priestesses interpreted the scrolls to suit their own self-interest. Have you ever been to Norge?"

"I have heard stories. It doesn't sound much different from the Southland."

"Exactly! For thousands of years, they grew and prospered while we roamed Terrapin Xon. Each year, we sent offerings and tithes. They grew in power, and we remained in squalor. That has ended. We will learn the secrets of the new unseen powers, and with both, the priestesses will have no defense against us."

Charara nodded. "As you say. Will there be anything else?"

"Yes, this Nigel Tomamark, send his family a small gift. Tell them their son is a hero of Terrapin Xon, and they shall be reunited with him soon."

"I will see it is done."

After Charara left, King Rathveil leaned back in his chair and steepled his fingers. Looking at his map, he chuckled, a deep-throated bass chuckle that held no mirth.

"We will have more than just new powers. We will have new allies."

Dressed in formal student robes, with a black shroud of mourning, Anton entered Mage Jedrowler's quarters.

Jedrowler didn't have much, a couch, a couple of comfortable chairs by the fireplace, a dining table with four chairs, and a hutch containing wine and other spirits. As Anton moved around the room, he ran his fingers over the furniture, his mind reliving the times he spent here.

On the window ledge sat the elvish flowers known simply as lovers blossom. They grew in the elvish land of Failon Gree. The petals, red with yellow streaks, reached out, arms looking for an embrace. It was said that as long as the plant lived, the blossom never died. The elves had a custom of giving the flowers as a token of affection to a loved one or a close friend. While living in Failon Gree, Jedrowler had become one such person. When he returned to Wintermist, he carried a plant given by the lord, whose house he stayed at.

An elvish trader had delivered these particular plants. This was a precedent, as the elves never allowed more than one plant to be given to a nonelf. Jedrowler had been nurturing four plants for a year, actually making them live in soil from the elvish lands. Anton never found out why he was raising them but had spent hours sitting with Jedrowler, admiring them.

He turned from the symbol of love and friendship, his lips moving in a barely audible whisper. "I'm sorry, Master, I failed. It's my fault."

The door opened, and Mage Master Gardner entered. The Mage Master was dressed in a formal robe with a mourning shroud over his shoulder. He carried his staff, the symbol of his office. Anton watched two guards take up position in the hall.

"I'm glad you agreed to meet me, Anton. I know your grief is great." He leaned heavily on his staff.

"It's okay, Mage Master. The cure for grief is to keep one's body and mind occupied."

The Mage Master nodded. "We shall be escorting Mage Jedrowler to the temple soon, so I shall get to the point. Please follow me."

Mage Master Gardener led Anton through a door on the left side of the room. A similar door was partly opened on the opposite wall. It led to a small sleeping chamber. This door led into Jedrowler's workroom. Mage Master Gardner walked up to the desk and laid his hand upon it.

The rolltop snapped open with the sound of air blowing through the mountain peaks. Anton resisted the urge to duck.

"This is Jedrowler's notes," Mage Master Gardener said. "Everything, all his research." He turned to the young student. "No one but Jedrowler knows what the second part of his spell is. It is imperative we find out."

"I understand. Do you have a mage in mind for the job?"

"Yes. With the blessing of your duke, you are permanently assigned to Wintermist Mage School. You will discover the second part of the spell."

"Me!" Anton's voice squeaked, his heart started beating faster. He shook his head. He could not do this. He could not risk another mistake. "There has to be others. There are mages with more experience."

"None has your experience. The past year, you weren't just Jedrowler's student. You were his assistant, a cocreator. You learned the intimate details of the first part of the spell. You understand what the completed spell will do."

Anton approached Jedrowler's desk. Piles of scrolls were scattered across the top, others stuffed in cubbyholes. He knew the drawers contained notes and books. The amount of information he would have to sift through was staggering. The endeavor would take weeks.

"It will take months."

"Possibly years. You have all the time you need. You and the Circle may not be able to draw on each other or the land. You may not be able to return energy to heal the land, but there are ways this spell is useful. When there are floods, drought, fire, and blight, the Circle can tell us where our resources are needed. We are at peace, but if attacked you and the Circle can alert the duke, and he can send his men. Anton, we don't need great display of magic to help mankind. Knowledge is a great weapon."

Anton ran his hand over the smooth wood. Many days and nights, he had spent watching Mage Jedrowler at this desk. There were times when Jedrowler would swing around, lean his chair back, and chat with Anton. Other times, he took his meals here, staying up all night to work out a minor magical problem. So many memories all gone because of a mistake.

"More than once told Jedrowler me of his respect and love for you, his belief you will be a greater mage than him. He left orders that everything was to go to you. Anton, this desk is yours."

Anton felt the lump rise in his throat, the tears build in his eyes. He looked at Mage Master Gardner. "I won't fail Mage Jedrowler."

Midday found the people of Wintermist lined up five and six deep along the road between the Temple of Odium and Wintermist Bridge. The market was empty, shops closed and the fishing fleet tied up. People respected this mage they never met, only knew by reputation.

On Wintermist Bridge, nobles waited. The duke stood in the center, his guards on either side and his advisors around him. On the school side, mages and students gathered in their formal robes.

Shopkeepers from the gorge stood by the stairs, while farmers and craftsmen from nearby villages stood near the lake.

Xantrawler placed his men behind the crowd, their unit patch covered by a black armband of mourning. At the doors of the school, two of his personal bodyguards waited. One guard held the flag of Lashtar, another the flag of Mead. Both flags slowly flapped in the breeze.

Drummers, their drums muffled with a black shroud, stood ready.

Chimes rang from the Temple of Odium, the notes floating over the crowd. Cries and sobs joined them, and the sorrow became a living being. As the large double doors of the Temple slowly opened, the chimes sounded one last time. As the last note floated through the crowd, the temple guards filed out. Their armor of gold reflected the glory of their god. With bronze swords drawn and wrapped in black, they filed out in a column of two and formed a line on either side of the road from the temple steps to the citizens of Wintermist.

As the muffled beat of the drums started, the murmur of the people died.

The High Priestess of Odium appeared. Flanked by acolytes, she sang the song of the dead. Her voice filled the courtyard and traveled among the waves of the lake. It was heard in the valley and on the plateau. Later, the men stationed on Wintermist Wall would report hearing it as clearly as anyone in the crowd.

The high priestess continued singing while she walked down the steps and into the temple courtyard. Her voice and the song subtly changed as she sang the plea to Odium to accept this soul.

The mage school doors opened and the procession of the Council of Mages, led by Mage Master Gardner and CynLisa, exited. Behind the mages, in a position of honor Anton slowly walked. He held the position of family. With grief threatening to overwhelm him, he held his emotions in check. He was determined not to disgrace Mage Jedrowler. Only his eyes betrayed his grief.

Six of Weaponsmaster Xantrawler's personal bodyguards marched to the slow beat of the drums as they carried the body of Mage Jedrowler.

Jedrowler was dressed in white formal robes. His death shroud, pure white with his personal runes and off-white images of the Spirits stitched in, was tucked around his body. His folded hands held a medallion of the school's insignia held in place with a silver chain.

As Mage Jedrowler reached the foot of the steps, the flagstaffs were lowered. Two guards stepped forward and slid black mourning shrouds over the flags. For thirty days, the colors would be restrained in memory of the mage.

Raising the staffs, the guards stepped behind Anton, and the procession continued.

As they passed the line of merchants, farmers, and craftsmen, the men removed their hats, and the women curtsied. So intent on the procession no one noticed the roar of the falls decreasing as the group moved toward the bridge. As they progressed across the bridge, the sound grew distant. When Mage Jedrowler reached the center, the falls went silent, the mist stopped rising, and a stillness hung in the air. The party stopped, and people stared at the flow of water tumbling from the lake without a sound.

Deep within the gorge, along the path of falling water, came the cry of sorrow, heard not by the ears, but by the heart.

The largest Spirit ever seen drifted into view. As tall as two men, the Spirit came over the railing and looked down on those gathered. Its lips were firm and unsmiling. Its eyes traveled over all, and its gaze peered into the heart of the people. When its eyes swept over the body of the mage, they halted, and the Spirit's face dissolved into grief. The eyes turned down, the lips parted, and a low moan filled the air and stabbed into the heart of all. Slowly, it made its way to Mage Jedrowler.

The Spirit reached out a nebulous hand, stroked the white hair, and traced the line of the jaw and the fullness of the lips. Gently cupping the chin, the Spirit bent and placed a kiss upon the forehead.

The Spirit looked at Anton.

Slowly approaching the young man, it placed its hands on the lad's shoulders. Spirit eyes met mortal eyes, and grief passed between them. For a moment of eternity, they shared their love, their sorrow. With the sharing, knowledge flowed into Anton. It wasn't a disgrace to show his feelings. Tears flowed.

The Spirit wrapped Anton in its arms. Two beings from two planes of existence shared a moment of time, a moment of eternity. When the Spirit released Anton, it turned toward the falls and let out a call that echoed in the mind of all.

A collected gasp ran through the crowd as Spirits poured from the gorge. A river of Spirits flew over Mage Jedrowler, paying respects to the mortal they loved as a brother. The stream kept flowing, wrapping around the bridge.

As the last Spirit passed the mage, the Master Spirit sent a silent command, and each Spirit flew. Along the line of people, along the path to the mage school, they looked.

Each Spirit sought an aura glimpsed through the eyes of Mage Kytril. Each Spirit had one mission. Vengeance, justice.

The Spirits found their man. He stood in the ranks of guards forming the honor guard at the steps of the mage school.

Xantrawler shouted, "Hold that, man!"

Nigel turned and fled across the courtyard, heading for the stairs to the gorge. Behind him, the Spirits followed.

Mage Kytril had been waiting. As Nigel fled, he brought his hands up; and with a twist, he unleashed the Vlynies.

Nigel felt the spell form, felt his feet grow heavy. He fell, striking his face on the granite. Pain lanced through his skull as his nose broke. Blackness swirled, and he grabbed his nose, rolling to his back.

The Northman was roughly jerked to his feet and found himself surrounded by the anger-filled faces of people he had known for a year. He felt no fear, only peace. He had succeeded, fulfilled his king's wish. A smile played across his face.

Weaponsmaster Xantrawler stepped through the guards and spat at the man's feet. "Take him to the Wall."

On the bridge, a Spirit and a young lad took a last look at each other. The Spirit bowed and slipped into the gorge.

As the Spirits returned to their home, Anton heard the crystalline song of justice. With the song, the roar of the falls returned. Anton should have been happy. The murderer had been caught, but his soul held an empty spot that would be a void for the rest of his life.

Before the procession could move, the Duke of Mead, Duke Altrid, stepped forward. He stood at the side of Jedrowler and knelt. Across the bridge, his court followed their liege and took a knee, the ladies curtsying.

For one minute, the duke held his position, his lips moving in a silent prayer to the god Odium.

When he stood, the duke nodded to his personal guard. Six took up positions with Weaponsmaster Xantrawler's men.

As Mage Jedrowler moved through the crowd, men took a knee, and women curtsied.

At the steps of the temple, six temple guards stepped forward. They bowed to the mage, nodded to the honor guard then assumed the task of bearers. In time with the chants coming forth from the priestess, they climbed the steps to the temple. As the doors slowly closed, the sound of the chimes swirled across the lake. The last note was swallowed by the mist.

Long after the doors closed, Anton stood, his tears wetting his cheeks. CynLisa approached and leaned his head on her shoulder. Her arms enveloped him, and he returned the hug. Mage Master

Gardner and the other mages gathered, sharing their grief and giving him their comfort.

Temple guards and Xantrawler's own men shepherded the crowd away.

As he leaned on a rock, Gunther watched the myriad of campfires in the valley. He saw vague shapes going about the normal routine of camp life. The night wind carried the sound of murmuring voices, shuffling animals, and the clanging of metal.

"How many do you think there are?" Gunther asked.

Halprin sat near the sleeping form of Wizard Amikin. Grunting, he replied, "More I can kill in single battle."

"They have set a quick pace." He stood and started pacing. "They even eat while traveling. We can barely keep ahead of them."

"Hunting trail ran out, now we follow game trails or what you call game trails. I call your imagination. That slows us down."

"They march at a steady, brisk pace."

"Good, they be exhausted reaching the Wall."

"They use the wagons to take breaks or grab horses, using them to help them along."

Gunther turned and looked at his two companions. The clouds had parted, and now the full moon made the area bright as an overcast day. Amikin was snoring lightly, curled up in his robes. "He's exhausted, not use to this much physical work."

"He been complaining enemy mages have done something to magic. Says a blackness here." Halprin put his thrower down and stood up. "I think need get off ridge. Get to road."

Gunther shook his head. "Not a good idea. They send scouts ahead. Sooner or later, they would spot us."

Halprin looked along the road to the Wall, the road and the stream crossing many times. Water glistened in the moonlight where the road met it. A few leagues ahead, the valley narrowed, the two ridges coming close.

Halprin eyes narrowed. "There, small band of warriors there. I make a few campfires."

Gunther peered into the valley. All he saw was the dark forest and silver stream.

"May the gods protect our men. Tomorrow is another battle," Gunther said. "We leave at first light."

Chapter Thirteen

Day Four

"Riders coming!"

Queen's Knight Marco Fensin watched the returning scouts from atop the barricade of logs. His men had accomplished much during the hours of darkness. Working by firelight, they fell trees, dug trenches, laid dead falls, and cut killing zones. Large branches, some as big as the maple and birch trees on his family's land, were dragged into position to form a makeshift palisade. Around the stream, he had pits dug, then covered with dried grass and ferns. The bottoms were lined with sharpened stakes, a nasty surprise for any of the invaders.

Along the roadway and the stream, no trees blocked the sun, and berry bushes took advantage of the sunlight. The growth created a nearly impregnable barrier, so Queen's Knight Fensin was using this cover, positioning archers just inside the barriers. Fallen logs had been dragged into the road, creating a maze to wind through.

The previous day, men-at-arms arrived around midday and added to the work force. With this complement of men added, the position was quickly secured. Not as fortified as a keep, it would still slow the invading army, giving the general time to prepare.

During the night, everyone saw the red glow from the enemy's camp. How they had arrived so fast was unknown. Queen's Knight Marco Fensin worried over the 125 men stationed at the outpost. None had appeared. He dispatched scouts to locate them, but none had been found. Now the last two scouts were returning.

"Sir, the enemy is slowly advancing," the scout reported when he came within speaking range. "They have a wagon in the lead being pulled by the strangest animal I have ever seen. We counted five people in robes. They had their hoods pulled up so I don't know if they are men or women."

Witch Cardura stepped around a crooked root and looked up at the rider. "Five you say?" At the scout's nod, she looked at Marco. "That would be their mages." She rubbed her eyes, the dark circles under them testifying to the state of her exhaustion. Through the night, she had placed magical defenses in the forest. "They would be the ones clouding the magic."

"Don't worry about it. When the fighting starts, I want you in the back, as far from battle as you can get. Even if you weren't exhausted, you can't battle five mages."

"Sir," the scout interrupted, "a group of warriors entered the forest a mile back. Light infantry, small shields, and short swords."

As if on cue, an explosion raked along the foot of the eastern mountain. It was followed by multiple flashes that lit the morning sky.

Other magical traps were tripped, their sound echoing through the valley. Witch Cardura cursed, "They shouldn't all be going off."

The traps flashed or exploded in a regular pattern. Some traps screamed, others cracked. Some were meant to harm, others to confuse and disorient. The spells kept being triggered at regular intervals.

"I sense the blackness," Witch Cardura was saying. "My spells are being triggered when the blackness touches them. Their damnable magic is triggering my spells!"

Marko shouted at his captain, "Captain Penmon, get a group into the forest, base of that mountain."

"If we do that, there will be weakness in our defense."

"Magic is triggering those spells, and you can bet the enemy is right behind the magic."

Captain Penmon swore as he mounted his horse, "Damn mages. May they burn in the abyss." Riding up the line of defenders, he issued orders to the sergeants.

Witch Cardura let out a yell and fell to her knees. Marco leaped from the pile of logs and knelt next to her, his arms around her shoulder. The scout slid from his horse, weapon drawn.

"The blackness! It hurts! It burns!"

"Esprin!"

"The magic is wrong. I was feeding myself earth magic. This blackness has corrupted it. It burns!"

Marco felt Witch Cardura shaking, shudders of pain throbbed through her body. He held her tight, gently talking to her. "I'm here. I won't let anything happen. Break your connection."

"I've broken the connection." She took a deep breath and looked up at him, pains evident on her face. "I burn from magical backlash, like I took in pure magic, unfiltered by the earth."

A shadow from a quick-moving cloud passed overhead. Looking up, Marco's blood turned cold.

Only in tales sung by bards did such creatures live. For a moment, Queens Knight Marco froze in fear and fascination. The creature was graceful in flight, its serpentine form flowing through the air. Watching the legend, the knight knew why there were no survivors from the outpost.

Arrows rose to greet the dragon. They were minor annoyance, and she roared her disapproval.

Captain Penmon rode up, and Marko shouted. "Order the men to pull back, retreat to the wall."

Captain Penmon reined his horse around and galloped behind the palisade. A bugler sounded retreat, and the cavalry scrambled for their horses, the infantry bolted from concealment. Panic was setting in, and confusion and terror spread through the ranks.

The dragon made another pass, and some of the braver archers fired. Arrows hit the thin membranes of the wings, one lodged beneath a scale, near the wing joint. Vella arched her neck and screamed in pain. She rolled, dropped her neck, and opened her mouth.

Flame stuck the ground and rolled into the forest, catching dry tinder and howled up the trunks of fir, hemlock and pine trees. The dragon laid down her path of flame from the road west, circling the fighters from Lashtar.

Fire filled the forest, and smoke surged into the air. High-pitched whinnies sounded from the panicking horses, and men shouted. Screams sprang from the forest where men were trapped.

Marko struggled to keep the terror from his voice. He yelled for his men to grab their companions to move east, away from the flames. He half helped, half dragged Witch Cardura.

Captain Penmon struggled to keep his horse under control. He spoke to be heard over the terror and the sound of burning wood snapping and crackling. His example calmed the men around him. Some of the men tied rags around their mouth to keep out the worst of the smoke. Gathering their injured companions and picking up what equipment they could, they made their retreat.

Marko grabbed a soldier, shoving Witch Cardura into the arms of the surprised young man. At the sight of a superior, the soldier automatically wrapped the witch in his arms and took her.

Now unburdened, Marko turned his attention to the raging chaos. Escape down the road was cut off as a tree roared to the ground, flames and sparks erupting. Directing the men east into the forest, they moved away from the fire.

The smoke burned his eyes. Ash clogged his throat. The heat singed his hair, and his metal armor grew hotter. Pushing his men, shouting orders, he got them moving into the untouched forest. It was the shadow passing overhead that made him see the error of his orders.

The dragon came out of the west. Her flame thrust through the untouched fir trees, creating another line of flame and smoke. Rising on thermal of her own creation, she spiraled higher and sounded a howl of triumph. Marko swore her face took on a smug look.

With tears created by the smoke streaming down his ash-coated face, Marko watched a flaming pillar dance from the smoke. Flames flicked around the body as the man screamed one last time and dropped to the ground. A sob escaped the knight's raw throat as he heard the cries of his men. Smoke filled the air, and he found himself disoriented as he stumbled through the forest. Dead branches jabbed him, glowing embers burned holes in his leather, and he felt the heat on his neck.

A shift in the wind parted the smoke. To his right, the road was twenty paces away. Men were making their way down the road. Others stepped out from the forest, dirty, burned, and disheveled. Captain Penmon appeared, cradling his right arm. A jagged red mark ran down the side of his face, a testament to the sharpness of the rock he landed on.

Marko smiled. They were hurting. Many had died, but they were going to escape. The enemy would not be able to continue until the fire died. They could make the North Wall and sound the alarm. There would be time to prepare, to build a defense against the dragon.

Captain Penmon fell soundlessly, a shocked look on his face. He landed on the side of the road, and Marko saw the arrow sticking from the man's back. The knight screamed as he pulled his sword and spun.

What Marko originally feared had happen. The enemy had moved men through the forest, and they now blocked the way. More were stepping from behind trees, swords in hand.

Witch Cardura allowed the young man to half carry, half drag her down the road. She heard the inferno behind her and felt the heat on her back as they struggled to escape the fate of the rest of the soldiers of Lashtar. She felt her body stop burning as the blackness lifted. It was like the first light of day as she felt the blessing of the goddess. Stumbling, she managed to get her feet working. She looked at the young man holding her and smiled.

Reaching out with her witch power, Witch Cardura embraced Mother Earth, once more welcoming the feel of nature as it refreshed her. It wasn't enough to do great magic, but she was able to travel on her own, freeing the young man to take care of himself.

Pushing herself away, she thanked him.

Turning, she saw other survivors stepping from the smoke and flames. She saw Queens Knight Fensin, men-at-arms behind him, his sword out, rushing toward black-clad forms of the enemy emerging from the forest. The two groups came together, and the sound of metal on metal added its voice to the chaos of the fire. She watched man battle man, a sight she had seen many times in the service of the queen.

Without her witch powers, she was a liability. Turning, she placed one foot in front of the other, slowly making her way down the road. The ones with her were too injured to fight.

She knelt at the side of a woman fighter who was half sitting, half lying on the side of the road. Esprin reached out and the touched the woman's shoulder and saw the arrow sticking from the opposite one.

Reaching across, Witch Varney grasped the shaft of the arrow. The two women locked eyes, and the fighter nodded slightly and took a deep breath. With a quick snap of her wrist, Esprin broke the shaft and yanked the other half from the woman. The woman grunted and bit her lip. Her eyes started to roll, then, with a gasp, her breath hissed out.

Witch Varney held the woman for a moment then murmured, "We must go." She helped the woman to her feet, and they started off down the road.

Esprin looked up as the passing shadow of the dragon flew at treetop level. Heaving its body, it coughed, and flames flew. Soldiers in front of her were gone. Only blackened piles lay where they had stood. The flames climbed the trees, and Esprin's only hope was heading east. She waved her hand, and the brush parted. The people nearby followed through the opening and made their escape. A part of her mind wondered how much was burning. It seemed the dragon had set half the forest on fire.

Smoke was growing thicker. To one side, she heard the sound of battle, to the other the snapping and popping of the fire. She felt the heat on her face, her cheeks turning red. Her magic was weak. She couldn't continue clearing a path, so she swatted at the dead branches, breaking them from the giant trees.

A tree flared next to her, flames shooting out, wrapping her in its hot embrace. She screamed as her robe caught, flames running up her back, catching her hair. Rolling, she narrowly missed a burning branch as it crashed to the ground. A shower of embers flew into the air, landing on her and burning her face. She opened her mouth, sucking in a mouth full of smoke and flames.

She cried in pain.

"Spirits of the forest, I command thee, hold the flames at bay!"

She knew that voice, a friend, a dear friend.

Hands slapped her, rolled her back and forth. The rough handling causing burnt skin to slide and roll, but she felt no pain. Blackness was around her, the sound of the fire, a distant echo, fading to a small point in her past. Peace gently enfolded her.

A hand brushed the remains of hair from her eyes. She could hear her breath wheezing, her breathing louder than the fire. Whoever had put the fire out was speaking. It was a friend. She should know him. She smiled to herself. She was not leaving on her trip alone.

"Esprin." It was a sob.

She recognized the voice and smiled. A companion from . . . where she was.

"Esprin, hold on. We will get you a healer. You'll be okay, just you see."

She was okay. The swirling gray was moving her down the tunnel. The pain was gone. She smelled the roses from her mother's yard, mixing with the tang of the herb garden. From the kitchen widow drifted the scent of fresh bread. The hearth held stew that bubbled in the pot. The cool spring wind blew through her hair, and her grandmother sang her favorite song. Her father's deep voice joined in. The swirling gray was lighter, flowing together.

"Damn it, Esprin, don't do this to me."

"Too late, wizard. She has the death rattle." A gruff voice carried the sound of compassion.

"No! Help me, we need to get her out of here. We can't let it end for her like this."

Esprin Cardura recognized the voice, the son she never had. She found the strength to reach back along the tunnel to cause tortured vocal chords to work, cracked lips to part. Her mouth was dry. The pain washed over her, her chest, one large torment, each breath sent pain rocking through her. She needed to talk, let the youngster know it was all right.

"Symill? Symill?" Her voice was raspy, like a file on metal. She would never chant her spells with this voice.

"Esprin, yes, it's me. Hang on. We'll save you."

Esprin felt her body, felt the damage. The gray mist was turning white. Her body was a trap, holding her in pain. Her dear friend Symill Amikin was so worried, but he need not be.

"Symill, it's okay. I need to leave you for a while. I'm going to another plane. There are others here, others coming to welcome me." She saw the figures through the white mist. She couldn't see their faces, but she felt who they were, felt the joy of welcome from them. "You need to let me go now."

"Esprin, *no*!" Wizard Amikin shifted his hold on the witch. "We have been through a lot in the past. You have survived worse."

"You need let her go. She no longer in this world," Halprin placed his hand on Wizard Amikin's shoulder. "Don't hold her in pain any longer."

Amikin looked down at Esprin and saw the blackened skin, the empty eye sockets, her hair withered to nothing. Her robe was a charred rag, fused to her charred body. Yet her face was holding a smile, an unnatural smile.

"Symill," Esprin's voice was just a whisper. He had to lean close to hear. "It is everything they said it would be. It's home. Let me go home, Symill. I will be waiting for you there."

Amikin felt the tears running down his cheeks. His eyes burned from the smoke, but the tears were from grief. He knew Halprin was right. He lightly kissed Esprin on the forehead. "Good-bye, sweet lady. I never thanked you for what you have done for me. Rest well."

Esprin took a last shuddering breath, and her body folded in his arms. Amikin laid her gently on the ground and looked up at Halprin. "She taught me how to use both my wizard ability and the spells of the druid I learned from my dad. She not only spent time teaching me, but also just talking. She became my friend."

Halprin shifted his stance and said, "Time to leave."

Wizard Amikin did not see the burnt face, the charred hair, or the empty eye sockets. He could not smell the nauseating odor of burnt flesh and the stench of crisped hair. He saw Esprin as she was when he left for the outpost, a lovely, laughing woman with a quick smile. He watched as she readily danced with him, teaching a shy boy the steps to entrance a lady. Her voice imparted words of wisdom on how to conduct oneself in the presence of a lady. He heard her laughter as he told her about his first encounter with life outside his father's forest. Her hugs. Her tender way.

"We must commit her to Mother Earth."

Halprin shook his head. "Your spell fading, the fire moving in. Besides, no time, the enemy still in these woods."

"We need to take her with us."

"No time."

Wizard Amikin looked up. Through the smoke, he saw five warriors of the enemy. He stood, brushing his hands on his robe. "I said we must commit her to Mother Earth."

"Wizard, more important things now." Halprin started advancing on the enemy, his war ax held firmly in his hands. "Behind me."

"No." Amikin stepped around Halprin and raised his hands. He looked at the black-clad warriors as he continued to march toward them. "Your mage's magic is gone. Now feel my wrath. Feed the earth from which I now call my powers!"

Magical energy streamed from Wizard Amikin's hands, the bandages Halprin had placed flared to ash as pure energy lashed out, striking the ground. The ground shook and split at the warriors' feet. Thrown off balance, two warriors slid on the collapsing earth and disappeared.

The other warriors stopped, looked at the opening as it slowly close. They looked at the wizard and saw unrestrained fury. As one, they turned and ran.

Wizard Amikin brought his arms up and mumbled the ancient tongue of the druids. In the common tongue, he said, "You love fire. You think it's proper to burn a witch, then taste fire!"

Wizard Amikin flung his magic into the flames. With a twitch of his arms, the flames followed the magic, streaming into the path of the fleeing enemy. It engulfed the warriors' bodies, exploding them into sparks.

Wizard Amikin lowered his arms and looked at the dwarf. "I said we need to commit her to Mother Earth!"

Marko blocked the thrust of the short sword, followed through with a quick jab, and watched his sword skid off the hardened leather as the warrior danced aside. Besides being as good as any men of Sir Carton, the knight that fostered him, these barbarians had a unique style.

Around him, the smoke and ash swirled, obscuring his view. He almost missed the second barbarian. Deflecting the blow, he was staggered by the force and feebly blocked a thrust from his first opponent. He avoided the second warrior's follow-through by sidestepping around a tree.

Marko found himself joined by a third person wearing the queen's colors. The new arrival was proficient in the use of the sword, scoring first blood on one of the warriors.

Marko redirected his attention to the other warrior, using his sword to hook the enemy's blade and spinning the sword away. With the enemy disarmed, he moved in, finishing his foe.

As his opponent slid from his sword, Marko saw his ally standing over the other warrior. The soldier turned and gave a salute.

"My lord, Corporal Dane of the Queen's army, at your service. Sorry we couldn't get here sooner, but it took us a while to find a path down from the mountain."

"Where did you come from?"

"The outpost, sir. My two companions and I are the only survivors. We have been following game trails, trying to make it to the North Wall."

Queen's Knight Marco nodded. "My thanks, Corporal. Let's gather my men and get out of this place."

"You are the last, sir." Gunther sheathed his sword. He saw Halprin and Amikin a short distance away. "My companions are over there. I suggest we get out of here before the fire overtakes us. The wizard's barrier is not that strong."

Marko noticed the flames were still creating a picture of destruction. Unmoving flames held in place climbing the trees, a limb held aloft by flames. Overhead tongues of flame were frozen in a wave.

"Someone has to have survived."

"I'm sorry. I watched the last man fall. Other than these two." He toed the one at his feet. "The rest of the Northmen have headed east, up the mountain."

"I have people on the road, heading back to the Wall."

"Nay, you don't," Halprin said as he approached. "Flying snake flamed road, everyone gone."

Around them, the flames started to move, heat closed in and a tree outside of the wizard's spell exploded. More smoke was curling into the area.

"We need to get back to the Wall."

"We have been using the game trails," Gunther said. "We don't want to get caught by the enemy's scouts."

"We don't need to worry about scouts. This fire isn't going to burn out anytime soon. What is important is that the general learns about this dragon."

They had been walking as they were talking, and Wizard Amikin heard the last part of the conversation. "You had horses. If we get to the road, I will call some to us."

Gunther and Halprin looked at Wizard Amikin. Halprin spoke, "Since when can wizards call animals? I thought all you were good for was calling lightning."

Amikin gave a dry humorless laugh. "My father was a druid. He taught me some of their ways."

Marko interrupted, "We need to get out of this fire. We can talk later."

Wizard Amikin shook his head. "No. I am not leaving Esprin."

Marko looked at the remains of Witch Varney and suppressed the revulsion and anger he felt. He had known her for a short time but had great respect for her.

Wizard Amikin shifted his position and faced Esprin's corps. "She worshiped the goddess. She worshiped Mother Earth. She will be rewarded for her devotion. She shall be committed to Mother Earth with honor. Her soul may be gone, but her remains will receive the blessing of the goddess and Mother Earth."

Wizard Amikin held his right hand up, palm out. Chanting the incantation of the earth, the prayer of acceptance, he slowly moved his arm. The magic danced from him to Witch Varney. As the four watched, the earth slowly rose, wrapping around her body.

As the earth settled, Wizard Amikin turned to the group. "She is safe now, cradled in the arms of the goddess and watched over by Mother Earth."

Chapter Fourteen

Warlord Thrawt reined his horse to a stop in front of the dragon. She was crouched in a clearing, whimpering. Her left wing was outstretched, her handler was underneath looking at the joint.

"What did you think you were doing!" the warlord demanded. "I gave you orders to scare them, no flaming!"

Vella whimpered more and held up her wing. The warlord saw the arrow holes in her membranes. She looked at him, and her eyes drooped.

"So you got hit by a couple of small arrows, that's no reason to burn down the forest and trap my patrol. I've lost thirty good men!"

"Warlord," the handler said, "she took a hit in her joint. The arrow penetrated into one of the ligaments."

Warlord Thrawt looked at the man. "And? We are warriors. Pain is part of us."

"The pain was too much. She went a little crazy."

The warlord looked up at the dragon. "Is this true, Vella?" His tone was soft. He cocked his head to one side. "Was the pain really bad?"

Vella bobbed her head.

"Well, too bad!" the warlord snarled. Vella flinched, almost stepping on her handler. "You don't allow a little pain to control you." He placed his hand on his sword pommel. "If you ever disobey my direct order, I will personally carve your hide. We're at war, and your actions affect my men."

The handler stepped out from under Vella and cleared his throat. "I can heal the ligaments, but she will need to ride one of the wagons for a day."

"Why does she need to cause undue strain on one of my beasts?"

"She can't fly. After I knit it, the ligament needs a day to fully heal."

"Then she can walk!"

"But warlord . . ."

"Will walking interfere with her healing?"

"No, but she should . . ."

Warlord Thrawt slashed his hand, cutting off the protests. He looked up at Vella. "A little walking will give you time to think about what you did."

Before another word could be spoken, he turned his horse and started down the road, passing the line of men who sat waiting. No one was going anywhere until the Force Shapers got the fire out. This delay was costly, throwing his time table off. Now instead of arriving at the enemy's wall early tomorrow morning, it was going to be after high sun. He had planned to attack at high sun. Now the enemy would have an additional day to prepare.

These southerners were proving troublesome. First, the incident at the outpost, now this. As Warlord Thrawt moved to the front, the fire started collapsing on itself. He watched the flames folded on themselves, shrinking into the charred remains of the trees. The smoke thinned and dissipated on the wind that blew up from nowhere. He imagined he could feel the Unseen Force being manipulated, the Force Shapers channeling the energy. As he witnessed the power, he knew the upcoming battle would not be the same as any encounter he had experienced.

This was not the same as attacking another tribe, nothing like going after a pack of wild beasts of Terrapin Xon. He was going to need the force shapers and Vella. He was going to use their abilities to his full advantage.

As he took his position near the front, he was already working out the new strategy. It had been determined the Force Shapers could neutralize the southerner's Force Shapers. He would have the upper hand with the Unseen Force, so he would use the Force Shapers to weaken the wall, perhaps take a section out. With no enemy force shapers an attack by Vella should put the defenders in disarray. With the defenders in a panic, he would have Vella take out the command staff. The spies at the wall had supplied the information on where they would be during an attack.

With the command staff gone, the fighters would be leaderless, confused. A few attacks by Vella and they should be on the run. No Unseen Forces being used against him, his own force shapers carrying out their orders and the dragon attacking should reduce his losses.

Thrawt uttered a sigh, force shapers and dragons. Times had changed from when it was warrior against warrior.

General Klaydon sighed. He had tried to finish breaking of the fast when a messenger came. Not for the first time, he wished he would break his fast upon awakening. Too many times, situations arose, and he missed his morning meal. His sense of duty would not allow him to do that. His command and his men came first. He needed the assurance that all was well before he could enjoy the morning meal.

First light had been spent walking the wall and gatehouse, watching the weaponmasters with new recruits and observing the knights and cavalry doing close quarter drills. He believed a man's horse was his responsibility, so he next went to the stable to groom his horse. The time with his horse was his quiet time, the time when he was able to escape the responsibility of command. This morning, it came searching him.

Stepping into the command room, General Klaydon looked around. The squires were manning the signal flags. Mage Margella was at the north side, polishing the air with a rag. A messenger stood to one side, the hood of her cloak pulled low. Colonel Fythe was bent over the map table, writing on the map and talking with three aides. He tapped the map, "Right here." He looked up as the general drew near.

"I fear Lord Fensin has run into more trouble than we expected." He jerked his head toward the north.

General Klaydon moved to Mage Margella, who was finishing his spell. In the distance, he could see a pillar of large and well-defined black smoke.

"On the map, it looks to be in the area Lord Fensin's message said he was. It's a good thirty miles away."

"They must have set half the woods on fire," the general said.

"More," Mage Margella said. He stepped aside so everyone could see the view that hung in the air. Small tongues of flames were wrapping around the black smoke.

"How long has this been going on?"

"About a mark." Colonel Fythe shook his head.

General Klaydon shook his head. "They have to be mad. The fire could turn back on them."

"Are you sure it's the enemy?"

"Gailton would never allow it," Mage Margella said. "It would hurt Mother Earth. Her witch powers could not tolerate it."

"This will buy us time," General Klaydon said. "The enemy can't advance as long as the fire rages."

"That may not be a problem," Mage Margella said. The two officers watched the smoke thinning, flames shrinking. The mage spoke, his voice hushed, holding a tint of awe. "For them to have the ability to quell a fire of that magnitude so quickly speaks of powerful magic."

"Can your mages handle them?"

"They can obliviously work together. That's the only way they can do what you are seeing. Our mages, witches, and druids are trained to do the same. There will be no problem, no matter how powerful they are." Under his breath, he muttered, "Unless they can protect themselves and take us out, one by one."

General Klaydon watched the flames slowly decreased. His extra time to prepare disappeared with the smoke. Thirty miles would bring the enemy here in three days, maybe two. They had to be ready.

"Prepare the men, Colonel. Double the patrol on the wall, pull in patrols that are out. Mage Margella, get with your people and work out a defense." He walked over to the map table. "You, squire, go to my officers and tell them to meet in my planning room in two hours." He looked at everyone in the command tower.

"Do not think for a moment this Wall is safe. What man can build, man can destroy. These barbarians have the force to do it."

Chapter Fifteen

Clouds had moved in during the night, dumping a cold rain on Wintermist. By dawn, the rain ended, but the sky was leaden, and a cold wind blew across the lake. The warm days of early spring had been replaced with the cold chill of late winter. People moved about wrapped in their cloaks or great coats. Others gathered around the fires of street cooks, and some hugged hot jada in their numb fingers.

The city was in mourning, but people needed to carry on the day-to-day routine of living. Meals needed prepared, so wives and servants were in the market. Goods were required, so merchants were busy striking deals. Assorted jobs necessary to keep a city functioning went on. Life continued. But on this day, it continued at a slower, quieter pace.

Ambrus clutched his collar and buried his nose in the fur trim. Crossing Wintermist Bridge, he noticed the falls were a quiet hiss. Along the railings, a few people gathered, peering into the falls looking for the Spirits. None had been seen since Mage Jedrowler's funeral march.

The Spirits appearance, the spell casting, his prophecy of the death of Mage Jedrowler caused him to be up all night. Needing to talk to someone and needing to rationalize the events, he sought the one person who would give him an honest answer. He sent

Duncan to the kitchen on an errand then slipped out and headed to see Sasha.

He moved across the table rock, down the ramp, and into the city. He made his way through the streets until he came to the main city market square. Stepping from the market and heading down the street to Magnate Bakery, he glanced over his shoulders. Ambrus gasped as the clouds parted, and a beam of sunlight broke through, bathing the Temple of Odium in a golden light. At that moment, the bells started ringing, calling the faithful to morning worship, their notes settling over the city. He stopped, as many others did, and stared at the sight. As the last note echoed across the city, the clouds closed in, constricting the golden beam to a point centered on the bell chamber. As it winked out, people whispered about the wonder of the gods.

Yesterday, Ambrus would have called them a bunch of superstitious fools. Today, he gripped his collar tighter and hurried on.

The warmth of Magnate Bakery was a welcomed relief, the heat bringing a tingle to his chilled cheeks and nose. Sasha's father was haggling with a couple of housewives over the bread. He directed Ambrus to the rear, then went back to his negotiations. Sasha was on the balcony overlooking the lake, the cold of the morning seeming to not affect her. She was working dough, getting it ready for baking into bread.

"Are you daft? You will catch your death in this wind."

Sasha looked up and blew a stray lock of hair off her face. The effort was wasted as the wind whipped it back. "After the heat of the kitchen, this is a refreshing breeze. You try standing in front of those ovens for three hours."

Ambrus shivered. "It's freezing!"

Sasha looked at him and blew the wisp of hair out of her eyes. "People who work usually get quite warm." She punched the lump of dough. "What brings you into the city so early?"

"I need to talk." Ambrus leaned against the railing, watching Sasha work, then hopped away and started to pace. Now he was walking in circles.

"The Screeching Owl is open this early. I don't think it ever closes."

Ambrus snorted. "I want advice, an honest opinion, not arguments and lectures." He looked at Sasha. Her hair was pulled back, a few strands escaping the hairband. Flour streaked her face and dusted her hair. She looked at Ambrus with a serious look. Ambrus felt tired, more tired than he had felt in seasons. "I respect what you say. Even with limited schooling, you have a natural intellect, one that sees through garbage."

"It's called common sense."

"Call it what you want. You have more insight than most others at the Screeching Owl."

"Okay, Sirdar Diamox, you can stop with the flattery. I was up before dawn. Never got to sleep until late and I'm exhausted. Please, get to the point."

Ambrus changed from a circle to pacing, first to the railing and Lake Mead, then to the building's wall. In his pacing, he looked down and noticed the toes of his boots were worn and made a mental note to see a cobbler.

"I want to know about the Spirits," he said to the wall, then turned. Walking passed Sasha, he said, "What type of magic makes them live? I saw them yesterday." He spoke to the lake before turning to the wall, "Saw what they are capable of. Before that, I watched forces swirling in the moonlight. I felt energy in the air I have never felt before." He turned and raised his voice to the lake. "What is the magic that is here?"

"Excuse me?"

"The magic, this force around us," he said, turning to the wall. "The energy that makes it possible for the Spirits to exist." He stopped and waited for the wall to respond.

"Excuse me!"

"Magic! The force you are always telling . . ."

"I know what you're asking. I just don't understand why you're asking. You're not telling me you believe in magic?" Ambrus turned from the wall and walked to the railing. Grabbing the rail and holding tight, he mumbled,

"Diamox, you need to speak up. I can't understand you when you talk to the lake."

Spinning, he clenched his teeth and snapped at Sasha's feet. "Yes, yes, I believe in a force you call magic!"

Sasha rolled her eyes. "Duncan is a prophet. The Grand Mauler is coming to worship at the temple."

"I'm serious!" He looked up at her, pleading in his eyes.

Stopping her chuckling, Sasha looked at Ambrus. He was her size, and she looked straight at him and saw his hollow eyes, his pale skin. His shoulders were slumping and under his cap, his hair, normally shiny, was drab.

"I'm sorry, Diamox. I didn't know. This is important."

"It is! If there's magic, if the Spirits exist then maybe, just maybe," he paused and quietly added, "what everyone says about me is true."

"What's true?" Watching the scholar, Sasha held her breath.

"I'm a prophet." Ambrus started pulling his beard. "I see the future. And with that ability, I can change the present." He dropped his hands and leaned on Sasha's table. "Xantrawler claimed I knew of Jedrowlér's death, that I saw it. If I am a prophet, I could have prevented that death."

Sasha saw the moisture in his eyes and the trembling of his lips. She reached her hand up, gently touching the side of his face. "Diamox, you didn't know. You had no way of knowing."

"If I had admitted my ability long ago, I could have learned to interpret them." His voice was low, on the verge of being a soft whisper. "I'm as guilty of Jedrowler's death as the assassin!"

"No!" She straightened and looked hard into Diamox's eyes. "Even if you had given the proper warning, Jedrowler would still be dead." Ambrus started to open his mouth, and she cut him off, "Xantrawler would have taken the same actions. There was no way to stop the assassin. If there was, then the precaution for the Mage Master would have protected Jedrowler."

"You weren't there."

"No, but Da talked with me yesterday. Da said it was not Xantrawler's fault. He explained how the weaponsmaster would have everything covered. He told me the tactics an assassin would use and . . ." She paused for a moment and pulled her lower lip, leaving a smudge of flour and some specks of dough on the side of her mouth. For a simple baker, her father knew a lot. She dropped her hand and looked at Ambrus. "Anyway, the assassin struck, and there is nothing we can do to change that."

Ambrus pushed away from the table and started pacing. "I need to understand this. What makes this work? There is a logical way magic works and prophecies exist."

Sasha blew her breath out and went back to kneading the dough.

Ambrus continued, "Everything functions under logical laws. Without logic, everything would fall into chaos. I need to learn the logic of magic, then I can understand it." He turned to Sasha, who glared at him. "You have been around magic. Exposure to the mages should have given you insight. Teach me about magic. Tell me how it works."

"Magic just is. It follows no reason I can explain. Believe in it and learn to use what little you have."

"I need to understand."

Sasha picked up her towel. As she wiped her hands, she walked around the table and approached Ambrus. She had never had the scholar come to her for advice, asking to be taught. He was the teacher. She was the student.

Grabbing Ambrus's shoulders, she gazed into his eyes. "Take a leap."

"What?"

"Go to Wintermist Bridge and leap."

"But why?"

"Faith. Surrender to faith."

"I don't understand."

"Ambrus Diamox, you have lived with logic all your life. You rejected religion, rejected magic. And for a while, you even rejected the sun traveling around the planet. Now you need to turn it around. Find faith."

"How can faith help me?"

"Faith gives you courage to carry on. Faith . . . well, faith just does."

"But a leap?"

"Leaping requires faith. When you pass through the Spirits' home, you will believe."

"Sasha, I don't know."

"Go take a leap!"

Ambrus started to say something, but Sasha pointed toward the door. He left, mumbling his good-bye to Sasha's father on the way out.

On the street, he allowed his mind to open, to expand, to wander.

When confronted with a new theory, Ambrus let his mind wander. It would combine facts, dismiss facts, and add new facts on impulse. His mind used everything he learned and put them in logical order.

The world dissolved into a blur as he retreated into his own little box.

The subconscious is a wonderful sorter of information. With free rain, it brings forward solutions the conscious mind would not discover. Ambrus stood back as an observer and enjoyed the process. He listened and watched his mind talk and argue with its self. He didn't understand what was said, but he did get flashes of images or words.

Ambrus never shared this with anyone. People would think he was crazy. The great scholar had lost his mind. He smiled at the thought of being crazy, jumping around making bird calls, swinging from the drapes, and chasing the cat. Ambrus started thinking of things to do to the people he didn't like, if he was crazy.

This was part of his pondering. While part of his mind worked on the problem, another part thought of whatever it wanted. Setting his mind free was a liberating experience.

When Ambrus returned to himself, he was on Wintermist Bridge. Subdued sounds of the falls washed over him, and the mist glistened in the midmorning light. He noticed he was next to one of the devices used for the leaps.

It was a simple mechanical device and stood in an opening of the railing. A large spool with 250 feet of rope. The interior had a complex series of gears and springs. As a person fell, the rope unwound, spinning the spool and tightening the springs. As the springs grew tighter, they slowed the leaper; and when they reached the end of the rope, the springs rebounded. The gears transferred the force of the springs to the spool, making it rewind and pull the leaper back up. A crank was used to haul the leaper the last few feet, if needed.

Drawing a deep breath, Ambrus stepped up to the spool. He indicated his intention to an attendant and was helped out of his jacket and into a harness.

Handing his hat to the attendant, he stepped around the spool and onto the ledge. The cold wind from the chasm caused him to shiver slightly. On the lake, the winds were bringing waves to the surface, many showing white foam.

From within the chasm, over the muted sounds of the falls, he heard crystalline voices singing. They sang the song of encouragement, the song of welcome, and the song of wonder. No human choir could achieve the skill of the crystal voices. Three different songs became one. They became his song, the song of Ambrus Diamox.

He felt his heart beating, his breathing just short pants as his toes curled in his boots. Sucking in a deep breath, Ambrus lowered his eyes and peered into the gorge. All he saw was the churning white mist. He heard the water echoing as it crashed on the rocks.

Holding his arms out, he closed his eyes and leaned forward.

Wind flowed past, cool mist touched his face, and Ambrus opened his eyes. Before him was the Spirits of Wintermist. Their crystalline voices sang the song of Ambrus Diamox, and he swore they were smiling.

As he plunged through the first group, he heard it. His song faded, and a new one started. The song of caring. The song of hope. The song of faith. A song for him.

A Spirit joined him, drew close, and reached out her hands. Giving her a smile, he reached for her hands. They were cool, but filled with warmth that had nothing to do with temperature.

Ambrus looked into the Spirit's face and smiled. She smiled back, and he was filled with a peacefulness he had never known. Happiness reflected on his face. The Spirit glowed as this emotion engulfed her.

With their fingers interlacing like lovers, their descent slowed. They started to dance the dance of the mist. Dancing and singing filled him with the love and care that was the Spirits of Wintermist.

Ambrus was welcomed, the Spirits overjoyed that he finally arrived. For years, they waited for him to join them in their home. And for the first time, he had a place to call home. No matter where he went and no matter where he lived, this would be home.

On Wintermist Bridge, people crowded the railing. Word had spread that a person had leaped, and the rope was slack. Men were frantically cranking the handle of the giant spool. Duncan Pentock pushed through the crowd and saw the jacket and hat lying beside the platform. He clenched his jaw and looked into the mist.

A Spirit drifted into view, dancing with Ambrus. He held his ladies' hand as he twirled her, swept her into him, and encircled her waist. They swirled together, their forms merging, then parting. His eyes never left her face as he was intoxicated by her twinkling eyes. He heard so much from those eyes as she told her story.

As the crystalline voices concluded the song, the couple stepped onto the bridge. Ambrus stepped back and bowed, and the spirit curtsied. When they straightened, she stepped forward and kissed his cheek. With a crystalline giggle, she was gone.

Ambrus stood for a moment, relishing the joy the Spirits had given him. He now understood. But understanding was just the start of his new journey. He reluctantly turned from the falls and faced the cheering crowd. The cheering was faintly heard above the roar of the falls. With the Spirit's departure, the fall's roar was louder, as if they were joining the people of Wintermist in cheering.

Duncan pushed his way to Ambrus, who saw the concerned look on the face of the bodyguard. He felt guilty, but the time alone was what he needed.

Ambrus grasped Duncan's shoulder and smiled.

Anton was laying his formal student robe out when there was a knock at the door.

All morning he had been attempting to prepare for Jedrowler's committal ritual. All morning he was interrupted by an endless stream of people offering their condolences. Most were fellow students, but there were a few low-ranking nobles.

Higher-ranking nobles or mages had not bothered him. Etiquette called for family to have the morning to grieve. Anton was Jedrowler's family, the person closest to him, so the honor was his. The problem was there were students from across the kingdom with other customs, and they were following theirs.

Now little time was left to get ready.

Before another knock could sound, he grabbed the door and yanked. His angry retort died on his lips.

CynLisa stood in his doorway, holding a bundle of reddish tan cloth.

"Good, you haven't dressed." The Cyn pushed by him, dropping the bundle on the bed. "We can't let you be seen in student's robes."

Anton looked at CynLisa.

"When you became Jedrowler's assistant, he went to the tailor." Unbinding the bundle she removed a robe. "And had your robes made. He was going to present them when the spell was done." She smiled. "Mage Master Gardner told me this morning. I made it my business to get them for you. Two work robes and a formal robe."

Anton reached down and touched the silk formal robe. He gently picked it up and ran his hand over the material, feeling the softness. His finger traced the stitching, following the line of the white trim. The reddish tan robe had a hood trimmed in gold and silver. Embroidered around the hem and cuffs, in white thread, were the runes he picked as his own when he first entered the school.

Anton noticed another pattern within. Pearl white stitching traced patterns around, and through his runes. patterns he recognized.

"All students achieving mage status," CynLisa said, "Receive robes trimmed in white, the color of the school. Within the color is your rune, intertwined with those of your teacher. Jedrowler's has always been white in recognition of the Spirits."

Anton looked at CynLisa and tried to smile. He found it hard with a lump in his throat. Finding his voice, he stammered his thanks. "But I can't wear these. I'm not a mage."

CynLisa waved his words off, "When you finish the spell, you will be. I talked with Mage Master Gardner. And we both agree, in honor of Jedrowler, you will be permitted to wear the mage robes for his committal."

She looked at Anton and smiled. "Jedrowler was my friend, one of the few I truly have. I knew his feelings for you, his hopes and his dreams. I know how you feel, how you look up to him. You can't properly honor the man with your student robes. You are a mage, not in name, but in spirit, one Jedrowler taught. Everyone at the committal ceremony needs to see that."

"There is not enough I can do to honor his memory."

CynLisa nodded. "You will do enough when you give the eulogy."

Anton turned pale. "Me . . . me? The priestess does that!"

"She gives the blessing. You, as family, give the eulogy."

"I was told I'm to occupy the seat of honor, the family seat. But I can't give the eulogy. You need to do it or the Mage Master. You knew him longer."

"How long you know a person is not relevant. It's how you feel in here." She put her hand over her heart. "That's what is important. We were his friends, but you were his son."

"Why me? The priestess is supposed to do it."

CynLisa let out an exasperated sigh. "We forget we have people from all across the kingdom. How is it done where you're from?"

"The priest says kind words about the deceased, talks about how wonderful their life was. Then he says how they are with the gods. He gives a blessing, and the deceased is taken to be buried."

"We do it differently. Only a close friend or a family member truly knows a person. So they say the eulogy. Then the priestess says her blessing, everyone pays their respects, and the family accompanies the deceased to the crypt. Afterward, the family joins everyone for the wake."

Anton moaned, "I hate wakes. The crying, the talk of death, wondering who is next. Do I have to go?"

CynLisa shook her head. "Our wakes are different. We talk of life. We celebrate the transition to a new plane. There is much food, much drink. And the bards play the favorite music of the deceased."

Anton sat heavily on the bed, absently rubbing the robe's trim between his fingers. He heard Wintermist Falls. He heard the crystal voices singing the song of transition and farewell. He thought of the times he had been with his master, the teachings, the lessons. There were many meals he took with Mage Jedrowler, meals where the mage talked of his first home. There were the tales of his travels around the kingdom and outkingdom.

In all his talks, Jedrowler had the Spirits close. When he talked of them, his eyes sparkled.

"I don't know what to say. I do, but how do I put it into words?"

"Say what comes from your heart. Believe in yourself, the way Jedrowler believed in you."

Anton looked at CynLisa and gave a weak smile. "I'll do my best. If you'll excuse me, I need to change."

"I'll be just outside your door."

CynLisa stepped out and waited. It wasn't long before Anton called her back. He stood in the center of the room, modeling the robe.

"How do I look?"

The cut followed his body, tight where it needed to be tight and loose where it needed to be loose. His waist was circled by a golden rope, tied with the mage craft knot. The mage sash hung around his neck, and its vibrate colors brought life to the room. He looked like he was born to the robe. She wasn't sure if it was the events of the past couple days or the robe, but Anton looked older.

CynLisa stepped forward and adjusted the sash. Leaning back, she looked him over, then brushed a lock of hair aside. When it fell back down, she giggled. "Well, maybe when you get older, you can train your hair to stay put."

Anton frowned. "That lock has given me trouble all my life. I should shave my head."

"Save the bald heads for the military and monks. Bald-headed mages look downright evil. Besides, look at the beards, I have yet to meet a wizard or mage that takes the time to properly take care of their facial hair."

"Master Jedrowler said he never had time. When his beard became a problem, he grabbed a knife and hacked off what he needed to."

"I remember him spending days in the archives and forgetting to eat. I would take food to him and force him to eat."

Anton nodded as he walked to his bedside stand and picked up an object. "There were many times we were working on an aspect of the spell, and days would go by. What we did last night was just the conclusion of weeks of preparation and spell casting . . ."

Anton got a faraway look in his eyes as he recalled the hectic pace in the last weeks of preparations. Time spent weaving spells on Wintermist Bridge, casting at the base of the falls, and even conjuring as Jedrowler did a leap. The mage had explained each spell and how they interacted.

Anton recalled one conversation where Jedrowler was explaining why the anchors were important.

"Time is important in any spell casting. We need to do this work before the actual casting. Otherwise, the effect of the protection spell will dissipate. The spell needs anchor points, and there is no time during the casting to create them. We are setting up anchor points for both parts of the spell now."

Jedrowler had explained what anchors were for which part of the protection spell. Being the student he was, Anton wrote down everything.

"I have it!" Anton turned from CynLisa and crossed to his desk. He started rifling through piles of parchments, glancing briefly before discarding it. "My notes contain information about a vital action."

CynLisa laid her hand on Anton's shoulder. "I'm sure it can wait. We have something more important right now."

Anton looked over his shoulder at CynLisa. "Jedrowler."

"The notes will be there tomorrow. Jedrowler needs us to be there as the priestesses send him off." She smiled. "Besides, it isn't like we are going to be invaded tomorrow."

"You're right, I got lost in the rush of the moment."

"You are a true mage, one track mind. It won't be long, and you will have a scraggly beard, unkempt hair, and a dirty robe."

Anton laughed. "Don't worry. I won't let myself get that bad."

"We will see."

Anton slowly made his way down the center of Wintermist Bridge. The gorge did not exist as long as he didn't look right or left.

He had been doing well, keeping his grief under control. But now, with each step, the pressure grew in his chest. His tears blurred his vision, smearing the white shape floating toward him. He wiped his eyes and looked deep into the white on white eyes. A hand caressed his face. And for a brief moment, he felt a connection, not through the spell, but direct with this Spirit. This was between the two of them, not to be shared.

The Spirit's crystalline voice sang the song of grief, the song of love. The song conveyed the Spirits loved of Jedrowler, how he was one with them. It conveyed the fact he had been taken, and there was nothing they could do. Now they looked to Anton. The young lad was the one who could finish the spell. All this poured into Anton unbidden.

During this rapport, Anton felt the presence of something black, but not evil. It was twisted and ugly, and the Spirits feared it. He knew, but he could not explain how he knew.

With a last look at Anton, the Spirit drifted over the railing and went home. His mind swirling in confusion, Anton watched the Spirit slide into the gorge. Master Jedrowler made the spell to protect the land, but the Spirit acted like it was to protect them. He must have misunderstood what the Spirit was saying.

As he stepped from the bridge, Anton stopped. Turning his sight beyond the falls, beyond Lake Mead, beyond farms and villages, he felt the blackness, a blackness calling him. It was evil to an extent he felt unclean sensing it.

Chapter Sixteen

The committal service was a blur. The blessing, the words of condolences, even the eulogy were just images in the white mist of the past. His mind and his being were focused on the pale body before the altar.

Anton rose when it was time and greeted the mourners. Through the numbness, he gave the proper response, said the proper words. As the last mourners left, he faced his mentor.

Kneeling, he clasped Jedrowler's cold hands and rested his head on his own. Sobs shook his body. "I'm sorry, Master. I'm sorry. I should have taken that bolt. It should have been me, not you."

A compassionate hand touched Anton's shoulder. He looked up, and Head Priestess Selaris gave him a sympathetic smile.

"You have not let Jedrowler down. He believed in you. He knew you would carry on in his absence."

"I have been given an impossible task." Anton turned his head and looked at the peaceful face of the Mage. "I must finish his spell, his dream, but I can't. I'm not the great mage he was."

She lowered herself, kneeling next to the lad. Taking his hands, she gave them a squeeze. "Mage Master Gardner said there are two mages in Wintermist history who have absolute power over magic. Jedrowler is one, and you are the other."

Anton slipped his hands from the priestess and stood. Looking at Mage Jedrowler, he bit his lower lip. He should tell her. Someone should know. He wanted to confess and tell the priestess that he caused Jedrowler's death. He lost control of the Ancient Magic and gave the assassin an opportunity to attack. Instead, he said, "He is wrong. I can't master magic like Master Jedrowler."

"Jedrowler could do no more when he was a new mage. Believe in yourself, Anton. Conquer your fear. Control it. Don't let fear prevent you from becoming the great mage you are." Selaris stood and took Anton by the shoulder. "I believe he saw this coming. Before he started the spell, Jedrowler came to me and asked me to give you something if he should die."

She handed him a slip of parchment. Anton started opening it, and Priestess Selaris closed her hand over his. "It is a spell of binding, one used by mages, but similar to the one we use in marriage ceremonies. It binds two as one, not as master and slave, but as equals. Jedrowler said you would know what to do."

"I don't understand."

"You will." She held her hand up. "That's all I know. Take your mind off it for now. It is time to attend to Jedrowler's wake, time to celebrate his life and his transition to a new plane."

The temple banquet hall held a fair representation of the different cultures in the kingdom. Common folks and nobles mixed at the buffet table, representatives of the dwarvish community gathered around the bards, singing dwarvish songs. Across the room, Duke Altrid was talking with the head of the Copper Guild. Nearby, the Queen's emissary was laughing at a joke a tradesman just told. Minor and greater landholders exchanged hopes on a bountiful crop while the military officers chatted with the priestess. The Master Healer kept circulating among the groups, and the emissary from the elvish lands was talking with Mage Kytrill. All these people had known Jedrowler.

Jedrowler had touched many lives. They came to honor the man, not the mage. Anton wandered among the crowd, talking with many and hearing tales of the mage's life and how it had been devoted to helping people, to the land. It was reflected in the stories of his life. He heard many praises, many stories. Mage Master Gardner told humorous incidents that occurred in Jedrowler's life which started a string of stories, each more outlandish than the last.

Anton broke away from the latest guest, who was explaining how Jedrowler saved his caravan from a giant. As he walked away, he had to smile. Jedrowler was taking on a larger-than-life reputation.

Anton had just picked up a goblet when his Duke approached.

"Mage Anton, may I speak with you a moment?"

Anton bowed. "Of course, Duke Fathom, my time is always yours."

"I'm happy to see you wearing mage robes."

Anton lowered his head. "Only for this day. Mage Master Gardner made a special exception in honor of Mage Jedrowler. Tomorrow, I will be back in student's robes."

"Yes, that was explained to me. Nevertheless, I expect you to be in mage robes by the next moon." The duke took a sip of his wine. "You're special. I saw it when you were first brought to my court. Others see it too. So special that Duke Altrid, Mage Master Gardner, and the elvish mage have talked with me."

"What about, my lord?"

The duke covered his mouth as he coughed. "They explained how important your work is, not just for the Dukedom of Mead, but for Lashtar. Mage Master Gardner told me this spell of Mage Jedrowler can be expanded to cover the entire kingdom. Is this true?"

"Master Jedrowler was working on ways to adapt it to other parts of the kingdom. He believed in time all would be protected."

"Yes, well, that is all good, but he is dead. These people think you are the one to continue his work."

"Mage Master Gardner has asked me to learn and complete the second phase of the spell. As for the rest, I doubt I'm the mage that can do that."

A stern look crossed Duke Fathon face. "That is a bunch of Underdweller droppings. You're one of my subjects. You come from great stock. Are you saying these knowledgeable people are wrong?"

"No, my lord, but the task . . ."

"The task is no greater than it was for Mage Jedrowler when he was your age." He paused and took a hard look at Anton. "I understand Mage Jedrowler looked to you as a son. He was grooming you to take his place."

Anton opened his mouth to protest.

The duke put his right hand on Anton's shoulder. "Just listen. I know I've been manipulated. I should be upset, and a part of me is. Our agreement is for you to return to my service once you attained mage status. That is no longer possible. Your Queen needs you." He looked over his shoulder and signaled Xantrawler to join them. The weaponsmaster had been standing off to one side at the request of Duke Fathon.

"Weaponsmaster, thank you for waiting." The duke turned back to Anton. "Wizard Anton of the Dukedom of Fathon, as your rightful liege, I proclaim from this day forth, you are released from my service and all vows made to me have been fulfilled. From this day forth, you are in the service of the queen. Complete Mage Jedrowler's spell and make our land safe. So say I in front of a weaponsmaster of the realm."

"Heard and bound," Weaponsmaster Xantrawler said. He nodded to the duke, turned to Anton, bowed his head slightly, and gave the lad a tight grin. With a click of his heels, he returned to the wake.

Anton stared at his duke, his mouth hanging open. The duke laughed. "Close your mouth, Anton. It's not dignified to catch flies with your mouth."

Xantrawler smiled. He enjoyed positive events that lifted people's spirit. Anton's duke would have bragging rights for producing a famous mage of Wintermist. It would raise his prestige and position with other nobles. For Anton, he was staying in a place he loved.

Still smiling, he walked over to the corner where Diamox and Duncan were standing. As required by his job, Duncan stood to the left and one step behind Diamox.

Xantrawler exchanged greetings and pleasantries. The scholar was holding a goblet in one hand and three different types of chesses in the other. He would nibble a slice of cheese, rinse his mouth with the wine then nibble on a different slice of cheese. In between, he managed to say whole paragraphs of empty words.

Xantrawler took advantage of a momentary pause as Diamox took an extra large bite of cheese. He looked at Duncan. "Perhaps you can join me tomorrow. I could use your thoughts and observations on what we have found. Afterward, we can have a mug of ale and chat."

"I would enjoy nothing better than to spend time and just talk, but I have duties. Someone needs to watch our educated friend here. As his bodyguard, I believe that is my job."

Xantrawler shook his head. "Never thought my best student would be doing a menial job."

"Makes you humble. The world needs more humble people."

"The world needs more competent people, ones who have certain gifts."

"I'm doing what I'm meant to do." Duncan's voice had an edge, an edge filled with sorrow.

Letting out a snort, Xantrawler turned from the table. "You and that scholar are one of a kind, both denying your abilities."

Diamox tried to deny the statement, but the mouth full of cheese made his words unintelligible.

"Ambrus isn't denying his prophetic abilities. Since his leap, all he talks about is seeing the future. I had to drag him to his room earlier today as he was cornering wizards or mages and grilling them on divination."

"He does go from one extreme to the next."

"No, it's just when he finds something new, he throws himself into learning as much about it as possible. He's been grilling me about the predictions he has made in my presence."

"Tell the weaponsmaster what you told me," Diamox said as he finally cleared his mouth of cheese. "Damn good cheese, but too soft and sticky."

"What did you tell him?"

"Not much. I remember one clearly. He had it when we were getting ready to leave for Wintermist." Duncan looked at the ceiling. "Legion plans as he slumbers, the king of the North his to command. Awaken the Northland does, their glory, their fall. A black river flows south, wasting its self on the Wraiths Falls."

Xantrawler shook his head. "Seers, no one knows what they mean until it is too late."

"That's why I'm trying to learn. I need to know what I am talking about. This ability can help me save lives."

"Do you know anything about the wraiths he mentions?"

"There is an old keep to the east, in Windlow Pass." Duncan shrugged. "I have heard it's haunted. Other than the Thanatos Range, I don't know where you would find wraiths."

"Maybe we should head there after everything is done here," Diamox said as he brought his goblet to his lips. "An expedition to explore old ruins may yield interesting information."

Xantrawler laughed. "That will keep you occupied."

Duncan voiced his concern with Ambrus's prophecies. The two of them talked of a black river, a river flowing south. They talked for a quarter mark, then Ambrus saw someone he needed to talk with and hurried off, Duncan following.

Xantrawler watched his friend walk across the room. It was then he realized the young weaponsmaster had managed to change the subject away from him.

Xantrawler let out a string of curses.

The sun had set, and the moon was partially obscured by a passing cloud. In the semidarkness, Anton, sensing the small tremors produced by the noise of the falls suppressed his fear but still felt the stone bridge sway.

Around him were signs of spring, of the land coming alive. Life was everywhere. Flowers were starting to blossom, the trees were budding, and ducks and geese were flying north. He heard the school's cats and their mating calls. He passed a couple holding tight as they hurried back to the city.

There were life and happiness everywhere, except in him. The man who taught him how to use his abilities, to harness the power and use it for the betterment of all was deep within the temple. Anton's soul cried for his teacher. The one comfort tonight was the stories.

CynLisa and Mage Master Gardner told of Jedrowler's lifelong pursuit of this spell. They told of his triumphs and his failures. They spoke how every step forward, every misstep strengthened his resolve. The tale helped Anton understand his task was surmountable. Still, he was afraid he would lose control of the Ancient Magic.

These were real fears. His fear of heights was in his mind, a product of his overactive imagination. His fear of Ancient Magic was real. He had manipulated it under the guidance of Mage Jedrowler, felt the power as it flowed through him. He had experienced the power of Legion when the Ancient Magic was used. He had seen the flash of Ancient Magic before Jedrowler died. He needed to secure the anchors for the Ancient Magic. If not, then Legion could consume them all.

He wiped the sweat from his forehead and entered the school through one of the student's entrance. The door no sooner closed when someone called his name.

"Da Antone, pretty gook time ye gut back."

"Hi, Smyth." The other student was taller by a hand and had dark hair cropped short. He wore gray breeches and a molted brown and black shirt. Smyth was one of the few students from Outkingdom. Smyth was here to study combat magic. Anton had spared with him many times but never reached the foreigner's skill level.

Mage Master Gardner believed all mages should learn to protect themselves in battle. The swordmaster and the weaponsmaster taught the students, with assistance from the mage master. Their lessons were driven home with wooden practice swords, sometimes with a resounding whack on the behind, but just as often with a hit upside the head. All the teachers were merciless, telling the students in a real situation their opponent would give no quarter.

After many bruises, Anton learned to erect a magical shield with only the utterance of a sound. As time permitted, he learned how to retaliate while being attacked.

The two young lads soon develop a strong friendship and would spend time talking about their area of expertise. Smyth helped Anton become proficient with the magic shields, enough to keep the weaponsmaster from giving him too many bruises.

Anton showed the Outkingdomer how to improve on simple spells, creating powerful enchantments with minute movement as the magic flowed through you. Smyth increased the power of simple combat magic with a flick of his wrist or a sound. Thanks to Anton's help, he outpaced the other two wizards learning combat skills. Because of his rapid advancement, he spent more time with veteran combat mages on intensive magical studies.

The last time Anton had talked with Smyth, the Outkingdomer told him he would be leaving in the spring. His trip would take all summer as he had to cross Lashtar then sail passed the Rolar Empire to his distant land.

"I have bent das far sas I dan here. Dis time to compeat dine lessons at home." Once there, they would finish his combat training; and in five years, he would join the ranks of his country's fighting mages.

Anton felt mages should not do actual fighting as they were not made for that. Both professions took intensive training to master. In five years, when Smyth turned twenty-three seasons, he would be a mage and a fighter, but not a true master of either.

"No master wit sword, nor wit magic. I be master mage fighter. Est of boat rules."

Anton was happy knowing how to defend himself. Why learn to fight? No one could take a mage once they called on the arcane forces.

"What did you do?" Anton said. Smyth had a smile on his face, his hands made little fleeting movements, and he was too relaxed.

Smyth pushed away from the wall and walked to Anton. "Olee dot mage master said. You gut new room and weed put stuff dare."

Anton's insides quivered. He knew where his new room was but hoped it wasn't. Smyth led the way, and with each step and every turn, his fear was confirmed. He allowed himself to be lead until they were in front of Mage Jedrowler's door.

Smyth turned to Anton. "I dot go to committal. I make myself useful, ready friend's new room." Smyth took Anton by the shoulders and held him at arm's length. "Mine family many losses, so I know ye hurt. Ye knee friend talk with ye see mine."

"Thanks, Smyth, I will talk with you. But tonight, I want to be alone."

Smyth nodded. "Ye have mourned now yea say gootby ye friend. Understood."

Anton hugged his friend then entered the room. He wandered, looking at Jedrowler's sparse possessions. He looked into the sleeping chamber where his stuff was piled on the bed. Looking at the wardrobe in the corner, he knew he would have to empty it before putting his stuff in it. He decided that could wait until morning.

Sliding the blanket from the bed, he dragged it to the couch. He lay down, pulling the blanket up to his chin. With a wave of his hand, he doused the lights and looked at Lake Mead. The night sky reflected in the water. He saw the moon, the clouds. This was a sight Jedrowler would have seen many times.

He pulled the blanket around him and silently started a private conversation with his friend.

Chapter Seventeen

Day Five

In the predawn darkness, General Klaydon inspected the wall. While walking the battlements, he caught himself constantly looking north at the sky full of stars and the black silhouette of the foothills. The fire of the previous day was gone, but the Night Watch reported a dim red glow in the north. He searched the canyon and saw the glow and knew it was the light from the campfires of the enemy.

On the northern horizon, the Thanatos Mountains' peaks were already gathering sunlight.

As the sun rose, he left the battlements to walk the base of the wall. He talked with the men and listened to their concerns and requests. Some he knew had children, and he inquired on their health. Others had sick parents, and he asked on their well-being. One man had recently been bonded to a local girl, and he spent a short time talking with him on the joy of being bonded.

His belief was an officer not only held a duty to his queen, but to his men. He made an effort to know as much about his three thousand man force as he could, and in return, they showed him loyalty.

The sun was still casting long shadows when the North Wall came alive. Washer women, peddlers, water boys, and others appeared. These were the people that kept the army going, the ones that did the work or provided the service that made the life of a soldier bearable. The peddlers knew military personnel rose early, so they hit the soldiers first. Later, they would be in the city, hawking their merchandise. Only a few peddlers cheated his men, and they were handled by the Merchants Guild, who were protective, of those who guarded them.

Passing the armorer's shed, he saw the apprentices sorting breast plates, shields, and helms. One apprentice was tossing leather armor to one side. Later, they would be sent to the leather workers for repair. The master armorer was at the forge, inspecting the work of his apprentices, nodding over some and scowling at others.

The arrowsmith was in his shop, bundles of arrows straining the table. The more enemies killed by arrows, the fewer the fighters had to deal with.

Engineers were combing the wall, reinforcing crucial areas, replacing ropes and chains, and pouring boiling water into troughs. During the attack, boiling oil would replace the water, and it would spray from the mouth of gargoyles.

Squires staggered down the steps, their arms hanging limp at their sides. Exhausted from spending the night resupplying towers with polearms, axes, arrows, and extra swords, they were headed to bed. On the battlements and around the grounds, pages were making their way back and forth, delivering messages.

General Klaydon saw extra oil, armor, and weapons being hauled up the wall. The extra supplies were stowed along the parapet, easy access for fighters needing replacements. Round stone was going to the top of the towers, ready for the catapults. Other towers were receiving bundles of javelin-size bolts for use by the ballista.

On the ground, artillerymen were honing their skill and speed; cock, load, fire. Twice a minute, another javelin-size bolt lodged in the thick oak target. The sergeant was yelling to move, be accurate, and keep hands clear.

The throop of a catapult caused General Klaydon to look up. The men were testing the range, learning where the missiles would fall and how they would bounce.

Soldiers were training with swordsmasters, while knights put their steads through riding exercise to prepare both rider and mount for combat. A group of pikemen marched pass, their sergeant calling out the cadence.

A group of soldiers was relaxing under a tree, joking and laughing about barbarians and their useless attempt at attacking the North Wall. They were boasting about sweeping the invaders from the wall or cutting them down in the ditches.

General Klaydon held no delusions. What man built, man could destroy. A prolonged siege, one with mages, would bring the Wall down. He needed to be ready. He needed his men ready. If the invaders found a weakness, if the North Wall was breached, the small company of three thousand and the militia from Trader's Junction would be outnumbered.

"Riders coming in!" the watchman called from the gatehouse. "They wear the queen's color."

General Klaydon hastened to the gatehouse.

As he reached the gate, the watchman called down, "Queens Knight Fensin leads them."

General Klaydon signaled for the portcullis to be raised.

Queens Knight Marko Fensin's horse sprinted from the tunnel. Frothing, its coat glistening with sweat and the mane singed, its sides heaving, the horse dropped its head. The other three horses were in similar shape. General Klaydon received a shock as he saw a dwarf, a dwarf on a horse. Dwarves never rode horses. They preferred the smaller and faster wong wolves of the forest.

Halprin slid from his saddle. Rubbing his rear, he glared up at Gunther. "Cheese and rice! I want wolf next time." Mumbling, he turned to his horse and started yanking his thrower and ax from the saddle. "Wong won fair and square. Leave it, won't need it he said. Stupid humans!"

Queen's Knight Fensin slid from his horse, calling to nearby soldiers to take the horses and cool them down.

Approaching the general, everyone but Wizard Amikin gave a salute.

"I hope you have a good reason for nearly killing my horses, Fensin."

Queen's Knight Fensin nodded. "A large force from the Northland. Corporal Dane and the Dwarf Halprin can give you a full report. Wizard Amikin has news on the enemy's mages."

"Where are the rest of your men?"

Marko Fensin's shoulders sagged. His head lowered as he spoke, "Dead, all dead." His voice held no emotions.

Looking the men over, General Klaydon saw their ash-smeared faces, their singed hair, and the dust clinging to every pore. The young knight had light burns on his exposed skin, and Wizard Amikin's hands were wrapped in bandages.

"Is the situation so serious you had to set the forest on fire?"

"We were attacked by a dragon."

A chill ran through General Klaydon. He knew they were not legend, not after what he had seen many years ago in the foothills.

"What size was the dragon?" General Klaydon had not heard Colonel Fythe approach. "Color, size of scale, bloated body or thin?"

"To tell you the truth, I was too busy trying to stay out of the flames to notice," said Marko.

"The beastie be thin, remind me of them tunnel snakes in mines," Halprin said. "Red brown scales size of me head. Claws long as me hand."

"You saw this?"

"When it flies ten feet and grabs fellow fighter hard not to."

Turning to the general, Colonel Fythe said, "I know of this kind. Legends tell us they dwell deep in the range. This one is young."

"Young don't matter, sir," Gunther said. "It wiped out the outpost in minutes. When it attacked Sir Fensin, it took three swipes of its flame to destroy his company."

"Three swipes are about all it can do," Colonel Fythe said. "That young can only flame three or four times."

"The mages can take care of the critter," General Klaydon said.

"Begging your pardon, but they have mages," Amikin said. "And some type of force that warps our magic."

General Klaydon looked at the North Wall. Mages and dragons, a combination he never envisioned. He had to face a dragon once in a war game. When the princess became queen, one of her first orders was to have her higher-ranking officers spend a year under Weaponsmaster Baylore's tutelage. He remembered that game he barely survived, but learned a lot about a no-win situation. This he could win as they had warning and could prepare.

"How many days before they get here?"

"Today."

"Today! That's fast for an army the size you claim. What are they doing, killing their horses to drag their equipment here?"

"They use horse for riding and large strange animals to pull their wagons," Gunther said. "Their infantry alternates marching, riding, and hanging onto horses and wagons."

"They sound a lot like the nomads of the southern plains," Marko said. "According to the reports, I read those people travel year-round and cover vast distance."

The general looked at his second. Colonel Fythe knew this country. He grew up here. General Klaydon had spent evenings with Wendell, sitting in front of the fire and talking over wine. The colonel spoke about dragons, how they were territorial and vicious. In the next breath, he laughed. "But everyone knows there is no such thing as dragons."

"Queen's Knight Fensin, I'm calling a council, and you will give a full report. Wizard, report to Mage Margella and tell him everything." Looking the two soldiers over, the general said, "You two can use a bath and real food. Report to the barracks, clean up and draw some rations. I will send a page for you later. Be ready to give a report to the council."

As everyone departed, General Klaydon looked at the wall once more. The earliest the enemy would attack would be tomorrow. No commander would have his men attack the same day, not after days' worth of force marching.

How was he to defend against a dragon?

King Rathveil sat his tea cup down as the door opened. Sighing, he wished just once his thirty minutes of free time would last longer, that no one would have an urgent problem.

He looked at the smiling face of General Thrawt.

"Does your expression mean good news? If not, I will be upset. I had one minute left."

"We have arrived." He tucked his gauntlets into his belt as he stood in front of the king. "Our forces are at the outskirts of the clearing. Tomorrow, we attack, and victory will be yours."

"I assume our Force Shapers have the Ancient Magic active?"

"They report that it covers the entire area."

King Rathveil smiled. "Good, good. How long before our warriors are ready to attack?"

"First light tomorrow."

"I did not ask when you were planning to attack. When will you be ready to attack?"

The smile disappeared from General Thrawt's face. "My lord, the men need rest. They have completed a force march of two weeks."

"We need to take the wall. These mages of the Southland are not novices. They are masters of the Unseen Forces."

"The men need rest." It was more a plea than a statement.

"They will adapt to this magic. They will counter our Force Shapers' spells." He slammed his book on the table, causing the fine china cup to dance on its saucer. "They will attack my pet with their spells! I don't want him hurt." King Rathveil pounded his finger on the table. "We need to attack while they are off balance."

"But, my lord . . ."

"If you have warriors too exhausted to fight, rotate them with fresh ones. I don't care what you do as long as you attack the Southland. Am I making myself clear, General?"

"Yes, my lord." General Thrawt bowed his head, submissively. "We will attack late sun. You should know some of our fighting will be after dark."

King Rathveil smiled as he stood. "Subduing the Southland in the black of night. What poetic justice. Their funnel pyres can light our victory." He stoked his chin, wondering where that thought came from.

Xantrawler leaned on the parapet and stared across the land. The sun was playing hide-and-seek behind the clouds, and he watched little dark and light patches pass over the land. Things were quiet, too quiet. The mages were staying in their quarters. There was little traffic through the gate, and his patrols reported no sign of Underdweller activity.

He didn't like it.

He pulled his sword, the one gifted to him by the dwarves, and held it. The magic within warned of immediate danger, and by concentrating, it gave warnings in advance, sometimes days in advance. The sword vibrated slightly.

Putting the sword back in its sheath, Xantrawler stood straighter, breathing in the fresh mountain air. It would rain tonight. He could smell it on the wind.

Listening to the faint sound of the falls, he thought his uneasiness was because of Jedrowler's death. This was a strike against the school. You do not make one strike. You attack, keep pressing your advantage. Whoever had ordered the attack was not going to stop, but the assassin was not speaking.

He recalled his meeting with Helena before the committal service. They were in his command room atop the gatehouse. Helena was holding a stone bowl, moving its pestle around, and tapping the sides.

"This is definitely what he mixed his poison in."

The rest of Nigel's possessions were spread out on a table, an extra uniform, a couple of pants, a shirt, and a worn cloak. Flint and steal, a sharping stone and a few coins were in a small belt pouch. A quiver held three bolts for the small hand bow. Beside the quiver was a crude dagger.

The only item of interest was a metal mirror with a piece of charcoal attached by a leather thong. Magical ruins were carved in the frame.

"I'm concerned with this device," Xantrawler said, poking the mirror with his finger. "It's magical, but what does it do?"

"I never saw anything like it."

Xantrawler turned to Captain Morse, who shrugged. "My mages never had anything like that."

"I'll have CynLisa look at it," Helena said, picking up the device.

"You won't find her," Xantrawler said. "She's going to Jedrowler's committal service."

"I'll leave it with one of her assistants."

Captain Morse turned to Xantrawler, "I don't think he was alone."

Xantrawler sighed, "I agree. Do discreet checks on the men. I'll have Helena do her own inquiries."

"It's a sad day, Weaponsmaster, when we have to investigate our own men."

Xantrawler leaned on the cool rock of the wall and wondered if his second comment was what was bothering him. He shook that thought off as over the years he had to question the loyalty of men and it didn't set his nerves on edge.

"A wonderful day, is it not, Weaponsmaster?"

Xantrawler turned as Mage Master Gardner walked up to him. Returning the greeting, he turned back and watched the land. Farmers were preparing their fields for spring planting; lumber men were dragging their loads from the mountain forest; and in one of the nearby villages, he could see a new building rising.

"You seem troubled."

"Too quiet. I don't like it."

Mage Master Gardner leaned on the wall. "I too have felt uneasiness. I had hoped with Jedrowler's committal, it would pass. Instead, it has become stronger. Something isn't right."

They were interrupted by a runner who handed Xantrawler a slip of parchment. The weaponsmaster quickly read the message. "Tell the duke I will be there in an hour."

Mage Master Gardner asked, "Trouble?"

"The North Wall reports a horde of barbarians moving their way. General Klaydon is asking for reinforcements."

"There are mages at the North Wall, along with well-trained men and knights who can fight. The attack will be over before the duke's men leave."

Xantrawler stared north, rapping his fist on top of the parapet. "I hope you're right."

"You know I'm right. The North Wall has never failed us. I would be more concern with a raid from the Underdwellers. This is the time of the year they come out of their holes and raid outlying farms and villages."

"A good time for an enemy to attack."

"My friend, I served with a merc unit for many years. It took me many more years to learn to relax and not see foes behind every rock. You need to do the same. Enjoy your retirement. You are useful protecting us from the occasional Underdweller party and teaching the next generation of defenders."

"A lifetime of paranoia is hard to break." Xantrawler sighed. "You're right. A barbarian horde is not much to worry about. They're small in numbers and not organized like professional men-at-arms."

Mage Master Gardner smiled. "You're right, but that doesn't mean you can't take advantage of the duke's paranoia. Take advantage of his hospitality, enjoy his wine, and spend the night in a soft feather bed. Your second can handle the details here."

"After this past week, I deserve a small rest, might as well let the duke provide it."

"Go and have fun. I'll send for you when the horde reaches us."

Both men laughed as Xantrawler left for the stables.

Chapter Eighteen

General Klaydon hastened up the steps of the command tower.

Late morning scouts returned with reports that the enemy was approaching quickly. They anticipated the enemy would reach the North Wall around lunch hour. Their estimate had proven accurate for as the officers were sitting down to eat, the enemy arrived.

Shortly before their arrival, the magic users became dizzy and disoriented. Because of Wizard Amikin's warning, this was expected. What was discovered was the severity was not dependent on the magic a person controlled. The degree of effect was random. Mages were flat on their stomach, trying to grab the floor to keep from sliding off, while wizards moved with little problems. Other mages had no physical problems, and students were the ones who feared falling from the floor. Others suffered extreme pain, and some were almost blind. Wizard Amikin was affected the least.

Witches and the two druids had similar experience. For each, their physical problems varied. What they had in common was their inability to use magic. Even master healers were having problems healing.

Mage Margella had said, “The magical forces have changed. They are brighter and sharper and flow differently. There is no gracefulness in their movement, and many report that it hurts when the flow passes through them.”

General Klaydon called another council meeting for the afternoon, and it was the one interrupted by a page with an urgent message from Colonel Fythe. The general's presence was required in the command tower.

Stepping into the command room, General Klaydon looked at the Northland's army. Men were at the edge of the field, beating their shields with swords and axes, others positioning themselves in a flanking position. Siege engines were moving along the road.

Colonel Fythe looked at the general. “You can see them making noise, but none is reaching us.”

“A quiet spell,” Mage Magnate had followed the general, “used to mask movement. But why bother? It's daylight, and we can see them.”

“To frighten us,” General Klaydon said. “We see men and wagons moving. You know animals are making noises, sergeants yelling, yet you hear nothing. It unnerves ordinary soldiers. Whoever is commanding that army is smart and cunning.”

General Klaydon looked at the sun. “Four candle marks before sun set. Not enough time for an attack.”

A brightly painted wagon rolled from the forest. Several highly colored banners flying and on top a flag of gold and black with a silver star burst in the center. “That's a mage wagon,” Mage Magnate said.

As the wagon rolled out of the spell of silence, the wagon's creaking and the snorting and snarling of the strange creature could be heard. The officers of the Wall watched as a figure dressed in a colorful robe dropped to the ground and stood on the road side. As the wagon followed the serpentine trail, mages continued climbing off. Finally, seven robed figures lined the road.

Stopping short of the missile fire, an eighth figure appeared. Stepping in front of the wagon, the enemy mage looked at the Wall. He started to chant an incantation, his voice building in volume.

"I don't like the feel of this," General Klaydon said.

Warlord Thwart sat in his saddle and watched. Behind him, the bulk of his warriors waited in the forest. The users of the Unseen Forces were positioning themselves along the road, readying a spell. The head of the Force Shapers stepped in front of the beast, pulling his wagon and started to chant.

Warlord Thwart motioned for one of his war chiefs. The young man leaned close and listened. "I want attack parties on both flanks. That is their weak points. I will have Vella concentrate along the center of the wall. Where is the force device?"

The war chief pointed to the gatehouse west tower. "I caught the signal where the tower joins the wall."

Warlord Thwart nodded. "Have three of the catapults aim on that location. When the first missile hits, have the Force Shaper set off the device. Let the southerners think we have magical exploding rocks."

He turned to another war chief, "Lantill, take your band and go for the eastern wall. Our spies report it is undermanned. Secure it before Vella arrives."

"Are we to remain on the wall?"

"No, I have fighters coming to do that. I want you over the wall and take out as many of the enemy as you can. Drive through their ranks and secure roads leading from the Wall. Hold their granary. We need fresh supplies and our beasts deserve to enjoy the spoils of war."

His two war chiefs rode off to prepare for their attack. His other chiefs knew their orders. They would hold back as the wall was softened up with stone throwers and spear tossers. Once the defenders were disorganized, they would charge the center of the wall. It wasn't the best of plans, but it was the only thing he had time to organize. He had little time to secure the wall, then he would subdue the other side in the dark. It was going to be quick and unorganized, with too much room for small mistakes to grow into big ones. Not for the first time, he cursed King Rathveil's lack of military knowledge.

He gave the command, and a bugler blew a three-note sound for attack.

The enemy mage brought both hands together.

Lightning raced from the foreign mage's clenched hands to the top of the gatehouse. Stone, wood, and soldiers flew as dust filled the air, obscuring the top of the gatehouse. Energy poured through the mage as he held the crackling blue, white bolt. He swung the energy back and forth, sending debris into the air.

On the road, the mages cast spells left and right. Water froze. Ice ran up the stream and under the gatehouse. On the Lashtar side of the wall, people watched ice race down the stream, the spell fading at the edge of the Terrapin Xon field of magic.

Within the ravines, the ground heaved and flowed, the sides sliding and melting. The marshes disappeared while rocks and small hillocks were sucked into the land. A wave of flatness swelled toward the North Wall.

As the notes of the bugler carried across, the Northland army men and animals rumbled across the flattened ground. Emerging from the spell of silence, their battle cry bounded off the sides of the pass and broke the unearthly silence. Seige engines came within range and stopped. Archers readied their bows as they took positions behind mantlets, large shield like device. Catapults lumbered across the ground, and covered cats rolled with troops underneath. Warriors ran across the field carrying ladders, ropes, and hooks. Two lines of barbarians arched across the pass, moving toward the North Wall's flanks.

On the North Wall, soldiers stood frozen at their post. Some looked toward the command tower, waiting for flags to rise. Many slid their weapons from their sheaths or holders. Younger ones slowly stepped back.

General Klaydon stared. His logical military mind refused to accept the enemy attacking. Slowly, he shook off his paralysis

"Sound the call to arms, raise the attack flags! I want every fighter on the wall. Have the knights ready to cover any breach. Hold till sundown, then they will be forced to pull back. I'll be damned if we can't hold them until sundown!" He looked toward Mage Magnate. "I don't care what you need to do, but give me magical protection!"

All along the North Wall, flags raised and horns echoed. From the barracks, stables and practice field soldiers poured, heading for their assigned post.

Gunther ran up the stairs, reaching his assigned post on the eastern flank. He gave a quick glance over the killing field. Behind the foot soldiers, the slower-moving siege engines were moving through the former swamp. He cursed as he realized the enemy's mages had neutralized a prime defense.

Glancing down the wall, he noted the position of the archers and the large gaps in the defender's ranks. He looked for the young recruits who would help repel anyone breeching the top. Everyone had been sure the Northmen would not attack until morning, so they were scattered, attending to what they felt were more important affairs.

His own sergeant had gone into Trader's Junction. "To get all, you lazy barrack rats, a reminder of why you fight." That little celebration was postponed.

Gunther saw the archer squad trying to fill in their gaps, and he called out to the closest one.

"Archer, where's your corporal?"

"He left earlier with our sergeant."

"Take command of your group," Gunther said.

Halprin approached with five other dwarves behind him. "Now, more what me like, enemy that believes in action."

"Halprin, can your throwers reach the enemy?"

Halprin laughed. "They won't fire mile."

"They're almost at the Wall!"

Halprin humphed and hopped on one of the steps made for dwarves. Looking through the merlons, his eyes went wide as he saw how close the enemy was and watched the northern mages dance and wave their arms.

"Bloody mages. No honor." He looked at the dwarves. "Come on, mates, show them how we dwarves respond to those without honor!"

The dwarves climbed on their perch and brought their dwarvish throwers to their shoulders. Taking aim, they sent off a volley of a half-dozen bolts. Most fell short or were deflected. As a unit, the dwarves recocked their throwers.

Gunther heard the *ka-thump* of the ballista in the tower next to them. On the field, he saw the projectile impact the ice near the oncoming siege engines. Nervously, he looked into the sky but saw no moving dot. He shouted down the line, "Swordsmen, look to the sky and watch for a dragon."

"Right, Corporal, since when do myths fly?"

"Watch you mouth or me thrower be aim in nother direction."

"Do as you were ordered, soldier." Gunther was not angry. Five days ago, he would have been the same. He turned to look at the mountain. The wall was built into the shear rock made smooth by workers over the years. The mountain face was left shear, and higher up, it contained sharp-edge rocks. In theory, no one could attack from that direction.

It also hid what was in the other valley. The dragon could fly over the ridge and be on them before they had a chance.

Wizard Amikin came up the stair, robes billowing around him. His hands had been healed by a master healer and were as nimble as when he was first stationed on the North Wall. He looked at the oncoming enemy and pulled down on his robe.

"Amikin, get out of here. You can't do nothing."

"I understand it. I know how it works!"

"Crazy wizard, what are you blathering about?" Halprin recocked his thrower.

"Esprin said, with limited power and an overwhelming force, look for a weak spot." Hopping on the wall, Amikin noted the enemy's position. He smiled as he spied the perfect target.

Gunther reached for the wizard. "You're going to get killed!"

The wizard whipped his arms up, his sleeves billowed, and energy swirled around his fingers. Shouting at the top of his lungs, he gathered then brought the magic into harmony, ordered it. A blue flash shot from his hands, impacting the ice. With a loud snap, cracks appeared and quickly spread.

Fissures ran along the sheet of ice, and a groan signaled the end. It gave way, dropping a catapult, two of the strange beasts, a supply wagon, and a dozen men into the cold muck. With the overturn wagon and catapult, trapped men and others were dragged to their death by their armor and weapons.

Wizard Amikin smiled as he picked his next target. "It's magic, old magic."

"Blasted wizard speak clear."

"Never mind," Gunther said, "just do it again."

"Where did that mage bolt come from?" General Klaydon demanded.

"Eastern sector, sir."

"Margella, who do you have over there?"

"None of my mages. We were all meeting, trying to learn a way to overcome this field."

"Well, someone has. Who is it?"

"The only one assigned to that sector is Wizard Amikin."

"A wizard? You're the best, and a wizard is performing magic when you can't!"

General Klaydon looked at the enemy force. Two segments were storming the western and eastern flanks. The rest of the barbarians lined up just outside of artillery range. General Klaydon looked at the situation table. "That commander is sending people into our flanks, thinking they're the weak points."

"He may be right. I'm not seeing much response from our flanks."

"The eastern flank will hold. They have a wizard who can do magic." He looked at Mage Margella who was deep in discussion with his mages.

On the field, a dazzling flash erupted within the eastern group of warriors. Sparks danced as ropes of pure magic slithered out of nothingness to wrap around the invaders. The sparks climbed into the air and screamed behind the mantlets. They chased archers from safety and into an onslaught of arrows from Lashtar's archers.

General Klaydon saw the enemy's mages join and face the eastern section. They raised their hands as one, and their chant rose above the sound of battle.

"Damn! Someone stop them!"

"*Get down!*" Gunther wrenched Amikin to the floor. The battlement rocked, the world turned white, and rocks and mortar flew as the parapet dissolved. Gunther's ears rang, and he smelled dust. The wizard beneath coughed and gagged from the lung full of dust he sucked in.

Slowly, the ringing receded, and the sound of screaming men and dwarves came to Gunther. He rolled to his feet, helped the wizard to a sitting position, before he leaned on the shattered wall and looked at the field. The enemy mages had turned away and were walking to their wagon.

The enemy had moved closer to the wall, men sat up siege weapons, and archers retook position behind mantlets. The enemy was being met with sporadic flights of arrows from the Lashtar defenders, the catapults were firing, and ballista bolts slammed through the tough hide of the creatures.

On the wall, commands were being yelled up and down the line.

"Shields, we need shields!"

"Archers, stand ready!"

"Bloody lime lickers, back on wall, still enemy to fight!"

"Get the wounded down the stairs!"

Fighters scrambled over the debris, looking for fallen weapons or shields. Others yanked their companions from underneath the stonework. Gunther saw another soldier, head back, mouth open, staring at the sky with sightless eyes. A group of recruits lay a short distance away, unrecognizable. Gunther was pushed aside as a couple of young recruits broke for the stairs. It was their first battle, and they had watched their friends die. With their bravado gone, fear rushed through them, and they were fleeing the carnage.

This was no different from what he had witnessed during the Underdweller War.

Flights of arrows came in waves, forcing the defenders into cover. Gunther shouted orders, but the men ignored him. He looked over to his right and saw Halprin and his dwarves crouched, ready with their throwers. During a break, they were up and firing.

When the first scaling ladder hit the wall, Gunther nodded at Halprin who clipped his thrower to his belt and brought out his war ax.

The arrows stopped as the first enemy came over the wall. Gunther and a few veterans met them with steel. Swords clashed with shields, and men screamed. Some warriors never made a sound, just watched a red flower blossom on their chest. As life left them, they silently tumbled backward to land on the unyielding ground.

Defenders came out of their daze, joined the fight, and fought to keep the black wave at bay. Men fought up and down the battlement.

Enemy and allies were cut down, many falling to the hard ground sixty feet below.

There was no plan, no tactic, just brute force against brute force. When a fighter fell, another took his place. A boiling mass of humanity, slashing and hacking. Soon, the combatants were covered with the result of battle. Screams of the injured and dying sounded all around. The defenders found themselves losing ground to the overwhelming number. With no defenders pushing the ladders away, enemy fighters were appearing every second.

Gunther and Halprin stood together, one with his sword and the other with his ax. As in the Underdweller War, they worked as a team, Gunther swinging high and Halprin chopping low. They held their ground longer but were eventually forced down the stairs. Two Northmen attacked Gunther, and he managed to block. He kicked and took the other one out, but his foot slipped on the blood running down the steps. He tried to regain his balance as he dodged a blow aimed for his head. Still unbalanced, he brought his sword up to block his unprotected front. The force took his feet from under him.

Gunther hit the steps, jarring his teeth. His head slammed into the stone, and his vison closed in with flashes of blackness. He felt his grip loosening, his sword slid from his fingers, and he fell into flashing, swirling blackness before the final impact drove him deeper into darkness.

"The eastern wall has been breached," Colonel Fythe said "Here, and here. The western side is being scaled here, but they're holding for now."

General Klaydon glanced at the map. "We have no choice. Send the first cavalry to the eastern sector."

Colonel Fythe gave the order, and a squire removed a yellow flag from one of the tubes and ran it up the pole. Snapping open in the breeze, the flag revealed a gold horse head. Beneath the flag, a green penned fluttered to life.

Walking to the window, General Klaydon surveyed the field. The enemy was holding, just out of catapult range. The two companies attacking the flanks moved like men who had saw combat together, organized with little wasted movements.

There was little to be done in the way of conventional defense. No boiling oil, no hot pitch as there was no mage power to instantly heat the substance. The enemy's field of magic was blocking his mages. He watched the western soldiers tossing large stones on the assault teams, but it wasn't enough.

A mage bolt took out a section of the parapet, giving the enemy an opening clear of defenders.

General Klaydon pounded his fist on the sill. "We need our mages!"

Mage Margella shot a glare at the general, then returned his attention to the two other mages. All three were waving their arms and muttering incantations.

"What is your estimate of the enemies force, Colonel?"

Colonel Fythe looked at the battlefield. The mages were gathered in a cluster on the side of the road. Men were appearing from the woods: mounted warriors, foot soldiers, swordsmen, pikemen, sappers, archers, and engineers. A battering ram was rolling down the road. In the western field, three catapults were being readied. On the eastern flank, the archers had redirected their arrows farther down the wall. From one of the towers now controlled by the enemy, a ballista fired into the soldiers on the wall.

"I've never seen so many barbarians. They must be close to ten thousand."

"I recognize those banners from descriptions in old reports. They're from the Northland."

"They never had mages, just shamans."

A mage stepped forward and waved his hand. A bluish green light flashed for a second, enveloping the gatehouse.

Twin explosions rocked two of the towers of the gatehouse. Screams of men cut through the windows as smoke billowed out.

"Margella!" General Klaydon yelled. "I have men dying."

"And I have wizards and mages dying."

Slamming into the curtain wall, a large stone missile took out a section of the parapet and spilled men to the ground. General Klaydon slammed his closed hand into a post.

"Damn it! At this rate, we'll lose the wall before sunset."

Colonel Fythe was staring. "I think we have more trouble."

From the forest, a new wagon rolled. Three of the large creatures pulled it clear of the trees and stopped. The wagon gave off a strong glow of magic, a glow even the untalented could see.

Queen's Knight Fensin spurred his horse around the East Wall barracks. Behind him, seventy-five knights raced. He saw bodies litter the ground of the eastern wing of the North Wall. A small band of defenders, no more than a hundred, were fighting the black leathered enemy at the base of the wall. Occasionally, a bolt of lightning struck the enemy on the battlements. Enemy archers took their place and returned fire. The defenders of Lashtar were slowly being decimated.

Queen's Knight Fensin thought of the men dead to the north. These invaders, these barbarians were responsible. Taking his anger, channeling it, and drawing strength from it, he let his resolve build.

"Drisidell, the left flank! Herrick, the right! *No quarters*!" Marko pulled his sword and charged through the parting ranks of defenders.

Sweeping their weapons, the knights attacked. Marko's warhorse kicked out, taking an enemy in the face. As the horse danced, the knight balanced in the saddle and slashed. Man and animal flowed as one. A sword bounced off the barding, and Fensin cut the man down. Drawing his blade through the exposed neck of another, blood spurted, covering horse and rider. Using his knees to turn the horse, he engaged another fighter.

With a fluid motion, the knights moved deeper into the mass of black armor. The enemy was scattering, men separated from their squads, officers isolated from their command.

The foot soldiers of Lashtar took advantage of the confusion. Following in the wake of the knights, they drove through the enemy. Within the mass of humanity, swords slashed, axes chopped, and horses' steel-clad hoofs crunched bone. The enemy was giving ground, pulling back to the wall. In the rear, the wizard cast magic at the enemy reinforcements coming over the wall.

The battlefield was a muddy mess of spilled blood. The moans of the injured hung in the air, but the dead made no sounds.

Marko's horse lurched, a high-pitched screech spilling from its mouth. A sword slid from the animal's side, blood dripping from the blade. Kicking loose from the stirrups, Marko smoothly left the saddle. Landing in a crouch, he looked for the one who killed his horse. The warrior was gone, melted into the formless mass of black-clad fighters. He brought his arm around, his buckler deflecting the blow aimed for his head. He staggered backward, regained his footing, and knocked another jab aside. Using his momentum, he thrust his sword through the leather armor. Without waiting to see the result, he engaged another opponent.

As fast as one enemy was dispatched, another appeared. His helm was dented, the buckler deformed, and his armor punctured by swords. He spouted bruises, his muscles protested, and blood flowed from a wound on his left shoulder. As the Queen's own weaponsmaster taught him, he blocked pain and concentrated on the battle before him.

Black stars dance on a field of dark blue. Blue sky dissolved, chasing the black stars. Clouds tinged with red floated into sight. Gunther moaned as his head exploded. Rolling to his knees, more black stars swarmed, blocking his view of the ground. Trying to gain his feet, the ground heaved and slanted at a crazy angle. His knees went out from under him, and he found himself sprawled on his face.

"Damn, human, don't move till feel better."

Turning his head, he saw the profile of Halprin standing with both hands on his battle-ax. Gunther looked at the multiple image of his friend. "Wha . . . what happened?"

"You took head blow, fell from stairs. Don't worry, fighters cushioned fall."

"We need to help them." Gunther struggled to sit and was rewarded with the sound of battle clamoring in his head.

"The knights here, things under control. Bloody wizard useful too. Impaled with wall."

Gunther squinted and saw enemy warriors swaying from stone branches that grew from the wall. The warrior's faces reflected terror as the wall's stone branches slowly impaled them.

Gunther looked and saw the knights and foot soldiers had the enemy backed up to the wall. The Northmen were putting up a losing defense. A number of the enemy was trying to climb the stairs, but Lashtar's archers were taking them out. Those who did reach the parapet grabbed bows from the hands of their dead countrymen.

Using his short friend to rise, Gunther climbed to his feet. "Where's my sword?"

"Lost when fell."

"Damn it, Halprin, the battle isn't over. Where's my sword!"

Grinning, Halprin snorted, "Stubborn like dwarf. Me knew you want to fight. Me grabbed one. It's beside you."

Bending down, Gunther fought the urge to vomit and grabbed the sword. The weight was right. It balanced nicely in his hand. With determination, he staggered toward the battle.

"Bloody hell, let's party."

"I have it!" Mage Margella yelled. To the other mages, he started talking excitedly.

General Klaydon shook his head. His present worry was the defense of the Wall. The western section had been breached. Just west of the gatehouse, the enemy was scaling the wall, breaching machines were moving down the road, and enemy archers were firing on his men. The enemy's mages had erected magical barriers around their fighters. The only good news was the eastern section had repelled the invaders.

"I want the reserves to move to this point." He indicated a spot on the map. "Signal our ground engines to move here, here, and here." Straightening, he turned in time to hear Colonel Fythe muttering. "If you have something to say, Colonel, spit it out."

"I said that is the fiftieth person to come out of that wagon."

"It's large."

"Not that large. They would have to be packed shoulder to shoulder."

General Klaydon watched a bolder hurl toward the gatehouse. He flinched in anticipation of the strike.

Just before striking, the bolder rebounded and crashed to the ground and rolled into a cluster of enemy troops. A cheer went up from the two mages in the command tower.

"It's not a magical field. It's old magic!" Mage Margella said. "The Northland mages have surrounded us with Ancient Magic. Just as Amikin said."

"What are you talking about?"

"Magical forces change as we use them, change as the land changes. We don't notice because it takes centuries. Some magic is untouched so remain unchanged. The Northland mages managed to pull in all those strands in the area and concentrate it."

General Klaydon waved his hand, cutting off Mage Margella. "You can use magic, that's good. Do your job."

"There is a catch. Ancient Magic is dangerous. It is powerful and hard to control. Not all will be able to use it." Mage Margella turned to the other mage.

Turning to Colonel Fythe, General Klaydon said, "We can win if they stop talking long enough to throw magic." Colonel Fythe smiled.

Magic streaked from Mage Margella's hands, scattering the enemy mages. Spells swirled and sparkled as the mage's concentration broke. Taking cover behind their wagons, they peered out.

Mage Margella sent mage energy around the battle field, erecting barriers and exciting the components of wood, causing the siege engines to burst into flames. He sent a charge of superheated air rolling across the field, broiling many of the enemy in their armor. Soon, his magic was joined by others as the North Wall's mages and wizards learned old magic.

Magic blocked arrows and boulders, sent ladders crashing and wound ropes around their holders. Cloth and wood burst into flame. On the wall, magic heated the contents of caldrons, so boiling oil spewed from the stone mouths of gargoyles.

The mages couldn't undo the spells upon the land, so the stream stayed frozen, the land level.

Men no longer took cover from magical attacks. Archers returned fire, their arrows no longer blocked. Catapults sent their loads into the midst of the enemy or crashing onto wagons and siege engines. Other fighters were repelling the enemy from the Wall.

The enemy started pulling back.

Warlord Thwart watched his warriors retreat. A few groups stood their ground. The eastern sector had men on the wall, and the catapults for the gatehouse worked to penetrate the barriers, but the rest of his attack was crumbling. The ram had stopped advancing, and his Force Shapers were hiding. As he watched, a ball of light rolled from the wall. It cut a path through his force, leaving unmoving men in its wake.

Warlord Thwart turned to one of his war chiefs, "Take the new arrivals and form up behind the ram. When Vella finishes, I want you to storm the gatehouse."

"A lot of good the dragon will do if the Force Shapers don't keep their users off us."

"I'll handle our Force Shapers." He looked at all his war chiefs. "They're weakened, their flanks opened. What resistance has developed will dissolve when Vella comes."

"Our men are panicking," another war chief said.

The warlord looked at the field. His war chief was right. Men were panicking. "Then control your men."

His Force Shapers were outnumbered. The enemy had a fortified position on high ground, and his men were tired and demoralized. He looked at the sun and knew there was little time left to take the wall. It was time to change the attack.

"Gardrid, take your band and reinforce Subchief Jenkrin on the eastern side. Once over the wall, strike for the gatehouse. I want you to cut off any reinforcements." He looked to the western sector. "Mantock, I want your band to do the same on the other side of the valley.

"Drankra, go to Vella's handler, have him instruct her to attack the gatehouse and that tower to the east of it then swoop along the wall. I want her to send the enemy into a panic, make them run. I want no mistake, like the forest."

The war chief turned his horse and galloped into the forest.

Warlord Thwart sat on his horse watching Lashtar's Force Shapers. He watched the shimmer of Unseen Force as barriers were erected and watched bolts of energy leap about. Lashtar's Force Shapers didn't always use force against force. Their magic would strike, and a wind storm would envelope his warriors. On the other side of the pass, his men became bogged down as the ground was saturated from a cloudburst.

These southerner's force shapers thought like military men and were true artist. His Force Shapers were children playing with flint and steel. His Force Shapers needed preparation time. The southerners just waved their hands, did funny little steps, and sent the force to do their bidding.

He had Vella, and he had spies. Two things that gave him an advantage.

Warlord Thwart urged his horse forward and approached the wagon of the Force Shapers. A magical barrier shimmered around their position. He found the leader, hiding under the wagon and gripping the wheel's spokes like the bars of a cell.

"Some leader," he allowed his upper lip to curl, "you hide like a young maiden about to meet her first mate."

"They're more powerful than we expected, Warlord."

"And they are working as separate units. You have practice working as a team. I suggest you come out of hiding and do just that." He looked toward the wall, then back at the leader. "If I start losing warriors because you decide to be a coward, I will kill one of you for every one hundred men I lose."

The Force Shaper dragged himself from under the wagon. As he dusted his robes, the rest of the force shapers appeared. "We will not let you down, Warlord."

"Vella is going to attack. When she does, set off the device our spy has in the gatehouse. After that, take out the Force Shaper in the tower to the east of the gatehouse. Then take out the rest of them one at a time."

Warlord Thwart knew that once they had the gate, it didn't matter what the southerners did. The wall would be his. He could march his troops through and combine with the other two arms of his force. This wasn't the plan the king had worked out, but he was not a warrior. He didn't understand that the best military strategy changes as a battle rages on, that it must constantly adapt to the changing situation and to the enemy movement. His plan of attack did not allow enough time to adapt to the enemy's counteroffensive. He should leave the fighting to the professionals.

He looked at the sky, half praying to the gods. The sun was too low in the sky, and he was running out of time.

As the sun slipped closer to the horizon, only small pockets of the enemy remained on the wall. General Klaydon gave a fatigued smile. One side of his face was lit by the setting sun, the other in dark shadows. "When the sun sets, they should pull back for the night. We can rest and prepare."

Colonel Fythe shook his head. "More than a hundred fighters have exited that wagon." He looked at General Klaydon. "We may be able to rest, but something tells me the Northland has a way to send more troops instantly."

"Mages can move from one place to another with magic, but whole troops?"

"You heard Mage Margella. This is Ancient Magic. Over the years, I've talked with Cyns, and they told me their records show Ancient Magic was more powerful than the magic we have now."

General Klaydon nodded toward his mage. "Margella told me once that there are still strands of Ancient Magic, but no mage can control it." As an afterthought, he added, "They don't seem to have any problem."

Mage Margella overheard the last statement. "That's because we're using simple spells. I don't think we could control the magic needed for more powerful spells.

"Ancient Magic is raw, untamed. A user of magic could do more with less, but it took longer to learn control, so there were less mages in ancient time. The magic users had powers that exceeded most gods. Nacromages, they were called."

"General, you grew up in this area, you know the legends of the before times. You know the stories of the gods warring with mortals."

"Legends, Wendell, are stories told to entertain or frighten."

Turning toward the battlefield, Colonel Fythe kept his comments to himself. His eyes caught movement in the air, and his heart stopped. A childhood legend, a nightmare was winging toward them. With a thud, his heart started beating, and he whirled.

"Dragon!"

Lazily flapping her wings, the dragon climbed high over the wall. Scales glowing crimson from the setting sun, Vella circled the gatehouse. With a roar, she folded her wings and dropped.

General Klaydon shouted for the men at the ballistas, but they were frozen in fear.

Spreading her wings, Vella came out of her dive and swooped along the wall. Fighters ducked or threw themselves flat as the dragon passed overhead. Flames shot from her mouth, engulfing the wall and the gatehouse. Smoke poured from openings as wood, cloth, oil, and rope started burning. Men's screams were cut short as fire consumed them. An explosion rocked the gatehouse, and halfway down the building, a cloud of vaporized stone and mortar shot from arrow slots. Large debris flew out windows to crash onto unsuspecting people in the courtyard.

Vella continued flaming down the wall. Yellow and red tongues of flames climbed into the air. She let out another roar as she rode the thermal into the sky.

Panicked voices chattered in the command tower. Unable to ignore the primordial fear the dragon invoked, frightened soldiers pushed each other aside. In the confusion, a bolt of magic shot into the command tower, striking Mage Margella. The mage flew onto the map table. He lay crumbled, not moving.

Chaos spread as men trampled each other in panic, overturning chairs and small stands. Pitchers of water smashed to the floor, the flag case was overturned, and General Klaydon was knocked to the floor.

As his sight cleared, the general was helped to his feet by Colonel Fythe. The general shook off the hand and hastily brushed his tunic and trousers.

"Margella is just stunned," Colonel Fythe said. "Chaos has free will."

Around the gatehouse, men scrambled to escape the wrath of the dragon. On the ground, knights fought horses that were wide eyed with fright.

The two commanders watched the enemy force's siege engines rumble closer. Groups of mages sent bolts toward Lashtar's mages. At the woods line, the large wagon was still disgorging fighters.

The colonel looked up at the dragon. "It's best we get to the ground."

Colonel Fythe lifted the stunned mage from the table. Turning toward the stairs, he caught a glimpse of the dragon folding its wings, coming at the command tower.

Shouting a warning, Colonel Fythe pushed the general down the stairs.

Lifting himself from the ground, Gunther watched fighters running in panic. Next to him, Halprin was yelling curses.

"Mages! Dragons! Bloody cowards!" Halprin yelled at the Northland warriors. "Why don't you come down and fight fair!"

Gunther watched the dragon flame the command tower, its flames pouring into the courtyard. Fire erupted as support buildings caught. Cries and shouting could be heard as black smoke curled around the flames. Flames spread through the central courtyard, and smoke engulfed the general's keep.

The sun was just touching the mountain top. Its light highlighted the wall, and the remaining towers glowed red. In the sky, the dragon was a dark red.

Sir Fensin limped toward Gunther. Watching the dragon circling high overhead, he curled his upper lip. "That creature killed my men." Looking at the flaming command tower, he let out a low growl, "It has killed the general."

He looked at the remains of the eastern sector's defenders. They were a mixture of knights, swordsmen, archers, and squires. A few dwarves stood with Halprin. The ground was covered with the bodies of both friends and foes. On the parapet, the remaining enemy stood, neither retreating nor attacking.

Lowering his gaze, he took in the condition of his men. All were battered and bleeding, many limping or holding injured sides or arms. A few gave out moans as they moved. He sucked in a deep breath and spoke,

"That beast killed my men. I will have my revenge."

"How do you mean to kill it, sir? That thing flies."

"On the tower is a ballista. They can penetrate two inches of solid oak. I'm sure it can get through the dragon's skin. I will shoot it."

No one laughed.

"Ye have a bloody wonderful idea," Halprin said. "Me no coward anyone tell you, but still a slime pit full of fighters on wall."

"We are only a few. I would be more than willing to secure the tower if we had a chance."

Marco glared at the huddled fighters. "Are you unwilling to defend your kingdom?" He stomped around the group, sword in hand. Blood trickled from a wound at his temple. "We've driven them this far. We can drive them from the wall! If we don't, they will overrun the entire kingdom!" Using his sword, he pointed at the tower. "Once on the wall, I can get on the tower and shoot the beast down."

"My lord," Gunther said, "they have the high ground."

"I can even the odds," a tired voice came from the huddled fighters. Wizard Amikin pushed through. His robe was caked with the same mud, blood, and gore as the fighters. His hair was matted, and his face was streaked. His eyes were sunken, and his complexion was that of a candle.

"If you have expended your energy, it would be no different than sending the men up without you."

Wizard Amikin pulled himself up straight. "I watched that thing destroy everyone at the outpost. It took the life of a friend, someone who taught me how to use all my abilities. She left us one weapon, me. I have my mother's teaching as a witch, my father's wisdom as a druid, and my own ability as a wizard. Esprin showed me how to use all three. I have enough in me, sir knight. I will get us to the tower, then I will bring the dragon to you. In Esprin's name, I will do this."

Marko nodded. To the rest of the fighters, he asked, "Are you with us?" Battle cries answered him. Without waiting, he started toward the wall.

Wizard Amikin's mother taught him the witches' way and encouraged him to learn his father's skill, the skill of a druid. As he grew, he acquired knowledge about the flow of nature, learned to call upon the goddess, and learned how to keep balance. When he approached adolescence, it was discovered he had wizard abilities. Upon being tested, his magical ability proved stronger than a witch or a druid. He retained the knowledge of a witch and the skill of a druid, but his studies were devoted to the wizard and mage way. He manipulated magic and formed it to his will.

Later, Gailton expanded his understanding. Gailton Esprin Varney was a witch, who was one with her ability. She understood the forces of nature and how they were interrelated with other magic. Esprin showed him how to combine the disciplines and use them to increase his ability. In all the kingdom, there was no other who controlled three disciplines of magic. His abilities in the three disciplines kept him going longer than any other wizard. He could manipulate magic longer without suffering a magical backlash. With the assistance of Mother Earth, he could refresh himself. Knowing nature, he could call upon the wild to aid him.

Coming within bow range, Wizard Amikin waited. When the enemy started firing, he called a wind from the east. A strong gust blew from the mountain and across the wall, sweeping the arrows from the air.

Climbing the steps, Amikin brought his arms up. Calling on the White Mother, he asked her blessing. He took a deep breath and felt the White Mother fill him with her blessing. Yanking his arms down, the force of the wind increased, buffeting the enemy and knocking them from their feet.

Reaching the parapet, Wizard Amikin channeled ancient magical energy, building it within. He felt it fight him, felt it try to find his fear and push. The raw energy flowed along his channels and burned, but it could not find his fear. He balanced the discipline within him. The magic was his to control. He crossed the thin boundary between wizard and mage. Pushing out, the magical force slammed into the enemy, scattering them. With a wave of his hands, the wind died, and he stood aside.

The soldiers of Lashtar charged. As the violence erupted, Queen's Knight Fensin grabbed one fighter and disappeared into the tower.

Knees buckling, Wizard Amikin slid to the stone floor. Rubbing his arms, he tried to get the tingling to stop.

"Esprin warned me," he mumbled. "Know your limits, don't exceed them. Magical backlash is something you don't want to experience."

A shout from the tower brought Amikin around.

"Now wizard!"

Staggering to his feet, Amikin struggled into the tower. In the deepening gloom of evening, he walked through the west exit. He could see a halo surrounding one peak, the hiding place of the sun. Dusk was here, but light flared along the wall from fires. He watched rocks slam into the wall. He could see the enemy mages around their wagon, magic spreading from their group. Nowhere along the wall did he see a return volley of magic. On the road, a large ram approached the gatehouse. He saw new troops coming to the wall, close enough that Halprin's dwarves were firing their bolt throwers.

The dragon flew around the gatehouse. She occasionally swooped down and rose with a horse, cow, pig, or something unpleasant in its claws.

Lifting his hands and collecting what energy he could, Amikin prepared the spell. Drawing upon magical force, reaching out to nature, and calling upon the goddess, he combined them with his natural talent. He molded the energy. The energy traveled through him, burning the skin and burrowing into his nervous center. He felt it coming together, using him like a human mixing pot.

Wizard Amikin channeled and balanced the power of nature and magic, then striking.

The lightning bolt lit up the valley. The enemy's force highlighted, shadows created by the fire dispelled, and across the wall, a hush descended as time stopped. The bolt arched high, striking the dragon at the peak of her climb. A silent explosion of light surrounded the creature. As the light dimmed, the dragon hung in the air, its wings crumpling inward.

Falling, tumbling from the sky, the dragon left a smoking trail, a path showing its end.

With a howl of pain that echoed up the valley, the dragon unfolded and spread her wings. Back flapping, the red-winged beast hovered, its eyes turning east. Issuing a bellow of rage, Vella headed for its tormentor.

Collapsing from his effort, Wizard Amikin felt magic burn within his body. His heart raced, and his head threatened to explode. He lay on the floor, conscious, but barely breathing. One breath from the dragon and he would be going to the peaceful place. There, he would find Gailton.

Gunther and the defenders of Lashtar had dispatched the last of the enemy. They turned in time to see the dragon flying overhead. Dropping to their knees and ducking, they watched as the dragon circled the tower. It hovered, looking at the two forms on the tower, and screeched. A bolt, the size of a man's forearm, flew toward her.

The creature dipped its left wing and turned from the missile. Instead of a clean hit, the bolt sailed through the wing's thin membrane. Screaming in pain and outrage, Vella spun, and Gunther watched in horror as the dragon swooped onto the tower, then rose, two struggling forms in each clawed hand.

"Bloody hell!" Halprin said. "Bloody creature . . ." The rest of his statement faded into raucous dwarvish curses.

Looking at the small band, realization filled Gunther.

The barbarians were heading toward their section. A large battering ram approached the gatehouse, and enemy troops were scaling the western section. Smoke filled the air as fire burned brightly on the command tower, flames danced in the courtyard and waved from the windows of towers. Mixed with the sound of the fire and the enemy battle cries was the sound of men suffering, of men dying.

The sun was all but gone. The fires gave light to see survivors making their way away from the wall, some heading west, others toward Trader's Junction. He knew Trader's Junction, with its high walls, was no haven. He looked south and knew what needed to be done.

Turning to the band on the wall, Gunther said, "We need to abandon our position!"

"Run away? You bloody daft!"

"Halprin, we have no choice. We weren't able to hold them when we had a stronger force. There is no way we can hold them now."

"It's unnatural to run from fight."

"When has it been unnatural to use your head? You've used strategic retreats in the past."

"Strategic retreat, blah! Name for cowardly fleeing."

"He who runs away," one of the fighters said, "lives to kick butt another day." He looked sheepish. "It's a dwarvish saying, and we know they can't rhyme."

"We have wizard!" Halprin said.

Gunther looked but didn't see Amikin. A quick search found him where he had collapsed.

"Easy, please," Amikin's voice was a horse whisper. "My skin burns."

"Can you stand?" Gunther asked.

"Better yet, how about bloody fireballs?"

Gunther glared at Halprin. "Amikin is not throwing any fireballs, lightning, or even a spark. You've worked with wizards and mages enough to know what is going on."

"Me ignored wizards and mages enough."

"You," Gunther said, pointing at the closest fighter, "help me." The two lifted Amikin, and the group started down the stairs.

On the ground, Gunther looked for a knight, but they were all dead. He started giving orders. "The wall is lost. We need to head south and hook up with other units. We will travel together and take turns carrying Wizard Amikin. It will be some time before the magical backlash wears off, and he can walk on his own."

"I'll be okay," Amikin protested. "It's not a backlash. I stop short of it."

"But you won't be using magic for some time."

"Where are we going, Corporal?"

"South."

"How far south?"

"As far as we need to find reinforcements, or we are forced to take a stand."

"We go south," Halprin said. "Get help from dwarvish miners. Only two-day journey."

"My village is south of here. I know the folks would be willing to fight."

"The village of Roltin has no garrison, but the folks have their own militia."

Gunther held up his hand. "We will talk and plan later. For now, let's get out of here. Halprin take point."

As the small band of fighters made their way from the wall, Gunther turned, taking one last look. He watched the smoke filling the sky, the fires lighting up the wall. Stars were coming out, and the full moon gave an eerie glow. Overhead, the dragon gave a loud cry and dove on the gatehouse.

General Klaydon had been sent, by Colonel Fythe, spiraling down the stairs as the dragon's flames filled the tower. Both the colonel and Mage Margella survived, landing on the general.

General Klaydon finished donning his armor and took the reins of his war stead. His chest plate had his family crest etched over his heart, and on the right shoulders was the seal of the monarchy. His sword hung from his belt, a dagger on the opposite hip. The gauntlets were plate over chain, but the boots were fine leather covered with bronze metal. A strange combination, but a gift from a duke's court.

Mounting his horse, he rode with Colonel Fythe at his side. Around them, the North Wall burned. Thick oily smoke poured from the openings of the gatehouse. The two nearest towers shot smoke and flames high into the air. Around the courtyard, barracks, shops, and stables were all burning. The evening air was lit by the dancing light of a thousand flames.

As he moved from the wall, the general entered a maze of chaos. Siege engines, overturned wagons, yelling men and baying animals were everywhere. Dead bodies were scattered randomly, some twisted and bent, others smoldering heaps of rags. Soldiers walked with blank faces, bumping into ones trying to escape.

Barbarians swarmed over the wall. The dragon's bulk became visible in the light of the fires, its red scales glistening. Climbing, it shot a stream of fire at the top of the wall where troops had gathered.

"Colonel, gather as many men as you can. I want you down at Trader's Junction."

"Sir, we should stay and defend the wall!"

"There's nothing to defend. Our men are panicked, many dead. What mages we had functioning are dead or incapacitated. That dragon can pick us off one by one, and shortly, the enemy will be coming through the gates. I need you at Trader's Junction. Seal the city's gates and hold off the enemy as long as you can."

"Then we need to evacuate it."

"There are fifteen thousand people. We would never get them out before the Northland had them surrounded. Better to die defending yourself."

"What about you, sir?"

"I'm going to gather as many men as I can and head for Wintermist. We need to warn the duke and get a message off to Gammount. The Queen's garrison of five thousand is there."

"What of Dyroam and Loc Berrie?"

"I'm sending Captain Ralen to Dyroam, and Captain Ceinture is already heading for Loc Berrie. I don't think those two cities have anything to worry about. It's Mead the enemy wants."

"The dragon?"

"If I'm correct, you needn't worry about that. This is an invasion, and they are going to take out our most powerful force. That will be Wintermist. They are unaware of what has happened, and if they remain blissfully ignorant as we were, Wintermist Wall will fall faster than ours. Then the mages will be defenseless.

"And they will have all the knowledge of the school and two major routes to the kingdom. With luck, while they are driving for Wintermist, the reinforcements that come from Dyroam or Loc

Berrie will be enough to defeat whatever force is left here. Then you can get the population to safety."

"As you command, General, but I hate giving up the wall."

"So do I, Wendell, so do I. Only a fool continues to fight when the odds are totally against him. We need to cut our loses and gather reinforcements."

"You think additional forces are coming south?"

"Only a fool would attack without additional force to hold what they have."

Colonel Fythe nodded and swung his horse around. Moving among the carnage, General Klaydon motioned for a rider to approach. The rider was on a light riding horse, leading another. The second horse contained the still form of Mage Margella strapped in so he wouldn't fall from the saddle.

"How is the mage?"

"He should recover in about twelve hours." The voice was soft, feminine. As the rider turned, reddish brown locks could be seen within the hood, and the feminine face of the rider was visible.

"Good. I want you to stay with me. In the morning, I will have reports and messages for you to get to the duke in Wintermist."

General Klaydon urged his horse forward. Making his way through the remains of his command, he gathered a sizable number of knights, cavalry, archers, and foot soldiers. Slowly, they worked their way through the moonlight, toward the western mountain range. As he rode, he worked on plans, worked out various strategies.

Behind them the gates of the gatehouse collapsed, and the enemy took the courtyard. Vella settled among the ruins and roared a welcome to the invaders.

Anton sat at Jedrowler's desk. Notes spread across the desktop, spilling on the floor. After hours of reading journals and notes, he was as lost as when he started. As he picked up a pile of notes, he lit a candle with a flick of magic.

He heard magic whisper of danger. He had fear for this Ancient Magic, fear he never had with the mage magic he controlled. No one could call this fear irrational. This fear was real. Ancient Magic was powerful and raw. So raw it would burn a mage's channels with one careless gesture.

Anton was mumbling, "End of my quest, it seems so simple. Ancient strands of magic not only to bind with the land, but the land with us . . . That has to be the clue." He started taping his front teeth with his finger while his other hand started rummaging through the pile of parchment. "I know I saw something on binding, something important."

Anton's eyes went wide as the channel with the land opened. The channel revealed a strange presence, an unclean presence. It was far away, at the edge of the land.

Danger from the north!

Anton felt agony mixed with the perceived loss of life. The feelings kept flowing, and the channels to the others open. Unity awoke.

Fear! Danger!

The emotion flashed into Unity with an intensity that caused him to scream. The scream echoed from all levels of the mage school. Emotions consumed him, emotions coming from hundreds of beings. Death taking hundreds of lives.

The fear hit hard. Fear of . . . the end of all they knew. Fear so strong it paralyzed Unity. Fear of the swirling blackness. Old, hateful, destroyer.

Struggling, Anton closed off channels to keep the rest from the intense mind-numbing emotions. As the channels closed, Unity dissolved into its individual parts.

The Spirits of Wintermist were screaming in terror.

Opening the door a crack, Duncan saw the concerned face of Sasha.

"I just got your message."

Indicating for her to keep her voice low, Duncan allowed Sasha to enter. "He's resting. The best I can figure is he collapsed at the same time as the ones who were bound got hit with the invasion."

"Invasion?"

"They received an image that the North Wall has been breached."

"That can't be!" She looked at Duncan who nodded. Letting the news slip from her mind, she cast her thoughts to her friend. She crossed the room and sat in the chair next to Ambrus's bed. The scholar's face was as white as his pillow. She took his hand and felt how cold it was. Stroking his forehead, she continued talking in a low voice.

"Mead is being invaded?"

Placing his hand on the hilt of his sword, Duncan nodded. "Nothing specific. Mage Kytrill said Anton shut down the channels, kept the rest from experiencing the full effect."

Sasha shook her head. "Could Anton have spilled this to Ambrus?"

Duncan shrugged. He crossed the room and looked down on the moonlit courtyard. Xantrawler's men were walking patrol, and a few citizens were staggering up the stairs from the gorge. "Both events convinced the Mage Master an invasion is real. Unfortunately, Anton is still out, so they can't question him."

"Do you think Ambrus saw the same thing?"

"Don't know." He turned from the window. He looked at Sasha. "I knew he was to meet you tonight. Sorry I took so long getting the message to you."

Sasha gave a weak smile. "I understand." Frowning, she looked at the scholar. "I'm worried, has he ever had these fits so close together?"

Duncan shook his head. "His fits are rare. In the six months I've worked for him, he's had two, and the second one was here."

They watched Ambrus in silence for a while before Duncan spoke, "He was looking forward to dinner. Said you were enjoyable company, one of the few people he finds a challenge."

"I enjoy my times with him. Since I was fifteen and first met him, I have listened to his stories of other places. He sends me letters filled with tales of different cultures and wonderful creatures."

"Why are you here? I mean here at Wintermist. You should be at the capital, at University becoming a sage, or at least studying in the academy here."

"I'm a woman and the daughter of a baker." Duncan raised his eyebrow. "I have the basic education the queen provides. Unfortunately, my father is not a noble, nor a rich merchant. He can't afford to send me for higher education. The only thing I can do is visit the Screeching Owl and the library."

"I took for granted everyone received the education they want. Xantrawler felt what sets a swordman apart from the common fighter is being trained to think."

"Your life has been filled with interesting times."

Duncan snorted, "Interesting times is a curse. When a sword swinger has interesting times, it means he's fighting for his life." He paused, then without thinking added, "That's what weaponsmasters attempt to do. Trains swordsmen so their lives are not interesting."

"Working in the queen's service makes it difficult to avoid interesting times."

Duncan wandered over to the wardrobe and opened it. He took an interest in Ambrus's evening wear. "That's why I'm a bodyguard. I only worry about myself and the person I guard. If I make a mistake, I'm the one in danger of getting hurt."

Sasha played with the corner of Ambrus's blanket. Talking to the quilt, she said, "I know who you are, Duncan of Pentock. My uncle attributes being alive to you."

Duncan looked at her sharply. "I'm not that person."

Sasha stood and faced him. "You are Duncan of Pentock, the most celebrated hero of the Underdweller War. The hero of the Valley."

"It wasn't me. It was many others. One man does not make a company."

"Da told me a good leader makes a good company. He said, during the Underdweller War, you were the best. He heard how you took care of your men, how your entire company was responsible for saving—"

"That's in the past! That was another person!" Duncan snapped, "After what I did, I have no right to be a hero! I killed those men!"

Sasha opened her mouth, but Ambrus started mumbling and tossing about. Putting her hands on his chest, she tried to comfort him. His thrashing became more violent, his mumbling louder.

Bolting up in bed, he sent Sasha sprawling. His eyes wide, Ambrus shrieked, *"They come for the wraiths! He is coming for them!"*

Chapter Nineteen

Day Six

King Rathveil adjusted his festive robes as he moved through the hallways of the palace. Today was a day of celebration.

He passed a set of guards and moved down the steps to the dungeon. It had not always been a dungeon. Before the changes, this had been an underground storage area. Each year, each tribe sent supplies for the ones who would stay, the guardians for the coming year. When Gareth became a permanent city, that practice was no longer necessary.

As he entered the dungeon, flickering torch light highlighted two guards standing on either side of a door. They stood straighter, their short spears held to their sides. King Rathveil nodded, and one of the guards opened the door. Beyond was a small room large enough to hold a wooden desk and chair. Oil lamps on all four walls provided light that contrasted the darkness beyond the barred window in the opposite door. Sitting at the desk was a large, heavy muscled man, the dungeon master.

The dungeon master rose, his head scraping the ceiling. "My liege, how may I serve you?"

King Rathveil smiled. “How is my guest?”

“Some complaining in the night. Calling for light, claiming she needs it for her prayers.”

“You didn’t give it to her?”

“She receives light as you ordered. During her one meal and the six times a day we check on her.”

“Good, good. Well, open the door. I wish to see her.”

The dungeon master shuffled sideways. Taking a large ring of keys from beneath his tunic, he unlocked the door. On the other side stood a beefy man, holding a wooden club. The walls were covered with moisture, the smell of decay hung in the air, and the sound of tiny feet scuffling away could be heard. Just inside the door was a small stool. A low stand held a half-eaten loaf of bread and a jug of water. An assortment of torches and three oil lamps hung on the wall. In one corner laid a pile of burned-out torches. As light flooded the passageway, the guard blinked repeatedly, trying to clear the tears from his eyes.

King Rathveil entered the dungeon. “Give me one of the lamps.”

The guard grabbed the nearest lamp and held it out to King Rathveil.

Rathveil looked at the guard for a few heartbeats, then sneered, “Light it, fool. It does me no good unlit.”

The guard grunted and removed a taper from underneath his leather vest, lit it from the torch in the outer room, and brought it to the wick on the lamp.

Taking the lamp, King Rathveil headed down a side passageway that contained one cell, a special one he helped build.

Once around the corner, the light from the outer room failed to reach. King Rathveil’s lamp brought everything to life. Scrubbed stone with veins of blue crystal had ruins carved into them. Overhead mahogany timbers held carved runes.

The light brought a scream from the special cell. Made of blue stone on three walls, the ceiling and floor, it swallowed the light from the lamp. The fourth wall was blocked with bars of pure silver.

The Lady Yolanda Trantro lifted herself from the straw-covered blue slab. Her once beautiful dress was ripped and wrinkled. Her hair was matted with straw tangled, and hanging at angles. Her once clear complexion held a spreading rash, and small scratches were visible on her face and arms. Looking closer, he saw crow's feet around the eyes, wrinkles at the corner of her mouth, and white twisted through her hair. Sitting up, her once firm breasts sagged. She held no radiance. She did not glow. King Rathveil did not find her desirable.

King Rathveil chuckled.

With one hand shielding her eyes, she blinked rapidly, trying to adjust to the sudden brightness. "Know that laugh." Even her voice was rougher, a sharpness grating on the nerves.

"I came to give you good news. We breached the Southland's North Wall last night. The Southlands are ours. I have declared a day of festival."

The Lady Yolanda brought herself to her feet. "You have violated the Sacred Scrolls."

"I have violated the scrolls for the betterment of all of us. From this day forth, Terrapin Xon will be a great and powerful kingdom."

"The violations of the scrolls were scarcely tolerated when it affected your land. Now you have endangered all. The Czaran will respond. She has not heard from me in days. Soon, she will be marching through the streets, and you will be punished."

"Your threats don't scare me. I have warriors heading for the border, and my Force Shapers are a match for yours."

"We are more powerful than you think!"

King Rathveil looked closer at Lady Yolanda. "Yes, I can see that. Without your Unseen Force, you look older. I thought you were around your twenty-fifth season. What are you, fortieth?" Lady

Yolanda crossed her arms, turning partway away from him. "You talk about how the scrolls forbid using the Unseen Forces. You Keepers of the Sacred Scrolls have no qualms about using them."

"What we do, we do to preserve what we have. We protect all that live above the Thanatos Range."

"You do it for the power." Rathveil chopped at the air with his hands and started walking back and forth. "Terrapin Xon is the savior. Everything is happening according to my vision."

Lady Yolanda turned toward King Rathveil. "You claim to have visions?"

"During my tenth season, I took the spirit walk. For three weeks, I spent my time in meditation, contemplation, and study. While wandering the lower slops of the Thanatos Range, my first vision came to me." He stopped and looked toward the ceiling. "I remember the moon was just a sliver. I had been meditating. And as I started moving out of my trance, it happened. My mind saw Terrapin Xon rise in glory. The city of Gareth had streets of silver. The palace was gold. My people were not suffering. There was prosperity for all."

"That was a false vision," Lady Yolanda's hoarse voice held a shiver at the edge of her words. "No vision in the Thanatos Range is valid. It is told within the scrolls that we keep."

"It is not in the Ten Sacred Scrolls!"

Lady Yolanda grabbed the bars. "The gods gave us our own set of scrolls, our duty to the land north of the range. King Rathveil, I plead with you, turn from this path of destruction!"

Laughter echoed in the chamber. "King Rathveil, is it? When you want something, you use my tittle. It is not going to work this time. Your Unseen Forces are gone, blocked by the magic within the blue stone. Without your Unseen Forces, you have no control over me."

He slowly stroked his chin as he looked at Lady Yolanda. "You call the vision false, yet from the vision, a spiritual guide came. He taught me to use the Unseen Forces. Each year, I choose the best and send them to the Thanatos Range, where this guide teach them. How do you think we have grown so powerful so quickly?"

His eyes were wide, unseeing. In his eyes, a spark grew as he looked at something Lady Yolanda could not see. "I am making Terrapin Xon great as it was eons ago. My army is moving through Mead. They will split, a three-prong attack, and they will sweep through the land. In days, they will meet at Wintermist, and once I have Wintermist, I will have the power within the falls. You will see, the land will be restored as I bring it under my control. With the Southlands people and the people of Terrapin Xon, we will pay you back for your past injustice."

"You must not. You can't stay in the Southlands. You will awaken the wraiths, and the terrors the ancients ended will be unleashed."

"Wraiths don't scare me. My spiritual guide promised the power to fight any obstacle."

"You will never have that power!"

King Rathveil lowered his eyes and smiled. "You are wrong, Lady Yolanda. I am a user of the Unseen Forces, and soon, I will attain a rank that has not been held in eons."

Stepping forward, he wrapped his fist around the bars. "I'm to be the first Nacromages in three eons."

Lady Yolanda felt her face drain of blood.

The farmlands of Mead lay like a chess board over the country. Roads wandered among the farms, connecting villages to villages. From time to time, the roads disappeared into forests to emerge on the other side, winding through a village. Farmers traveled the roads, taking their goods to market. Craftsmen passed from village to village, selling their services either in the streets or at fairs. Merchants journeyed to reach far off markets. Now no one traveled these roads, except for messengers carrying news of the invasion.

General Klaydon had watched the army from the north spilt, the largest heading through the heart of Mead and the smallest on the western flank. They left men behind to hold the North Wall and a group to take Trader's Junction. Still, in his judgment, the enemy's strength had not decreased. If anything, the army was larger. His force had killed hundreds, thousands. The North Wall was littered with their dead bodies. Yet their size had not diminished.

A fast-moving black dot caught General Klaydon's eyes. He watched it spiral down and land among the enemy's forces in the center column. He sneered, "Enjoy your victory. You head for Wintermist, and I plan to make sure the duke will be ready as well as the mages."

He turned to the young lady warrior dressed in lightweight leather armor, a short sword on her hip and a dark brown cloak, the hood shadowing her features. She sat astride a riding horse that was dwarfed by the heavier war steads. A small bow was tied to her saddle, which was nothing more than a small formed piece of stiff leather with fasteners. Two bags were nestled behind the saddle, bulging with documents.

"Are you ready?"

"Yes, sir." Her voice was soft, but echoed in your mind and lingered long after she finished speaking. "Reports from Mage Margella, your command staff, and your own report."

"Good. Get them to the duke at Wintermist."

The rider nodded then spurred her horse. The general watched as she urged her horse up the mountain side and disappeared.

Wheeling his horse around, he shouted, "Lieutenant! We're following this group all the way. Wintermist will not stand alone."

Ambrus listen patiently as Duncan explained the danger. When his bodyguard paused for a breath, he interrupted and calmly explained that if the invaders made it to Wintermist, there would be time to escape.

Now, as they made their way through the hallways of the mage school, Duncan was trying another tactic. Ambrus gave him credit.

The man knew that if one tactic didn't work, attack from another angle.

"Your vision was adamant about them coming for the wraiths."

"I'm still working on that vision. I don't know who's coming or where these wraiths are. There's no wraiths, except at Windlow Pass. That is . . . how many leagues from here?"

"Don't change the subject. For all we know, this invasion may wake something that has been dormant for hundreds of years."

"Trust me, Duncan, if there were wraiths near Wintermist, the mages would have woken them a long time ago."

"Oh, and now you're an expert on magic?"

Ambrus stopped at the head of the stairs and turned to Duncan and said, "Good one, very good. When your opponent makes a preposterous statement, turn it around. You weaken his argument that way."

"Ambrus, this is not one of your debates at the Queen's university. This is real life, and you can get killed."

"I appreciate your concern. But remember, you are my bodyguard, not my babysitter."

"The gods know you need one."

"Duncan, I'm old enough to make my own decisions. Right now, I have decided to stay."

"You'll just get in the way."

"I may be of some use. There is something I may have foretold that can be of use."

Before Duncan could respond, a voice called up the stairs, "Ah, Duncan, I have been looking for you."

Xantrawler took the last few steps and stood next to Duncan. "I need to talk to you. More to the point, I need your help."

"I would be more than happy to help you." Duncan looked at Ambrus. "But only if you can convince this old man he needs to get to a place of safety."

"I am as safe here as anywhere, isn't that right, Weaponsmaster?"

Xantrawler held up his hand. "I don't know what I've walked into, but you two are not dragging me into it. I only handle one conflict at a time." He looked at Duncan. "That's why I need you. The duke and the rest of his council feel the enemy won't reach Wintermist. They think Dyroam or Loc Berrie will counterstrike from the rear, giving the Queen's army time to get here from Gammount."

"Makes sense if General Klaydon got messages off to the other two dukedoms."

Xantrawler shook his head. "Figure the time to assemble and prepare troops. Think of the distance. How long for reinforcements to arrive?"

Duncan nodded. "At least five days."

"Five days to assemble and march on Mead, then, additional days to fight the enemy at Trader's Junction. Then marching through resistance along the way here. Say six days. Eighteen days and the reinforcements will be here. The enemy force can reach here within the week."

Duncan pulled on his lower lip and nodded. "What do you need from me?"

"My men are good. The trouble is, they are either old soldiers or young kids. Anyone between is either inexperienced or lame."

Duncan put an edge to his voice, "I see where this is going and you know my answer."

Xantrawler's eyebrows came together, and he clenched his jaw. "I need you. Your Queen needs you. You can't turn your back on this!"

"I have my contract with Ambrus."

"Oh, that's easy to take care of," Ambrus said as he reached into his belt pouch. "You've been a good bodyguard, but your kingdom needs you more." He pulled out a stack of coins and slapped them in Duncan's hand. "There, that should make us square. Your pay for the year. I release you from your contract. So say I in front of a weaponsmaster of the realm."

"Heard and bound," Xantrawler said before Duncan could speak.

Duncan looked from Ambrus to Xantrawler. Jingling the coins, he said, "This doesn't change a thing."

"You're not a simple sword swinger. You're not a man-at-arms. You took an oath, made a vow the day you left my salle."

Duncan half turned, his fist clenched. "I made another vow five years ago." It was a hoarse voice, one that jerked and conveyed pain.

"A fool's vow!"

Duncan swung back, almost knocking Ambrus to the floor.

"The massacre was my fault."

"It was war time. You had no choice."

"I had a choice. How many did I murder?" Duncan's voice echoed down the stone corridors. A few heads poked from doorways, saw who it was, and quickly retreated.

"You did what had to be done."

"It was my responsibility!"

"Your responsibility is to your Queen, to this kingdom."

Duncan turned from both men. As the sound of metal upon metal rang in his ears, his eyes locked on the floor. He felt the spray of blood on his face, heard the screams, and heard the quiet of the dead. He smelled death, the deaths he set loose in The Valley.

His voice was barely a whisper, "I was in command. My orders lead to their deaths. I allowed the slaughter to happen."

"Another one is about to take place."

"I being here is not going to change anything."

"Weaponsmaster, do your duty!"

Without looking up, Duncan placed his hand on the hilt of his sword. His fingers caressed the leather then slowly wrapped around the hilt. His body trembled as he spoke, "I can't."

Xantrawler's face turned red. "I never thought one of my own students would fail to answer the call!"

Duncan strode away. Xantrawler attempted to follow, but Ambrus stopped him.

"Let him go."

"Someone needs to get his head on straight, or I swear I will rip it off!" Xantrawler shook the hand off him. "I wish he had taken a swing, then I could have knocked this foolishness out of him."

Ambrus shook his head. "He hasn't healed."

Xantrawler's shoulders slumped, his hands hung loosely at his side. "If he doesn't heal, he will be lost to us."

Ambrus nodded. "I talked with a mind healer, and he felt bringing Duncan here, letting him be around you, would start the healing process. Unfortunately, none of us foresaw a war."

"Why, why did the gods pick now?" Xantrawler tilted his head back and looked at the rock ceiling. "He was starting to talk. He mentioned Corporal Wheatfield's family and the farm the man left behind. He told me it was a farm Wheatfield had earned in the queen's service when he was younger. He made the comment on how the man had already done his duty for his country and should have been home with his family."

Xantrawler ran a hand over his face. "If he doesn't get over what happened, he is going to self-destruct." He nodded to Ambrus. "Master Diamox, I will talk to you later."

Ambrus watched the weaponsmaster walk away, his head bowed. He could empathize with the old man. From what he had been told, Xantrawler had treated Duncan as a son. Sighing, he turned and started down the stairs. He needed to hurry before something else delayed him.

The stairs wound down the center of the mountain and opened between the main banquet hall and kitchen. There were many of these stairs placed to enable servants' quick access to any part of the school. Because of this, most mages used them to save time.

As Ambrus rounded the corner, he ran into a mage. The impact caused him to slip and land on his rump. A whoosh of air escaped, and he heard a familiar voice, "Oh my, Master Diamox, I'm so sorry."

Ambrus looked into the concerned face of Anton. The look on the youngster's face was comical. He couldn't help but chuckle.

"That's okay, lad, we both should be more careful." Anton reached down and helped him up. "What has you in such a hurry? Find something to do with your research?"

"I don't know," Anton said as he brushed Ambrus's clothes. "I'm hoping CynLisa can tell me."

Ambrus pushed Anton's hands away. "Where is the Cyn?"

"At this time in the morning, she should be working with the younger students. But she isn't in the classroom. No one has seen her, so I'm checking the archives."

"Anything I can help you with?"

Anton hesitated a moment, then nodded. "You might. I had a vision this morning, one that was shared with Mage Kytril."

"Seems to be a lot of visions happening lately."

Anton ignored Ambrus's comment and proceeded to explain what transpired. He explained how Mage Kytril felt they had received a message from the Vlynies, and it may have something to do with the invasion and the spell of protection. Ambrus listened patiently, only interrupting to clarify a point.

When Anton finished, Ambrus said, "I know a little bit about these Vlynies. I spent some time in the archives at Western High Peak Mage School." He pinched the bridge of his nose and tried to recall what he had learned. "That was many years ago. By the gods of knowledge, I wish I had the recall abilities of your Cyns."

Ambrus started wandering as he talked, causing Anton to be nervous as Ambrus would go down two steps and wander that step before ascending. Meanwhile, he kept talking, unaware of his surroundings. More than once, his swinging arms almost caught a passing servant's nose.

"They are a type of elemental creature composed of pure energy. They know no distance. They are here and now, and there and now." He started mumbling, so Anton had to strain to hear him. "If they are here and now, why can't they be then and there? Could they have shown you a vision of the future?"

Anton shook his head. "Mage Kytril said the magical energy showed it was a vision of past events."

"Hmmm. Well, if anyone should know the Vlynies, he should. This vision sounds much like my visions. The future is cloudy, but I wonder if the Vlynies could be relaying that future to me and others like me."

"That's an interesting theory, but I don't think it has anything to do with what I saw."

Ambrus stopped and looked at Anton. "Oh, but it does. These Vlynies, these elemental creatures, must have their own way of communicating. They're bound to the land like the rest of you. Well, I assume they are as they showed you what the land knows. They don't speak the same language we do and can only communicate in the simplest terms. This can cause a lot of confusion. That's why visions are so often misinterpreted. Do you think the Vlynies could be responsible for my visions, just like they were for yours?"

"I don't know. There are very few of us here who knows much about them."

"Of course, of course. It's getting along toward midday. I bet Sasha will be at the Screeching Owl. She may be able to help." Mumbling under his breath, Ambrus hurried down the stairs, leaving a confused Anton standing on the steps.

Chapter Twenty

The timing candle showed King Rathveil exactly one half hour had passed. He sat his cup down and waited. General Thrawt was a creature of habit, predictable in everything. Every day, right after the midday meal, he would come and give an update.

King Rathveil marked his page and closed his book. Standing, he placed his book on the table, then headed out the door. His personal guards waited, and Herald Gilmore stood nearby. Since the herald didn't seem concerned about the missing General Thrawt, Rathveil allowed a sigh of relief to escape. He turned and started walking down the hallway. His personal guards fell into step behind him.

Herald Gilmore took a position on the king's left. "General Thrawt sends his apologies, but a problem has arose that requires his personal attention."

"Very well."

As they made their way along the hallway, the white curtains draping from the ceiling rippled in the breeze. Winter was ending, and the afternoon wind held the scent of warmth and the promise of blossoming flowers.

The party moved around a corner and approached the study. Castle inhabitants stopped and bowed, and King Rathveil smiled, not because he commanded power, but because they respected and loved him. His people were prospering, enjoying a life their parents never dreamed of. When he had started on this path, his intent was to unite the tribes and bring a better life to all who dwelled north of the Thanatos Mountains.

He had succeeded, and they showed their honor to the man who lead them out of barbarism. All this had been foretold in the Sacred Scrolls. Now, he continued preparing for He Who Would Come.

He reached his study and entered with Herald Gilmore behind. Settling in his chair, he nodded.

"My lord, General Thrawt reports remnants of the Southland's army attacking the western army flank. It's a small force, only a couple hundred mounted fighters and a handful of foot soldiers."

"This doesn't sound like anything that should take up the general's time."

"No, sir, not normally, but these skirmishers seem to be aimed at the transportation wagon. The general wants to ensure its safety, so he is supervising its move into the center of his column. At the same time, he is sending a detachment of your own mounted fighters to discourage the Southlanders."

"Looks like they have smart people in the south." King Rathveil shrugged. "Any other messages?"

"A couple from your operatives at Wintermist. Tomamark was captured."

"That's too bad, and I had planned to reward him richly, a hero to our people." King Rathveil sighed, "Let us pray we can rescue him before they kill him."

"Would you like the operatives to attempt a rescue?"

King Rathveil pulled his lower lip, before shaking his head. "Can't risk exposing them. Send for his family, I will tell them personally of their son. It will be small consolation for their sacrifice."

Gilmore waited for King Rathveil to continue. When he didn't, the herald proceeded. "They report the Southland mage was able to cast his spell of protection. It happened before Tomamark was able to eliminate him."

King Rathveil sat up straight, a curse escaping his lips, "That was what he was supposed to stop!"

"It's okay, my lord, it was only half the spell. They are scrambling to find the rest."

"Let us hope they're not successful, Gilmore." He leaned his arms on his desk and squinted at the map on the wall. He turned his head, as if listening to an unseen voice. "Send a message to our operatives at Wintermist. I want them to find who is leading the search for the spell and eliminate him."

"Yes, my lord." Herald Gilmore walked over to the mirror hanging by the window and picked up a piece of charcoal.

General Klaydon dodged his horse around a tree, then reined it to a halt. Five horsemen assembled, all breathing hard and showing signs of battle. A couple had their bloody swords out.

A horseman with lieutenant's chevrons rode up and reined his horse next to the general. Leaning forward and holding onto the pommel of his saddle, he said, "I believe we lost them, sir. They may be good in a fight, but they don't know their way around our forests."

General Klaydon nodded. "The forest of Mead may be our savior yet."

The sound of approaching hoof beats brought the fighters to full alert. As the riders came into view, everyone relaxed as the queen's colors flashed through the branches. Two riders, just as battle weary, approached. Slung across the rear of the saddle of one rider was a bound man in black leather armor. They unceremoniously dumped the prisoner on the ground.

"A prisoner for you, sir."

General Klaydon looked at the prisoner, who struggled to his feet. The man was average in height, with dark short-cropped hair, and a clean-shaven face. The armor was blackened, boiled leather with no special adornments. The man's breeches were of a dark brown cloth, or light leather, laced over dark boots.

The enemy stood straight, his arms bound in front of him.

"What's your name?"

The man remained silent, and the rider that captured him kicked him in the shoulder. "Answer the general!"

The enemy fighter glared at the mounted man, then turned back to the general. He brought his head up and threw his shoulders back, keeping his face expressionless.

"Who are you people?" the general asked. "Why have you invaded? Why have you attacked?"

The prisoner snapped out unintelligible words.

"Someone get me Mage Margella."

In short order, Mage Margella was brought to the general. He looked the prisoner over and asked a few questions to which the prisoner spat at him.

"Not very friendly." He pulled a small pouch from his sleeve. The mage threw a pinch of powder at the prisoner and spoke an incantation. When he was done, he asked, "Now are you willing to talk?"

The prisoner's eyes widened, and he blurted, "They said you would not be able to use the Unseen Forces!"

"What is your name?" the general asked.

The prisoner looked at the general. "Lotar of the Grass Cat tribe."

"Well, Lotar of the Grass Cat tribe, I am General Klaydon of Lashtar. Why have you attacked us?"

"The ruler of us all, the ones the Sacred Scrolls spoke of, commanded it."

"Who might that be?"

The prisoner scowled, "I do not expect barbarians to know, but soon you call him master." Lotar smiled. "You shall bow to King Rathveil of Terrapin Xon."

General Klaydon asked a few other questions but got nothing useful. Finally, he asked about the large wagon.

"That is our transport, as the users of the Unseen Forces say."

"The wagon?"

"No, device it carries. Yesterday, I was in Gareth. King Rathveil ordered Grass Cat here. We replaced faithful of Terrapin Xon you murdered. We walked through door in palace and exit in wagon."

"It's not possible," Mage Margella said. "It's not possible."

General Klaydon looked at his mage. "What's not possible?"

"If what he's saying is true, then that wagon contains a portal, a, ah, a magical gateway between here and there. Legends have it that before the present time, when man first learned magic, they were able to create these portals."

"So why isn't it possible? I have watched mages disappear from one place and appear at others."

"Yes, we do that. We can even teleport groups of people, but no mage has ever created a portal. The magical energy required to keep something like that open is beyond us!"

"I tend to believe him. Fighters have been exiting that wagon far more than what it can hold."

The prisoner smiled. "You don't have transport. You barbarians. We do you favor by coming and teaching you civilized ways. You will learn duty to king."

"Take him away," General Klaydon said. As the prisoner was escorted away, he looked at his lieutenant. "We need to get a messenger bird off to Wintermist."

"We only have a few left."

"This is important. With a magical device like this, they can resupply faster than we can. The gods only know what else could come through that portal."

Chapter Twenty-One

Day Seven

One of the perks Mage Master Gardner enjoyed was his room, actually a suite. The living room provided a lovely view of Lake Mead, the falls, and Wintermist. At night, he sat on the balcony enjoying the city of Wintermist sparkle, lights flickering from thousands of windows. Taking advantage of the natural curve of the mountain, the living space blended into a formal dining space. A three bay window in the dining room was filled with a view of the falls and the Temple of Odium.

His bedroom and a smaller bedroom were on the traditional right side. Next to it was a small library. Tucked in a crevice on the left was a short hallway that led to his personal laboratory.

What delighted Mage Master Gardner the most was a small alcove to one side of the dining area. Mornings were the only time of the day that was truly his own, so often, he enjoyed a private breakfast with a guest.

This morning, Wizard Anton had joined him. The table was set with a large pitcher of juice, a pot of herbal tea, a platter of sausage, a special dish from his home of Hawks Beak, and hot biscuits complemented by a pot of honey.

Anton had filled the Mage Master in on his vision of Legion and his talk with Mage Kytril and Ambrus. The young lad's inability to locate CynLisa disturbed him as she had been ordered to be available to Anton at any time.

"How do you like the quiche?" Mage Master Gardner asked.

"It's interesting," Anton said around a mouthful. "May I ask what the ingredients are?"

"Normal things, eggs, seasonings, and a special seaweed found in the coastal waters of my land."

"It's very good, adds a certain tang, Mage Master."

Mage Master Gardner looked at Anton. "Please, I hear that title all day. No titles. Please, call me Sholem."

"I'm sorry, sir, it's hard to break a five-year habit."

Sholem sighed then smiled at the young lad. "I know, but you need to learn. You're an equal here, and soon you will prove it. Any progress in your search?"

Anton laid down his spoon. "I can't locate anything on phase two. I've looked through all his notes, every scrap of parchment, but there is nothing."

"You may be going about your research the wrong way. Looking through a mage's notes is not the same as looking something up in the archives. We tend to be secretive. Notes are vague or written in code. It means nothing to anyone, but it triggers our memories."

Anton nodded. "I remember looking at some of Jedrowler's notes on phase one. At first, I didn't understand them. But over time, they made sense."

Sholem reached for a biscuit and broke it in half. "That's why I want you to look for the second half. Of everyone here, you alone understand how Jedrowler thought, how he kept his notes."

"I thought I did, but . . ."

"Don't look for whole passages. You may have to make a connection between something written now and a phrase wrote days, maybe years later. Look for common threads, for references to other spells. We don't create spells out of nothing. They are built on what was learned before us. Look for things that connect with the information you have."

"I'll try, Mage Ma . . . Sholem. This wasn't the only spell he was working on."

"You need to concentrate on this spell. I know the pressure is on, that there are just a few days before the enemy arrives, but I have faith in you."

"I'm glad someone does. The mage council shook my confidence."

Sholem waved his hand, as if to brush off a bothersome insect. "Ignore most of them. Too many are old and set in their ways."

"I'll try."

"One thing, keep in mind that you're redoing Jedrowler's research. The only difference is you don't have to travel the world or spend years only to discover you're on the wrong track."

Anton nodded as he returned to his meal. "Master Jedrowler said once we finished this spell, I would be a mage."

"I won't delude you, Anton. I don't know why Jed said that, but just casting a spell will not make you a mage. You know what the last hurdle is you need to cross."

Anton looked into the Mage Master's living room. The muscles in his neck tensed as he refused to look to the side at Wintermist Falls. What the Mage Master said gave him an idea what part of the spell involved. He held back telling Sholem.

For a moment, he felt the resistance of magic and his fear.

Duncan folded the last of his clothes and thrust them in his saddle pack. The pay from Ambrus would keep him for some time, and he thought to travel south. He had never been to Kreun Durn. It was a costal country, and they wouldn't know him. He should find plenty of work with the merchants.

He sat on the edge of his bed and laced his pack closed. He was tired of the constant moving, the constant traveling. Ever since he escaped the healers, he had been on the move. He needed to move, keep going. If he kept his thoughts busy, his mind didn't see it, didn't see them.

Duncan put his head in his hands, and the massacre was there in vivid color. He heard the screams, saw the crumpled bodies. He kept screaming, screaming, and screaming. He slashed his sword. Blood flew, and his men cried out. His voice filled the air, giving the order, one order he regretted.

"No retreat! No quarters!"

Nothing made it stop, not his yelling, not his killing. The blood was there. He saw it every time he washed.

No matter how many times he washed, no matter how much he bathed, he was dirty. The blood still flowed. No one understood. It was his command that he had slaughtered. He wasn't crazy, just guilty. Guilty!

And there were them. He sealed their faith. He ordered their death.

> Forget them not, honor their name.
> The Hero's Nine in a circle they lay
> A giant rock holding their name . . .

Duncan softly sang the words, his voice just above a whisper, then dying and only his lips moving, his eyes fixed on the floor. As his voice returned, he was in the chant of names:

> Husband and father, he lead the Nine, he made them shine
> Quen Lon a thief, in the Nine he found his honor he left this plane with no shame

Direhound Silverrose a dwarf who made his clan proud,
he held the Nine's ground.
Gilvilanna Blue, Odium's chosen, led the Nine to the
heavens, blessed them all
Bodice Cain a pauper's son, rich without gold, bestowed
grace to the Nine's name
Katrice Cobbler her family slain by Underdweller malice,
a mother to the Nine
Staven Lorshire the farmer's son, sowed the seed of honor,
the Nine's honor
Tallen Drone, the bard, his music lent voice to the Nine.
Jasphan Lumber a mountain of a man, he held the ground,
the last of the Nine to stand

A knock interrupted Duncan. He pulled himself together, wiped his face, and sniffed back the sorrow. Opening the door, he found Xantrawler standing there.

"May I come in?"

Duncan opened the door wider. He watched as the Weaponsmaster quickly took in the room, from the single bed, the small stand by the door with the pitcher and wash basin, to the small desk and chair by the fireplace. The eyes lingered over the packed bags then they settled on Duncan.

"You're leaving." It was a statement.

Duncan closed the door and went to his packs. While he talked, he toyed with the straps. "I'm no longer Ambrus's bodyguard, so I can't stay."

"I have room in the gatehouse towers."

Duncan turned to face Xantrawler. "Those are for officers."

"As a weaponsmaster, you have the right to request quarters from any military outpost."

"I gave up that right when I walked away."

Xantrawler shook his head. "You never lose that right. It was decreed long before either of us was born. That is the reward the monarchy bestows on those who dedicated their life to the service of their kingdom."

"You're not listening. I gave up that right. I'm no longer a weaponsmaster. I am Duncan Pentock, simple sword for hire."

Xantrawler's face drooped. His eyes held no sparkle as he looked at Duncan. "I said something yesterday that I regret. I know what happened was hard. It would affect any commander. That's not a reason to turn your back on everything, on your country."

"I haven't turned my back on my country. I am helping those I can in my own way."

"What about the ones about to die? We have received numerous reports. The enemy is coming straight at us."

Duncan bit back his retort. Instead, he asked, "They're not fortifying their positions? Not holding the ground they have taken?"

"The only place they have any manpower is the North Wall and Trader's Junction."

"That doesn't make sense."

"It does if they have an important objective. That objective is Wintermist."

"All the Queen needs to do is get her army around and attack from the rear."

"Remember what we discussed yesterday. By the time any rescue comes, we will already be defeated."

Duncan shook his head. "I can't believe Wintermist Wall will fall, not with what you have done and the caliber of mages here."

"The North Wall was manned by seasoned troops, fighters in their prime. I have old men and young recruits. The duke's soldiers have some experience, but there's not many of them. The North Wall had mages, wizards, and witches. The wall was four times as thick and twice as high. It fell!"

Duncan turned back to his packs. “There’s nothing I can do.”

“So you’re leaving?” Xantrawler waited, and when Duncan did not immediately reply, he said, “Despite everything, you’re still a weaponsmaster. You can’t leave and let innocent civilians die.”

Duncan clenched his fist and squeezed his eyes. He could see it. He shook his head, but it wouldn’t go away. If he left, he would not be responsible for the slaughter. In his mind, he heard the counsel Xantrawler gave all his students.

“Those who fail to stop the act are as guilty as those who commit the act.”

He held his head down, and the scene changed. He saw it, a massacre, men, dead men on Wintermist Wall, bodies of old men, young men, and the mages killed by an enemy no one knew nine days ago.

At the gatehouse of Wintermist Wall, a lone figure laid. Still defiant in death, Xantrawler’s unseeing eyes looked at him, not with accusation, but with sorrow.

Duncan opened his eyes and looked at his clenched fist. On his bed laid his sword. The scabbard worn, the leather shiny in spots from rubbing on his leg. The wrappings of the hilt needed to be replaced. The guard was bent from countless blows. It was a good weapon, and he could never part with it as it was given to him the day he left Xantrawler’s salle. A gift from his teacher.

“I will stay. I will fight this enemy.”

Xantrawler allowed a small smile of victory. “Good, I’ll have a room prepared for you in the tower.”

Duncan faced Xantrawler. “I said I would stay. I’ll fight this enemy with all the training you gave me. I will fulfill my duty to the Queen. I will stand beside the men, die beside them if need be. I will not lead, and I will not command.”

“That’s what you want,” Xantrawler’s jaw jerked from the pressure of holding back what he wanted to say. “Report to my quartermaster this afternoon. He'll assign you a company." *And I know just the company for you.*

Ambrus wove among the crowd in the marketplace. He had planned on getting up early and catching Sasha at her home, but a late night at the Screeching Owl had caused him to sleep late.

The crowd pulsated as the people of Wintermist went about their daily business. An invading army may be heading their way, but life continued. Meals needed to be cooked, clothes washed and mended, children cared for, and animals tended. War could only interrupt, but never stop the way of life.

As Ambrus pushed through the crowd, he caught a glimpse of dark hair, a flash of rust-colored clothing, and the harsh voice of a person he knew. He pushed through the crowd, and as he got closer, he heard Sasha arguing with the owner.

"Two krunt! For a rabbit! That's outrageous. On the other side of town, they're only one krunt and five shillons."

"What do you expect, Sasha, war is coming. People want fresh meat and . . ."

"And you would take advantage and rape me of my money! I'll give you one krunt and four shillons. Four shillons, mind you, because you tried to cheat me."

"I'm not trying to cheat you." The meat merchant held the rabbit over his head. Ambrus could see it was a plump animal, larger than most. In the capital, it would have gone for three krunts easily. "I live outside of the wall. When that army gets here, they'll ruin me, steal my animals, and take my grain and fodder. I need funding to start backup. One krunt and eight shillons."

"Oh no, don't use the sympathy ploy on me. I happen to know you live up the shore, a long way from the line of attack. One krunt and five shillons."

"Oh, but they still need to forage. I'm not so far from an army of thirty thousand that they won't come after me." He stroked the fur on the rabbit's leg, causing them to part and revealing the plump meat on the inside. "One krunt and seven shillons."

Ambrus knew they were about to make their deal at a price agreeable to the two of them. If buyers didn't haggle with the sellers, the marketplace would not be entertaining.

"Skin it for me and I will give you one krunt and six shillons."

"I charge for the skinning." He took one look at Sasha and added, "But for you, I'll do it free. Come back in one mark and it will be ready. Do you wish the head?"

"Keep the head, and don't try to cheat me with a scrawny rabbit from the back of your booth."

"I won't, Mistress Sasha, in one mark then."

Sasha turned and bumped into Ambrus. She was about to let go a tirade of admonishment when she noticed who it was.

"Ambrus! How are you?"

"Same as I was the last time I saw you."

Sasha peered through the crowed, twisting her neck and swinging it back and forth. "Where's your bodyguard? I don't see Duncan." She looked at the scholar and glared. "You didn't give him the slip again, did you?"

"No, I paid him off and released. It's more important he serves with Xantrawler on Wintermist Wall."

Sasha's face lost its glow, but she kept her voice cheerful, "Well, you're just in time. I need a nice, strong man to carry my basket. After all, I am such a fragile lady."

Ambrus snorted, "Weren't you the one who told me she throws hundred stone weights in flour bags?"

"Okay, I just want someone to carry it." She shoved the basket in his hands. "Now follow me so I can get my shopping done. I saw some nice-looking winter apples over there."

Ambrus followed Sasha for the next hour from one booth to another. At one, she stopped briefly to confirm her father's order. At another, she got into a heated argument, which was beyond the semijoking bartering normally done. In the end, she stalked away, mumbling that if she had Duncan with her, he could have convinced the lout she was right.

After they picked up the skinned rabbit, Ambrus steered her to a small kiosk. It was one that served fresh food and drink to the market patrons. He ordered for them, and shortly, they each had a trencher of some type of stew and a mug of weak ale.

"Four shillons for this," Ambrus said as he bit into a half-raw carrot.

"You don't expect Lakeview quality from a peasant's vendor, do you?" Sasha asked as she noisily slurped her stew from her spoon.

Ambrus winced. "No, but I did expect my lunch guest to maintain the manners she has shown in the past."

Sasha laughed as she picked up the wooden mug and took a large gulp. Sitting it down, she burped loudly and looked at Ambrus. "So what do you want?"

"What do you mean?"

"You didn't come all the way from the school and hazard the marketplace just to eat bad stew and drink weak ale with me."

Ambrus looked at Sasha a moment then said, "I need your opinion." Sasha shrugged, as she had a mouthful of stew, so Ambrus continued, "I believe my power of prophecy is nothing more than me being sensitive to the Vlynies."

"You're not trying to explain your abilities away, are you?" she asked around a piece of grizzle. "If you are, I swear I will throw you off Wintermist Bridge when the Spirits are looking the other way."

"Not trying to explain it away, trying to understand it. If I can understand what is happening, I may be able to interpret the visions better."

"What do the Vlynies have to do with it?"

"I'm thinking, they're not just in the here and now, but the here and to come. We know they communicate immediately across vast distances. We know they reveal things from the past. If they communicate with their past selves, which were their present selves in the past, then why can't their past, future selves communicate with their present, past selves? Their present selves should be able to communicate with their future selves as they are the future selves' past selves and the future selves are the past selves' present selves."

Sasha stared at Ambrus, her spoon halfway to her mouth, her mouth hanging open. When she found her voice, she virtually squeaked, "I think I have just been Diamoxed."

"You've been what?"

Sasha shook her head, laid her spoon down, and reached for her mug. "It's a term we use at the Screeching Owl. It's named in your honor. Whenever you have your opponent on the run and you want to totally confuse them, you use the same type of circular logic you just used."

"There's no such thing as circular logic. Logic is logic."

"Not what you just did. You went around and around until you were back where you started, and anyone who tried to follow you is dizzy."

"There is nothing circular about what I said."

"Let me see if I have you right. You are trying to say you believe the Vlynies are not only able to talk with their past self, but their future self."

"See, you understood what I said. You repeated it perfectly."

"Why didn't you just say it that way?"

Ambrus looked shocked. "What? And take a chance on it being misunderstood?"

Sasha threw her hands up in the air. "You are impossible."

Ambrus cocked his head and looked at her. "But what do you think? Is it possible?"

"I think you need to overcome your own argument." At Ambrus's quizzical look, she added, "Where you state that if you get a message from the future and act on it then that future does not exist and you could never have gotten the message."

"I said that?"

"Well, you used your circular logic, but yes."

"I don't have an answer to that, but I have to be getting the message from somewhere."

"Why can't it be just your present self going ahead in time and seeing what is there, then returning?"

"Hmmm, never thought of that. But how would I know where to go? Perhaps the Vlynies are a sort of guide. They show me the way, and I go and look. The whole thing would be like a dream so that's why it would be ambiguous."

"You are hung up on the Vlynies."

"Well, it makes sense."

"Then go see Mage Kytril. He's the expert on the Vlynies."

While they had been talking, they finished their stew, and now Ambrus started ripping his trencher apart. "A little coarser than I'm used to, but very good. It has the taste of the stew right into it."

"So are you going to talk to Mage Kytril?"

"If he will talk to me."

Sasha narrowed her eyes. "Ambrus, what did you do?"

"Nothing, just voiced my opinion when he was on the Council of Mages."

"Ambrus!"

"We got into a discussion on magic. Okay, it was an argument. He doesn't have the sense of humor the mages here do. Anyway, I told him his Vlynies are nothing but a bunch of hot air he shoots out his rear."

"Rider coming in!"

Xantrawler stopped on his way up the stairs and hurried back down. Only a messenger of the Queen would bring a cry from the tower. The portcullis was up, and the doors were wide open. As Xantrawler reached the gatehouse, foot traffic was scampering aside as the rider wound around the wagon traffic. The rider brought the horse to a stop and leaped from the saddle. Xantrawler caught a glimpse of reddish hair and the slim build of a female. Female couriers were preferred since their light weight made for a swifter run with less strain on a horse.

As Xantrawler approached the messenger, she was calling for a fresh horse. She slid from the saddle, unbuckled it as she hit the ground, and slid it from the horse's back. The horse's sides were heaving as it struggled to draw in air. Froth was foaming at its mouth, and the coat had a bright sheen from perspiration. These messenger horses were a special breed, and seeing one in this shape told a tale of a hard ride.

"What do you have messenger?" Xantrawler asked.

The messenger gave the weaponsmaster a brief glance, noted who it was, and went back to her task. "Documents from General Klaydon for the duke."

Xantrawler smiled. He remembered every student that came through his salle. He had been operating his salle for a number of years when the king died. Upon the coronation of the Queen, she made a decree that all officers would spend a year at his salle. General Klaydon—just a captain at the time—was one of the first. He went on to serve the Queen in many pivotal campaigns and rapidly advanced. His posting at the North Wall was a reward, a time for the general to relax and prepare for retirement.

"Should have known the old fox would make it through."

"Just barely, sir," the messenger said as she was handed a blanket, which she immediately threw over her horse. A soldier took the reins and started to walk the horse, cooling it down. "We lost many fighters. The general only has about three hundred men."

"Did he send anything for me?"

"Yes, sir, only one phrase."

Xantrawler arched his eye brow. "Yes?"

"Baylore's myth lives."

Xantrawler frowned. He had forgotten the mythical war games he used to play with his students where he would give them scenarios using mythical creatures, just so they would learn how to handle the no-win scenario.

"It sounds like the general feels this was a no-win situation."

The messenger glanced at the weaponsmaster as she picked up her saddle. "You could say that, Weaponsmaster."

The horse trainer came up with a fresh horse, one of the special breed kept for the messengers. After turning it over to the messenger, he turned to the soldier cooling down the horse and yelled at the poor man to get the horse in the shade, get water, and feed and admonish the man to be sure the horse didn't drink too much. The last thing he wanted was a horse that was floundering.

As the messenger went on her way, Xantrawler continued his circuit. Since the death of Mage Jedrowler, he got into the habit of walking the wall and the mage school twice a day. He was determined there wasn't going to be a repeat.

He was on his way back from the lake tower when one of the duke's messengers caught up to him, a squire in his early teens. The message was brief and to the point. Duke Altrid had called an emergency meeting of his council and wanted Xantrawler and Mage Master Gardner to attend immediately.

Duncan tossed his bags on the bunk and started to unbuckle his sword. The barracks were simple affairs, three long buildings around a central courtyard. Each held seventy-five men. Bunks were placed around the walls. One wall contained bows and quivers of arrows. The center of the room held long tables and weapon racks. Each man was responsible for his personal weapon, which was kept near at hand.

The room had a fresh scrubbed smell, and the pails of dirty water stood by the door. The men were enjoying their off duty time the way all soldiers do. A few had drawn their daily ration of beer and were sitting and talking. Others played a dice game, while another group sat, playing a card game. Others stood by the windows reading letters from home or sat at the table writing letters home. The Queen's insistence that her subjects know how to read and write had sparked an abundance of mail, an event Duncan approved of as it raised morale.

The spot between his shoulder blades itched as it always did when he was being watched.

"Sir," a young voice said behind Duncan. He turned and looked at a boy, old enough to shave, but having few hairs to justify a razor. The lad wore light brown leather, a short sword on his left, and a long knife on the opposite hip. Dirty brown hair covered his head in a tangle, one that no comb could straighten. He looked familiar, but Duncan was unable to place him.

"Yes?"

"We were wondering, the guys and me, are you who we think you are?"

Duncan finished unhooking his sword and laid it on the bunk. "I'm just a sword hire."

The boy's face fell. "We thought you may be Weaponsmaster Pentock."

Duncan saw the other soldiers listening, waiting for his answer. He bit his lip, torn between telling an outright lie, being evasive, or admitting who he was.

"I'm Duncan Pentock."

The boy's face brightened. Sticking out his hand, the boy said, "I'm Joshua. Everyone calls me Josh."

Duncan took the offered hand and grasped the wrist in the tradition of warriors and equals. "I'm pleased to meet you."

"The pleasure is mine, Weaponsmaster. I've heard much about you from my father. He was a corporal in your company."

"I had a lot of corporals, every one the best in the queen's service." For the most part, it was true. All his men were the best. And the little voice that followed him whispered, *"Look how you rewarded them. This child is lucky his father is alive, no thanks to me."*

Joshua gave a slight smile. "I've been told I have my father's spirit. No one was surprised I joined the Queen's army. Well, not quite the army yet, but this is where I was sent."

Duncan was getting an awkward feeling. Did this boy's father die under his command? Was that the real reason he came over? He turned the subject from the boy's father.

"Weaponsmaster Xantrawler is the best to learn from."

"Yeah, I know. But in the battle that's coming, I won't be fighting. They gave me an ax and a long-handled pole arm. I'm supposed to push over ladders and chop rope."

"That's an important assignment. When the enemy starts coming over the wall, it will be up to you and others to try to stop that."

"But I want to fight like my father. I want to use my father's sword." He slapped the sword at his side.

"There will be plenty of time for that, lad. Learn the basics. Don't be in a hurry to die." His words were harsher than he meant.

"I know. Father's letters said that battles were the last place a sane man wants to be, but someone has to do it."

An older soldier came up and spoke, "Joshua is great at quoting. 'A glorious battle leads to inglorious death and grieving families.'"

Duncan looked the new arrival over, a man in his later years, more white in his hair and beard than dark. His face was heavily lined, and he could see built-up callouses on the man's hand. He also noted a slight limp as the man approached.

"Swordman Kentell Quintal at your service, Weaponsmaster." He thumped his right arm across his chest in a salute.

Duncan waved his hand. "There are no titles in the barracks. I'm a simple swordsman like you, Kentell."

"Sorry, Weaponsmaster, but I can't think of you as a swordsman, not when I owe you my life." Duncan gave him a quizzical look. "I was part of a scouting party that got pinned downed by a bunch of those screaming white brassards. If it wasn't for you coming in time, we all would have been killed."

Duncan shook his head. "I believe I had helped. I couldn't have done it without the men of my company." He was getting nervous. Why did these people want to talk about the war? They needed to forget it, forget him.

"A good leader makes a good company. You made them as good as they were."

Yes, as they were. The thought went through Duncan's mind. Not was, not is, but were. *A massacre had a habit of changing the tenses.*

"In letters, my father said he was in the best company in the kingdom. He told how you took care of your men, worked them hard, but rewarded them greatly."

"That's what I'm talking about, Weaponsmaster. I've been in the service of the kingdom since I was this lad's age. I've seen a number of commanders. The good ones put their men first."

Joshua nodded his head. "Yep, father said that about you. You ate with your men. You checked on the sick and the injured. He said you never left a man behind. He told us how you were the first to rise and the last to seek his bed." Josh stopped long enough to take a deep breath. "My dad told me he learned true honor from you. He knew there were things in this life worth dying for, that you showed him . . ."

Duncan snapped, "Don't go making me no hero. There's nothing special about me."

The lad was not fazed by Duncan's outburst. "Father thought you were special. So much, he had concerns about you. Why in his last letter, just before the Valley, he said a bunch of them were going to . . ."

"He should have been concerned about me. I got him killed." He had heard what he needed, another child who grew up without a father because of him.

Joshua started to say something, but Kentell placed a hand on his shoulder. "Come, lad, we have bothered the weaponsmaster enough for one day." Josh reluctantly wandered back to his bunk. The old soldier turned to Duncan, fire in his words, but sadness in his eyes. "We'll let you get settled, Weaponsmaster. Just remember what you said. In here, there are no titles. We're all brothers. If you can't go to your brother for help, who is there?

"So you know, the boy's name is Josh, Josh Wheatfield." He nodded to Duncan and turned. "Your words, remember the Hero's Nine."

The duke's keep was built in the days when Mead was settled. It sat on the side of the mountain, overlooking the pass to Gammount. Grouped around the keep were barracks, the duke's own Temple to Odium, and stables. The kitchen butted up to the rear of the keep, and a wing had been added for dignitaries and visiting nobles.

A curtain wall, complete with a gatehouse, circled the keep. A section ran down to the twin towers that guarded the pass. They had their own gate to seal the pass, barracks for more soldiers, and a small village of houses for the family of officers.

In the four years Xantrawler had served the mages of Wintermist, he had only been to the duke's keep a handful of times. Mostly state functions, only a couple visits had to do with his job. Now, as he walked the corridor escorted by the duke's own personal guards, he felt the weight of the situation descend on his shoulders.

The guards brought him to a set of double doors flanked by two more of the duke's personal bodyguard. Both were dressed in full chain, swords at their side and holding short lances. Neither was dressed in ceremonial garb. They were dressed for war. One opened the door, and the other remained alert.

Xantrawler entered Duke Altrid's council chamber and saw the rest of the advisers were already present. Most acknowledged him with a nod while a few, like the Lord Marshal, ignored him and continued talking with their neighbor.

Xantrawler was not surprised to see Mage Master Gardner. Mages had ways of moving that the common man was incapable of. He took the only vacant seat at the table and listened to the talk around him.

The talk was speculation. Many were of the mind that General Klaydon had a plan that involved the knights and fighters of the dukes. A few dissenting voices did not believe Duke Altrid's five hundred men, the Wintermist Wall guards of two hundred, and whatever force General Klaydon had, would be enough against the invading army. They believed they were going to evacuate the city to the south

Xantrawler agreed with the smaller group. Any force that could breech the North Wall would overwhelm the small force at Wintermist. The only hope would be the Queen's force at Gammount arriving in time.

Xantrawler tried to determine the number of warriors he was facing. After stationing rear guards at Trader's Junction and other crucial locations, their numbers would be depleted. The question was, were they depleted enough that they could be held at the wall. While he was thinking, Duke Altrid entered, carrying a bundle of papers. He went to the head of the table and sat.

"General Klaydon has sent a full report to me." Duke Altrid started without a preamble. "It's worse than we were led to believe. While the messenger birds reported a large army, we had no idea of its size." He paused and looked at the top sheet. "General Klaydon estimates the enemy's strength at ten thousand men."

An uproar filled the room as all the advisers started talking at once. Their combined voices mingled into an unintelligible babble. Xantrawler felt he was back in the mages' council chamber. It didn't matter what class you were. There were people that wanted to express their own self-importance. Xantrawler leaned back in his chair and waited. Across him, he saw Mage Master Gardner doing the same.

The duke allowed his advisors to carry on for a few minutes, then stood, holding his hands up for silence. As the room quieted, he revealed the rest of the information: the number of mounted fighters, foot soldiers, archers and mages, the siege engines, and the strange creatures. He laid the report aside and looked up.

"I have two other important pieces of information, and both will affect how this upcoming battle will play out. Just this morning, I received a messenger bird from General Klaydon informing me of a magical device of the enemy. According to him, the enemy has a magical portal through which they move men and supplies."

"Impossible!" one of the advisors said. "If there was such a device, our own mages would have it."

"Do not grow overconfident about our mage abilities," Mage Master Gardner said. "There is more to magic than we know."

"Mage Margella thinks it is possible," Duke Altrid said. "Another message had two words, 'Ancient Magic.'"

A thoughtful look appeared on Mage Master Gardner's face as he played with his beard. "In the days before present time, magic was young and not developed. Ancient scripts tell us this magic, though harder to control, was powerful. There were few users of magic, as it had a tendency to turn on its users. The ones who did control magic were called Nacromages.

"Not much survived from that time, only a few scraps of parchment. We do know some type of cataclysm took place, possibly from the use of this raw energy. It took hundreds of years for the world to heal. In the years after, the cataclysm magic evolved, matured. Still, there are strands of Ancient Magic around."

"What does it mean?" another advisor asked.

"It is possible to gather in the strands of unrefined magic as Mage Jedrowler did for his spell. It appears the mages of the Northland have harnessed Ancient Magic."

The duke nodded. "There is a report for you from Mage Margella. He speaks of the enemy mages deploying Ancient Magic to cripple the mages at the wall. His explanation goes into nonsense words." He pulled out a couple of sheets of paper and had them passed to the Mage Master. "You can read it, and plan accordingly."

Mage Master Gardner took the parchment with a nod of thanks.

Duke Altrid took a deep breath. "The next information is equally disturbing. According to General Klaydon, the enemy has tamed and controls a dragon."

The news brought silence to the room. The duke expected some type of reaction, but not silence. He waited a couple of moments, then spoke.

"General Klaydon says the dragon's flaming breath killed hundreds of his people, burned most of the North Wall, and totally demolished the morale of his fighters."

"There is no such thing as dragons," the Lord Marshal blurted out.

This broke the spell, and everyone started babbling at once.

Xantrawler's mind was racing. He now understood the general's message for him. He had used dragons and other mythological creatures in his war games.

"Counselors, please," Mage Master Gardner's used the same voice he used in his own council meetings to bring order. "We know dragons don't exist. And even if they did, according to legend, no one can control them. They are creatures as intelligent as man."

"I have a cousin who is a merchant," the duke's economical advisor said. "And he claims to have seen dragons when he was at villages in the Thanatos Range foothills."

Mage Master Gardner nodded. "Over the years, there have been reports of flying creatures in the foothills. These sightings have been unconfirmed. This dragon could also be an illusion cast by the mages of the Northland at the same time as a spell of fire. This could cause anyone to think they were being attacked by a myth."

"That would have to be a powerful illusion," the duke said. "I have reports from four of General Klaydon's officers that describe the dragon. Even Mage Margella mentions it in his report."

"I could dismiss something," Xantrawler finally spoke, "if it was one or two people. When a number of people report the same thing, it's either true or the group is suffering mass insanity."

"Illusion can be a powerful spell. Cast it with Ancient Magic and what can we get?"

"What can we do to combat an illusion?" the duke asked.

"Now that we know its existence, we can cast anti-illusion spells," the Mage Master said.

"And if it is real?" an older advisor asked.

"I do not believe it's real. What type of creature flies and spits flame?"

"It doesn't fly," Xantrawler said. "But fire lizards breathe flame." He was not going to argue the possibility of a dragon. It was not worth the waste of time. He would give them something familiar to deal with. "They have been known to do a lot of damage and break the morale of the strongest of armies."

"Could the Northland mages have a fire lizard?" the Lord Marshal asked. "And rather than casting an illusion spell, cast a spell of flying on the creature?"

Mage Master Gardner said, "It could be possible. If so, all we need to do is neutralize the magic."

"Everything you are saying, Mage Master," the duke said, "indicates the problem are the mages. We need to eliminate them."

Mage Master Gardner nodded. "Before I came to Wintermist, I used my talents for a number of years in combat. The first thing each side tried to do was locate the mages and eliminate them. Even the Underdwellers know this."

"General Klaydon reports there are at least eight mages."

"We have three times more at the school. That's not counting the visiting mages and wizards, the witches and the druids. The difficulty comes with this area of old magic. We have tried to scurry where the enemy is and found a blackness."

"So we let this beast decimate my men while you mages hide in your school?" the Lord Marshal snapped.

"They are not your men, Lord Marshal," the duke said. "They are the Queen's, and Wintermist Wall is under the command of Weaponsmaster Xantrawler."

"My duke, I'm responsible for your safety and in charge of your soldiers, not that old man!"

The duke slapped his hand on the table. "Youngster, you will show respect to the weaponsmaster! As for Wintermist Wall, that is a duty handled by the mages of Wintermist School for centuries."

"I meant no disrespect, but I am the Lord Marshal. Therefore, I'm the highest-ranking military officer for the queen, next to you, my lord."

"Weaponsmasters are in the direct service of the queen. Once charged, Weaponsmaster Xantrawler can override my commands."

"I would never do that, my duke," Xantrawler said softly. "I reserve that privilege for the terminally stupid."

The Lord Marshal shut his mouth.

Duke Altrid looked at his Lord Marshal for a moment, his eyes flashing in displeasure. He had excused much because of the lad's inexperience. But on this matter, too many lives hung in the balance. Weaponsmaster Xantrawler was a man of honor. He had never allowed his rank or position to swell his head. He was well respected throughout the kingdom. The man would follow orders, even the Lord Marshal's, unless he believed the orders foolish. Then he may hesitate before overriding them, and in battle, that moment of hesitation could cost lives.

Duke Altrid sat straighter in his chair and looked around the room. His eyes caught each advisor. "These reports indicate this is not a simple raid. The events unfolding show this is not a border skirmish. For that reason, I issue the following order." His eyes returned briefly to the Lord Marshal, then turned to Xantrawler.

"Weaponsmaster Xantrawler Baylore," his voice was the voice of authority, the representative of the queen. The weaponsmaster rose for he knew the duke spoke not as the Lord of Mead, but as the Queen's representative. As such, his words were those of the Queen.

"I formally declare in the name of our Queen, witnessed by nobles, knights, and advisors of my council, that our kingdom of Lashtar has been invaded. From this moment forth, until such time as the Queen herself declares a truce, we are at war with the land beyond the Thanatos Mountains.

"Weaponsmasters, do your duty."

The last time a duke charged weaponsmasters with their duty, the country was at war for three years with the Underdwellers.

Xantrawler brought his right arm to his chest, his fist clenched in a salute. "Heard and bound!" With those simple words, all weaponsmasters of the realm were bound to this war.

Lashtar was officially at war.

As Xantrawler sat down, Duke Altrid continued, "The Lord Marshal brings up a good point. Is there anything you can do until the mages are ready to strike?"

Xantrawler knew what could be done. It all depended on one man. *Well, I'll just have to make him cooperate.*

"I know one man who can handle fire lizards. Duncan Pentock."

"The Duncan of Pentock? The Hero of the Valley?" the Lord Marshal asked, his eyes wide. "The one who took out three firelizards single-handedly!"

The duke leaned back and steepled his fingers. "Weaponsmaster Pentock is one of the few who understands firelizards, but no one knows where he is. He dropped out of sight at the end of the war."

"You've seen him, my lord Duke. He was the man guarding Ambrus Diamox the night Mage Jedrowler was killed."

The duke sat up. "He's been here all this time?"

Xantrawler felt the morale of the room rise. Duncan did not know nor would he ever accept the impact he had. His deeds, his actions, inspired many and gave hope to more. Now these men, many who had met great people in the past, felt hope because of the man credited with winning the Battle of the Valley and ending the Underdweller War.

The Valley was the last major battle of the war. In any war, there are battles that create an impact, and it doesn't matter if other places have the same name. Everyone knows what you're talking about.

The battle lasted six hours, but the fiercest fighting of the war occurred there. The Valley where over five thousand of the queen's men died. Twice that many Underdwellers, many their leaders. One company held the pass, and many were dead when the Queen's army rode in. But because of their sacrifice, the army of Lashtar stopped the Underdwellers.

With most of their leaders slain, the Underdwellers retreated to their tunnels and caverns. There were only a few raids after the Valley, and soon they stopped. Now, only the normal, small bands of Underdwellers, attacked isolated surface dwellers.

The battle changed the outcome of the war and one man's life.

The duke held his hand up for silence, "Weaponsmaster, when can you speak with Weaponsmaster Pentock?"

"I will meet with him tomorrow. He's presently settling into his new quarters."

Chapter Twenty-Two

Day Eight

Anton rubbed his eyes as morning light spilled through the window. He was at the dining table, having given up the workroom in the middle of the night. He had spent the remainder of the night reading Jedrowler's journal from ten years ago. At that time, Jedrowler had finished his research.

For the fifth time, he reread the same entry: *I have finished. Now that I am at the end of my quest, it seems so simple. A two-stage spell, one to bind us with the land and one to bind the land with us. Besides the anchors around the land, each side will have an anchor to direct the entity that will be created.*

The Spirits is the logical choice for the land, as they understand the Ancient Magic.

For the human channel, I need to find the appropriate candidate. They must be strong with personal magic; able to grasp, understand, and control Ancient Magic; and capable of channeling large amounts of the Living Magic. They must be grounded in reality and have a strong sense of self. Without this, we will have what I call the Legion effect. Without the strong sense of self, every person in the circle will be absorbed by Legion.

If that happens, if Legion is awoken, I will lose my friends. I am prepared for that. Before I allow Legion to take over, I will use my staff for a mage strike and destroy the falls, the mage school, and half of Wintermist. I will take my time in looking for this person. Too much is at stake to have the wrong person, one who will resist the Legion effect.

Anton shuddered. Whatever this Legion effect was, it scared Jedrowler enough he was willing to destroy his beloved falls. He thought back to the night of the casting and remembered laying out the staff because Master Jedrowler had said it was needed.

"Legion effect, Legion effect." Anton flipped through the pages. He had been repeating this for candle marks and was unable to find any other mention. As he scanned the pages, he yawned deeply and rubbed his eyes.

"This is getting me nowhere." He slammed the journal shut.

The sun was shining, bringing out the red in the blooms of the elvish flowers. He inhaled the scent of the flowers carried on the cool morning breeze. Standing, he stretched, feeling his back pop. He would have to get one of the other students to water the flowers. He had been faithfully finding someone each day, but they were starting to look wilted. He needed to find out if there was a special nutrient. Maybe CynLisa would know.

"You idiot," he admonished himself. "CynLisa should have the answer."

Anton hurried out the door and through the hallways. This early, there were few people, so his journey was swift. The archives were in the middle of the mountain, where it absorbed all that was known, all events of the mage school. CynLisa's assistant was at the desk, sorting piles of scrolls and timidly pointed Anton toward the stairs leading to CynLisa's private office.

History hung in the endless black cavern from white salt crystals. Words floated on diamond dust glistening in the air currents. Jade told the story of the mage who discovered the combination for shape-shifting. A black onyx held the tale of a mage duel that crushed an evil empire. Black stone from the lake disclosed the building of Wintermist Wall.

Simple stone divulged tales of simple times. Sand flowed through the history of the early years of the school. Every thought and every utterance built the columns that supported the Cyn's room, created the steps to the Cyn's office. A quartz steeple sang the song of the dwarf who spent his life forging the special bell that rang when Wintermist appointed a new Mage Master. The steeple rose high to disappear in the darkness. Its top sat on the summit of the mountain.

The steps, slate stepping stones, to CynLisa's room hung over an endless chasm, and it never bothered Anton to walk them. This was the one spot his fear never struck. Clear crystal enveloped the office of Cyn, where CynLisa sat at her desk committing another scroll to the chamber of knowledge.

CynLisa welcomed Anton with a hug, then held him at arm's distance. "You look like hell. When was the last time you slept?"

Anton shrugged. "I've been busy."

"So Mage Master Gardner told me. I need to apologize. I'm supposed to be available to you, but there was a slight misunderstanding. I was finishing some business, and I told my assistant I was not to be disturbed but failed to tell him to send you to me when you needed me."

"That's okay. What I need to know is anything you have on the Legion effect."

CynLisa's body stiffened, and her arms dropped from his shoulders. Her eyes glazed over and took on the stare of her Cyn trance.

"Hear you who have come to what I say. This information is sealed for all eternity, except to those named. Do you vow to keep my information in trust and use it for the betterment of the kingdom?"

Anton felt himself wide awake and shaking. He swallowed around the lump in his throat and nodded, then realized that he needed to give a verbal reply. "I vow."

CynLisa's eyes closed. "Within the vault of Forbidden Knowledge is an animal hide scroll. Upon this scroll is the tale of the before time, when the land was young and magic was new.

"In those days, the users of the Unseen Forces delved deep into the mysteries of the living invisible force. Powerful in this force they became. Their power was greater than the shamans of the people. They outstripped the power of the earth and the elements as used by the witches. They were the Nacromages, and they used their power to build a great civilization. The people celebrated the bounty of the Nacromages' rule."

CynLisa bowed her head. "The Nacromages were benevolent. They had the best interest of the people at heart. That was their downfall.

"The minor gods were cruel. Their goal was to destroy the gods to be the only gods. They used people as pawns, so the people suffered. The major gods took no interest, having their own agenda. The Nacromages fought the minor gods, but individually were not powerful enough.

"In an effort to defeat the minor gods, the Nacromages used the living force to combine their powers. With the use of magic, they bound themselves, their strength, and their power. In the end, they became one. They became Legion."

CynLisa paused, her eyes coming into focus for a moment. In a normal voice, she said, "The Legion effect consumed them. That is what you resisted. The desire to be one all-powerful being." Her eyes unfocused, and her voice returned to its monotone.

"Legion defeated the minor gods by becoming the minor gods. They battled, and Legion absorbed them. Or they absorbed Legion? In the end, Legion became all-powerful. Legion now set out to finish the job of the minor gods. Legion was a god.

"His was a regime of terror. He forced more and more people to worship him. Worshippers give gods power, and Legion was part god, so he drew on the power of his worshippers. Legion grew by encouraging all users of the Unseen Forces to become proficient. When the users of the Unseen Forces were powerful enough, they became a Nacromages and were absorbed by Legion.

"In time the major gods took an interest, Legion had enslaved a large part of the sentient population. When gods battled, mortals suffered. In the end, Legion was defeated, and humanity was decimated. All this is locked away in the vault of Forbidden Knowledge."

CynLisa's eyes closed, and her chin dropped. Anton moved as she started to collapse. He caught her and quickly lowered her to a chair. Her breathing was regular, but a soft moan escaped her lips. After a moment, she opened her eyes and looked at him. She gave a weak smile.

"Opening the memories to a sealed file takes a lot out of me."

"Master Jedrowler had sealed that information." CynLisa nodded. "But why me? Why open them to me when you wouldn't open them to anyone on the council?"

CynLisa looked up at Anton. "You are very naive. Jedrowler believed in you. He knew if anything happened to him, you would need access to all the information he had. This spell is dangerous because of the Legion effect. The binding is powerful enough that the channel could be overwhelmed and another Legion could form."

"Then why pick me? I could have ruined the entire spell." Now that he knew what he was facing, he felt the fear, heard the magic give a warning cry.

"No, Anton, Jedrowler knew you were strong enough. You have a hard time believing you are powerful and that you are respected by many. It is a weakness when it comes to a personality trait, but a strength when dealing with something like Legion."

"What if he had been wrong?"

"He wasn't."

"He could have been, then everything would be lost, everything is. They're asking me to do the impossible. Now you come along with this information, and I'm scared. What if the second part of the spell requires another confrontation with Legion? Can I resist this time?"

"You did once. You will again."

"You don't understand. I almost gave in. The power is tempting. Now knowing if I give in, I will be lost, along with the rest of the circle, I'm scared."

"You will resist for that reason. You know if you gave in, Anton would cease to exist."

Anton turned from CynLisa and walked across the room. He leaned his head on a cool spun crystal column and let out a groan. Around him, the rooms slanted and started to spin.

"I can't do this. We have to turn it over to someone else." His whole body trembled. "This is real fear, a true fear, not the imagined fear of heights."

"It is that fear," her voice was soft. "What was the first thing you were taught when you came to this school?"

"How to command higher magic."

"Before that."

Anton looked at CynLisa. "You mean all that history? Or do you mean the lessons in meditation and mind relaxation?"

"The lessons in magical force."

Anton walked over to a glass shelf and looked at the tiger eye stone of feline control. "Magic is a power that surrounds us and we can use to create. It is an energy force."

CynLisa sighed in frustration. "The most important lesson in magic is living energy. A mage controls the most magic. We control the energy strands by channeling them through us. You are on the threshold of becoming a mage. A very powerful one. You can channel more magical energy, pour forth an untold amount of force. But if it senses fear, it is gone."

Anton walked from the shelf over to CynLisa's desk. The Cyn followed and leaned against it, crossing her arms. She waited for him to speak, to make the first statement or ask the first question.

Anton felt the power of magic inside. It squirmed, and a little leaked out. He knew CynLisa was right. He wasn't a simple wizard. But he wasn't a mage. He had controlled the power of the spell, allowed the magic of all the disciplines to flow through him. Ancient magic responded to his command.

And I lost control of Ancient Magic, allowed it to fill the banquet hall and push our magic aside. The mage lights disappeared and gave the assassin an opportunity to strike unseen and unobserved. Mage Jedrowler is dead!

"I can't control the magic." It was a half whisper, but CynLisa heard it.

"You can and you do. Now master and control your fear."

"That fear caused me to kill Master Jedrowler!"

CynLisa stepped back as if Anton had delivered a physical blow. He believed it, thought he had killed Jedrowler. Slowly, she stepped to her desk and laid her fingertips on the top.

"Anton," her voice was soft, "you had nothing to do with the assassination."

"I was responsible for placing the magic in the anchors, all the magic. I failed, and the Ancient Magic escaped, giving the assassin the opportunity."

CynLisa stepped from her desk and approached Anton. She laid her hands on his shoulders and looked into his eyes. "Is that why you are holding back? Is that why you are afraid to do the second part?"

Anton tried to look away, but the Cyn's eyes held him as they bored to his soul, laying the truth behind. Slowly, with just a brief movement, he nodded.

"I think we better see the Mage Master."

Mage Master Gardner listened as CynLisa briefed him on her exchanged with Anton. The young man was standing next to her, eyes downcast and shoulders slumped. He had failed to look at the Mage Master when he came into the room.

"I thought it best he heard the findings of the investigation from you," CynLisa finished.

Mage Master Gardner leaned back in his chair and intertwined his fingers. "You actually see Ancient Magic? You know it on sight?" Anton nodded but refused to look at the Mage Master. "And it was your responsibility to anchor the magic around the kingdom?"

"It was important to anchor it. The concentration Master Jedrowler called could overwhelm our magic, did overwhelm it." He closed his eyes. "I failed. I failed in anchoring the magic, and it escaped."

"Anton, you did nothing of the sort. You have strong control of the Ancient Magic. You understand it better than any mage."

Anton opened his eyes and looked up. For a moment, hope glistened in them. "I understand it. It was used to create the circle, and it almost created Legion." Then the hope faded. "I can't control it."

"You have strong control over the Ancient Magic. From what you're saying, you are the only person in Lashtar who can control it."

"I saw the Ancient Magic flash. Our magic was lost."

"The Ancient Magic was from a device the assassin had. He used it to counter our magic."

Anton looked at the Mage Master. "He set the Ancient Magic lose?"

"He brought Ancient Magic with him. He carried a device, and he used it."

"I still control the Ancient Magic? It's still anchored?"

"Reach out to the anchors. Feel how solid they are."

Doubt appeared on Anton's face, which rolled into concentration. The Mage Master waited as Anton's eyes closed, his brows grew together. A smile spread across the face of the lad. "They're all there, and the Ancient Magic is accounted for. I didn't do it." Then the smile faded, replaced with anger. "These invaders made it possible for Master Jedrowler to be killed."

Mage Master Gardner nodded.

Anton turned to CynLisa. "I want to see all that Master Jedrowler had sealed away. I will learn how to use this spell to defeat these creatures."

"Anton, I need another favor." Anton faced the Mage Master. "We need to understand this Ancient Magic, and you are our expert."

"When, not if, I complete the second part of the spell, all in the circle will have my knowledge of Ancient Magic."

"That's good as one of them is a combat mage. Anything else?"

"I want to be on the wall when they attack. I want the bassars!"

As he wandered the hallway, Ambrus's stomach grumbled. He wished he hadn't been so hasty dismissing Duncan. He was accustomed to having someone get him food or remind him of meals.

The thought made him realize that there had always been someone to remind him to eat, to bath, and to change his clothing. He could not recall a time he had not had a servant. Part of him enjoyed the feeling of independence. The scholarly part hated it. This was interrupting his research on the Vlynies, prophecies, and visions.

As he passed a door, it opened, and Mage Kytril stepped out, almost into Ambrus.

"My pardon, scholar," Mage Kytril said, looking down at the shorter man.

Ambrus nervously rubbed his hand on his fur collar. He had spent hours convincing himself he didn't need to see the mage. Now the man stood before him.

"Ah, Mage Kytril, so nice to see you." Trying to appear unruffled, he stopped rubbing the fur. "I had been meaning to consult with you." In a debate, start out strong. Never let your opponent think you're unprepared.

Mage Kytril raised an eyebrow. "How may I help you, Sire Diamox?"

"I have a theory, and you're the expert. I thought I could get your opinion and advice." Ambrus explained his theory on the Vlynies and prophecies.

Mage Kytril listened, his thoughts not spilling on his face. When Ambrus was done, he nodded. "I have never known the Vlynies to exist in the future and the now, but I am not saying it isn't possible." He tapped his lips with his finger. After a moment, he looked at Ambrus. "What we need is someone to test this theory. Someone familiar with prophecies."

"Yes, that makes sense. Do you have anyone in mind?"

"You, you overeducated twit."

"Me!"

"You're the one who recently had a personal experience with prophesying. I can teach you to contact the Vlynies. Can you get your simple mind around the concept of meditation and the astral plane?"

Ambrus nodded. "I once took a course on meditation as a form of relaxation."

"This is not relaxation. It's work. We start now. Come to my quarters."

"Well, ah, I'm on my way to break my fast."

"Excellent! You know lesson one. Meditation is best done when the body has been cleansed by a ritual fast. We can proceed to lesson two, turning your mind in on itself." Ambrus was not feeling well as he entered Mage Kytril's quarters.

Duncan looked at the bowl of biscuits with sausage. His other hand held a large mug of jarda, and on the tables were bowls of fresh fruit and plates of sweets. When he tasted the jarda, it was hot and strong, the way he enjoyed it. Barracks life was one of the few luxuries he made sure his men had, and this meal showed whom he learned that from.

As if thinking his name was a call, Xantrawler stepped into the mess hall, saw Duncan, and motioned for the young man to accompany him. He made his way to the older weaponsmaster and bowed his head. "Weaponsmaster."

"Duncan, we need to speak in private."

"I've just drawn my rations."

"Bring them with you. I need your advice on a matter that shouldn't be discussed around the men."

Duncan followed Xantrawler down the hall to the small officer's mess, where he was briefed on the meeting at the duke's keep.

"I don't agree about it being a fire lizard levitated by magic," Xantrawler concluded. "I believe it's a real dragon."

"No one has seen a real dragon."

"Not true. There have been reports of something in the Thanatos Range that matched what we call a dragon. At Unity Fort, both the Vercracken soldiers and ours reported a flying worm-type creature. A dragon makes more sense than diverting mages to make a fire lizard fly. From the reports I read, whoever is in charge of this army is smart, too smart to squander his resources."

Duncan nodded as he took a bite of food. After chewing for a bit, he asked, "So what do you want from me?"

"I believe a dragon is related to a fire lizard. They both spurt fire and are types of reptiles. I need someone who knows fire lizard to devise a plan of attack."

Duncan's face clouded. "I know fire lizards too well!"

"I know. What can we do to defeat this dragon?"

Duncan hesitated, his eyes glazed as he looked over Xantrawler's shoulder. "We used crossbows and dwarvish throwers made out of ironwood on fire lizards. First, hit the gas bladder, but not when it's full!"

"You used crossbows and dwarvish throwers?"

"Only up close, after the lizard had expended most of its gas. That's the trick, getting the damn thing to flame without killing anyone." He pushed his half-empty bowl aside "Hit a full gas bladder and the flame ball will kill everyone within a hundred paces."

"Can we kill it at a distance?"

"Perhaps. The problem is the scales. I'll say shoot the belly. Hopefully, it is soft."

"Well, you did it a number of times."

Duncan shook his head. "Fire lizards are basically dumb creatures, easily tormented. Just have a group attack the weak points. Sometimes, you get the gas bladder. Other times, you get the soft plate in the roof of their mouth."

"I can't afford to have this thing breathing up and down the wall. According to General Klaydon, this thing is capable of flaming a large section at one time."

Duncan nodded as he pulled on his lower lip. "We need to eliminate it before it has a chance to do any damage."

"You have a plan?"

Duncan nodded slowly. "The trick is getting it to breathe without killing everyone. Then we can hit it at a closer range." He swirled his jarda and stared at the whorls. "I may have to alter a couple of your ballistas."

"That's no problem. We have some in storage, use those."

"I need your blacksmith to make strong metal tips for the bolts. The underside may be soft, but it's tough. I'm hoping the dragon has the same weakness."

"Anything else?"

"Four men to operate each ballista, and one other thing," Duncan paused, "I will not command them."

Xantrawler held his tongue, but his anger was evident on his face. "As long as you train the men to kill the dragon, I don't care."

Sasha stepped out the back door and allowed the cool breeze from the lake to flow through her hair. Midmorning and the last of the customers had left. It had been a brisk business, people purchasing more bread than normal. The sweets had moved, but not as well as the bread. People knew war was coming, and the sugary sweets would not last like bread.

"People are hoarding food in fear of a shortage."

Sasha turned to her father, who was leaning against a rain barrel. Around him were baskets of bread and sweets he was taking to the wall.

"I thought you had left."

"No, Argun is running late. He sent a messenger to tell me he had an emergency at the brewery and would be along shortly."

"So you hid out here in the coolness while your poor-wretched daughter slaves away in the shop?" Bran laughed at his daughter's attempt to look severe. She finally gave up and smiled. "They're not all hoarding. Lady Curthush's servant placed an order for next week. Apparently, they plan on having a large gathering."

Bran pushed away from the barrel and walked to his daughter. "The word is out. Duncan of Pentock is at the wall. People believe the hero of the Valley will defeat the invaders."

"And you heard all that standing out here?"

"No, last night at the pub. While having my pint, news came that Weaponsmaster Pentock had arrived." He chuckled as he rubbed his hands together. "The stories were, to say the least, interesting. They had him coming out of the gorge on a white horse. Others told of him summoning the Nine from the falls where they dwell with the Spirits."

"I'm surprised they don't have him leading a battalion of the Queen's troops."

"Oh, that story went around, but the teller was branded a braggart. Everyone decided it was a company waiting in the gorge."

He looked at his daughter. "You don't look surprise to hear he's at the wall, don't believe it?"

"Oh, I believe it. I knew he would fight."

"Oh, and how did you know, Miss. Smarty-Pants in a dress?"

Sasha smiled at her father's pet name for her. She had not heard him use the term in a long time, and it made her feel close to him. "I knew since the night we found out about the invasion. I sat with him and watched over Ambrus. He's not as distant and gruff as he tries to make people believe. He truly cares and wants to help them." She cast her eyes down. "I got to know the man, well, a little."

Bran shook his head. "I don't think anyone truly knows that man. The Valley changed him. It hurt him."

"I sensed that, but he won't talk about it. What happened there?"

"That, my dear daughter, is something he will have to tell. Trust me. The bards don't have half the story."

"I know he walked away from his duty." She looked at her father. "He needs to do his duty, or it will tear him apart." The last she said in a rush, her voice stepping up.

"And you know this how?"

"I feel it here." She put her hands over her heart, and Bran watched a tear slide down her cheek. He wrapped her in his arms and held her, rocking her slightly. This was the closest his daughter had come to tears since her mother died.

"What's wrong with me? This isn't logical thinking. He hasn't said anything, really, but the way he talks, how he reacts, I see, no, I feel the hurt go through him." She brushed the wetness from her eyes on her father's shoulder. "What's wrong with me?"

Bran pressed her head back onto his shoulders. "There are things that cannot be explained with your logic," he paused and smiled. "You have strong feelings for him."

"No, I can't. I mean he's a man of violence."

"He's a man of peace. He only uses violence when it's necessary. You feel strongly for him, and you want to help."

"Yes, but how? I mean he has all these people around him, Weaponsmaster Baylore, Ambrus. There has to be other weaponsmasters that could help. If they can't help, there's nothing I can do."

Bran took his daughter's shoulders and held her away from him. He looked her in the eyes. "Duncan has not sought help in the last five years. Now he is where someone knows him, and there is a war. Weaponsmaster Baylore is busy getting a meager defense set up. He has engineers on the wall, shoring up weak points, stocking up on ammo for the artillery, and preparing his men to die. Somehow, he is going to bring the bridge down when the wall is breach, and he still has to figure out a way to protect everything at the school."

"So Duncan has no one to talk to."

"Not right now. Even if he did, he may not talk. Sometimes, it is easier to talk with someone you don't really know." He gave her a smile. "Or someone who cares deeply." He watched a blush spread across her face. He kissed the top of her head. "There is nothing wrong with what you're feeling. Don't let the fact that he comes from a long line of nobility intimidate you, not that much does."

Sasha stepped back and looked at her father. "And how do you know he comes from a long line of nobility?"

"It's common knowledge. The Pentock crest hangs in the capital."

"You know this how? For that matter, Father, you know a lot about military matters more than you would have learned from your brother. How do you know they are going to take the bridge down? Artillery? Not catapults and whatever the overgrown crossbows are called. I have listened to you over the past few days, and there is no way a simple baker would know this stuff."

"Sasha, this is a conversation we should have some other time, indoors."

Before Sasha could respond, she was interrupted by the sound of hooves on cobblestones, and the brewmeister came around the corner.

"We will talk, Father," her voice was soft, with a small hint of concern.

Chapter Twenty-Three

In the gathering gloom, Ambrus headed for the base of the falls. He didn't know why, but he was drawn here. And after this day, he needed a place of peace.

Mage Kytril kept him until midday, teaching him meditation and showing him how to reach for the astral plane. Ambrus was able to slip into a trance. He felt the swirl, and his body became light, but he could not reach the astral plane the mage talked about.

"You are too grounded in the earth. Get rid of that stupid logic you carry. Let go and find the magic." A half hour later, after spending twenty minutes asking questions and ten minutes reaching for the astral plan, Mage Kytril threw his arms up. "Enough! It is past the midday meal, and I'm hungry. You, it would do you good to fast another day. Spend the day fasting and stop thinking logically. And no more questions!"

Ambrus could not stop asking questions, stop being logical. His whole life was questioning everything, learning the inner secrets. It would be easier to stop the sun from rising than to turn off his mind.

Ambrus climbed onto the rock and settled in. The sound of the falls drowned out everything, its rhythmic voice soothing. He felt his tense muscles relax, his breathing slow. He crossed his legs and put his hands on his knees. It was a pleasure to sit, listen to the falls, and think of nothing.

As he sat, his mind thinking of nothing, two Spirits drifted down and settled on either side of him, their soft crystal voices blended with the falls. His breathing slowed more. Slowly, his eyelids closed, and peace wrapped around him.

Ambrus's mind was still, not a thought whispered. His body swayed to the thrum of the crystal. The blackness inside his mind expanded, spinning. Lines of gray and black spun and twisted in front of him. He felt the weight lift from him, the pressures of his life recede. As his breathing slowed to nothing, he drifted within the crystal sound.

Anton stared at the flickering candlelight. He was in his new room, Master Jedrowler's old bedroom. The mage had kept a spartan bedroom, claiming it was for sleeping, not enjoyment. There was a single bed, a wardrobe, and a nightstand with a pitcher of water.

In the doorway, a Spirit was singing the song of understanding and magic. Turning his head, he saw CynLisa in the brown stuffed chair next to the bed, one of the large archive's books on her lap.

Anton shifted and sat up. CynLisa smiled and closed the book. "Good evening, are you feeling better?"

Rubbing his eyes, Anton said, "A slight headache. But otherwise, I feel fine."

"And the circle?"

"The channels are closed."

"All of them?"

Anton nodded as he reached for the glass. "I'm not letting anything back or forth, not until I understand what is going on."

"Anton, we need information. You can't shut off everything."

Anton nodded as he sat his glass down. "I know, but I'm waiting before I restore the circle."

"Restore?"

"I learned a lot from the Living Magic."

"I'm sorry, Anton, this is all my fault. I thought you would be able to handle it." She looked down at her folded hand on the book, "I didn't think of the fact you don't have your fear under control. I almost killed you."

Anton recalled the events after his meeting with the Mage Master. He had accompanied CynLisa back to the archives, where she introduced him to the vault of Forbidden Knowledge. The vault was a pillar of crystal that disappeared into the granite of the mountain. Here, knowledge deemed dangerous was locked within the lattice of the crystal.

Only a Cyn could guide a mage to the knowledge they sought, and only a mage could command the magical energy needed to travel the paths of crystal. Anton slipped into his trance and called the Living Magic to him. The magic flowed through him and carried him into the crystal, with CynLisa leading.

He found the knowledge, and CynLisa allowed it to flow into the young wizard. As the information grew, Anton understood what Master Jedrowler was doing, the power he was playing with. That was when everything went wrong.

Anton panicked as fear filled him. The fear caused the magic to leave, and he found himself trapped in crystal, unable to move and unable to breathe. He tried to recall the magic, but his fear drove it farther away, which increased his fear.

The rest of the circle felt his panic and reached out to help. Without the complete spell, there was nothing they could do, and his panic feed into them, which in turn came back to him. It was a vicious circle, and Anton had no choice but to close the channels.

As he sealed the channels and resigned himself to his fate, a calmness rose in him. He knew his death was imminent. Instead of fear, he felt peace. It was then he saw the Spirits.

Five Spirits came through the lattice and enveloped him. As they did, the magic returned. He doesn't know how it came to be or how the Spirits moved through the crystal, but he regained control. With the Spirits there, he reached deeper into the magic and was almost overwhelmed. He felt the mage channels burning. He was approaching a magical backlash.

That was all he recalled until he awoke here.

Anton looked at CynLisa and nodded. "No, I almost killed myself." He sat up and stretched. "My fear, my phobia, is preventing me from completing the spell. The magic knows what is needed. The Spirits know. They have told me."

CynLisa looked at Anton skeptically. "Magic doesn't speak, and the Spirits are only able to communicate in a rudimentary fashion."

"Master Jedrowler understood them." He waved his hand to dismiss that thought. "Magic talked to me. The Spirits sang to me. There is a language to both of them, one I'm not understanding." He threw his covers off and slid to the edge of the bed. "Master Jedrowler must have something in his notes."

"Jed did research on speaking with the Spirits, but nothing about magic."

"Magic speaks. It's alive. We know that. It can speak, trust me. The problem is I'm ruled by fear, just like Master Jedrowler, the Mage Master and you keep telling me."

CynLisa shook her head. "The archives say people who have been touched by magic, like you, have a hard time distinguishing between what was real and what was hallucination. You were near death. Whatever you thought you heard was your mind trying to make sense of what was happening."

"Magic wants me to unify the circle. That's why I was in the nexus, the center of the spell."

Anton stepped away from the bed and went to his wardrobe. He didn't say anything as he pulled out a student robe. He looked at CynLisa who sighed and turned. He took his time, folding the sleep clothes, slipping the robe on, and tying the belt around his waist. As he knotted the rope, he looked at CynLisa's back.

"I need to know everything about this Legion."

"Why?"

"Magic is scared of Legion. The Spirits are more than terrified. I need to find out why. I need all the information locked away to understand the Legion effect and avoid it."

Lines of white, blue, red, and orange flowed to life. They slowly resolved, forming a rainbow. Ambrus half jerked, half shuddered, before he regained control. This was the path Mage Kytril taught him. He stretched out his arms and allowed the black wind to lead him. The different planes were streaming by, multicolored ribbons of lightning that wrapped through the astral plane.

White pinpoints flashed in and out of existence. Some raced. Others crawled. He reached out and touched a few. They settled on his finger and danced. Slowly, he pulled his hand in and looked at his forefinger. Millions of points of light danced, and sound rose from their sparkles. The silvery points were talking, speaking a language he could not understand.

As he brought his finger to his eyes, the Vlynies swarmed, streaming from his fingertips to his face, covering his eyes. Images formed, and a story unfolded.

At the base of Wintermist Falls, the Spirits of Wintermist maintained a constant vigil.

Ambrus's body started to shake, his mouth went slack, and he started to drool. He fell, but the spirits cushioned him. On the cold hard rock, he laid, his limbs twitching, his eyes rolling into his head. Words streamed from his mouth, but no one was there to hear his prophecy.

Ambrus opened his eyes. He felt like he did after one of his fits. He didn't question the milky white light or that the stairs were not shrouded in mist.

He lifted himself on his hands, mumbling, “I need to see Anton. He needs to know.”

Ambrus’s arms gave out, and he struggled to lift himself, to pull himself toward the stairs. He managed to lift his head and mumbled. The effort was too much, and he laid it on the hard rock. Sleep took him and spun him into the abyss of dreamlessness.

Spirits moved from the mist and draped themselves over his body. Others circled, looking up and down the gorge, the entire time emitting a crystalline gibberish.

Chapter Twenty-Four

Day Nine

The incessant pounding woke Anton, and he muttered for the intruder to go away. He had spent the night reading the scrolls CynLisa had brought him, retiring when sunlight crested the eastern mountains.

Anton rolled over and felt himself falling, his arms instinctively flailing the air. He hit the floor, and the air whooshed from him. He shook his head and blinked rapidly to adjust to the bright glare of the morning sun. He turned from the window and tried to bury it in the base of the couch. It was easy to fall back into slumber, a contented smile on his face.

He jerked awake as the pounding came again. The pounding had an urgency. Rolling to his feet, he moaned and stumbled to the door.

Anton opened the door to find Ambrus Diamox, his arm upraised to knock again. The scholar's hair was a mess, his clothing rumbled, the fur collar matted. Bags under his eyes gave him a haunted look.

"By the gods, Sire Diamox, what happened?"

"Anton, good you're awake." Ambrus stepped past the youngster. "I was hoping you would be up." He crossed the room and poured a drink from the decanter of wine. After taking a large swallow, he set the goblet down and turned to Anton. "Oh please, close the door. There are strange people around this time of the morning." He started pacing. "I've had another prophecy, and it concerns you. Keep in mind I'm new at this, so I'm not sure what it means."

"Ambrus, please sit down."

"Oh yes, thank you, I will, but you need to listen." Ambrus stopped pacing. "I had a talk with Mage Kytril, and he taught me to meditate, how to reach out to the Vlynies' home."

Anton crossed to the couch and sat, indicating for the scholar to join him. "I'm sure that was interesting, sire, but what does that have to do with your condition?"

"My condition?" He looked down and noticed his clothing. "My, my, I must look dreadful." He shrugged and stepped in front of the couch. "Come, lad, let us sit. Enough walking around, you don't look well rested." He sat on the couch and leaned back. "Ahh, so much better."

Anton fidgeted, waiting for Ambrus to continue. When nothing was said for a few minutes, Anton prompted him.

"So what happened to you?"

"Oh yes, what happened. You need to learn patience. In your profession, you need it. Well, like I said, I learned how to meditate. And last night, I did it."

Ambrus leaped from the couch and started to pace. "I left my body. I went to where the Vlynies dwell and had a vision. A vision of you!" He turned, pointing his finger at Anton.

"I'm going to die?"

"No, you're not going to die. At least I don't think you are. The vision wasn't that clear."

Anton scowled. "You're not being very reassuring."

"I'm sorry, lad, remember this isn't an exact science."

"Ambrus, what did you see!"

Ambrus looked at Anton and blinked. "Ahh, that's just it, it's not what I saw as what I was shown, or I should say told. The Vlynies are not good at telling us things, but they did tell me this." He took a deep breath. "Wintermist Wall is under attack, and you're standing on Wintermist Bridge. There is blood pouring from you, from your side actually. The sky is on fire, and lightning is crashing all about. Suddenly, the bridge starts to shake and crumble. You scramble for the mage school, but pieces of the bridge fall away. The Spirits are crying, but they make as much sense as the Vlynies, so I don't know what they're saying.

"The Priestess of Odium is on her side of the bridge. I don't know where she came from. She throws you a rope. You ignore it and keep working toward the opposite side of the bridge."

"Do I make it?"

"Make it? No, the bridge crumbles, and you fall into the chasm."

Anton slumped against the back of the couch. Ambrus ignored Anton's reaction. "This is great. It is the most wonderful thing that could happen!"

"How could you say that? I died!"

"What? Oh, the vision. I wasn't talking about that. It's great I remember the vision."

"Ambrus, I hate to dampen your enthusiasm, but your vision shows that I fail. I don't find the spell, and Wintermist falls to the attack."

Ambrus stopped pacing and sank to the couch. "You're right. I never thought of that." He appeared to think for a moment, then slapped Anton on the knee. "Don't worry."

"Don't worry! Mage Master Gardner trusts me, and you tell me not to worry."

"The future is not set in stone. This vision gives a warning. It means something. It tells us something. If we figure it out, you will change the future, and this vision will not come true."

"Ambrus, I don't have time to decipher your visions. In three days, they will be here. I need to find the secret to the spell."

Ambrus looked at Anton before replying, "I don't expect you to interpret my vision. That's my job. You need to do your work. Now answer this. Is there any reason you would be on the bridge?"

"No!" Anton was quick to answer.

"Are you sure? Perhaps your ritual needs to be performed there."

"Master Jedrowler would never have me going near the bridge or any height."

"But you were up on the plateau."

"That's different. I didn't have to look down. Besides, being up there is no different from being here. We have nice solid rock under our feet, nothing that would give way like the bridge."

"You're afraid of heights!"

Anton sheepishly nodded his head. "All my life. My Da couldn't send me into the loft to get hay for the animals. I slept on the lower floor and never helped with the apple harvest."

"Hmm, I wonder, the Spirits could be saying something about your fear."

"I don't know. What I do know is that I need to find that spell. So if you will excuse me." Anton rose and walked to the door.

"Of course, I need to get to work on this vision. I wonder if CynLisa can help me."

"I'm sure she can." Anton opened the door for Ambrus.

Ambrus stopped and looked at Anton, "You know you need to get over that silly height thing. When you do, you can take a leap. It's wonderful to fall among the Spirits." He turned and left.

Anton stared at the scholar's retreating back, then slowly closed the door. He stood a few moments, his exhausted mind failing to function. Ambrus's words reminded him of something, but it was being elusive. The harder he tried, the further away it slipped.

Giving up, Anton headed for the workroom. He sat at the desk and pulled out the battled journal. He had only skimmed through it still, parts stuck in his mind. He flipped through the pages until he found the passage he was trying to recall.

Master Jedrowler had been at a recently discovered crypt and talked of finding notes on a spell that eventually lead him on his life-long pursuit. *Soon my dreams of protecting the land will be a reality. It can't happen soon enough, since the feeling of dread has been growing. I fear for the Spirits and all in Wintermist. Last night, my old dream returned. Fire rained down on Wintermist, and I watched the bridge crumble. In the dream and even now, I feel the blackness in the north creeping this way.*

Anton leaned back in the chair and ran a hand over his weary face. The date of the entry was thirty years ago.

There was more, but he was so tired he barely kept his eyes open. Even as the thought of bed ran through his mind, sleep carried him to oblivion.

Sasha climbed down from the wagon as the brewmeister brought it to a halt. Soldiers were marching in unison in front of their barracks, the sergeant yelling cadence.

As Sasha made her way to the rear of the wagon, another group ran passed, each looking younger than her. She knew recruits and older fighters were assigned here, but she had never paid attention to how young or old they looked. Now, with an invading army growing closer, the youthfulness of many of them surprised her.

To one side, she saw an older fighter showing a lad barely old enough to shave how to handle a sword. The child swung, and the veteran easily blocked him. The older man grabbed the kid's sword hand and held it up, shaking the arm to emphasize his point.

She heard swords clanging, quarter staffs clacking, and officers yelling. She had never seen this much activity at Wintermist Wall. The soldiers had always moved at a sedate pace, relaxed, never a sense of urgency.

Sasha had accompanied the brewmeister today, with little effort at convincing her father to let her hand out the baked goods. In all the years her father had been donating, this was the third time she had accompanied the deliveries. The other times, she had looked on the soldiers as crude and unrefined. Between her association with Duncan and the conversation with her father the previous night, she saw them with new eyes.

"You think they want this war?" her father asked as he settled in his chair. "The youngsters may be excited, but they have never seen a man die in battle. The older ones, they know. They have watched friends cut down and viewed an enemy end a promising life."

"Then why do they want to fight?"

Bran stopped with his jarda halfway to his mouth and looked at his daughter. "Did you even listen to what I said?" She opened her mouth, and he cut her off. "They don't want to fight. They need to. If they don't, who? You think your friend Ambrus can stop this horde? Will any of those philosophers of yours be able to hold a sword?" He gave a chuckle.

"They don't know how to fight."

"My point. They're willing. They just don't know how. Now who makes it so you and your friends can sit around and have your great discussions?" He pointed in the general direction of the wall. "People who willingly go where you and they fear. Oh sure, there are some who do it because they love a good fight, but most do it because they feel it's their duty or they want to give back to the kingdom. Many want to be sure their families are safe.

"Soldiers are no different from you and me. Some are good, some are bad." He now took a drink of his jarda. When he put the mug down, he looked at his daughter and smiled. "What are you planning?"

Through her hemming and hawing, he got out of her that she wanted to help Duncan. She pushed her father for what happened to the weaponsmaster in the war. He wouldn't answer but suggested she talk to the man herself.

"What if he won't talk?"

"Do what you do to me. Keep badgering him until he has to do it to shut you up." Bran smiled at his daughter and stood up. Before she could respond, he kissed her forehead and disappeared to his bedroom.

Now she was handing out sacks of fresh-baked bread and cartons of sweet pastries and helping with the other donated items. In short order, the baked goods, meats, and kegs of ale were unloaded. Sasha jumped from the wagon and told the brewmeister she would make her own way back to town. He dismissed her with a sly smile.

Sasha stopped one of the soldiers and inquired on Weaponsmaster Pentock. He indicated the weaponsmaster was behind the set of barracks near the gatehouse. She thanked him and headed in the indicated direction.

The road was clogged with wagons, animals, and people fleeing the approaching army. The guards at the gate were searching wagons and checking people. Sasha made her way through the throng of refugees and wondered where they were all going to go. The city's inns were already full, camps were springing up along the shore, and the open space in front of the temple was overcrowded.

Between lack of food and the increase in people, the market was running out of the basics, and prices were climbing. Her father had enough to last a week, but if this became a protracted engagement, they would be short on essentials.

Sasha found Duncan with three other men gathered around a strange contraption made of wood and metal banding. To her, it was a conglomerate of wooden pins, posts, crosspieces, twisted rope, and gears, all mounted on wheels. It looked like those overgrown crossbows she could never remember the name of. A hundred paces away, there was a dragon-shaped target with short javelins scattered around it and stuck in it.

One of the men was scratching his head. "I don't know, Weaponsmaster. We can up the tension, but I don't know if the arms will hold."

Duncan sighed as he looked at one of the men who was bald and had thick arms. A heavy leather apron covered his broad chest. "Do you have any metal flexible enough?"

"No problem. But I not have anything to replace the wooden pins and dare not be enough time to make ones."

Duncan rubbed his face. "We need more power." He indicated the target. "We're only sinking the bolts two inches. We need to do better if we want to puncture the gas bag."

The first man said, "My men will take a shot when they see the opportunity."

"No!" Duncan's voice was crisp, with an edge of anger. "I want no one shooting that creature within one hundred paces."

The third man, who was dressed in brown breaches and wore a rust-colored shirt, ran his hands over the contraption as he studied the framing. "This will penetrate chain at one hundred fifty paces. How powerful does it need to be?"

"A fire lizard's skin is tough and elastic. I have watched crossbow bolts bounce off at fifty paces. I've penetrated one at forty paces, but it had expanded most of its gas. The ballista needs enough force to penetrate . . . Let's say plate at one hundred paces."

The first man shook his head. "Those pins won't hold." The pins he was referring to were the size of a man's forearm and passed through the twisted bundles of rope. "We cock the machine to its fullest, and something will give."

"Ironwood would work," the third man said.

The first man shook his head. "There's no ironwood."

"I know where there's a stand, just an hour ride from here."

Duncan looked at the soldier and nodded. "Grab some men. Pick up saws, axes, and a cart. Bring back as much as you can cut in a day."

The soldier nodded and started to turn when the master carpenter spoke, "Take extra axes. You'll need them with ironwood."

Duncan looked at the other two men. "Get your teams to work on the modification. I'm going up on the wall to determine their best position."

Duncan turned and almost ran Sasha down.

Sasha gave a weak smile. "Hi, I, ahm, delivered some bake goods and thought I would say hi."

"This isn't a good time."

"Well, I was hoping you would have a few minutes. We haven't had a chance to talk lately."

"I need to check on things, figure out where these ballistas should be placed."

"That's okay, Weaponsmaster," the carpenter interjected quickly. "It will be hours before I move them up onto the wall. Need to be careful when you break them down. Those twists of rope could hurt you if they let go."

Duncan shot the man a look while Sasha's face brightened. "Good, you do have time."

Duncan was looking uncomfortable. "Well, yes, a little bit. But I don't think it would look proper for you to be seen alone with a single man."

Sasha got a mischievous smile on her face. "Is the big bad sword swinger afraid of little ole me?"

"I just don't want anyone to get the wrong idea. I worry about your reputation."

Sasha laughed. "The people of this town know me. They know I have set more than one guy straight on where my purity stands."

Duncan saw no graceful way out. "On the condition we walk along the lake. It's private but in plain view."

Sasha took Duncan's arm. "Lead on, oh mighty warrior."

"You've been around Ambrus too long. You're starting to sound like him." Sasha laughed as they headed for the lakeshore.

They walked along the lake in silence, each lost in their own thoughts, but enjoying the company of the other. Their meandering took them closer to the falls. As they approached, Duncan stopped and brushed off a seat on the lake wall. From where they sat, they could look at the lake and see the mist rising from the falls. They watched people traveling the roadway and the bridge, but none of the sounds of daily life reached them. Only the gentle slapping of the waves on the shore filled the air. A scent of clean air was carried on the wind, and the sun slanted on their face.

As they enjoyed the warm spring sun, a piece of the fall's mist broke free and came closer.

Duncan finally spoke, "I like this spot, so peaceful. I've been coming here at night to relax."

The crystalline music of friendship softly settled over the area.

Sasha looked up at him. "It's hard for you to relax."

"What do you mean?"

"There is something about you, Duncan Pentock, something I can't explain. You're more than a simple weaponsmaster. You have this thing about you I find tantalizing."

Duncan turned his head away. "You're not going sentimental on me, are you?"

Sasha laughed. "Don't worry, brave warrior. Remember, I don't find sword swingers alluring." She turned his head toward her. "I consider you a friend."

Duncan gave a wan smile. "I can get used to having a smart mouth lady as a friend. It's better than the moon-eyed ones in court."

"I'm glad you feel that way." She gave a dramatic pause, "I'm worried about you."

"Don't be, with Xantrawler's defenses, I'm as safe as anyone. As for the dragon, I'll have him taken care of."

Sasha shook her head. "I mean another way. I sense the hurt, see the pain in your eyes."

"I don't know what you're talking about." Duncan's voice was flat, emotionless.

"Don't shut me out, Duncan Pentock! My father knows, but won't talk. Ambrus, well, if he thinks something should be a secret, the Queen's own inquisitors couldn't get it out of him. The few soldiers I know claim to not know anything."

"We're a tight-lipped lot."

"Yes, and you're the worst. Duncan, I want to help. No one will tell me what's wrong, what happened. They say you have wounds that haven't healed."

Duncan jumped to his feet. "It's my business. My own personal torture."

Sasha stood, but did not touch him. "It does not have to be, not with friends. That's what friends are for. Your friend and brother warriors. We're here to help each other."

Duncan snapped his head around at her words. The words of Swordsman Kentrell sounded in his ears, *"If you can't go to your brother for help, who is there?"*

The Spirit started singing the song of sharing.

The old swordsman was right. Who do you talk to when you can't talk to your brothers? Duncan felt his chest tighten, as it always did when he thought of the Valley. His eyes stared across the lake but saw neither water nor shore. The Queen's troops marched past his eyes, many being helped by comrades and others being carried. Only a few were able to move without assistance.

"Duncan, what can be so bad you won't talk, not even to your closest friend."

Mixed with the notes of sharing, the song of trust enveloped the two.

He needed to tell someone. Someone needed to know the truth. The healers had talked to him when he was recovering, but they never fought, never took a life. They didn't know. They wanted him to talk about the Valley, to share his pain. Since the war, he had tried. He talked to others who had been in battle, but none understood.

"No one understands, not even Xantrawler. They think I should move on, act like nothing happened. Some suggested I see a mind healer." He dropped his eyes to the ground. "I'm not crazy."

"Your friends are too close, but at the same time not close enough. They may have been where you were, but did they experience it to the degree you have? I know nothing about being a fighter. Tell me and I will see it in a different light than your friends. Duncan, nothing can be as bad as you are making it out."

How little she knew. Her whole life spent in a quiet city, hearing the glorifications of war from her uncle and sitting in the protected environment of the Screeching Owl. He shook his head. Someone had to know, why not her? Sasha was just a woman, someone he would never see again. Maybe if he told her, a sort of confession, he could get rid the demon enough to make the nightmares stop.

"I killed my own men!"

Sasha's blood froze. The air became the coldness of deep winter. The Duncan she knew could not have done what this man just said.

The crystalline voice sang of acceptance, of understanding. The Spirit moved closer.

"Duncan, I . . . I don't . . . I don't believe it!" she shouted the last. "There is no way you would have killed your men."

"Because of me, they're dead."

"Duncan, it was war. People die."

"They were slaughtered! A massacre of my own creation." It sounded so trite, so self-centered, but it was the truth. He was the weaponsmaster, so he was in command. He gave the order. And he sealed the Nine's fate.

The Spirit's face was full of concern, filled with empathy. It reached out and touched Duncan.

Duncan stiffened. His face contorted with grief. This was the truth, one that needed heard. A warning to others who play gods with men's lives. He knew Sasha would hate him, but someone needs to know the truth and tell the kingdom what transpired that day.

"Men die in war, but mine had no choice. I ordered their death." He turned from Sasha. His fist pounded the rock wall.

Sasha touched his shoulder. "Duncan, I don't know what happened. You need to tell me."

The Spirit ran its hands over Duncan in a loving caress as it returned to the song of sharing, of grief shared, of love and understanding.

Duncan opened his mouth, then slowly lowered his eyes, his head dropping. For five years, he had remained silent. For five years, he kept the secret. Now this woman, whom he has known for a few days, wants to know what happened. She wants to help. "How can you want to help? Why do you even want to be near me?"

"Because I'm your friend. Friends stay beside you in the bad times as well as the good."

"I had friends once," his voice was hoarse, just above a whisper. "My men, I considered my friends. They fought beside me, defended the country with me." He ran his hands over his face. "As I told you at dinner, swordsmen and warriors are family." His mind raced as he thought of the times spent with his men. They had always been there for each other, always helped each other through the bad times, the loses, and the deaths.

Duncan looked at Sasha, his eyes glistened with moisture. "My men were getting a well-deserved rest when the order came."

He took a deep breath and in a stronger voice continued, "We were called upon by the Queen's Lord Marshal to do a simple mission. A troop of the Queen's men was camped in a valley, mostly injured and recovering from battle wounds and sickness. The Underdwellers came out of the ground with a fire lizard, with no warning. They had our men trapped in the valley."

"The battle of the Valley. The one where you were made a hero. The bards sing about it all the time."

Duncan scowled, "A fool's hero." He put his hands down and leaned on the wall, looking toward the mage school. "It was a simple mission I turned into a slaughter. Do the bards sing of how my men lived through the war then I killed them in the valley?"

"Stop that!" Sasha snapped, "You may be able to get away with talking like that to others, but not around me."

"You will see." Duncan's eyes saw the past, the lay of the valley, and the hundreds of the queen's troops filing out through the narrow pass.

"We killed the fire lizard and defeated the Underdwellers, with few casualties. The Queen's men were a different story. They had been taken by surprise. They fought, but too many had already been injured in other fights. Now the injured were killed by Underdwellers or flamed by the fire lizard. Our arrival made it possible for them to escape."

"That doesn't sound too bad. The bards made it sound like a full scale war. As one put it, 'all the battles of the war rolled into this war within the war, the battle of the Valley.'"

Duncan gave a laugh. "That little skirmish was the prelude. We had most of the queen's troops out when the ground opened up, and two fire lizards and scores of Underdwellers poured out. Two fire lizards, and one is hard enough to control. How they controlled two, I will never know." He rubbed his hands across his eyes. "I immediately saw what was happening. Across the valley, holes were opening up. Not only did they have troops coming out, but many machines of war. Underdwellers poured from other holes riding strange creatures. This was the most complicated battle plan the Underdwellers ever used. They were going to erect a base in the middle of our country.

"We stood between them and escape from the Valley. If they got control of the valley, they would have a foothold. Covering the pass, they could hold our army at bay. They would have captured land that we could not regain without massive loss of life." He saw the valley now, saw the Underdwellers exiting their burrows. He kept his eyes closed as he watched and revisited the massacre.

"I sent a detachment with volunteers of the queen's troop to take care of the fire lizard on the left flank. I warned them not to puncture the gas bag, stressed that point. As they moved off, I reformed my men. We needed to hold the pass long enough for the queen's men to get away and reinforcement to arrive."

As he talked, the past came alive. He felt the chill, heard the growls and cries of the Underdwellers, the shouts of his men as they took up position. He was there with his men one last time.

"What about the queen's troops, couldn't they fight?"

"Not many were in any condition to fight."

The pass was narrow, a low rock outcropping on one side and a steep-sloped hill on the other. A creek flowed through the center, not more than hip deep. The entire valley was open, offering little cover. What trees there had been were used long ago.

"Did you have a choice." It was a statement, not a question.

Duncan shook his head. "If we had turned and ran, everyone would have been cut down."

"And the Underdwellers would have the land," Sasha's voice faded away. There was just him and the Valley. He talked, the story pouring out of him.

I brought my horse around and shouted to my lieutenant. I wanted the second platoon cavalry to form up in front of me. We were to drive a wedge through the mass of white, orange, yellow, and green creatures. I then turned to my second, Duke Royfound, "What do you think?" Nothing Xantrawler had taught me had prepared me for this type of massive attack from these creatures.

Duke Royfound shook his head. "I've never seen so many of the various species working together. Look, in the back, the orange creatures are experts at riding. The yellow goblins bassads are good at close quarter fighting."

I nodded. "They learned. Mounted fighters in the front, foot soldiers behind."

"With missile troops in the rear." He shook his head. "Fight them like any human enemy. The gods know they're using our tactics. I wonder who managed to get them to work together."

"Worry about that later. I want a horn of a dilemma. Take the right flank. When they finish the fire lizards, I'll have the detachment attack the left flank. The second platoon cavalry will charge the center. I'll stay with the foot soldiers and hold the pass."

The valley was a box. The farthest end was a steep hill with springs that formed a lake of blue. The stream flowed south, weaving through the valley, to pour from the pass we stood in. The narrow pass was the only exit.

The last of the queen's troops left. The only fighters were my men. One company against hundreds, thousands, of Underdwellers and two fire lizards.

I was talking with my captain when a voice called my name. Looking down and around, I saw a full platoon of dwarvish fighters complete with dwarvish throwers. Many were wounded, and a number wore makeshift bandages on their head or arms. All were covered with mud and gore.

"We the Goldlief clan and ready to serve, Weaponsmaster." The one talking wore the patch of the clan's Warboss.

"Are your men up to it? You look done in."

"Ye mean these little scratches?" His clan laughed. "We ready to fight, Weaponsmaster."

I gave him a curt nod. "Warboss, I want throwers up on that rise. Shoot anything that doesn't look human or dwarvish. But don't shoot the fire lizards. The rest of your platoon hold the rise."

The Warboss turned to his dwarves, "You hear! We part of Pentock's company. Show them what Goldlief clan can do!"

As the dwarves moved off, Corporal Wheatfield and his squad ran up. His squad had nine mixed fighters in it. His sergeant had been killed in our last battle, and I had planned on promoting him during our break.

"Weaponsmaster Pentock, the last of the queen's troops has left the valley."

"Good, stand by." I gave him a slight smile. "Sergeant." I watched him stand a little straighter. He was a good man, as were the other eight.

I turned my horse and started to give orders when the left flank lit up, and heat licked the side of my face.

The left flank had punctured the gas bag. Unfortunately, they were on top of the creature. The scene was one of devastation. A number of Underdwellers were dead or dying, but so were my men. On the ground were fiery bundles that use to be human beings. I saw the ones still alive stumbling around, half blind and their skin burned black. The Underdwellers were the first to recover, and they started to hack my men to pieces.

I don't know what happened. I think madness grabbed me. I growled and turned to my captain. We looked at each other and understood. There could be no breakout. We were vastly outnumbered, but we had to hold the pass and pray reinforcements arrived soon. "We stop them here! Not one Underdweller is to leave this valley. They want our kingdom then they will pay the price."

I knew what I was saying, what I was committing my men to.

"We stand together!"

"Yes, sir, we will."

"Captain, no quarters."

My captain smiled. "Of course, Weaponsmaster." He held his sword high and shouted, "*No quarters!*"

The call rang up and down the valley as my men moved to engage. Behind me, I heard the words, words that I have never told anyone about. It was Sergeant Wheatfield.

"Okay, you nine, you heard the weaponsmaster. No quarters, now hear me. We protect Pentock to the last. He has a battle to run, so you keep him safe. Any of you slack off and I will personally see you out back of the latrine!"

"My vow and my oath to Odium was to serve and protect Weaponsmaster Pentock!" It was the feminine voice of Gillanna Blue. She had joined my company many months previous and was a chosen of Odium.

"I am not allowing anything past my ax!" It was Quen Lon's voice I heard next, "By my honor, I swear to you Sergeant, I will protect the Pentock!"

"Agreed?" Sergeant Wheatfield said. "Then we swear the oath! Weaponsmaster!"

I turned automatically, my mind on other matters. I heard, but paid no attention. This time, when all nine spoke as one, I responded automatically.

"Our oath till death is to protect and shield Weaponsmaster Pentock and hold Lashtar safe. So we all vow!"

"Heard and bound." Then I turned back to the valley, not realizing what I had done. That was when I heard the other female in the group, Katrice Cobbler.

"The thrice-damned creatures took my husband and children. They will not take me from my family this time."

I stopped listening and urged my horse forward. I charged. I shouted orders, and my buglers and drummers sounded them out. I moved through the mass of creatures, and soon, my sword was dripping gore.

It is believed the Underdwellers come from two or three different species. Interbreeding has given us brown, green, and even yellow scaly-skinned Underdwellers. Some have tough leathery skin, others hard carapace like bugs. Some had long stringy white hair. Others were bald. What they had in common were razor-sharp teeth and talons, eyes adaptable to the underground, and a howling that screeched on your nerves.

My horse was a well-trained battle steed, and with pressure from my knees, he was up on his hind quarters, his front hooves flashing. The wet sound of his blows reached my ears. Even the best trained team of man and horse can't withstand the onslaught of the magnitude surrounding us. It wasn't long before I found myself unseated. I regained my feet as the nine surrounded me. With a battle cry of my own, I plunged into the fray. To my right, I heard the high-pitched whine as my horse lost its own battle.

The fire lizard slid from my mind, but a jet of flame that flamed the outcropping of the dwarves reminded me. Small bodies scurried, dragging injured companions to safety. Those not injured attacked. Thrower bolts struck the fire lizard's mouth, nose, and one eye. Gore ran from countless wounds in the underbelly, none deep enough to penetrate the gas bladder.

In battle, there is never a want for weapon. Spying a long bow, I sheathed my sword, plucked an arrow from the quiver of an unmoving man, and focused. Without a command from me, the nine shielded me, giving me the time I needed to aim and shoot. The arrow was true and hit the soft spot on a fire lizard. The arrow sank to the feathers, lodging in the joint where the front legs joined the body. I had the angle right, and it hit the gas bladder. Because it had been flaming, it had little gas, just enough to explode its chest. Its feet collapsed, and it slammed into the earth, the mouth reflexively snapping at death.

As I pulled my sword, I saw one of my men drop to his knees, a wound in his side. The creature cruelly twisted its weapon, yanked it out, and pushed the man over with his foot. Then it used the fallen soldier as a stepping stool.

I screamed. I pushed through the crowd and rammed the point of my blade between two bony plates over its chest. Greenish yellow blood streamed from the wound, and the creature looked at me, disbelief in its slowly dimming eyes.

"Get behind us, Weaponsmaster!" It was Jasphan Lumber, and he was a mountain of a man, over six and a half feet tall.

I looked to my left, and Sergeant Wheatfield was blocking blows with his shield.

"We got you, sir." I looked to my right, and Bodice Cain stood, gore dripping from his helm, mixing with what I believe was his blood. "Move back to where you can command. We can hold these creatures. Just tell us what to do."

I found myself behind a wall of nine, even our bard, Tallen Drone, took out the occasional Underdweller. He held a sword in one hand and a horn in the other. When I shouted orders, he blew the horn to relay the message to other horn blowers and drummers. It was hopeless. There were too few of us and too many of them. I started using tactics I had been taught but never thought I would use. I used tactics Xantrawler had taught in his fantasy wars, ones we laughed about. They worked.

My captain was fighting straight in front of me, his left hand gone, the stump spurting blood. I watched Sergeant Wheatfield go down when he moved to protect me from a rear blow. I could not stay here, not behind them as they died to protect me. I moved forward, grabbed my captain, and shoved him back. His face was pale, his eyes glazed. I brought my sword around and caught the creature he had been fighting and cut it from crotch to sternum. Before I could do more, I felt myself being surrounded by the nine, Wheatfield hobbling with a twisted leg, blood pouring from the wound in his side.

Direhound Silverrose went down as he took one out low. I stepped up and stood over him, swinging on a third. I never saw the club. It crashed into my shoulder, driving me to my knees. I felt *a sword slide into my side and I felt the blood soak me.*

Then hands were pulling me back, and someone shouted, "Pentock is down. Fulfill your oath. Protect the weaponsmaster." The remainder of the nine closed around me. Behind us, I heard the horn, a battle horn playing the sound of attack.

It was one of ours.

"That's all I remember till I woke in the healer's tent, bandaged from countless wounds, broken arm, smashed leg, and a couple of back teeth missing." Duncan rubbed his face and shook his head to clear it. Sasha sat, not saying a word. He waited for the outburst, the condemnation. He took a deep breath and continued,

"I found out that Queen's Knight Fensin brought his men into the valley. He was a new knight, just received his spurs, and it was his first patrol. He was assigned to a quiet area, one with no fighting." Duncan snorted. "His move saved me and the survivors of my company. He held the pass until an entire battalion of the queen's men came rushing from the east. To the south, Weaponsmaster Hendrel brought his company. And by midday, another force of the queen's troops arrived. You want heroes? There's many from that day. Just not me."

Sasha was quiet, digesting Duncan's story. Her father was right. The bards didn't have half the story. Looking at his hands, she saw the thin white scars. His nose was not straight, and she recalled that he walked with a slight limp, one a casual observer would not notice. His eyes were hollow, his skin pale. He kept fit, but there was an aura of emaciation about him.

"You are a hero." He looked at her as she added, "You prevented the Underdwellers' escape."

"My men did because they followed a fool, a fool who led them into a massacre!" He thumbed his chest. "I killed every one of them!"

The Spirit slid from the outburst, then moved to place its arms around Duncan.

"You took them on a mission to save people, and they went willingly."

"Only because they didn't know what they were getting into."

Sasha was getting frustrated. Every time she used logic, he went off on the emotional angle of . . . She smiled to herself. Ambrus's rules of debates, when the enemy is not responding to logic, hit him with emotion.

The Spirit sang softly with its crystal voice, the song of calmness.

"I should have come up with a battle plan that would not have put my men at risk."

"But it was a glorious battle. It's one they sing about to this day."

"Glorious battles bring glorious death and grieving families!"

Sasha blew her breath out in exasperation. She broke with traditional debate and used the only thing Duncan understood.

The blow caused Duncan to see stars. His head snapped as the flashes of light danced before his eyes.

"Of all the self-centered, egotistical people I have ever met, you are the number one." Sasha was on her feet, her red hair billowing as the wind blew from the gorge. "Oh poor, Duncan, lost his men in a war. *War where men die*!"

Duncan wiped a trickle of blood from the corner of his mouth. "You don't understand. You don't know what it's like to watch your men die." Duncan came to his feet yelling, his eyes growing moist. "The Nine sacrificed themselves for me! I was supposed to watch over them, not the other way around."

"You are so full of yourself. You don't even know what you're saying."

The Spirit changed its song to one of listening, of awareness.

"I know what I'm saying. I have been telling myself the same thing for the past five years."

"Wallowing in self-pity you mean."

"What?"

"Do you see grieving families? I may not pay attention to things military, but you would have to be dead not to have heard of the Battle of the Valley. I know about it since my uncle regales us with stories of the battle and the great Duncan of Pentock."

Sasha got right up to Duncan, pushing her chest into his, coming face-to-face with him. "You gave your men and the Nine something no one else could. You showed them there are things worth dying for, fighting for. Things outside of us that make us great. Uncle told me how the families who lost sons or husbands were treated like heroes. How the kingdom expressed their gratefulness for the mothers who gave the ultimate sacrifice.

"Remember the Hero's Nine and their sacrifice!"

She stepped away from him. "Are you honoring their names, like you implored everyone else?" She, over her shoulder, added, "All you're doing is taking from the dead the honor they deserve. They were brave men and women and from what you told me, thought highly of you. In case you weren't paying attention to your own words, listen to mine! Your men kept putting themselves between you and the battle. Anytime you were in danger, they were there to protect you. You did not force them. They did it willingly!"

The Spirit sang the song of acceptance.

Sasha turned back to Duncan. "Don't you see, you didn't lead these men to their deaths. You did something wonderful. You took your teaching as weaponsmaster and taught it to them. You instilled in them honor and devotion." She took his hand and looked deep in his eyes. "The Heroes Nine did not get death. You gave them something."

"What?"

"Corporal, excuse me, Sergeant Wheatfield, he learned how to lead men, and he passed your learning to his squad.

"Katrice, her family was killed by the Underdwellers. Not only did you give her a way to vent her vengeance, you gave her a family, a family she was able to care for and love.

"Quen Lon, I understand he was a thief. He didn't die in some back ally with a knife in the back. He died defending what he believed. You gave him honor.

"Bodice Cain came from a poor family. I'll bet his parents are proud for the first time in their life. That's something no one can take from them.

"Shall I keep going? Are you as thick headed as I first thought all sword swingers were?"

The guilt of the past five years crushed Duncan. The emotions he kept buried, the fears, and the nightmares erupted. The truth, the truth he shared with no one, not even himself, rolled over him. His heart stopped, his vison blackened, and he dropped to his knees and screamed.

"I took their oath. I bound the Nine to their death!"

The Spirit was slammed by the emotional outpouring. It let out a shrill screech that echoed into the gorge. Within the mist, the cries of hundreds of Spirits came. On the bridge, people paused as they felt sadness and despair wash over them.

Sasha felt tears erupt as she watched the weaponsmaster bury his head on the ground. She had opened a wound that festered. A wound that would kill as quickly as any sword thrust.

From deep within the gorge, a bass crystal voice rang out. The song of empathy spread across the water, followed the shore, and settled around Sasha. As it washed over her, she felt Duncan's pain. She felt it drive her to her knees to face the haunted eyes of the weaponsmaster.

"I watched them die saving me."

The Spirit returned and settled behind Duncan. From the falls, the Spirits of Wintermist started singing the song of love, the song of healing, and the song of closure. The Spirit at Duncan's side echoed the song.

"Before she died, Gillanna Blue gave me her personal blessing from Odium. She finished her fight, died without the protection of her god." He cried as he continued, "Direhound stood in front of me, never once moving, even when the spear came directly at me. He took it full on.

"Tallen kept playing the orders I was trying to get out, orders that moved the company into better position, sealed breaches. He kept playing, even when he was shot full of arrows.

"Jasphan held me. He made it so my men could see me. He was the last. He took the sword meant for me, swung me like a doll, and used his body as a shield.

"Why did they do it? Why didn't they defend themselves?"

Sasha reached out and laid her hands on his shoulders. She felt his body shaking as emotions shook him to his core. She didn't hear the song of empathy, but she felt Duncan's pain, felt it pour into her. She couldn't explain, but she knew somehow, someway, she was helping the man. She wrapped her arms around him and pulled him close.

The Spirit settled around, holding the contact he had with the female. The anger, the self-hate, he drew from the weaponsmaster, through the stronger person and into his ethereal being. This was positive energy of a powerful kind. It could and would destroy, but it was energy created from love. The Spirit fed on this energy and in return sent compassion, acceptance, and love back.

Duncan hung onto Sasha, hung on for his life as he started to speak. His words were random, jumbled. He jumped from one subject to another. He started a new thought in the middle of another. Sasha let him go, held him, and rocked him as a mother rocks a hurt child. She allowed him to ramble.

After a time, he slowed, and the words finally stopped. They were leaned up against the wall, and Duncan had his arms wrapped tightly around Sasha's shoulders, his face buried in her hair. He lifted his head and sniffled.

She smiled at him.

"I have lost men, but never in this number. Before the Valley, we kept each other's morale up."

Sasha's voice softened, "And then there was none."

"There were a few, but like me, they were in a state of shock, disbelief. Part of it was because we thought we should be dead."

Sasha laid her hand on his arm. "All these years, you have never talked to anyone, let anyone close."

"I felt empty. I needed someone to blame."

"So you blamed yourself."

Duncan nodded as he looked at Sasha's hand on his arm. He lifted his face and looked at her. Her face held no hatred. There was no disgust. There was just caring, understanding. He reached for her and pulled her into his embrace. Her arms went around him, and he gripped her tight. There were no tears. They had been shed. There was warmth flowing into the empty space he thought would never be warm again.

The Spirit's song was one of contentment.

After a while, Duncan leaned back, still holding Sasha. "You're a good friend, Sasha Magnate. Also, you have a terrific right hook."

Sasha laughed and reached up with the sleeve of her dress to wipe the blood from the corner of his mouth. "Duncan Pentock, you're the most frustrating male I have ever met."

Duncan put his arms on Sasha's shoulders and clasped his hands behind her neck. He looked deep into her eyes and moved closer until their foreheads touched.

"I have never met a lady like you. The women at court are bubbleheaded, interested only in social climbing. You, I find exciting."

"How exciting?" she asked softly, feeling the heat rising to her checks.

Duncan smiled. "I would like to get to know you. How about another dinner date?"

"Without Ambrus?"

Duncan pulled back to Sasha's disappointment, but his throaty laugh, which she had never heard, made up for it. "He's not my employer. I think I can say it will be the two of us."

Sasha smiled. "I would like that, where would we go?"

Duncan got a mischievous grin on his face. "An evening cruise from the Lakeshore Parlor." He enjoyed watching her eyes roll. "Before that, I have one thing I need to do. What's your favorite flower?"

Duncan reveled in the look of astonishment and happiness on Sasha's face.

The Spirit sang the song of happiness. From the gorge, happiness spread.

Midday meal was over, and Duncan had missed it. He was use to missing meals. He was heading to the wall to talk to Xantrawler. He had duty.

Before reaching the steps of the gatehouse, Duncan noticed a group of recruits near the lake training. They each had a long pole with a metal horseshoe-shaped ends. He stopped to watch the young lads' drill. The sergeant had them running along the lake wall, thrusting up, thrusting down, and thrusting out. Each thrust followed with a yell.

Duncan watched for a few minutes before the sergeant noticed him and called a halt. The weaponsmaster signaled for them to be at ease and asked for Josh Wheatfield. The young man came running and stopped in front of the weaponsmaster and gave him his best salute.

The pair walked a short distance and sat upon the lake wall.

"How are things going, Josh?"

The boy made a face. "Okay, I guess. All the sergeant wants us to do is work with this silly pole. I want to learn to use my father's sword." He touched the short sword at his side.

Duncan took the pole from Josh and held it out. "This is an important, versatile weapon."

"But Sarge says all we're going to do is push ladders over with it."

"True, that's your primary job. You and the rest are responsible for keeping the enemy off the wall. Besides shoving ladders over, there will be others chopping ropes. We also have to worry about siege towers and who knows what other devices this enemy has."

"But they will be on the wall sooner or later. Shouldn't we be working on our sword work?"

"Pessimistic little lad, listen. Once the enemy gets on the wall, you need to stop other borders, as well as fight. Look at this end." Duncan pointed at the horseshoe end. "It has points that will penetrate leather and chain. In addition, you can do this." He placed the horseshoe around Josh's neck. "Give a little twist and you break the neck or send the man falling."

Duncan stepped close to Josh. "See how my hands are?" Josh nodded as he watched. Duncan thrust the weapon and twist at the same time. "You can put a lot of force behind your thrust and twist. Besides the neck, you can grab an arm or a leg." He handed the weapon to Josh who copied the move.

Duncan stood behind the boy, guiding him until it flowed with him.

Josh gripped the pole closer to the head and hefted it. He pulled his sword and gave it a couple of swings. "You could use both at once."

"Not before you learned the basics of both. One trick at a time, youngster."

"But . . ."

"No buts. Recruits follow orders in my company without questions."

Josh's face lit as he smiled.

Duncan looked down and became serious. "Your father was a good man, and I want to make sure his boy grows up to be half the man he was." Duncan sat down and told Josh about his father and the events of the Valley. They talked for a quarter mark before Duncan sent him back to his group.

As Duncan headed for the wall, Kentell Quintal walked up to the weaponsmaster. "Thank you. No one truly knows what went on at the Battle of the Valley. You've given him what he needed. That's more than I can say for a couple of the men, who think it's great sport to pick on him."

Duncan looked hard at the swordsman. "Are those men in our barracks?"

Quintal hesitantly nodded.

"Tell them I want to see them after evening meal on the practice field. Tell them to bring their edged weapons. I am back into teaching."

Quintal smiled. "It shall be a pleasure, Weaponsmaster."

Xantrawler came out of the gatehouse, spotted Duncan, and immediately headed toward him.

"Duncan, how is the dragon slayer coming?"

"The blacksmith is pointing metal tips on the missiles. I have the engineers redesigning the firing mechanism and increasing the tension, and a team is out gathering ironwood."

"Sounds like you are as efficient as ever. Can you be spared for a day to do something else for me?"

"Anything you need, I will."

"I need a scouting expedition to head up the center of Mead. We have little information on that column."

"Heard and bound!"

"I know you don't want to lead, so don't think of it as . . ." Xantrawler stopped, "What did you say?"

"The other day, you gave me a command."

Xantrawler sputtered, "You can't do this! I've worked up a good argument that would leave Diamox gasping. You can't . . . Oh damn! What changed your mind?"

"A good swift smack to the face."

Hearing those words caused the weight of command to lift, even if slightly. He looked Duncan over. "If I knew that was all it took, I would have done it years ago."

"You're not as good looking as the one who hit me."

Xantrawler chuckled. "The good-looking ones have the fun. Since you're ready to lead, I will order your gear moved to the gatehouse."

Duncan shook his head. "Captain Anraye commands my company. Think he would mind a weaponsmaster?"

"When I asked for volunteers to take you in, he was the first and most vocal. He always did take the best."

"Then I will remain there. My bunk is off to one side, so I won't bother the men. We have only a few days to get ready, and I want them to understand how I work."

"We have three days. Anton informed the mage council a candle mark ago."

"Hence, the need for the scouting expedition." At Xantrawler's nod, he asked, "Do we have the full complements of noncom?"

"The company is short one sergeant. Otherwise, all the ranks are filled."

Duncan gave him a strange look. "Still being sly? Never mind. I want my new sergeant to be a swordsman named Kenteu Quintal."

"That's no problem. But if you want to gain the man's respect, it would be best if you promote him yourself after checking with Captain Anraye."

"Will do that. When's our briefing?"

"After evening meal, can you make it?"

"A couple of unfinished business, but I will be there." Duncan had a wily smile on his face.

"Good. Assemble your team and have them be at the briefing. I want you to move out before first light."

Duncan nodded then turned and walked away. As Xantrawler watched him leave, he shook his head. For a brief moment, he thought he saw a Spirit around Duncan, but that was impossible. They never ventured this far from the falls.

Chapter Twenty-Five

Day Ten

Ambrus swung the doors to the Screeching Owl open and stepped inside. Outside, the wind drove a cold spring rain against the door. The cheery fire in the corner quickly chased the chill from his body.

As he swung his cloak off, the bartender called out, "Ambrus, it's been a while."

"Been busy, Koaldeck, with this invasion business and all."

"Been busy getting in the way you mean!" a voice called from one of the tables.

Ambrus stepped down to the main floor and crossed to the patron. "Draytack, the last time I saw you, you were running from the city watch."

"That was three years ago, and I was avoiding being caught with a married woman. How was I to know she was the wife of a watchman? Besides, you saw me a week and a half ago."

Ambrus took a seat at Draytack's table. Sitting with him were two other people, a short man with a bald head and a stocky lady with a bad wig.

"I don't remember much from that day. Not only did I forget my vision, but a lot of the day's events."

"Do you remember them now?"

"Well, I remember the one I had last night. Mage Kytril taught me some meditation tricks, and I had a vivid vision."

"Ah, now yea believes what we be telling you all these years," the lady with the bad wig said.

"Well, when you anger a weaponsmaster, watch spirits chase a murderer, then have your own close encounter with the Spirits, you start believing."

"It's about time," Draytack said as he took a drink of his tea. "We have been telling you for years that you had the gift."

"Yea, ye ability and ye knowledge, ye will be the famous prophet we know ye to be."

"Sweet Lileela, I don't plan on becoming famous."

"If not famous, then maybe you can prevent some bad wars. If you had paid attention to your own prophecies, you could have prevented this invasion," Draytack said.

"What are you talking about?"

"One moment." Draytack pulled a small note book from inside his tunic and flipped through the pages.

"What did you do, write down every prophecy I make?"

"Not just yours. I believe if we could gather them all together, we would have a map of the future."

"You're crazy."

"Crazy or not, here is what you said eight years ago sitting in this same room. 'Legion slumbers, but his sleep is disturbed. The king of the north disturbs the killer of gods, and a black river will flow. The Northland has arisen, but their glory will be their fall. The black river is coming, flowing through the range of death. In the south, it shall waste itself on the fall of wraiths.' That's what you said eight years ago."

Ambrus rested his chin in the cup of his hand. "Hmm, I hear the enemy is dressed in black."

"Ye know the unclean and the worshippers of evil wear black. Yea thine souls are even black."

"Could be evil, but I don't understand the wraith thing," Draytack said. "There are wraiths over in Winlow Pass."

"Could this be a diversion?" Ambrus asked. "Are they going to come in at Winlow Pass? That way does open up the country to them."

"Perhaps you should look at the last prophecy you made when you were here," their short stocky companion said.

"I don't see where that fits in," Draytack said.

"I'm not talking about the one you all listen to. I'm talking about the other one." His voice was pitched deep, sounding like two bulldogs tumbling together.

"I don't recall another prophecy, Mckirtchen."

In a perfect imitation of Ambrus's voice, Mckirtchen started speaking, "From the north, the black river flows, consuming all it encounters. The land is corrupted and cries for help. Only the land of the mist can turn the river back, send defeat to the god of the north. The leader of the Spirits lay dead, killed by the blackness of the north. Only the young leader of the mist can save the land by surrendering to his fears."

Ambrus leaned back in his chair, lost in thought. The other three at the table started debating back and forth. Ambrus rolled the two prophecies over in his mind and compared them with the one he had during the night.

Ambrus leaned forward and slammed his hand on the table. Everyone jumped, Draytack spilling his tea. "That goes with the vision." He went on to explain what he had seen.

When he finished, Leeliela spoke, "Aye tis clear to I, the priestess represents faith. Young Anton needs to find his faith."

"No, you're wrong," Draytack said. "Anton needs to go to the temple where he will find the answers he seeks."

Ambrus sighed, "It is a warning. If Anton doesn't cast the second half of the spell, then Wintermist will fall."

"We already know that. You don't need to prophesy it."

The four of them started to argue and debate the prophecies. The bartender threw down his rag and shrugged as another patron left his table and joined the debate. He called back to his cook and told him to prepare finger foods for he knew these debates could go on for hours and no one would want a normal meal.

King Rathveil sat in the council chamber and watched his advisors, some still rubbing the sleep from their eyes. He sighed. As the lives of the tribes improved, many of the higher-ranked leaders developed bad habits. Tribal leaders use to be up before the sun, ensuring their people's well-being. They would have attended to unfinished business from the day before, checked on the less fortunate, and made sure the stock was okay.

Now they were lucky to be out of their chambers many sun marks after dawn.

Shaman Charara Kilar was sitting in the chair normally occupied by Warlord Thwart. The warlord was standing at the end of the table, waiting to give a report, then return to his men. Kilar normally did not attend these meetings, but King Rathveil had been asking him to come, so he understood the workings of the council. It had been reinforced to the shaman that he was to take over the council when Rathveil was not able to.

King Rathveil's other plans were for Charara to rule the land of Mead as governor. The shaman was the perfect choice, dedicated to the welfare of the people, honored the gods without being controlled by them, successful when new tribes joined Terrapin Xon, and, most important, he was not a user of the unseen forces. With the knowledge Wintermist contained, the wrong user of the Unseen

Forces could become very powerful. That person may not have the people's best interest at heart.

As the advisors settled down, King Rathveil sat straighter in his ivory seat and looked around. "The invasion is going as I planned. In a few short days, we will completely control that land. Before Warlord Thrawt gives his report, Shaman Kilar has some new information."

King Rathveil nodded, and Charara nervously got to his feet. He held a slip of parchment, and his voice squeaked, "This morning our spies in Wintermist attempted to send a message but were surprised by one of the officers and had to eliminate him."

Charara stopped and took a sip of water. His hand shook slightly as he brought the cup to his lips. Putting the cup back down, he continued, "Our man who eliminated the Force Shaper Jedrowler is being held captive. Our other men report that he has revealed nothing and has remained loyal to Terrapin Xon."

Rathveil looked at the general. "As soon as the wall is taken, I want Nigel found and rescued. If he's dead, find who killed him. Bring them here for execution."

King Rathveil nodded for Kilar to continue.

"The message added that a Wintermist Force Shaper, Jedrowler's assistant, has been assigned the job of finishing the spell. We do not know if this person is what they call a mage, but we do know he is an expert in our Unseen Force and will teach the other how to work with it."

King Rathveil leaned forward. "That cannot be allowed to happen. Their duty is clear, kill this mage."

Kilar made a note and sat down. King Rathveil turned to his general.

"The warlord of the North Wall has amassed three hundred fighters. He's using them on the western column with constant raids," the general said.

"Are they going to be trouble when you attack?"

"No, except for the user of Unseen Forces he has with him. That user has been able to function within our user's environment. This user is as strong as some of Czarana's voices."

"We don't need to worry about users," Tribal Chief Dztard said. "My men have handled them in the Thanatos Range."

King Rathveil nodded. "I am aware of that Dztard. That's why I'm not sending your men to Wintermist."

Tribal Chief Dztard pounded his fist on the table. "My men are ready, and they're the best!"

"I know. That's why I'm reassigning them. After we finish the Southland, your troops will lead the way, the Keepers of the Sacred Scrolls."

Tribal Chief Dztard smiled.

Warlord Thrawt grumbled, "I may need those troops."

"Warlord Thrawt, you have ten thousand of our best warriors."

"My eastern column has been losing fighters. At the dwarvish mines, they were repelled by the dwarves and a handful of humans. They have been delayed by landslides, missing bridges and ambushes. Someone has rallied the people and recruited fighters. I don't think they will make the battle at Wintermist."

"Can you take Wintermist with what you have?"

Warlord Thrawt hesitated, "Yes, but . . ."

"Then I want Tribal Chief Dztard's troops transferred. The Lady Yolanda may be locked up, her powers stripped. But I fear the Czaran may be planning something."

Warlord Thrawt pushed himself upright. He frowned, but he knew better than to argue. "As you wish, it shall be done. May I return to my troops?"

"Yes, Warlord. One more thing, have our users drop their field when they get near Wintermist. None of our Unseen Force is to be felt by these mages. It appears these mages can use it given enough time."

Warlord Thrawt clenched his teeth, bowed, and left the room.

Xantrawler strode from the gatehouse, heading for the lone robed figure leaning against the top of the wall on the western side. Mage Master Gardner was intensely staring north, his eyes open, but unseeing.

"Good evening, Xantrawler," the Mage Master said.

"Evening watch, Sholem, but I wouldn't call it good."

Mage Master Gardner's eyes came into focus, and he looked at Xantrawler. "Something more than your normal worries?"

Xantrawler nodded. "We found Captain Anraye dead in a storeroom this afternoon."

Mage Master Gardner turned back to the north. "The invaders were cloaking themselves with Ancient Magic. Now they've dropped their shroud."

Xantrawler leaned on the wall. "Why drop their shroud? It makes it possible for us to see into their camps."

"They have magical sentries. As soon as I get close, they clamp down with shields." He gave a humorless smile. "Simple shields, one our students could bypass with no thought."

"Will they still be here when Mage Anton predicted?"

"Day after tomorrow, but he doesn't know the exact time."

"Jedrowler's spell?"

Mage Master Gardner sighed, "I know Anton can do it, but I fear we're out of time. Any mage compiles lots of notes through their lifetime. Much is nonsense, and it is that nonsense that he has to work through. Anton could spend hours, even days following the wrong trail, a time we don't have."

"So it's hopeless."

"No, Jedrowler was his mentor for five years. They ate, worked, and slept together for the past six months. Their entire energy was tied up with this spell. He knows how the man thinks." He looked at Xantrawler. "Above that, there are two other things. The lad knows Ancient Magic, and starting tomorrow will be teaching us about it."

"That may be the edge we need. When we lose you mages and they still have theirs, then all could be loss. What is the other thing?"

"The Spirits of Wintermist are with him."

"I don't understand."

"Neither do I. Only that Jedrowler told me once that the Spirits have accepted Anton as their own."

Chapter Twenty-Six

Day Eleven

Anton unrolled the parchment and placed a weight on one end and a mortar on the other. He stepped sideways, tilted his head, and looked at another parchment spread on a pile of similar parchments. He looked at it for a couple of seconds then turned to the table behind him and picked up the parchment lying there. He glanced at it then allowed it to fall to the pile at his feet.

He moved back and forth, placing spells and notes in piles around the workroom. At the same time, he jotted his own notes and placed them in the center of the table. Occasionally, he would consult one of two books lying on the desk. While doing this, he mumbled various phrases he recalled Jedrowler using.

He knew many doubted him. The previous evening, he had voiced this concern to CynLisa. She told him he was letting worries interfere and suggested he meditate and isolate himself from those fears and doubts.

Anton took her advice. Later, he arose in the middle of the night and set to work with renewed vigor. Looking through his notes on what he pieced from Master Jedrowler's journal, he found a pattern.

He sent a student to Mage Master Gardner as he needed the sage advice of the Mage Master.

A knock on the door broke his concentration, and he called out to enter. He heard movement in the outer room then Mage Master Gardner stepped through the doorway of the workroom.

"I see you've been active."

"Mage Master, I'm glad you came."

"Anton, what did I tell you?"

"I know, Master, but this is not informal. I need your advice as Mage Master."

Mage Master Gardner walked to the table and looked at the piles of parchment. Occasionally, he would pick one up. He studied Anton's notes and glanced over components on the table.

"It appears you have everything for the first part of the spell."

"Yes, dust, leaves, branches, and such."

"And?"

"There are two minor spells that are important. Without them, the whole thing falls apart, unraveled. We have the spell of binding," He picked up parchments from various piles. "It's modified for each form of magical energy." He handed the spells to Mage Master Gardner.

"Then there is this one." From a large pile, he took a parchment. "This spell of binding I used to bring everyone together in the circle. This spell made us a whole."

Mage Master Gardner nodded his head. "This makes sense. Each of these spells and components represented each type of magic's source of power."

"Yes, that way, not only were we bound, but so was our magic."

"What is the other spell?"

"The spell of calling used to bring the Spirits into our circle. The Spirits and I are channels. We link the circle with the land and each other."

"So you're linked with the Spirits?"

"In a way, yes. I am channeling power and information from the land through them. No one knows it, but Mage Jedrowler spent years preparing the Spirits to be part of this spell.

"Water is everywhere. That is why they are perfect. That's why the falls is the heart." Anton picked a book up from the table. "This is Mage Jedrowler's journal, and this is what he wrote:

"'*The Spirits will be the channel for the land. They are already part of the land. They have been for over three thousand years. They are the only choice.*'"

"So this first part of the spell will bind you with the land, and the next part will bind the land to you."

"And we will work as a team, able to use the other as a source of power and energy. That's the simple explanation anyway."

"We know this. What we don't know is how. Do you know how to bind the land to you?"

"I don't. No one can."

Mage Master Gardner turned and stared at Anton, his arm with the parchments in it dropping. "Are you telling me there is no way to finish this spell?"

"There is a way, but not the way you put it. I can't force the land, or in this case, the Spirits to bind with me. They have to do the binding."

"How?"

"I think it's already done. At some point over the years, Jedrowler set this spell into motion. All we need to do is complete it."

Mage Master Gardner looked at the parchment in his hands, then looked over the notes in the middle of the table. "How do we complete it?"

"I believe I need to cast the spell of calling, cast the spell of binding, and use the spell component. I need to find the component."

Mage Master Gardner was rifling through the parchments, looking for something he had seen. "I believe you have it right. I knew you would do it."

"I'm not finished, Mage Master. I need to figure the component out."

"You will, you will. My advice," he looked up from flipping through the parchments, "look for something simple and symbolic." He went back to flipping through the sheets. "Jedrowler said part of this spell was based on old magic and it was always simple. Perhaps that is why it was so powerful. It didn't use up energy on complicated formulas. Ahh ha!" The Mage Master pulled out a sheet of parchment.

"What is it? Did you find the component?"

"No, but here is the last part of your spell. There are three major parts, the binding, the calling, and the spell of completion. This spell needs to be sealed. Otherwise, the magic would fade away."

Anton took the parchment and started scribbling his own notes. "Thank you, Mage Master." Anton hooked his foot around a stool and dragged it closer. "Now I need to make sure I have the proper wording and the proper order." He went on mumbling and writing.

Mage Master Gardner watched the young mage for a while, then chuckling, left the workroom, commenting, "He is a true mage. The rest of the world doesn't exist when you have found your spell."

At midday, Duncan and his party came riding through the gatehouse. All had the eyes of ones who have seen death riding their way. Duncan dismounted, threw a quick acknowledgment to Xantrawler, and turned to his men.

"Have the stable hands take care of your horses, then get over to the mess hall. If the cook gives you any trouble, send him to me."

The men dismounted, and Duncan turned back to Xantrawler. He signaled they needed to talk in private. They entered the gatehouse and went to Xantrawler's office, a small room on the same level as the battlements. One window looked out on the mage school and the barracks. Another showed the woods and farmlands to the north.

Xantrawler poured them wine then sat down. After taking a sip, he asked, "What did you find?"

"It's worse than we were led to believe. If this is a third of the force, then your wall is not going to stop them. We couldn't begin to count the number of fighters, both on foot and mounted. We did count twenty siege machines pulled by strange beasts and many supply wagons and one wagon definitely for mages. They're the only ones I know who have brightly painted and decorated ones. But that is not the worst."

Xantrawler waited while Duncan took a drink. He heard fear in the young weaponsmaster's voice. "It's a dragon, not a fire lizard being flown by magic."

"We were planning on that."

Duncan shook his head. "We were not planning on the size. This dragon is three times larger than any fire lizard."

Xantrawler looked at him in disbelief. "You must be mistaken."

"I wish I was. We didn't see it at first, then it came flying from the west. It had a full-grown steer in its claws, a steer! It ate the whole thing. I don't care how well disciplined your men are. They're going to panic."

Xantrawler took a moment before he found his voice, "Can you kill it?"

Duncan shook his head. "I don't know. Its hide may be thicker than I planned. Even if it isn't, a thing that size must have a large gas bladder. At a hundred paces, the fireball would wipe out the men on the wall."

Xantrawler put his goblet down and stood. He walked over to the window and looked at the barracks. His men were coming and going on various missions. He could hear the sound of the blacksmith. In the distance, he watched a mage exit the school. The bridge had people carrying on their daily lives.

Duncan stood and looked out the window. "We don't have time to evacuate them all south."

"The mages wouldn't go anyway," Xantrawler said. "Our only hope would be to hold them at the wall as long as possible." He looked at Wintermist Bridge. Without that bridge, the enemy would need to use ferries to cross Lake Mead.

"Duncan, do you think the engineers could bring the bridge down?"

Duncan stared at Xantrawler.

"You want to cut off this side of Wintermist?"

"It would buy us time. The chasm is too wide to bridge, especially if there is a constant rain of arrows."

"And the dragon?"

"I have faith in you. I'm worried about the army."

Duncan looked at the mage school, the many openings that would need sealed. Xantrawler followed his eyes and laughed. "Don't worry about the school. The mages will take care of the entrances. We must deny them the use of the bridge. Their only recourse will be to cross by boat, and we have enough catapults to sink the boats."

"We could meet them with our own boats. But we need to have everyone on this side take their boats across or burn them."

"Good idea. Keep in mind that I want to make destroying the bridge a last ditch effort. We will do our best to defend the wall."

Duncan thought for a moment, his hand on the hilt of his sword. He paced the office, looking at the floor. "I want the eastern side cleared. The only ones east of the gatehouse will be me, the ballista operators, and volunteers from my company."

"That will leave that wall vulnerable."

"We'll try to prevent that. But I want as few men as possible. We may not survive."

"What do you have in mind?"

"We'll hit the dragon on its closest approach."

"The fireball will kill you and your people."

"I'm hoping not. I hope he has expelled some of his gas." He looked up. "I want tarps, lots of tarps. Soak them with water, the wetter, the better."

Xantrawler smiled. "So when the dragon breathes or explodes, you have a place to hide." Xantrawler picked up a pile of papers from his desk. "Let's get this plan in motion. Dispatch the fastest riders we have. I want them to spread the word up and down the coast, as far as they can in a day. We need to evacuate as many people as we can. Talk to the engineers about the bridge. I hate to do it. But to save the land, we have to. I'll see the dwarves. They have the best, and many of them have worked with this rock, carving the rooms in the mage school.

"Effective right now, you are my second in command. Are you ready?"

Duncan felt his stomach knot up. He had come full circle. He was now involved in another hopeless battle, with the death of him and his men certain. He looked at his old teacher and knew that this time, he wasn't alone. "I'm a weaponsmaster of the Queen. I'm always ready."

Xantrawler smiled as he laid a hand on Duncan's shoulder. "Good. I'm off to see Mage Master Gardner. We have limited time, so I want him to send a mage message to the duke's mage."

The bloated sun hovered over the summit of the mountains, casting their shadows across the plateau. Anton was in the only sunny spot, the pedestal in the center of the pentagram. He gazed over the lake. He knew how high he was, and his fear tried to rise within him.

He felt the tremors inside, his heart churning like the Hellion River at the base of the falls, his breath caught in his throat. All he needed to do was turn away from the view, and he would forget the height, but he chose not to. Everyone was right. He needed to conquer his fear. If he was going to finish the spell, he needed to channel and focus more magic than any mage before him.

He had come to study the pentagram. Jedrowler's notes indicated the pentagram was instrumental in both halves of the spell. *"It will hold the magic for linking both sides. Without all being linked to their channel and their channel linked to them, then the channels cannot link."*

He did not understand what Master Jedrowler was saying, and after examining the pentagram, he was not closer to a discovery. It was a standard pentagram, except for the pedestal in the center. The runes around the circumference were runes of protection, the alpha and omega runes, containment runes and shielding runes. He tried studying the runes woven among the lines inside the pentagram, but they were indescribable.

Anton figured they were ancient, and he needed a rune book from the archives. As he was not ready to return, he sat on the pedestal and looked out over the land. When he felt the shakes start, he pressed his lips firmly together and resolved not to give in to the fear.

As the sun sank lower, he felt a cool wind move across his face. He smiled. This was the longest he had stared his fear down. He dropped his eyes, not from fear, just exhaustion from fighting so long. He found he was not as afraid of heights as he had been. He wasn't ready to go near the edge, but it didn't bother him to sit back and look over the land.

He sat, looking at the graceful curve of the rune inside the pentagram. A curl started, then arched up and over, before it descended and circled to form a tail. Anton marveled at the way the mage had flawlessly drew the Nath.

He stopped in midthought. He had read the rune. It was not an ancient rune. It was a normal rune meant to be read from inside the pentagram, from the center. He stood and looked at the other runes. Slowly, he turned and read the runes interwoven among the inner lines.

Master Jedrowler had danced with these runes. He had twisted around each one, moving right to left, spiraling in with them. Anton recalled how Master Jedrowler danced around and back, how the power bent in and flowed through the center, flowed into the channel. The dance activated the power of the runes.

Anton stopped. The last three runes were different. The line spiraled closer to the center when the last three jumped toward the outer rim. Then they stepped back to the center. He thought a moment and remembered Master Jedrowler had not danced around him. The mage had dance in front of him, then repeated the steps.

He hopped down and knelt, looking closely at the nearest rune. He could see the individual grains and feel the roughness of the design. All the rest had been fused by magic, became smooth as glass, and part of the mountain. These runes had not had their power activated.

Anton sat back on the heels of his feet and translated the meaning of each and the order they were laid out. Community, One, Union. He shook his head. This was too simple. If all that was needed were these three runes to be activated, then it could have been done the night of the spell casting.

Master Jedrowler wrote, *"It needs to be a multistage spell composed of a number of spells and steps."*

"Multistage, not two stages, not two parts," Anton said as he stood and stepped up on the pedestal. Still talking to himself, he slowly turned, looking at the design of the pentagram, the layout of the runes, and the position of the various participants. "The first phase was not one spell, but a number of spells. Each cast by a person in the circle. I focused them, and Master Jedrowler combined them."

He stopped turning and looked at the last three. "A community of one, a union," he whispered. "We are not a Legion, many who are one. We are a union, one who is many. I made us a union by not allowing us to fuse into one. We can operate as one, but we are individuals."

Before he could think of what he was doing, Anton slipped into his mage trance. He breathed in the mountain air and felt the wind swirl. The magic was there, and he took it into him.

Moving to the outermost, nonactive rune, he started the dance. He had watched Master Jedrowler practice the dance many times, so Anton knew the steps. He spun around the first rune, magic gathering to him, growing in potency, power pounding the ether. He heard the throbbing of the drums.

He moved closer to the center and danced with the second rune.

Power flared, and he channeled it, built it, and shaped it. He circled the rune of Union, and magic flashed down the line of the three. They shimmered as their energy grew. Anton reached into the mountain and drew on the magic there. He brought in the magic of the plains to surround the positive energy flowing from the falls.

Anton danced to the first rune and turned, sweeping his arms up. The three runes rose, spinning with the power of their magic. Phantasmal energy danced in a pulsating cylinder around each. He danced with the power as power crackled through the mountain. Jedrowler had laid these runes so a lone mage could activate them, bring them to life, and start the next step of the spell.

The young mage swept onto the pedestal, and with a simple flick released the magical energy he was channeling. The three runes flared, then settled into the mountain top. As they fused, magic flashed through the rest of the runes.

As the last rune came to life, Anton held his arms up. The power of the circle came to him, and he held it. It was there. He felt them. He didn't just sense them. A small part of the people had been left in the circle that night and now flowed within the circle, passing through him.

As he brought his arms down, Anton watched the magic recede. Power settled out of the pentagram and returned to where magic comes from.

Anton stepped from the pedestal and looked at the containment rune. As it slowly dimmed, it dawned on him that Master Jedrowler had not needed him for this spell. The containment rune would have held the magic. Then the mage could have danced among the runes and activated them before stepping onto the pedestal and channeling the power. He could have cast the spell with no help from Anton.

Mage Jedrowler did not need Anton. He wanted him. Why?

Fatigue raced through him as his body and mind responded to the massive magical manipulation he had just done. He had not realized it at the time, but the casting drained a lot from him. He had come close to a magical backlash.

It was done. He was one step closer to completing the spell. Now to return to the workroom. As his stomach growled, he amended, eat first. Food was the curative for magical exhaustion.

Anton started to turn when he heard the sound of metal sliding on metal. He threw himself to one side and shouted the incantation for a shield.

"I need as many men as you can spare to evacuate the coastal area," Xantrawler was saying to the image of the duke. He was in Mage Master Gardner's office, and the Mage Master had set up a connection with the duke's mage.

"I have a number of squires and retired soldiers I will send. The Lord Marshal will be along in the morning with my . . ."

The duke's words were interrupted as three spirits sailed through the open window and circled Xantrawler. They tried to push him toward the door.

"What the? Gardner have you seen this behavior before?"

"No. Something has them agitated, and they want you somewhere."

Xantrawler turned and opened the door, and the Spirits rushed him down the hallway. He shouted to his personal guards, "I don't know what's going on, but assemble the men."

As the small procession made their way down the hallway, the Spirits nudged people aside. As they made their way up another set of stairs, Xantrawler realized where the Spirits were herding him.

The short sword bounced off the invisible barrier around Anton's arm. He rolled away from his assailants. As he came to his feet, he found himself facing two of the Wintermist Wall's guards.

"Nice move, user of the Unseen Forces, but it will be the last." The man was stocky and just slightly taller than Anton. His accent was heavy, coming from deep within the chest. The other fighter, who was small and agile, smiled and pulled his sword.

"Yout be hood and we make quick, udder wise yout suffer."

Anton could not keep his eyes on both, and his shield spell had been a quick small one. The spell did not hinder his ability to cast, but he was close to magical backlash. He dodged back and brought his shield arm around to block the slash from the smaller opponent.

He had no choice. He brought his arms up and twirled his hand, unleashing a blue bolt at the first assassin. Before the bolt impacted, an amulet the man was wearing glowed, and the blue bolt rebounded at Anton.

"King Rathveil say South and user's spells ould fail against his god-given power, surrendor yout fate."

Anton saw the other assassin out of the corner of his eye. He shouted a command as he whirled. Mage force shot out, throwing the assassin across the rocky floor. Immediately he turned to block a sword stroke. He never saw the dagger in the other hand.

Struggling backward, Anton clasped his left hand to the wound. He felt the first trickle of blood soak through his robe and run down his side. Pain lanced through his brain, breaking his concentration. The shield on his arm drew his personal energy, and he knew he was on the edge. Only Weaponsmaster Xantrawler's training had kept him alive this long. As one of the men rushed him, he swung his left arm and blocked the blow. The blow drove him to his knees and jerked a scream from his lips.

Years of training at the mage school and working with Jedrowler took over. Anton let himself slip into a trance, a light one, but enough for his purpose. The pain slid from him, and his mind cleared. He slowed time, watching the two Northlanders advanced. Their movements reminded him of molasses pouring from a jug.

A sword swung and he made a gesture and magic formed a barrier between him and his enemy. The sword struck the invisible shield as he formed the words for the next spell.

Flames erupted under the feet of the two fighters, and they danced away.

Anton slowly got to his feet, his trance keeping the pain at bay. He knew he was losing a lot of blood and could feel his breathing becoming labored. He had one thing to do before he died. He opened the channels in his mind, poured out what was happening and burning the image of his assailants in his mind and the mind of each person in the circle. He was going to die, but everyone in the circle was going to know who did it. As he felt the rest of the circle respond, he felt the backwash of anger. He felt frustration as they tried to figure out where he was. They clamored for his location, but Anton wanted everyone to know the enemy. He blocked all sight of his surroundings and let the assassin's face fill his vision.

"You killed my friend, murdered him like you have me. Before I die, I will have you burning in the tenth hell of the abyss."

The Northlanders stopped, and the leader smiled. "Brave words, you would have made a fine addition to the king's subject. Now die."

"*No!*" Anton shouted as he thrust both hands forward and poured the last of his power into a mage force. Both Northlanders flipped into the air and were flung toward the doorway. Anton dropped to his knees, magical backlash slamming into him, and he barely maintained his hold on consciousness.

Xantrawler took the final flight of stairs, two at a time. Not knowing what he was heading into, his sword was out. He stopped short of the open door and looked.

Anton was on his face, blood pooling around him. Two of Xantrawler's men were shakily climbing to their feet, swords in.

The weaponsmaster stepped through the door and shouted for the men to stop. Both turned, and with no sign of fear took up defensive postures against their commander.

Xantrawler's pulled a short sword, the movement so swift the weapon seemed to appear in his left hand. His other sword was not a sword of simple blacksmithing. It had been gifted from a dwarvish clan by one of their warriors. The blade was made magical by a mage in the distant history of the world. It was lighter and stronger than other swords, imbued with magical powers he rarely used, preferring to let his own natural abilities do the work.

Xantrawler gave forth his battle challenge and moved to engage.

Xantrawler immediately disarmed the larger of the two, the sword flying to skid uselessly many feet away while the dagger was sheathed by Xantrawler in the enemy's thigh. The weaponsmaster used his short sword to bypass the other's defense and scored a blow across the leather armor. No wound, but the opponent backed away.

Xantrawler turned to the one he had disarmed and caused the fighter to stagger back with a blow from the flat of his sword upside the head. He grabbed the man's wrist, giving it a twist, and heard a satisfying snap. Before the man could scream in pain, he slammed the pommel of his sword into the man's chin. He then jerked the man down, sending him sprawling to the ground.

Xantrawler turned. "If you think you can take a weaponsmaster, then come on. Just keep in mind that I only need one of you alive."

The Northlander hesitated, until a voice sounded from the doorway, "And if you can take a weaponsmaster, then you will have me to deal with." Mage Kytril stood outside the door, energy crackling between his hands and a cloud of Vlynies around him.

"Surrender," Xantrawler said. "There is a whole school of mages below and a barracks full of fighters on their way. With the Spirits on our side, you won't be able to hide."

"You have defeated me." This one's command of the language was better than his companion's. "You will not defeat my king. The might of Terrapin Xon is coming and you shall learn what it means to defy King Rathveil."

The man of the Northland brought his sword up, nodded at Xantrawler, and with a pledge to his king, charged.

Xantrawler watched as his sword slid into the man, the light fading from his eyes.

By this time, others had made it to the plateau. Xantrawler's men immediately trussed up the unconscious foe. Mage Kytril knelt in Anton's blood and rolled him over.

"You needed to give us more information. It took me a moment to figure out where you were."

"I . . . I didn't think you would get here in time," Anton gasped. "I wanted everyone to know who the enemy was. That was more important. Know the enemy and stop them before they kill others like they did Master Jedrowler and me."

"Stop sounding like you're going to die," a new voice said. A man in healer's robes flanked by Spirits stepped through the crowd and knelt. After a quick look, he muttered, "Damn heroes, think they need to die for the cause." He looked at Anton. "I'm not going to fool you, lad, it's bad. I'm a master healer, but this may be beyond me." Placing one hand on Anton's head and the other on the wound, he entered the healer's trance.

Xantrawler had seen master healers at work many times and experienced it once. He knew it wasn't pleasant and Anton was going through the worst pain he would ever experience. He was locked in the trance with the healer and was unable to voice his pain.

Mage Kytril moved beside Xantrawler. "I'm not a healer, but I possess the healer's vision. The lad is hurt bad and has lost a lot of blood. He is also suffering magical backlash, and his body does not have the energy to heal."

"Is he going to die?"

"With so many Spirits, I doubt the specter of death could get to him. What I do not understand is why the magical backlash. He didn't use that much magic during the battle."

Around the rim of the plateau and within the falls, the Spirits of Wintermist sang their song of healing and love.

From the falls, the bass crystalline voice of the Patriarchal Spirit rose. He sang the song of power, sending his own power to the one that needed it.

After being allowed to pass by three of Xantrawler's personal bodyguards, Ambrus crossed Anton's living space. He glanced behind him at the men, each was dressed in plate, wearing long swords and holding pikes.

As he swung his head back, Ambrus caught sight of Helena blending with the shadows in a corner. She never moved, just sat watching the whole room.

Weaponsmaster Xantrawler was taking no chances. Twice, mages had been attacked by assassins, attacked by his own men. He now openly checked his men, verifying who they were and where they came from.

Approaching Anton's sleeping quarters, Ambrus noted the student standing outside the door. He had seen the lad, but never dressed as he was now. He was attired in hardened leather armor, a helm of a dull gray metal, and on his side was a bastard sword. One would not expect a mage to have a sword, especially one as heavy as a bastard.

The student eyed the scholar suspiciously. Ambrus nodded and stepped to the doorway. In the low light from the bedside table, he saw CynLisa holding the pale hand of the boy. From the corners of the room, he heard the song of healing in the crystalline voices of the Spirits.

He was not surprised to see Spirits. Outside, they were still being seen, the waning moon adding an eerie spectacle to their presence. All of them had raised their voice high so that it was heard above the falls. Their voices echoed around the lake.

"Hello, Ambrus," CynLisa's voice was weary, her face drawn, and he noticed lines that had never been there before.

"How's he doing?" Ambrus entered the room. The Spirits turned, their song faltering until they saw who entered.

"Master Healer Fenton says he shouldn't be alive. He claimed the damage and the loss of life energy was far beyond anything he could save, yet he stopped death. He said when he was in his healing trance, it was like someone was with him, feeding him the power he needed."

Ambrus sat on the edge of the bed, placing his hand over CynLisa's. "I had a vision I shared with Anton. The vision indicates a different future. This is wrong. It shouldn't be happening."

CynLisa patted Ambrus's hand. "The future is always changing. What you saw was the future at that moment."

"What I saw showed the attack on Wintermist, showed Anton on Wintermist Bridge."

"Anton won't be going anywhere for at least a week. That is, if he makes it through the night."

"Healer Fenton has his doubts?"

"Anton is not able to replenish his life force. Between magical backlash and his life energy being drawn down so far, he doesn't have the power. If there was another master healer, he could give Anton the energy to make it through the night."

"Healer Fenton can't?"

"He's been drained too much by the initial healing. He'll be back in the morning. And if Anton is still alive, he will do more healing."

Ambrus looked at the young, pale face. He had heard the story. All of the school had, and it was spreading through Wintermist.

When he first met Anton, he didn't think much of the lad, just another charlatan learning to play mage. Now, after accepting there was a force called magic and learning what being a mage meant, he had grown to respect the lad, know the man.

"Will he be able to finish his work?"

CynLisa shook her head. "He won't be awake for another day, possibly two. Then he will be too weak to move. I'm sorry to say we will not have Jedrowler's spell to protect us. Ayndough is ranting about how he was right all along and is blaming the Mage Master."

"Can't any of you find the spell?"

"It's not that simple, and I won't go into it right now."

Ambrus was silent for a long time, just listening to the Spirits in the room. Their song was different from the one the others were singing, but the two blended together. It made him feel refreshed and revitalized.

"Will that song they are singing help?"

"Who?"

"The Spirits."

CynLisa looked around the room, then at Ambrus. "They aren't singing. They've been here since Anton was brought down, and they haven't made a sound."

"I tell you they're singing! That's the song of healing. Listen to the song coming from the Spirits in the falls."

CynLisa's eyes went wide. "Have you become sensitive to the Spirits?"

"What?"

"Only a few people ever hear the Spirits. They claim to understand their songs, what they want. Many times, Jedrowler told us what the songs were about. He saw the Spirits when others didn't and was known to have a number of them around him in times of danger or when he was sick. And he was hardly ever sick." Her voice trailed off.

"The Spirits came to Anton's rescue," Ambrus said. "Master Healer Fenton received power from an unknown source, and we have four Spirits singing the song of healing."

For a moment, CynLisa's face glowed, then her shoulders sagged. She released Anton's hand and slouched back in the chair. "They will keep him alive, but he will never be ready to finish the spell before the enemy arrives. That is if he knew it."

Xantrawler stepped onto the deck of the lakeshore tower. He was exhausted, and his shoulders sagged. It wasn't the work, and he knew it. It was spending the evening grilling his men. He hated casting suspicions on any of his fighters, but he had no choice. He couldn't risk another attack from an unknown assassin.

"It's always bad when you have to suspect your own men," the voice of Duncan floated softly to him from the wall.

Xantrawler walked over and leaned on the wall with the younger man. In the same quiet voice, he responded, "It's something a good strategist would do. Get spies in the enemy's camp and try to eliminate the largest threat."

"Shows they have been planning this for a long time. I fear this may be why the North Wall fell. How many spies were there? How much sabotage was done before and during the attack?"

Xantrawler shook his head. "I only hope I've found them out before they weakened my defense. We don't have much as it is." He straightened, stretching tired muscles. "What did you want to show me?"

"The enemy will be here in a little over a day." He pointed to the northwest where a red glow lit the low clouds beyond the spur of the mountain that reached into the valley. "I would say they are about twenty miles away." He pointed to the north where another large glow danced on the bottom of the clouds. "A little closer, but those roads are better."

Xantrawler nodded. "About where I expected them."

"Did you expect that?" Duncan pointed to the northeast.

"What?"

"That."

Xantrawler shook his head and blinked. He still couldn't make out what his second was talking about. He saw no strange shape, no unusual movement. It was a peaceful countryside.

And he knew what it was, and he felt like a foolish old man.

"There's no enemy camp that way."

"General Klaydon said the enemy split into three columns, and they should arrive at the same time. I do see a faint red glow way off. I would say the enemy is well over fifty miles away."

Xantrawler's smile was unseen in the darkness, but the pleasure in his voice could be felt. "They've been delayed. That means the enemy will be down by a third. If they wait for their eastern force, we may have reinforcements from Gammount."

Chapter Twenty-Seven

Day Twelve

Duncan lowered his end to the floor of the battlement. The last of the ballistas were in place. He looked along the eastern section of Wintermist Wall and watched his men prepare for the dragon. Canvas was laid out on the battlement, barrels of water were spaced at intervals, and extra weapons were placed.

The normal complement of soldiers would be reassigned, half to the gatehouse and half to the lake tower. They would remain until the dragon was destroyed or Duncan's men were killed. For a brief moment, the thought took him to the Battle of the Valley.

He had spent the night at one of the watch fires along the shore. Earlier, he had been talking with his men, asking for volunteers, so none would feel pressured they were to come to the fire. In ones, twos, and threes, they came. By the time the sun rose, every man had gathered.

He tried to talk young Joshua out of being on the wall, but the lad had the same stubbornness as his father. "You need someone to repel the invaders. Me and the other recruits are ready." He brought his shoulders up and stood straight as he looked at the weaponsmaster.

"You don't want us to shirk our responsibilities, do you?" He put Joshua in charge of the lads.

Kentell walked past Duncan with two other soldiers, each carrying strawmen with helms and broken lances.

"Kentell?"

"Morning watch, Weaponsmaster."

"What's this?"

"Well, we'll be short, so me and a few of the lads thought we would make some dummies. Fool the enemy into thinking there's more of us. Might even get that dragon to come at us first. Save the rest of the wall from having to deal with it."

Duncan smiled. "Good idea. Carry on." Duncan turned and started walking the wall. While helping a couple of soldiers rearrange some canvas, a squire came running up with a message that Xantrawler wanted him in the gatehouse. He left his men with words of encouragement and hurried off.

Duncan found Xantrawler with CynLisa and Helena. They had some items laid out on the table and were going over them.

"I'm not sure what these are," CynLisa was saying. "I don't recognize the magic. But I can tell you it's Ancient Magic."

"These mirrors," Helena said, holding one up, "you say they're magical?"

CynLisa nodded. "Once more, Ancient Magic. It's similar to the magic used to send Mage messages. They're like the one the first assassin had. I believe that's how our assassins kept in touch with this King Rathveil."

Xantrawler acknowledged Duncan, "These are the devices we found with our two assassins."

"Have you gotten them to talk?"

"The one who killed Jedrowler is still going on about this great king of his. The survivor of Anton's attack is keeping mute. Helena will be questioning him later."

"Don't expect much. These people are fanatics. They're hard to break," the assassin said.

"How about a mage truth spell?"

Helena shook her head. "Unless they talk, it won't work. Besides, there could be a geste that activates when a spell is cast. Then we lose our informant."

CynLisa set the two boxes to one side. "I'll have Mage Leone look these over. She has worked with ancient devices, so will have the best chance of determining what they do."

Xantrawler picked up the mirror. "How does this work?"

CynLisa pointed to a charcoal stick on the table, "That was with it. So I would say you write your message on the mirror, and it's received at the other end."

Xantrawler picked up the charcoal stick and wrote a brief passage.

Duncan smiled as he looked at the mirror. "Not very subtle."

"The time to be subtle has passed. Remember my rules of engagement. That is an application of one of them."

"An angry opponent is an unthinking opponent."

"Never take anything your opponent says personally. What if he has read your book?" Helena asked

"I'm counting on him being like most kings, sees little combat and lets his generals do the fighting. With luck, he will be angry enough to give us the small edge we need. At this point, I'll take anything we can get."

"How bad do you think it is, Weaponsmaster?" Helena asked.

"If they attack in the morning, by the afternoon, we will be on the other side of the bridge."

CynLisa picked up the two box objects. "Then I had better get these to Mage Leone. They may be something we can use."

Xantrawler watched the two ladies leave before he turned to Duncan. "With everything that happened last night, I haven't been able to fully brief you on my meeting with Mage Master Gardner."

"You said he agreed to evacuate the school and assist in destroying the bridge."

"Reluctantly agreed. He still feels the Northlanders can be stopped."

Duncan walked around the table to stand and look out the north window. This room was one level below the battlement and provided a view on both sides of the wall. Doors on either side lead through small passageways that ran through the center of the wall. He looked at the refugees pouring into Wintermist, mostly farmers herding stock. Others were driving carts filled with the remains of their winter stores and seed grain.

The air still held the smell of wood smoke from the boats that burned through the night. Many fishermen had been reluctant to burn their extra ships, but they didn't have the manpower to sail them across the lake. They understood the danger the abandoned boats held for Mead, so they sacrificed their livelihood to provide for the safety of all.

"We're not the only ones who stand to lose a lot," he said, still staring out the window.

"That's what I drive home to all my students, not just you weaponsmasters."

Duncan turned and looked at Xantrawler. "Nothing drives it home like reality. I saw this scene played out many times during the war, families losing their homes and children losing their parents. Now I'm seeing it happen again. This time, it's not creatures, but man doing it to us."

"Man has been doing it to each other for thousands of years. And thousands of years from now, we will still be doing it."

"Will it ever end?"

Xantrawler shook his head. "As long as there is one person who can control others and craves more power, it will never end. I have seen it played out all my life, from large scale conflicts like this to the petty maneuvering in court."

"I wish I was a simple farmer. All they ask is to farm the land, take care of their family, and have a little enjoyment in their lives."

Xantrawler laughed. "You were born a noble, just like me. You don't know what it's like for them. You may dream their life is idealistic. But in its own way, it's as harsh as ours. The only difference is we have the best food, the best drink, and the best healers."

"How do they endure?"

"The same way we endure. They know no other life. We look at the other and envy them and dream to someday be like them."

"If they only knew what our lives are like, they would be happy with what they have."

"I believe they say the same about us."

King Rathveil ground his teeth as he stared at his mirror. He turned and paced back and forth, Shaman Kilar stepping out of the way to avoid being knocked down.

"Where is he!"

"He should be here soon, m'lord."

A knock on the door announced the arrival of King Rathveil's visitor. Rathveil snapped an enter, and Warlord Thrawt stepped in.

"I hope there's good reason you recalled me. We are only a few hours from Wintermist, and I need to be with my men."

Rathveil ignored the lack of title. "Look at that!" He pointed at his mirror.

General Thrawt squeezed past Rathveil and looked at the mirror. In shimmering black, the barely legible scrawling of the Southland glowed at him.

"I'm not fluent in this uncultured tongue."

"That is a message from one who calls himself a weaponsmaster. He warns us to leave or be destroyed."

"I wouldn't worry. Tomorrow evening, we will be walking the streets of Wintermist."

"This weaponsmaster calls Vella an overgrown fire lizard." King Rathveil slammed his fist on his desk. "And says they kill fire lizards for sport. He has the insolence to promise the mages will roast my pet and serve it at their victory banquet!"

Warlord Thrawt chuckled. "I think I could like this weaponsmaster."

"Tell me the joke, Warlord, so I can laugh too."

"Your Majesty, he is using an old trick. He's goading you, hoping you will make foolish decisions. Ignore these childish taunts."

"He's right, milord," Kilar said. "He may have a mirror and most likely your spies, but the rest is just a bluff."

King Rathveil turned to his shaman. "I don't take threats lightly. Vella is a gift from a god! A god that we will all honor." He swung to Warlord Thrawt. "You, go back. Tell the Force Shapers to keep the field effect down! They are not to erect it until you're ready to attack. When you attack, the first thing you do is activate my surprise. Then you take the wall. You're not to use Vella in this attack."

Warlord Thrawt pulled himself up to his full height. "We can't take the wall without Vella. My eastern column is being delayed and won't be at Wintermist when we need them. Either we use Vella or we wait for them."

Warlord Thrawt held up his finger. "One, setting off your surprise early is no advantage. We don't even know if the men have them planted." He held up a second finger. "Two, the defenders always have the advantage. Without Vella, we have no way to efficiently cut down the defenders and open up an avenue of invasion. With Vella, most of their defenders will either be dead or running. Why do you think their Northwall fell so easily?

"You have eight thousand men. Take the wall and conquer Wintermist!"

"Those eight thousand can be cut down by the defenders on the wall, and I have no reinforcements. You sent my reserves to Norge, remember?"

King Rathveil waved the warlord's concern aside. "If it's that bad after you have tried four times then use Vella for one or two passes. No more!"

"If I wait that long, I might as well not bother. By that time, we will have suffered heavy losses. I like this plan less than the original. My flanks are not covered. The few men I left at the North Wall are vulnerable, and there is a whole city of potential warriors waiting to strike."

"You will do as ordered!" King Rathveil stepped behind his desk and leaned forward. "Those are my commands."

Warlord Thrawt clenched his fist, but he saw the shaman out of the corner of his eyes grip his staff. He relaxed, not wanting to give the shaman any excuse to use his abilities. As a youngster, he had experienced a soul slap from his tribe's shaman. It had been days before the pain died enough for him to move. He could not risk being placed out of action, not with the king out of control with anger. Someone needed to be on the front line who would not be afraid to countermand the king's orders.

"I'll take that damn town for you. I swear I will use all my abilities and resources to succeed."

"Good. Return to your men and prepare. You will still attack tomorrow?"

"We're on time. We'll arrive late afternoon and rest through the night." Warlord Thrawt was smiling on the inside. The king's anger was working in his favor as well as the enemies. King Rathveil was not paying attention to what was being said, only what he wanted to hear.

"Thrawt, please understand, what we get from Wintermist is worth the risk. Carry out your duties, Warlord." As the warlord left, King Rathveil turned to Kilar. "Prepare my entourage. Tomorrow, we walk through the portal onto the courtyard of Wintermist Mage School. I will finally return to the falls!"

As the shaman left, Rathveil walked over to the window and looked at the Thanatos Range. He felt himself calming, the anger leaving. He snapped a look at the mirror and waved his hand. The writing faded.

He turned back to the mountains and muttered, "Soon my destiny shall be fulfilled."

Accompanied by his guards, Mage Master Gardner exited the mage school onto the battlement of Wintermist Wall. He quickly covered the space between him and Weaponsmaster Xantrawler, who waited halfway to the gatehouse.

Two columns of soldiers were advancing toward Wintermist. They were spreading out from the roads, covering the fields. The defenders were encircled in sound echoing from the mountains. The combined voices of men and animals, the creaking of wood, and the thudding of feet, all combined into a calliope of noise.

"They have finally arrived," Mage Master Gardner said.

Xantrawler nodded. "They are everything General Klaydon said."

"Will you be able to repel them?"

"If you are able to neutralize their mages."

"It all depends on this field of Ancient Magic. It hasn't reached us yet, so I don't know how it will affect us."

"Do you sense it?"

Mage Master Gardner paused a moment. "There's nothing. Everything is normal."

"That's not the way it was in the general's report."

"Perhaps they are conserving their power. Magic is not endless."

Xantrawler snorted as he watched the enemy start to set up camp. While watching their movements, he saw the Lord Marshal approaching.

"Weaponsmaster, Mage Master," the Lord Marshal said. Xantrawler watched the man stare at the enemy encampment. He was fidgeting with the buttons on his great coat, and despite the cool spring afternoon, his face had a sheen of perspiration.

"I never imagined it would be so large, so huge. How many men would you say are there, Weaponsmaster?"

Xantrawler did a rapid calculation, "Hard to say with all the movement. The wagons also give it an appearance of being larger, especially the way they are setting them up. I would estimate no fewer than six thousand."

"By the gods, that is a lot of men."

Xantrawler looked at the man. "You have never been to war, have you?"

The Lord Marshal continued looking at the enemy in fascination. "No, during the Underdweller war, I was just a squire serving the Duke of Wayebrin. Not to worry, Weaponsmaster, my father was a great Lord Marshal and served in the Underdweller War. I learned from him and our swordmaster."

"Huh, huh." Xantrawler looked at the Mage Master, who in his youth had been a combat mage. The Mage Master just shook his head.

"This is like seeing one of my father's books come to life. I've read about armies this size. But until you see them, you can't comprehend them. The sheer mass of humanity is staggering. The battle will be glorious!"

"Leading to glorious deaths," Xantrawler muttered.

"Xantrawler!" The weaponsmaster was saved from making a comment he would regret by the appearance of CynLisa. She came running, her hair and robes streaming behind her. She ran up to the three, her breath coming hard and fast. "Xantrawler . . . we know what the devices are."

"Slow down, woman," Xantrawler said, "catch your breath, there's no need to hurry."

CynLisa nodded her head yes as she gulped air. "The devices . . . They are . . ." She paused to try to get more air before continuing.

"Cyn! Remember yourself!" Mage Master Gardner said.

CynLisa looked at the Mage Master and let herself slip into a light trance. Immediately, her breathing slowed, and the flush of her checks disappeared. She composed and straightened up in one smooth motion.

In the monotone of a Cyn, she spoke, "The devices are of an ancient design. Magical forces are contained within, held by a spell. When this spell is dissipated, the magic instantly rushes forth, consuming all within a set radius."

Xantrawler looked at her and arched an eyebrow. Mage Master Gardner quickly explained, "Releasing a large amount of stored magic at once will create an explosion, the size depending on how much magic."

"The magic involved is enough to take out the gatehouse or one of the towers."

"By the gods, that is ghastly," the Lord Marsha said. "How do you defend against something like that?"

"You lock it away under the tightest shields you can," Mage Master Gardner said. "In rooms deep within the mountain." Turning to CynLisa, he said, "Take them there immediately. I want them in separate chambers."

"Wait," Xantrawler said, "I have a better idea."

Mage Master Gardner frowned. "We don't know what spell triggers them or when the enemy will set them off."

Xantrawler smiled. "Return them to their owners."

"Are you crazy!" the Lord Marshal said.

"Not at all. Tonight, under cover of darkness, I will send out a team. They will plant them in the enemy's encampment."

Mage Master Gardner smiled. "Are you sure you're not a strategist?"

"Not much of a difference. This is another rule of mine, never toss a weapon the enemy could turn against you. They violated it, so we use it to our advantage."

"Do you want my men to deliver the devices?" the Lord Marshal asked.

"No, I have someone else in mind. Where is Duncan?"

"Walking along the lake with Ambrus's friend," CynLisa said, "Sasha Magnate."

The Lord Marshal snorted, "A commoner. Know what he has in mind."

Xantrawler's hand fell to the hilt of his sword. "If I ever hear you disrespect the Lady Sasha again, I will personally challenge you. If you manage to defeat me, then you may fight Weaponsmaster Pentock for the honor of his lady."

The sun was setting when a low moan escaped Anton's lips. The nurse the duke had sent was quickly at his side, along with four Spirits. Taking a wet washcloth from the bedside stand, she placed it on his forehead. Anton opened his eyes and looked at the nurse. "There really are angels in the heavens." His voice sounded like he had inhaled a bucket of sand.

"You hush, I'm old enough to be your mother," the nurse scolded. "Now behave. If the master healer catches you doing anything foolish, the gods themselves don't know his reaction."

"I know what I will do." The healer stood in the doorway, flanked by two Spirits. "I'm here now, you may go." He waved his hand at his escort, and his ghostly escorts faded into the living chamber. "I hope you're healed soon, Master Anton. These Spirits of yours won't leave me alone, not even to use the chamber pot."

Anton gave a weak smile. "I have no control over them." Hearing his voice, he asked, "Can I have a drink of water?"

"I have tea I want you to drink. It will take care of that dry throat and help your healing."

As the nurse left to fetch the tea, Anton asked, "How long have I been asleep?"

The healer stepped up to Anton's bed and placed a hand on his forehead. "A little over twenty-four hours."

"Twenty-four hours!" Anton struggled to sit, but the healer pushed him back.

"Lay there. Your injuries were critical, and I'm surprised I was able to save you."

"But the invasion!"

"Is already here. The Northland army is camped a mile away."

"I don't feel that." Anton looked at the Spirits. "You're blocking me. Let it in. I need to channel for the circle."

The healer snarled at the Spirits. "I don't know how to threaten something not alive. But if you care for him, then you will not put any undue strain on him."

"This isn't right." Anton tried to sit up but fell back into his pillow. "We need to get the second half of the spell done. We need to stop the invasion."

"You need to rest! I'm not telling you again. Next time, I'll give you something to make you sleep."

"But I'm so close. I've activated the first stage of the second phase."

The nurse returned with a cup of tea and handed it to Anton. He sipped the hot liquid and tried to appeal to the healer, "Can't you at least let me have my notes. If I finish the spell, we can use it to defeat the enemy."

"You're going to be in no shape to cast any spells for two weeks, if then. Your life force was severely depleted. The only thing that will restore that is rest."

"If I finish it, someone else can cast it, Mage Kytril, Mage Master Gardner. Any high-ranking Mage."

The healer looked down at Anton, then snorted, "Mages, fighters, and fanatics, all the same. If I don't get you your notes, you'll kill yourself trying. Okay, you can have them. But only if you promise to rest. Understand?"

Anton nodded.

Ambrus settled into the rock seat at the base of the falls. All day he had been possessed with an uneasy feeling and an urge to return to this spot.

He had spent the day with Mage Kytril, learning more on the art of meditation. When he had conveyed to the mage what had happened, the mage became excited. That set him off on spending the afternoon teaching the scholar how to tap his center and to secure himself in this plane so he could drift free, yet return.

He looked up at the falling water and the mist and sighed as he placed his hands on his knees. "Okay, let's see what it is you want to tell me." Armed with this new knowledge, he settled into the rock and started the relaxing exercise.

Chapter Twenty-Eight

Day Thirteen

Duncan slowly parted the grass. He watched dark figures moving among the wagons and tents. His eyes searched for movement that shouldn't be there. He studied each shadow for one that was too symmetrical.

He heard a horse neigh off to his right. And ahead, one of the strange animals made a noise, a cross between a dog's growl and a hawk's screech. The low murmurs of the night watch reached his ears. The smell of wood smoke filled his nostrils.

It had taken most of the night to get here. A mile was a short distance, unless you wanted to move unseen by alert troops. The three-quarter moon had not helped. They used shadows, ditches, and gullies. Now the moon had set behind the mountains, their movements were slightly faster.

Duncan had picked men who had been in the war. The three volunteers had scouted the Underdwellers, and anyone who could move around an Underdweller's camp undetected would be able to move around a human camp with ease. Presently, two had moved toward another part of the camp while he was accompanied by a dwarf. All four had dressed in dark lightweight leather. Their weapons, composed of long knives and daggers, were tied down and secured to their side. The dwarf carried his dwarvish thrower as well.

Duncan saw what he had been looking for, a shadow among the shadows. Slight movement within a bush a hundred feet from the edge of camp.

Shifting his head slightly, Duncan studied the bush and after a moment made out three dark human shapes clustered so they observed all directions. He reached behind and tapped the dwarf on his leather helm. The dwarf looked in the direction Duncan pointed and nodded. Sliding to the side, he made his way in the opposite direction of the enemy watchers. Duncan marveled at the way something as big and bulky as a dwarf moved so quietly. Moving silently himself, he followed the dwarf.

Half a candle mark found them within a stone's throw of the next hidden watchers. They were in a small patch of trees that offered cover, but left blind spots that were being exploited by the two from Lashtar.

Another quarter candle mark brought them to the edge of the enemy's encampment. Now the true danger began. The area they were in was dark, a gap of blackness between watch fires. This was their last hiding spot. Duncan eyed the distance to the nearest wagon, a distance he could cover in a few seconds. He worried over those few seconds. A guard behind them could turn and spot him. He knew the watch patrol routine, but they could change. He had his men change when he was in command of a company. Then there was the lone soldier. An enemy soldier, who walk to heed nature's call or just to stretch his legs, could appear. More than one mission had gone awry because of the random factor.

"What do you think?" Duncan whispered.

"That catapult. It will have the most men around it. I also see an officer's tent behind it."

Duncan smiled. He didn't want to leave the magical device in just any spot. He wanted to do the most damage and cause the most confusion possible. Any catapult required a large number of men to operate. This one was large, and from the look of the harness, so was the creature that pulled it. It was flanked by rows of tents and a larger officer's tent with two guards.

"I'm going to place the device at the base of the arm. That way, it will move with the machine. If anyone sees it, hopefully, they will ignore it."

The dwarf smiled. "If it is discovered, maybe they will give it to an officer."

Duncan smiled, then got ready to sprint across the open ground. When the dwarf tapped him on the rump, he shot out and was quickly crouching in the shadow of the catapult.

He slipped the device off his back, slithered under a beam, and crawled on his back to where the massive-throwing arm joined its pivot. He studied the workmanship, noting the design differed little from what they used, but the craftsmanship was better. This was not a hastily constructed machine, but one built to last and endure hard travel. What impressed him was the foresight to build such machines to travel a great distance and still function. Most siege machines were built on-site, since they were too heavy to be moved long distances. Construction took time, and with siege engines ready to go to work, you didn't have to worry about your enemy counterattacking while you were building them.

He jammed the device between a crossbeam and supporting brackets then took a moment to use the length of rope.

Duncan readied himself to sprint when the sounds of multiple hoof beats caused him to freeze. He turned slowly and watched soldiers ride up to the officer's tent. As they reined in their horses, an officer stepped from the tent and gave a salute to one of the men on a horse.

Duncan studied this man. His armor was plate with etchings throughout. His helm was a simple design and held one long multicolored feather. His face was clean, his lips set in a tight line. His sword appeared to be similar to a long sword, the scabbard a bronze-type material wrapped in silver ribbon. There was no mistake who this man was. The enemy's general.

Duncan's sword hand fell to the hilt of his sword, and for a brief moment, he visualized leaping from cover. The thought passed as quickly as it came. There were ten soldiers with the general, the officer and his personal guards and the night watch.

He mentally shook his head. Even if he killed the general, that would only delay the battle. With all armies, there were many layers of command. The general was the one at the top, but right below him was his second, ready to take over.

The only way to end this was to defeat the army, then take it to the Northland to King Rathveil.

Duncan spent a moment ingraining the man's face in his mind. He would meet him on the field.

As morning light spread across the sky, Xantrawler paced in front of the gate. From the shadows, four figures appeared, causing the gate guards to draw their weapons.

The weaponsmaster waved them back and waited. Duncan sent his men off to rest, then turned to Xantrawler, "The packages have been returned."

Xantrawler smiled. "Let's hope they enjoy them as much as they hoped we would."

Duncan looked to the east. He shivered slightly, not sure if it was from the cold or the army on the other side of the wall. "They're getting ready for the attack."

Xantrawler nodded. "We're ready. I have the duke's men spread out and stationed on the western half of the wall with a handful of my men. His mounted cavalry is saddling up in case we need them."

"The men in the shore tower?"

"In place, with orders to fight from the tower. They won't come out unless your company is overcome by the dragon."

Duncan looked in the concerned eyes of his friend. He slapped him on the shoulder. "Don't worry. My men will take that creature. It's one less thing for you to worry about." He looked toward the bridge. "Is everything ready there?"

"The dwarvish engineers will weaken it enough so the mages can take it out with mage bolts. Let's pray to the gods it won't come to that."

"I'm afraid it will. We both know we can't hold out against this force."

"Don't give up so soon. Your mission may help even things up."

"Don't count on it," Duncan explained to Xantrawler what he had seen. When he was done, the sun was above the mountains and spreading its rays over the lake.

The Lord Marshal came out of the gatehouse. "We have company." He pointed toward the Temple to Odium.

In a column, three wide, the temple guards marched. They had already crossed the bridge and were approaching Wintermist Wall. They were in full ornamental garb. Golden breast plates, silver helms, and chain mail embraced their exposed extremities. They wore long swords, the scabbards made of maple, stained a deep sunburn. Longbows were slung over their backs, and they carried round shields, emblazoned with the fruit of the land. In the center, an opal gem radiated golden thread.

Each guard was female.

They marched up to the three men in the shadow of the guardhouse, and the Captain of the Guard presented herself.

"Xantrawler Baylore of the Dukedom of Centaurea, third son of Sir Baylore, Weaponsmaster of the Queen, I present myself and my Soldiers of the Light. By order of he who watches us, bringer of our lives, and holder of our soul, we are yours to command for the coming crises."

Xantrawler bowed. "Praise to the wonders of Odium. I thank you, Lady Captain, and extend my thanks to the head priestess for this honor."

"Weaponsmaster, the Matriarch, she who speaks for our lord, has not commanded us."

"Then I am doubly honored and triple blessed."

"Ladies, your presence would be most welcome, but . . ." The Lord Marshal never finished his sentence as Duncan hit his breastplate, causing a loud gong. Xantrawler took the time to quickly divide the temple guards to the western section and the shore tower.

As the temple guards moved off, Xantrawler turned on the Lord Marshal, his eyes blazing, his hand once more rested on the hilt of his sword. "If I didn't know you were stupid and uneducated, I would cut you down and throw you to the Northlanders or feed you to their dragon!"

"I am the Lord Marshal, and I don't have to take that from you." His own hand fell to his sword. "I look out for my duke's people. Sending those ladies to die is unholy."

"You are twice a damned fool," Xantrawler said. "I have tolerated your dung-filled speeches since your father died. You're why titles should not be conveyed solely on hereditary lines."

"Do you know what you almost did?" Duncan asked quietly.

The Lord Marshal turned to Duncan, "What I did?"

"You almost angered a god."

"Those women are the edge we need."

"The edge? Gold armor, bronze swords, silver helms? I may not be a weaponsmaster, but I know soft metal won't last under combat."

"Your education is sorely lacking," Duncan said.

"Their weapons and arms are blessed by a god!" Xantrawler's voice was settling down, but still held a harshness. "Their metal is harder than anything man made. Their aim with the bow matches the best bowman in the Queen's service."

"The captain of the temple guards said they were sent. It is not often he intercedes in the realm of mortal man," Duncan added.

"I didn't know."

"You should have," Xantrawler had resumed his normal speaking voice. "Temple guards are warriors for their god." He started walking toward the gatehouse. "To your posts, we have wasted enough time."

Anton stared at the sunlight coming in the window of the living chamber. The elvish flowers looked wilted, and he felt guilty for not seeing to their watering. He should have the nurse give them the special fluid Mage Jedrowler had made up. He looked to his left and saw the nurse sleeping, little puffs of air escaping from her lips. He had felt her moving in the night, making sure he was covered, putting wood in the small fireplace, and feeling his wrist

He smiled and reached for his notes. He didn't want to disturb the nurse, so he stifled a moan of pain.

Anton knew the Spirits was the key to the spell. The notes in Mage Jedrowler's journal hinted the Spirits needed to play a large part in the spell. He became so absorbed by his research that he didn't hear CynLisa enter. She placed a bowl of thin porridge on his stand, and he looked up and smiled a thanks.

"You need to take a break."

"I've only been awake a short time, not even a quarter candle mark." CynLisa gave him a stern look. "Honest. Besides, it's important I finish. I have the first stage of the second half activated and all I . . ."

"You've started the spell?"

"Didn't I tell you?"

"Anton, you've been near death. Other than hounding the healer to let you have your notes, you haven't said much."

"Well, I discovered one stage of the spell and activated it. That's what I had finished when I was attacked. It's also why I was able to communicate with the circle so well. I not only sense them if I wanted to, I could tell you what each one was doing."

"What do you mean?"

"We are a union. We can be one if need be, at least when the spell is completed."

CynLisa gasped, "Anton, that's the Legion effect."

"No." Anton shook his head and immediately regretted it as the room swam around him. He closed his eyes for a moment, waiting for his stomach to settle.

"Legion is many who are one. No identity, except Legion. Unity is a union, one who is many. Separate beings working as one," he paused. "Where did the name *Unity* come from?"

"The whole thing sounds like Jed. He had an inclination to split hairs. I think it would have been interesting to have him and Ambrus debate."

"I just need to figure out the spell component. Then Mage Kytril or one of the high-level mages of the circle can cast the last spell."

CynLisa sat on the edge of his bed and took his hand. Keeping her voice low so as not to disturbed the sleeping nurse, she said, "Anton, Ambrus and I have been talking. We believe the spell needs you to make it work."

Anton gave her a puzzled look. "Why me?"

"Do you hear the Spirits in this room?"

"Yes, they are singing their song of healing and love."

"I'm not attuned to them. You, Jedrowler, and Ambrus are." She explained what she and Ambrus had concluded. While talking, the nurse woke up and quietly left the room to come back a few minutes later with a cup of medical tea.

"But we need to finish the spell," Anton pleaded. "The Spirits are trying to block it, but I feel their fear. The Northland army needs to be stopped."

"Weaponsmasters Xantrawler and Pentock are doing everything they can."

"You don't understand. The Spirits fear this army and know we can't stop them. This spell is the only thing that will defeat the Northland."

"You're getting this from the Spirits?" At his nod, she asked, "Have you read all the scrolls on Legion?"

"I read some and skimmed the rest. There's a lot there and I didn't have the time to read it all."

CynLisa took a deep breath, "There are things you need to know, important things." She stood up and started pacing. The nurse tapped the cup of tea, and Anton picked it up and sipped. "How much do you know of the Spirits?"

"They are filled with love and caring, dwell within the falls, come out during the day, and enjoy being around the people of Wintermist. Oh, and their singing is very relaxing."

"Things were not always that way in Wintermist. Of course, it wasn't called that in the time of Legion. Legion was the living god that walked the earth. They set up a religion and gathered worshipers. Without worshipers, a god will cease to exist or in Legions case lose power. They acquired a few worshipers from the congregations of the minor gods, but not enough.

"He wanted more power. He needed more to defeat the other gods and become the only god. They needed thousands more worshipers."

CynLisa stood in the doorway, looking out the living quarters window. "They absorbed magic users when they reached Nacromages level, but they needed the power of worshipers. They needed to force people to convert. Legion was willing to use whatever means he could.

"Legion came to Wintermist. At the time, it was the population center of the world. The people already worshiped their chosen god, including the one we have today, Odium. They refused to bow down to Legion, so Legion created something to help the conversion process."

CynLisa turned to the nurse, "Can you leave us for a few? What I'm about to say is for mage ears only." The nurse left, closing the door behind her.

CynLisa walked over and sat in the chair. She looked at his almost full cup of tea and smiled. "Healer's brew tastes worse than witch's brew."

Anton smiled and took a sip. "Legion made something for the conversion to his faith?"

CynLisa nodded. "If you had the time, you would have read it in the scrolls. This is more sealed information."

She settled back in the chair, arranging her robe, and entered the trance of a Cyn. "Legion came to the land of the falls, the land of the big water the natives called Rho Mantrin. 'God's gift' in the native language. Legion brought his most faithful followers, his strongest priests, and his newest Nacromages. For a fortnight, they worked on converting the simple farmers of the land. They were unable to shake their belief in their gods.

"Legion cursed the gods and their followers. He ordered his priests to bring ten worshipers of the ancient gods to him at the bridge overlooking the falls. The victims were brought, and Legion offered them up as sacrifice to him."

CynLisa's eyes lost focus, and she looked Anton in the eyes. "He was using blood power, godly power given up eons ago by the gods." Her eyes lost their focus. "Legion used this power to reach into the abyss and pull creatures to this world. Once here, he tied them to the falls.

"They were wraiths, and they were hungry. Legion had removed them from their plain of existence, and they had no way to feed. Now Legion reached to the negative plain of the abyss and pulled its energy through the falls to the wraiths. They fed, but only so long as they maintained negative energy flow in this realm."

CynLisa fell out of her trance and looked at Anton. Smiling, she said, "Finish your tea, then eat your porridge."

"Yes, Mother dear," Anton said with a smile. "But how were the wraiths used to convert the people of the land?"

"The wraiths needed energy, emotions to draw from the negative plain. Everything had to vibrate with negative energy. They instilled fear in the inhabitants. Fear and hatred. One by one, the people bowed to Legion to escape the great fear and the nightmares that haunted their dreams. Only through Legion were they able to live with the negative energy emanating from Rho Mantrin." CynLisa continued to recite without her trance. This part she had studied extensively.

"Worshipers grew for Legion. He became powerful. His followers flowed across the land, raiding villages and forcing the worship of Legion on others. Those who resisted were subjected to the wraiths. The wraiths would fill their lives, their dreams, with fear, hatred, and pain. This made them powerful."

"I can't picture it. This area controlled by wraiths."

"The negative energy changed the landscape, twisting it into something horrible. Not even Legion could stand living here, so he gave this area to the wraiths. Legion used this area as a place of punishment and rewards. Unbelievers and transgressors were sent to suffer. Those who were rewarded were sent here, blessed by Legion and capable of bathing in the negative energy. They participated in the torture of the innocents."

"The gods let this go on?" Anton looked disgusted.

"The gods take little notice of mortals, except when it suits them. For most of them, it's not because they don't care, it's because they allow us to make our own destiny. The gods do interfere when there is no other way to stave off total destruction."

"Then Ambrus may be right. There is no such thing as true prophecy."

"That is a different matter for another time." She sat forward in her chair, closer to Anton. "In the time of Legion, the gods were waiting to see if mankind would surmount the burden of Legion. There were those who fought him. Whole armies rode this land. The forces against Legion used magic but were always in fear of losing their magic users. When any powerful Nacromages were captured, they were absorbed by Legion. It became clear to the gods that Legion was too powerful for mankind to defeat. They intervened."

CynLisa saw that Anton was done with his tea, so she took the cup and gave him the porridge. "Eat, you need your strength."

"The gods must have been losing worshipers. I don't understand why they didn't step in and stop it right away."

"I have my own theory. I think this life is a crucible, a testing ground. Here we grow and become something greater or whither. The gods watch us and wait. I'm not sure what they may be waiting for."

"My mother use to compare them to parents. They let us go so far, then step in when we would hurt ourselves."

CynLisa nodded. "I have heard that at many sermons. If they interfered in our lives, then we would become dependent and not grow." She shook her head. "As I said, we can have a theocratic debate later."

While Anton ate his porridge, CynLisa continued, "The gods were almost too late to stop Legion. He had amassed a wide range of followers, trained up magic users to Nacromages, then absorbed them. He had the power of a god and the abilities of mortals. Cut off from his godly abilities, he had the combine power of the Nacromages. If he was isolated from magic, he had the god-given abilities to use. He could not be cut off from both simultaneously.

"What followed was a true battle of the gods. In any battle where great beings are involved, the smaller beings, in this case mankind, suffer. Believers on both sides died.

"I don't know what happened. The scrolls don't say. We know the gods won the war, but we don't know what happened to Legion.

To this day, you and I are the only ones that know about Legion, the wraiths, and the battle of the gods."

Anton set his empty bowl aside. "Then that must be the fear I feel from the Spirits. They are afraid that the wraiths will return."

CynLisa clasped her hands and hung her head. "They don't fear the wraiths. They are the wraiths."

Anton's blood froze as he shot a glance at the four Spirits in the room. His mind refused to believe the words of the Cyn. As he reviewed the story she just told, he came to accept it. After long moments of silence, he looked at her but was unable to speak.

"Jedrowler had the same look."

Anton found his voice and when he spoke it, trembled, "But how? I mean the Spirits, they are full of love. They care for us!"

"For that, you can thank Lord Mead. By the time man returned, the wraiths were dying. There had been no humans to terrorize in eons. The small animals in the area were not enough. Their connection with the negative plain was fading. And with it, so were they.

"The land healed. The wraiths were unable to corrupt it, so it returned to a beautiful peaceful spot. When Lord Mead and his people arrived, they saw the wonder of the falls. They stood on the bridge and sent praises to Odium for a wondrous creation. The wraiths saw food. In an act meant to cause fear, they flew from the falls and knocked Lord Mead from the bridge. They then waited for the fear, the hatred to pour from the assembled people. They waited to suck the fear from Lord Mead as he fell.

"Instead, the people misinterpreted what happened. They thought the Spirits, for that is what they thought the wraiths were, had chosen Lord Mead. As for Mead, he was euphoric that he was given such an honor. The wraiths were bathed in these positive feelings.

"Wraiths draw power from both the negative and positive plains. While the positive plain's energy is stronger, it is harder to maintain. Now, with all the positive energy around them, a path opened, and the leader of the wraiths grabbed the opportunity. All of them started feasting on the positive power. When one of them saved Lord Mead, the positive energy grew stronger."

"That was the first leap."

"That is what really happened. Not the story we have told the past five hundred years."

"So the Spirits are afraid Legion may return and they will become wraiths?"

CynLisa nodded as she stood. "They know they will become wraiths. Legion will close the path to the positive plain, and they will have no choice but to return to their evil ways. We have created the Spirits, made them what they are. They remember the old days and do not wish to return."

She looked at Anton. "Now you need rest."

Anton was about to protest when a wave of dizziness swept over him. His world tilted, his vision blurred, and he clutched at his bedsheets. The dizziness passed, but he still felt disoriented.

"I think you're right. I suddenly don't feel so good."

CynLisa's voice held fear. "The enemy has dropped their field of Ancient Magic on us. The attack is about to begin."

Chapter Twenty-Nine

Xantrawler, Duncan, and the Lord Marshal stood atop the gatehouse, watching the approach of the enemy's force. The sound of thousands of feet, the creaking of wood and leather, and the multitude of noises from different animals reached their ears.

All Xantrawler's people were in place. Extra weapons were scattered about, horses saddled and readied. The duke's cavalry was mounted and ready to respond. The catapults and ballistas had extra missiles. Cauldrons of boiling oil and water were in strategic spots. In the gatehouse, men waited at the murder holes if the enemy breached the outer portcullis.

Canvas was laid on the battlement, dripping with water. The mages had cast spells, so they held more water than they were designed for. In Xantrawler's command room, canvases were ready to drop over the windows. The men had been briefed on what to expect from the dragon. The one concession he gave the Lord Marshal on intelligence was the idea of having bards visit nightly and sing the horrific songs of dragons. Hopefully, the stories, many more horrific than fact, would reduce the panic.

On the western section of the wall, Mage Master Gardner and a group of mages waited. They appeared disoriented, leaning on the wall. Some doubled over others being assisted by soldiers. He could only assume the enemy mages had launched their attack.

"They're within range," the captain of the artillery reported.

"Hold your fire. I want them closer."

The captain picked up a flag and signaled.

Duncan smiled. "And they still keep coming."

"That's good, right?" the Lord Marshal asked.

Xantrawler nodded. "They're well within the range of our catapults, and once they secure their weapons for firing, there will be no hasty retreat. Duncan, join your men. The dragon could come at any time."

Duncan nodded and exited through the hole in the roof. The Lord Marshal turned to Xantrawler, "Thank you for putting me in command of the catapults. I won't break your trust."

"I put you where you'll do the least damage. My captain knows his job, and as long as you listen to him, he won't throw you from the tower." Xantrawler headed for the hole. "Captain, the tower is yours, fire when ready."

Mage Master Gardner leaned on the wall and tried to get his eyes to focus. The sudden formation of the field of Ancient Magic took them all by surprise. They had been expecting it but did not expect how strong it was. He felt the sharp magic burning along his channels as if someone was rubbing sand on his nerves.

"That is quite an experience." The Mage Master turned at the sound of the familiar voice.

"Where did you come from Kytril? I ordered everyone not involved in the battle across the bridge."

"I'm here to offer my service." He looked at his hands as he flexed them. "I got hit with this field on my way here, and I must say, I do not like the feel."

"You are not part of my mage school. You don't need to stay."

"I am part of the circle and the kingdom. I'm honor bound to defend it." He dropped his hands, and his eyes took on the stare of a mage watching the strands of magic. "If you fail, I would have to fight them sooner or later. Hmmmm, yes, this is what I saw during Jedrowler's casting."

Mage Master Gardner smiled. "Perhaps your Vlynies can do more than ordinary magic."

"Perhaps they do not seem affected. Still, I need magic to manipulate and control them."

"I think you are about to be put to the test." The Mage Master was looking at the enemy setting up their siege machines. "Anyone who can, be ready to shield."

The arms of the catapults snapped, sending rocks flying. The mages flung their magic, but the ancient field of magic reacted differently. Spells fizzled into silvery sparks, and others roared as thunder. The spells that reached the flying boulders cause them to shiver. Only one spell successfully blocked a rock, sending it crashing to the ground.

Mage Kytril screamed as he started shaking his hands. Mage Master Gardner used his mage sight and saw a swarm of Vlynies massing on Kytril's hands.

"They're burrowing into my skin!"

The mage who had deflected the boulder ran up. "Hold still. I see the knot!"

"So do I, I can't undo it!"

The mage passed his hands over Kytril, twisted his fingers then gave out a yelp. The Vlynies fell away and scattered to the wind. Kytril immediately clasped his hands and dunked them in a nearby barrel of water.

Mage Master Gardner ran to his friend. "Are you okay?"

Mage Kytril shook his head. "I lost control. The magic twisted at a strange angle."

"You may have only conjured at the edge of the force," the mage that freed Mage Kytril said.

Mage Kytril looked at him and scowled, "I have been working with magic and Vlynies before you were born. I learned from my mother, so don't tell me how to work Vlynies."

The mage shrugged. "As you wish, but remember, I threw a successful spell."

Mage Master Gardner looked at him. "How did you manage that?"

"I was using mage sight when the field descended. I watched how the force changed. It's the same magic, just less refined. The edges are sharp, the center less malleable. Knowing that, I adjusted the flow."

The ka-thump of the gatehouse catapult sounded. Mage Master Gardner looked at the gatehouse and ordered the mage, "Grab two other mages and protect the gatehouse. Teach them, then send one back to teach us." He saw Xantrawler heading their way.

As the mages left, he turned to Mage Kytril and in a voice no one else could hear, said, "Can you work your magic?" Mage Kytril shook his head. "Then you must leave the wall."

Xantrawler had reached the group and looked at Kytril, whose hands were still soaked in the water. "Is he going to be okay?"

"I'm fine," Mage Kytril said as he pulled his hands from the water and quickly slid them into the sleeves of his robes. "Just a little problem."

"Let me see your hands!"

Mage Kytril pulled himself up to his full height and held his head up. "I can assure you, Weaponsmaster, I am okay."

"Hands!"

Mage Kytril reluctantly withdrew his hands to reveal a mass of blisters and flaming red skin. Some of the blisters were leaking fluid, and the fingers were twitching in pain.

"Off my wall now!"

"I will be fine, Weaponsmaster. I shall remain and assist Mage Master Gardner."

"You're injured and cannot function. You will leave, or I will have you removed."

"You do know who you are talking to?" Mage Kytril brought his shoulders back.

Xantrawler sighed, "What is it with mages. I know who you are. Are you aware of who I am? I am not risking anyone on this wall because of an injured man. No further argument, either leave now or I shall have you carried off."

"You wouldn't!"

"I would!" Both men stared at each other until finally, Mage Kytril said, "Okay, I'm leaving."

Xantrawler watched the mage leave. "This is just the beginning, just them testing our strength. It won't be long before we will have their full force attacking us." He turned to Mage Master Gardner, "I hope you can use magic soon. That first round missed anything major. We won't continue to be that lucky."

"I have one mage who can work in the field. He is covering the gatehouse and teaching two others." Gardner looked at his hands. "Mage Margella's report has been some help. We know what we're dealing with."

Xantrawler nodded.

The explosion caused everyone on the wall to look toward the enemy's camp. In two spots, dust filled the air. Men and beasts were running and dodging falling debris.

Xantrawler smiled. "Looks like we scored first blood."

The sounds of the dural explosion still echoed from the mountains as General Klaydon leaned on the pommel of his saddle and looked at the enemy encampment.

For the past two days, they had stopped raiding, keeping under cover and watching. The closer they came to Wintermist, the harder it was to stay hidden. Farmland replaced the forest, until finally, they were forced to lag behind and move forward in small groups.

Now his force of three hundred waited on the edge of a large wood lot, an abandoned farmhouse nearby. The original force had grown as they gathered survivors from the wall or local garrisons that had been overrun. Half the force were mounted soldiers and knights, the rest various swordsman and bowmen with a few pikemen.

"I don't know how he did it," General Klaydon said to himself. "But Xantrawler always finds a way to equal the odds." He grabbed the reins and brought his horse around.

His men were fatigued, dirt-streaked faces, unkempt hair peeking from under helms. The only thing that held any semblance of cleanliness was weapons. A good soldier took care of his horse first and his weapon second. Everything else could wait.

"Listen up! You've seen what happened. I don't know how they did it, but the defenders on Wintermist Wall have managed to strike first," General Klaydon paused to let the small cheer die. "Now it's up to us. I don't ask you to do this for me, for your Queen, or for your country. I ask you to do it for them. We've been there. We know how hopeless it is. Battling that dragon is bad enough, but when your enemy replenishes his manpower as fast as you eliminate it, it reduces your chances."

General Klaydon urged his horse to make a slow pass up the line. "We need to eliminate that problem. We need to take out that wagon with the magical portal. We're going to ride into the heart of the enemy encampment. Most of us are not going to survive, but the Northlanders will know the people of Lashtar do not yield.

"Mage Margella is riding with me. It is important we get him to the wagon for he alone can neutralize the portal. Whatever you do, ensure the mage's life. If I should fall, forget me. I am unimportant. Grab Mage Margella. Footmen, men-at-arms, and pikemen set up that farm as a defense. If we survive, we will return and fight with you." He withdrew his sword and shouted, "Are you ready?"

Battle cries roared from every lip as weapons were raised and shook. Men beat their shields, and trumpeters blew their horns. Horses stomped eager to get moving. These fighters had felt defeat and were ready to return what they had been dealt.

General Klaydon reined his horse around.

The mass of Lashtar fighters surged down the mountainside, their battle cry echoing from the mountain.

Warlord Thrawt urged his horse through the settling dust. Around him, the air was filled with the cries of the wounded and the ground littered with wood, rope, and metal. A horse, its saddle empty, dashed past, the animal's eyes wide in fear.

He had ordered his mage to set off the magical devices, and instead of seeing sections of the enemy's wall dissolve in rubble, twin explosions shot from his force. He watched the blacksmith's wagon lift off the ground, then disintegrate into countless pieces. The main catapult was being readied to move to the front when it became the center of destruction.

As his horse made its way carefully through the debris, Warlord Thrawt looked toward the wall. He thought of his opponent, whoever it may be, and smiled. He found respect growing for this warrior. The enemy had found the devices and determined what they were, then planted them in his camp.

A soldier, half his face covered with blood and his right hand clamped over his eye, came struggling through the dust, almost tripping over a shattered rock. Another soldier was kneeling and looking at his bloody hands. Around the warlord, injured men wandered in confusion, and the ones uninjured dashed around in a blind panic. The enemy had accomplished their goal. The army was in confusion.

Warlord Thrawt rode free of the dust cloud. He could not let the enemy succeed. As he entered clear air, he saw two of his war chiefs trying to bring order. He slowed and shouted at them.

"Find the Force Shapers. I need them to assemble here immediately." He pointed at the other war chief. "Send up our battering ram and scaling units. We attack the wall immediately. The Force Shapers will provide magical cover. Now go!"

Warlord Thrawt never waited to see if his orders were carried out. He needed to get to another siege machine.

A short gallop brought him to a strange-looking device. A boxy skeletal framework surrounded a multitude of grooved planks. Upon each plank laid a four-foot-long arrow. Masses of pulleys and ropes entwined through the machine. The whole thing was tilted at an angle. The operators of the machine huddled a distance away, staring at the machine in dread.

"Get your sorry hides over here and man your post!" Warlord Thrawt yelled. Hesitantly, they moved from the trees they were hiding behind. "The thing is not going to bite. It's time to show the enemy what kind of people Terrapin Xon has. Or are you going to let your king down?"

The mention of their king spurred the men to their post. General Thrawt smiled. The Southlanders may have smart leaders, but they had nothing to match the loyalties of his men. He looked over his shoulder and saw the battering ram moving toward the wall.

It was time to act.

"Shields!"

Xantrawler looked to his left. He saw men scramble to get their shields up. From the enemy camp, a flight of arrows came toward the west side of the wall. As they approached, he saw they were not normal size. Before he could yell an additional command, they arrived.

Men screamed as the heavy four-foot-long arrows penetrated shields. Cries of pain rolled up and down the wall, but the silence of the dead was deafening. The weaponsmaster turned from the sight. He was accustomed to seeing sudden death but never became use to it. Only those who experienced it could understand the subtle difference.

"Archers, ready!"

The archers of Duke Altrid, temple guards, and Xantrawler's own men notched arrows and brought bowstrings taut. He gave the command to fire.

The arrows flew, only to bounce off invisible objects or be diverted by a gust of wind. Only a few found the enemy. Those fired by the temple guards always found a target.

A large share of the Northland's army was still in disorder, but here and there, groups were forming up. A giant battering ram was being pulled around the remains of the catapult. A wagon loaded with ladders moved forward, and Xantrawler spotted the colorful robes of mages.

Seeing the mages made him wonder if there was something about color and magic. No matter who the mages were, they had a bit of color about them.

He shook the thought off. This was not the time to be thinking of anything but the approaching army. They may be disorganized, but they were still a large force. A hail of arrows from the enemy's own archers and a volley from three catapults slammed the wall. The mages at the gatehouse managed to defend it, but the rest of the mages were still not functioning.

The black river of the enemy forces flowed as arrows flew from the defenders' bows. The enemy returned fire from behind mage shields, their arrows taking out many defenders and causing others to seek cover. With the Lashtar soldiers behind cover, the enemy maneuvered into position, unharassed.

Scaling ladders and ropes slammed against the wall, and men started climbing. On the battlement, young boys ran back and forth, pushing ladders away or chopping ropes. Swordsmen stood ready, and when the enemy did reach the battlement, they were met with steel. Swords swung, and in the eastern section, the recruits used their polearms as Weaponsmaster Duncan had taught Joshua.

Joshua watched the guts spill from his barrack mates, heard the man scream, and saw the red life fluid flow. He smelt death and fell to his knees. Bile rose in his throat, and his breakfast spewed from his mouth. Joshua Wheatfield wiped his mouth and saw the enemy soldier turning. His eyes narrowed, a scow appeared, and he felt his heart beat faster. Ignoring the roiling in his stomach, ignoring the shaking, he felt he cried his rage. He gripped the polearm tighter, rose to his feet, and jabbed.

The enemy had not finished his turn as the twin points of the weapon punctured the leather. With a twist of his hands, the young lad tore the chest and unbalanced the enemy. As the Northland warrior fell, the recruit yanked his weapon from the dead body. More by accident than design, the butt of Josh's polearm caught the enemy behind him. Unaware of that, he turned to the wall and slammed the horseshoe end into another enemy's throat.

With rage filling him, Josh turned on another soldier on the parapet. Once more, he caught the enemy by the neck and this time twisted as the weaponsmaster had shown him. He was oblivious to the screaming and cursing coming from his mouth as he returned the enemy's ferocity.

From cauldrons, boiling oil and water rained down on the invaders as they brought their battering ram to bear on the portcullis. Mage fire ignited the ram, only to be doused by an enemy mage. As the mages of Wintermist learned how to work old magic, the mage battle started. Magical energy crackled back and forth. Mage Master Gardner directed his mages as Weaponsmaster Xantrawler directed his fighters.

Wintermist Wall was soon painted in the blood of both allies and foe. The field north of the wall was littered with the black armored bodies of the enemy. On both sides, unmoving fighters lay sprawled at the base of the wall. Soldiers too old or too injured to fight moved among these bodies, seeking friends still living. The living were moved a short distance to the master healer, who worked with a couple of young healers and a small group of assistants.

As the sun climbed the morning sky, the defenders slowly regained control of the wall. Their spirits strong, they triumphed one small victory at a time over superior numbers.

General Klaydon charged his men into the heart of the enemy encampment. He could see what was happening at the wall, but his determination centered on eliminating reinforcements.

His attack was simple. His knights rode in a V formation, while other mounted soldiers followed. Mage Margella rode pillion with him in the center of the formation. Around him, the best horsemen he had repelled any of the enemy that got past the knights.

With robes whipping behind him, Mage Margella had a smile on his face. He yelled, "Just like the Underdweller War!"

General Klaydon nodded. "Are you ready?"

"Just get me inside that wagon and I will do the rest."

The battle to the wagon was quick, the fighting sparse. Most of the real fighters were at the front lines, battling to take Wintermist Wall. The men of Lashtar pulled up to the large wagon and encircled it. As General Klaydon and Mage Margella reached the back of the wagon, the flap opened, and a man in colored robes stepped out.

General Klaydon's actions were instincts honed sharp from years in battle. He launched from the saddle, grabbed the platform, and swung himself up. As the surprised mage looked at the general, he buried his dagger in the mage's stomach.

Mage Margella climbed onto the platform and followed General Klaydon into the wagon. The inside was empty, saved for one large frame that held a shimmering view of a room.

"Fascinating," the mage said, "I thought you never could combine those magics, farseeing, and transmovementation."

"Analyze later, now destroy." General Klaydon was breathing hard, gulping in lung fulls of air. Outside the wagon, he could hear the sound of battle grow as the enemy launched a counterattack.

Mage Margella raised his hands and muttered a few nonsense words. Bolts flashed from his hands, striking the door frame. Sparks filled the interior of the wagon with a silvery light.

Mage Margella swore, "Have to think old, not new." He brought his hands up again. This time, the interior of the door frame started to swirl. The distant room spun and melted. With a loud pop, the image vanished. A mage-created flame struck the door frame, and it started to burn brightly.

Both the mage and the general made a hasty exit into the chaos.

Mage Master Gardner turned from the mage who had just taught him. He had watched, listened, and learned how to function with old magic and was ready. He had allowed the rest of the mages to learn, and now their combined might was focusing on the enemy. Now that they understood Ancient Magic, they could show them what real combat mages were.

Mage Master Gardner grasped the magic and twisted it, forming a shield of pure magical energy. His hand swiped the air along the wall, and ladders and men fell to the ground.

Climbing atop the wall, the Mage Master had a clear view of the enemy's army. With his mage vision, he found the concentration of magic that signified mages at work. The Northland mages were not trying to hide.

Years of combat with mage, repelling the magic of powerful mages and learning from veteran battle mages, all flowed through his motions. As Mage Master Gardner wove his spell, his years of experience flowed into the casting. He manipulated the convolutions of the Ancient Magic and focused them on his target.

Within the ranks of enemy mages, screams erupted as their magic turned. Spells wrapped around the mages, flowed along channels not meant to experience such power, and flared along nerves never meant to feel such energies. For some, their minds literally fled, leaving a gibbering hulk on the field.

Mage Master Gardner felt the energy flow back to him as a magical shield slammed down around the enemy. He dropped the force he wove, letting it unravel before any backlash could touch him. As he went to his knees, he felt strong hands pull him to the parapet. He looked at the concerned face of the weaponsmaster.

"Are you all right?"

Mage Master Gardner nodded. "That spell took a lot out of me. They are short a number of spell casters, and I have found out something interesting. These are not ordinary mages. When my spell touched them, I felt the way magic flowed through them. It is more like a witch or a shaman."

"What do you mean?"

"The magic flows around them, not through them. They don't take it into themselves like a mage." He turned to look at the enemy. "That is why they need this field of old magic. They feed off each other, calling upon each other's power."

"What does that mean?"

"Just as we were unable to use the Ancient Magic, they wouldn't be able to use Modern Magic. We eliminate this field and they will be helpless."

"So eliminate it!"

"It's not that easy. We have to know how they called the Ancient Magic."

Xantrawler clasped the Mage Master on the shoulder. "I know you can do it."

Warlord Thrawt pounded his fist on the pommel of his saddle. His eyes narrowed as he watched his men fall from the wall, then a snarl escaped his lips as he watched the majority of his Force Shapers collapse in screaming fits. His assault on the gatehouse was failing. The catapults' rocks were falling harmlessly to the ground after bouncing off invisible barriers. The arrows were swatted from the sky.

"Any news on when the other company will get here?"

One of his war chiefs answered, "No word, Warlord. Even if they defeated that band of barbarians, they're still a day's ride away."

"No reserves to call in and reinforcements a day away!" He had committed a large share of his men to the attack. It had been a gamble, but he needed to the wall before the enemy Force Shapers were able to overcome their disability. Now he knew he had lost that advantage.

He quietly gave the order, "Have the drummers sound recall."

"Is this going to be a siege?"

"No, not with those Force Shapers. That and the warlord on that wall is too smart. I'm sure he has more planned if we decide to just sit here. Besides, we have no security behind us and he can call up reinforcements from the south."

Warlord Thrawt sat in his saddle and looked at the wall. Off to his left, the sun glittered from the lake. To his right, mountains towered with sides too steep to climb. All that stood between him and his objective was a wall smaller than the first one they took.

He had told his thrice damned king that attacking a place containing so many users of the Unseen Forces would be risky. Attacking any place filled with users of the Unseen Forces that studied and taught would be a fool's campaign. Only the promise of unlimited manpower and his own Force Shapers convinced him that it could be done.

As the drums sounded recall, he looked over what he had left. A quarter of his warriors lay dead or injured. His siege machines were useless, and looking at his users of the Unseen Forces, he knew they were no longer an asset.

He spurred his horse and crossed the field toward the Force Shapers. Upon reaching them, he looked at the nearest one. The

Force Shaper was holding another, who was spouting gibberish and drooling. There were more, some sitting and others wandering around.

"Will they recover?"

The unaffected one looked up at the warlord. His eyes were sunken, and what color the man had was drained from him. "I don't even know what was done to him. It's like his mind is gone."

"How many of you are functional?"

"Warlord, we are not machines."

"Are you capable of using your power?" After this war was over, he was going to petition the king to return to the Sacred Scrolls' prohibition of the use of the Unseen Forces. These Force Shapers were too superior in their attitude.

"There are a few of us, but we can't risk going against their users."

Warlord Thrawt jumped from his horse and backhanded the force shaper. The man cried out as he sprawled on the ground. The force shaper he had been holding crumbled in a heap and shouted howls of laughter.

"If you are capable of combating the enemy, you will do your duty to your king."

The Force Shaper wiped blood from his mouth and looked at the warlord. "They have their abilities back. They may kill us."

Warlord Thrawt's sword was out, and he thrust it into the Force Shaper's chest. Blood blossomed on the robe and as he gave a twist more spurted from the wound. Pulling the sword from the unmoving body, he looked at the rest of the Force Shapers.

"Anyone else afraid of dying at the hands of the Southerners?"

The Forces Shapers said nothing, just moved closer together. Warlord Thrawt nodded and sheathed his sword. He walked to his horse and swung into the saddle.

"Come up with an attack to use on the wall. Blast it like you did that pile of rubble in the pass if you have to. I don't care."

He pivoted his horse and moved back to his command position, his war chiefs closing around him. He looked over his shoulder at the wall. The Force Shapers should be able to take a section, but that would not be enough. His army was already depleted. He needed to bring the advantage back to him.

There was only one way to win this battle.

"War Chief Fath, I want the dragon brought in."

"Sir, King Rathveil forbid . . ."

General Thrawt spun on the man. "Damn King Rathveil! He's not here to see this mockery. If he wants that wall and if he wants to be sitting in Wintermist tonight, then we're just going to have to risk his precious little pet!"

The war chief shook in his saddle but acknowledged the order.

"Tell Vella's handler to have her hit the gatehouse first. After that, I want the side closest to the mountain taken out. That's where I have seen their Force Shapers."

General Thrawt looked at Wintermist Wall. "Let's see how you do against fire from the heavens."

Chapter Thirty

Anton awoke with the screams echoing in his mind. The four spirits were screaming, their crystalline voices echoing from the rock walls of the room. Fear swept over the room to such an extent that the nurse showed signs. She was pacing, wringing her hands.

Anton clamped down on the channel to the rest of the circle to stop the fear. Fear is what the wraiths generated, used to draw substance from the negative plain. That's what corrupted the land, corrupted them.

"Stop it!" Anton beat his fist on the bed. The nurse whirled, staring at the young mage. "Stop, don't you see what it's doing? What you fear is going to happen. Only it's going to be your own fear that opens the negative plain. You will corrupt yourself."

There was a brief surge of fear, then a comforting hand passed over the room. A paternal touch that held them all. Anton's heart slowed. The Spirits quieted, their song trailing into a soft, gentle sound. The fear from the Spirits lessened to a feeling of dread, then dwindled to an uneasiness. Anton released the channels. He sank into his pillows as this small effort had taken a lot out of him.

Voices could be heard in the outer chamber, and CynLisa appeared with the master healer. One look and the healer was at Anton's side, peering at him with healer's vision.

"What happened? You're drained, and my nurse looks like she's about to pass out."

"The Spirits," Anton's voice was a low, hoarse whisper. "They're afraid. Their fear filled the room. It's okay now."

"No, it's not. Any more shocks like that and you won't live." He glared at the Spirits. "You hear me, he won't live." Turning back to Anton, he felt the boy's pulse. "It's a good thing we're here to evacuate you."

Anton struggled to sit up, but CynLisa pushed him back down.

Anton protested, "No, you don't understand. I'm close. I can't leave. The Spirits need me to finish Jedrowler's work!"

"The Mage Master has ordered this," CynLisa said. "The defenders don't know how long they can hold the wall. If the dragon attacks and they don't destroy it, the wall will fall."

"They won't destroy it," everyone turned to the new voice. Ambrus stood in the doorway, his clothing damp and his hair plastered to his head. He had bags under his eyes, and his skin was wrinkled, as if from a long immersion in water.

"You look like hell!" CynLisa said.

"You try spending the night in the cold gorge with the Spirits yammering at you and the Vlynies showing you things you don't understand. Then you can tell me I look like hell."

"How do you know they won't destroy it?" Anton's weak voice came from the bed.

"I understand my vision, or at least part of it. It's both a glimpse of the future and a message from the Spirits." Ambrus walked across the floor and half collapsed, half knelt next to Anton's bed. "The Spirits need you. Only you can save them and the land of Mead."

"He can't save himself," the master healer said. "He's too weak to do anything."

Ambrus looked up at the master healer. "Then heal him."

"I don't have enough life energy to give. Your young mage almost died. That much damage needs to recharge on its own. All I can do is give him enough to keep his soul with us."

"Polywash!" Ambrus spit out the word as he climbed to his feet. "You know as well as I that healers have given life forces to enable others to finish their mission. Leaders of armies, kings, and people of power, all of them received more of this so-called life force than you would normally give. Enough to make it possible for those individuals to do what needed to be done."

"Ambrus, it doesn't matter. I don't know the spell."

Ambrus was on his knees, holding Anton's hand. "Yes, you do. Don't you see, the Spirits have shown me, shown you. The vision with you and the bridge, it's going to happen if you don't succeed. They are going to destroy Wintermist Bridge."

"Destroy the bridge?"

"That is why we need to evacuate you," CynLisa said.

Ambrus waved CynLisa to be quiet. "The high priestess throwing you a rope is symbolism." He rubbed his forehead with his free hand. "That was driven into me during the night."

"And what does it symbolize, oh great seer of the future? The high priestess is going to hang him if he doesn't get across the bridge?"

Ambrus glared at the healer. "Stick to healing and let me do the prophesying." He turned back to Anton. "Faith, that's what they have been telling me. You need to have faith in yourself. Yes, faith in Jedrowler's work, in the Spirits, but mostly in yourself. Faith in your abilities and faith in overcoming your fears."

"I have faith in all of that. Right now, I can feel the land. I can feel everything that is going on all because of his spell. I do believe I can find the rest of the spell given time."

"Do you? Are you willing to show it? Listen to one that has just recently learned faith. You can talk all you want. But until you show faith, you will never have it. Once you have it, anything is possible."

"You showed your faith, how?"

"I took a leap."

Anton went pale and started to tremble. The healer pushed Ambrus aside and laid a hand on his forehead. "I can't. The height. No."

The Spirits started singing their crystalline song of comfort. The song stroked deep into Anton's soul, and from far away, he heard a voice, a familiar voice.

"I hear the voice too, Anton," Ambrus said. "This is the clearest the Patriarchal Spirit has ever been. This is taking a lot of energy for him to be so clear. Listen."

"Don't give into your fear."

"Faith will carry you far, believe in it." Ambrus's voice blended into the song, and Anton looked at the scholar. "Faith will carry you through your fear."

"It's too simple. There has to be more than that."

"You know the spell. You know what needs to be done."

Anton slowly nodded and looked at CynLisa. "I have suspected it, and it came to me right before the attack. I know the major component to finish the spell."

"Love!" It was CynLisa. Everyone looked at her, and she shrugged. "All my life, growing up in Wintermist, we knew of Jedrowler's love for the Spirits and this land. Love he demonstrated many times, with multiple leaps, leaps he always dedicated to the Spirits."

Anton's brows came together, and his words whooshed out of him, almost too fast for anyone to follow. "Love, faith, and love to be demonstrated in the ceremony of the leap. It's clear to me. For the land to bind to us, the Spirits need to know that we have faith in them and love for the land. The leap shows our faith."

"What of the love?"

"By going through everything needed to be part of the circle shows a great deal of love. But this spell needed a component, a component that means love. Something that is everlasting and given out of love."

As if the same hand touched them, everyone turned and looked into the living chamber. Looking at the window sill, their eyes fell on the large arrangement of red elvish flowers sitting there.

"Where's Mage Jedrowler's journal?" Anton started frantically, patting the bedsheets. He had been reading the journal before dozing off. The master healer reached down and picked it up from the floor.

Anton started flipping pages until he found the entry he wanted. "Here it is. This was written after Mage Jedrowler returned from the elvish lands. He had been gone four years, and he wanted to celebrate his return with a leap. He had brought one elvish flower with him to give to the Spirits." Anton fell back into his pillow, his eyes rolled back. When he opened them, the master healer took the journal from him and pushed it into Ambrus's hands.

"You read it." Looking at Anton, he said, "You rest and calm yourself."

Ambrus started reading, and everyone in the room remained silent, even the Spirits had stopped singing.

"Something extraordinary happened on my leap. I released my offering of the elvish flower, but instead of it drifting down, it dissolved, becoming part of the mist. I never reached the end of the rope for the Spirits surrounded me, their love filling me. And for a moment, I saw the mist through their eyes. Not just the mist, but the lake and the land. I even sensed the far away mountains boarding the south shore. I felt something else, a great pleasing power, a peaceful flow of power that filled me. All of this happened in a moment, then the moment was gone and I found myself being deposited on the bridge. The largest Spirit I had ever seen set me gently on my feet, caressing my face. For a moment, until it dissolved back into the mist, I felt the emotion of mother, of father. Then it was gone, along with the Spirits."

Anton opened his eyes and looked at all around him. "That's it. That is the second part of the spell."

"That's all?" Ambrus shook his head. "That's so easy, so simple."

"Simple enough that no one would ever think of it," CynLisa said. "Anyone who witnessed the complicated and involved first part of the spell would be looking along those lines for the second part."

Ambrus laughed. "That old fox. I wish I had got to know him better. I would love to have debated him."

CynLisa made a face at Ambrus. To Anton, she said, "So what needs to be done? Can one of us do it?"

Even as Ambrus shook his head, Anton said, "It has to be me. I know, look at Jedrowler's last entry."

Ambrus flipped to the last page and read,

"It worked! I can feel the land. Anton did not fail me. Not only did he resist Legion, but he channeled all the magical energy better than I expected, better than I ever dreamed. His bonding with the Spirits was smooth. The link is complete. Now we move on to the second phase. Once I have him activate the spell at the pentagram, Anton shall take a leap of faith."

Ambrus closed the journal. "What's a Legion?"

"He knew I would overcome my fear. He was pushing me to the extreme, just like he did with his roommate and the ant. That's why he was convinced I would be named a mage."

"But what's a Legion?"

"He would do that," CynLisa said. "I recall the story of him and Mage Quinland."

"The Queen's mage?"

"Will somebody tell me who Legion is!"

"Later, Ambrus." CynLisa waved the scholar off.

The master healer cleared his throat. "That still doesn't help me. I don't have enough life force to give. I've been drained just healing him. I'm unable to tap into the life force around. I'm that weak."

"I don't think you have to worry about finding a source," Ambrus said. He pointed to Anton and the Spirits around him. "Have you noticed that our young mage is appearing a little healthier?"

The master healer looked at Anton, and a sigh of disbelief escaped him. "There is a small tendril of force entering him, not much and nothing I have ever seen."

Ambrus nodded. "The Spirits are giving him the energy he needs."

The master healer shook his head. "They're not giving him enough to enable him to stand, let alone cast spells."

"Mages have been known to work together," CynLisa said, "Combine their magical forces to create something more than if they did it individually. Jedrowler's spell of protection is an example. Do you think you could work with the Spirits and give Anton what he needs?"

The master healer thought for a moment. "I believe I may have already." He looked at Anton. "By rights, you should have died on the mountain. I may be good, but you were too far gone. I don't think any healer could have saved you." He looked around at the group. "I believe I can do it. I suggest we wait until we get to the bridge so Anton will be fresh. Send in the litter carriers."

Duncan knew it was out there. He knew it was waiting to attack. He absentmindedly stroked the wood of the modified ballista. The arms were cocked, the wood creaking with the strain. The metal tip of the bolt glistened in the sunlight. Down the wall, the other ballista stood ready. The men manning the weapons stood ready to track the dragon and send death toward it.

"They're moving," Kentell said.

The enemy slowly moved away from its camp. Some reluctantly approached the idle siege machines. Others carried ladders and ropes while behind them archers prepared.

"Get ready," Duncan called out. "Archers, you know your duty. The rest of you, have shields ready. Anyone with a free moment, I want these canvases constantly watered. When that dragon breathes, I want us well insulated."

No sounds came from his men. They were good men, and he feared this day would be their last. He toyed with the idea of ordering them off the wall but knew they would not listen to that order. They were here to fight for Lashtar, to protect the people.

Drums sounded from the enemy. Rapid, steady beats. *Thrump, thrump*. It was a code, just like the flags and trumpet calls used in Lashtar. Some command, the enemy soldiers understood,

The enemy stopped advancing, and Duncan took to scanning the sky. This had to be it, but where was it? Something that big should be sighted miles away. But the sky was clear, no birds, no clouds.

It burst over the mountaintops, soaring on a downdraft to skim the length of the wall. Men cried in fear, instinctively ducking, others stepping back from the monster, stepping into emptiness and screaming as they fell.

Duncan ducked with the rest, yelling to hold fire. The creature was moving too fast. As it passed overhead, the wash from its wings blasted their face, blowing dust and other lose material into the air. The dragon soared just over the top of the shore tower. As it passed, its rear legs stabbed down, knocking stone and mortar into the lake. The screaming body of a fighter plummeted with the rubble.

Duncan watched the dragon drift over the lake, making a leisurely turn. It let out a bellow that echoed off the mountains. "Come on, come on." He wrapped his fist on the ballista. He watched as the creature soared toward them at wall height. As it got closer, he could see the neck muscles working up and down, convulsing as a fire lizard does before it sets loose its fire.

"*Cover!*" he yelled. Immediately up and down the eastern wall, men dove under the soaked canvas tarp.

"Just follow it, follow it." The creature was coming right at them. A better shot they would never get. As it passed the first ballista, he yelled, "Fire!"

The men yanked the string. And immediately, two missiles, the size of a man's forearm, shot toward the dragon. Not waiting to see what happened, the men dove under the tarp.

Duncan watched, holding his breath as the first one, then the other imbedded in the creature's side, right where the gas bladder would be on a fire lizard.

The dragon let out a yowl of pain and flapped its wings, gaining altitude. Both bolts lodged under separate scales, but Duncan could see the missiles had failed to penetrate much beyond the scales.

He watched the dragon circle, gaining altitude while pawing at the wooden slivers in its belly. With a screech of rage, it knocked both bolts loose, then dived. Its neck muscles convulsing, it opened its mouth in a silent scream.

The flames slammed into the gatehouse.

The dragon circled, keeping the flames on the stone structure. As the flames died, it arched its neck and shot a stream of flames down the eastern side.

With a curse, Duncan dove under the wet canvas and felt the heat as the flames turned the water into steam.

The dragon winged over the enemy encampment, screeching its victory. On the ground, the enemy soldiers cheered and with renewed vigor surged toward the wall.

The canvas was still hot, but cooling as Duncan flipped it back. Up and down the wall, anything that had not been wet was in flames. The straw dummies were burning brightly. The top of the gatehouse spurted smoke from small fires. The ropes on the ballista were in flames, the wood charred.

Duncan leaped to the ballista and started patting the flames on the ropes, while yelling for his men. Shortly, the fires were extinguished, and injuries were being assessed. Most of the men came through the encounter unscathed. Only a few had burns from where bare skin had touched the canvas. The other ballista, closest to the gatehouse, was useless. The one he was looking over was badly damaged.

"It will fire," the operator said. "But we don't dare ratchet it fully back."

Duncan shook his head. "Doesn't matter, we can't penetrate that thrice damned hide. Dragons are tougher than fire lizards." He watched the dragon make lazy circles around the enemy camp. He could hear the drumbeats. Their rhythm had changed, and a new cadence was sounding.

"We need something that can penetrate those scales."

"There is nothing, Weaponsmaster. The smith made those points as sharp as possible. We couldn't twist the rope any tighter without snapping the supports." He hesitated, "What if we wait until the dragon was on top of us point-blank?"

"We would be killed by the fireball."

"I would rather be killed taking that thing out, than like Weaponsmaster Xantrawler, unable to defend myself."

Duncan looked at the gatehouse. White smoke poured from the doorway. The windows had smoke curling from around the canvas out. On top, the catapult blazed, sending up its own column of black smoke. He knew his friend lay dead.

"Evacuate everyone. Once across the bridge, take it down!" He turned to the soldier, "I'll man the weapon, no argument. When the queen's men arrive, tell them what we have learned."

The dragon was swooping over the lake. Its wings tipped as it started its turn. As it came around, it stretched its neck and roared a challenge.

"Now go!"

The soldier started running, shouting the order to retreat. Duncan turned to the ballista and started to ratchet it back. He had to stop to wipe the tears from his eyes, tears he blamed on the smoke. He thought of Xantrawler, of all the times with him. He would see him soon, in the place where the faithful went.

He thought of Sasha. He would miss her. Her smile, her laughs. He chuckled quietly around his sniffles. He would miss her debate with Diamox. He was sorry he had not met her a long time ago. Maybe he would not have spent five years in self-pity.

The ballista clicked on the last tooth. He had brought it all the way back, despite the advice of the operator. The arms groaned, and the ropes quivered.

Duncan picked up a bolt and slapped it in the groove. Making sure it was properly seated, he brought the weapon around, tracking the rapidly approaching dragon.

He watched the creature through the remains of the sights. As it came closer, he was able to make out every detail. It was not like a fire lizard. The dragon was graceful, the body not bloated. Even with the scales, he watched muscles move gracefully, the smooth flow of the wings. They may have been related, but a fire lizard was not a dragon.

Then the dragon was just above the merlons. When it got within a stone's throw, Duncan let lose with a battle yell and let the bolt fly. It would impact as the dragon was overhead. He watched it going for the joint in the forward leg, the spot that would lead right to the gas bladder.

Something slammed Duncan in the back, and he hit the parapet hard. Blackness smothered him as the wet canvass fell over him. He did not remember anyone rewetting the canvass. Then everything was orange and white as flame billowed around him. The water instantly disappeared, and heat drove the wind from his lungs. He struggled to draw air as flames appeared in front of him. The canvass had caught.

He felt a body next to him move, and the heat flipped away. The cool, but smoky breezes flowed in his face, and he opened his eyes.

He was flat on the parapet with a bug's view of the lake. He had never seen anything so lovely.

"Are you all right, Weaponsmaster?"

Duncan knew that voice, and he turned to look at Josh. The lad was sitting up, one side of his face bright red, but he was smiling.

"I ordered everyone off the wall and that meant you."

The boy shook his head. "My father would not have liked me leaving you. Besides, your orders were countermanded."

"Who dares to countermand the orders of a Queen's weaponsmaster?"

"I do." Duncan looked up at the figure striding toward him. The face was blackened, hair singed. "The last I knew, I was still in charge of this wall."

Duncan was on his feet and clasping his old teacher by the shoulders. He stopped short of hugging the old man, but Xantrawler saw the emotion and smiled. "If you kiss me, I will have to take you out back."

"But how? I mean I saw the dragon flame the gatehouse. I know you were in it."

Xantrawler held up his sword, the gift from the dwarves. "Never fought dragons before, so I didn't know it had the ability to shield us from flames. I instinctively brought the sword up when the dragon came and watched the flames wrap around us. My captain, his aide, the Lord Marshal were saved. Tables, chairs, and maps were gone."

Duncan kept smiling but turned north toward the enemy. He could see them pulling back, pulling away from the people who destroyed their dragon.

"They'll regroup shortly," the Lord Marshal said as he approached. "Your captain has spotted their leader from Duncan's description. He's moving forward."

"He's going to lead the next charge," Xantrawler said. "His troops are demoralized, and he needs to motivate them."

"I don't think he will hold anything back this time," Duncan said.

Xantrawler nodded. "Bring the reinforcements out of the shore tower and the lake tower. We may not stop them, but we will make them pay the price."

"More news, Weaponsmaster. The captain reports that General Klaydon is holed up at a farm. It doesn't look good for him."

Xantrawler shook his head. "There's nothing we can do for him."

"Sir," the Lord Marshal said, "I would like to take a group of men and try to rescue the general."

Duncan looked the Lord Marshal in the eyes and saw something he had not seen before. The Lord Marshal looked older than his young age. Perhaps just a little wiser as well. "It's a suicide mission, you know that?"

"General Klaydon is out there fighting alone. He needs reinforcements."

Duncan looked at the man and shook his head. "This is worse than what I faced at the battle of the Valley. Most likely, none of you will come out alive."

"All the more reason for me to go." He turned to Xantrawler, "You said something about the men not seeing us lose it, being bad for morale. Seeing one of us leading the way into battle with the enemy will be something to raise their morale. Perhaps enough to make them fight just that much harder, hard enough and long enough to give everyone a chance to evacuate."

Duncan gave a weak smile. "I think you just earned points in Xantrawler's salle. Not many can take his own words and throw them back at him so he can't argue. Very well said, Lord Marshal."

The weaponsmaster nodded. "Only volunteers, ones who know what they are facing."

"I'll go with him." The Lord Marshal looked at Duncan. "Not as the weaponsmaster in command, but as your equal."

As Duncan ordered the squires to find volunteers, the captain and Mage Master Gardner came running from the gatehouse. "Weaponsmaster, you had better see this." He pointed south.

Xantrawler and the other two looked at the pass. A thin line was spilling into the land of Mead.

"The Queen's men," the Lord Marshal said.

Xantrawler shook his head. "Too late. They won't get here in time." He turned to the two men, "Continue with your mission. May Odium watch over you."

"What in the name of the sacred codex are they doing?" Mage Master Gardner said. Taking a rag from his robe, he swiped the air, creating a hazy distortion in front of him. The magic was not as good as what he was used to, but it showed activity at the bridge.

Mages were stopping people from crossing, while others hurried the ones on the bridge. On the roadway, Anton was lying on a litter, a man in healer's robes bending over him. Around the two, mages had taken defensive stances, including CynLisa

From the mist, white vapor twisted toward the group, encircling the healer and Anton.

Anton stared at the bright blue sky. The sun was warm on his face, and a cool wind blew from the falls. He smelled the freshness in the mist and a slight fragrance of spring flowers. The songs of the Spirits mingled with the birds' melody.

Knowing what was happening on the wall, he felt this was wrong. There shouldn't be beauty, or peacefulness, when today was the darkest day of Wintermist.

He felt drained. He didn't have to move. Everyone else had done the work moving him to the litter, carrying him through the hallways and downstairs. But even the small effort for the trip was exhausting. If the master healer was not able to give him the life energy he was lacking, he would not be able to cast the spell.

"How are you doing?" CynLisa's concerned face hovered over him. She knelt and took his hand. "Give the master healer a moment to enter his trance."

Anton gave a slight nod, too weak to even speak. His head pounded, and he was shaking from the chill. For a moment, CynLisa's face blurred, blackness ringed her face, and everything grew dim. He heard her speaking from far away, down a tunnel swirling in black and gray.

A hand was laid on his forehead, and the blackness receded. "Relax, I will do all the work," the quiet voice of the healer came echoing in his mind. He felt the slight discomfort as the healer started feeding him energy, life energy.

Anton felt himself spiral into a trance, one not of his own doing. He felt the healer guiding him, taking him beyond a place of peace. He tried to resist. Now was not the time. He needed to pull the energy to him, not languish in a meadow of flowers, enjoying the solitude and peace.

Don't fight me, lad! I need you to relax, let this energy flow into you. I will do the work you lay here and take it.

Anton tried to do as he was told, but his instinct wanted to rebel.

Relax, don't fight. The mental voice gave a grunt, and Anton felt something change, something new in the flow. *What have they done, what is this?* The healer sounded confused, then he relaxed. Anton could mentally feel him adjusting to energy that was different from the life force. *Easy, easy.* The mental voice was talking to itself. *This is more powerful than anything. Don't grasp for it, lad, let it flow at its own pace. Otherwise, it will burn you and me out.*

As Anton reached for the energy, a flash showed him the energy trail. The Spirits of Wintermist were channeling their own energy to the master healer. Power from the positive plain of the abyss filled Anton.

Suddenly, the trance was gone. Sight, sound, and smells rushed at Anton. He was engulfed with the buzz of conversation, the rustling of cloth, and the gentle sound of the falls. He heard no singing. No crystalline voices greeted him. Then a hand was on his shoulders.

"They await you," Ambrus said.

Anton sat up, expecting a wave of dizziness, but nothing happened. He felt alive, energized, and ready to do what needed to be done. He looked at CynLisa and Ambrus.

"I'm ready." His voice was strong, clear, and without any sign of slurring. "Do you have the flower?" There was no time to waste. He didn't know how long this was going to last, how long before the positive energy of the abyss would be used up, and he would once more be near death.

Ambrus shoved the potted red elvish flower in Anton's hand. "You can do it. Hold your faith and show your love."

Anton smiled at Ambrus, then plucked the flower. He handed the pot to CynLisa. "I will vindicate Master Jedrowler's faith in me."

The group parted, and Anton stepped onto Wintermist Bridge. He kept his eyes focused on the far side, on the solid ground there. His eyes drifted neither right nor left. He looked at the solid rock of the bridge and the base of the twin spirals. He forced from his mind the vision Ambrus had of the bridge falling and told himself there was no way the solid rock of the bridge could fail.

His legs trembled, his stomach lurched, and sweat beaded his forehead. Despite the coolness of the mist, Anton felt hot, his mouth dry. He faced the falls. He watched the water slip over the edge. The roar magnified in his mind a hundred fold. He felt the hum of the bridge through his feet, the tremor running back and forth as the bridge resonated with the sound of the falls. He felt the bridge sway and give a lurch as it dropped. For a moment, he almost lost his footing. He stared at the opening from which people made their leaps and watched the stone railing quiver. He heard and felt the creak as somewhere a small imperfection gave way and a vital section of the bridge moved.

With jerky movements, he approached the opening. He had to get there before the bridge collapsed completely. For the spell to work, he needed to leap on his own, not be thrown into the gorge by the collapse.

Anton felt the underside of the bridge break away. First, minor pieces tumbled toward the river, then large chunks started falling. Each chunk caused more to follow as their separation sent up vibrations, vibrations causing the bonds that held the rock together to separate. He heard the rocks hitting the water. The swaying caused him to tumble, almost took him to his knees. Only his own will and determination kept him upright. He could see the underside of the bridge slowly dissolving as more rock separated and fell three hundred feet to the river.

Anton felt the bridge give a lurch. His stomach flipped, and he was thankful he had not eaten. The temperature was starting to rise, and he wiped perspiration from his forehead. His sweat drenched his robe.

Anton watched a bird fly overhead in panic. He tasted the fear in the bird's flight, tasted blood where he had bit his lip. He stopped and clenched his fist to his side. He shook as he tried to fight down his fear, fear of what would happen when the bridge fell. When the solid rock bridge tumbled into the gorge, stone by broken stone, he knew his broken body would be bashed by the rubble as he plummeted to the river.

He looked ahead at the lip of the leap platform, looked at the water, failed to see the lake. He saw the frothing white water falling over the edge. The water striking the river with such force that it smashed into mist. What will the fall do to him? He staggered once more as his stomach fell and his head swam. His ears roared with the shattering of the bridge. He closed his eyes and screamed, dropping to his knees.

Anton knelt on the bridge, his heart racing and his breath ragged. He squeezed his eyes shut as he trembled, shaking like a leaf in the breeze. He bent forward, touching his head to the cool stone, trying to gather his thoughts. He felt the energy from the positive plain leaving him, rushing from him as he consumed it in his panic.

And he felt no magic.

His fear of the bridge, no, of the height, had driven the magic away.

The bridge is solid. This is all in your mind. Have faith in yourself. Have faith in yourself. Have faith in yourself.

Anton repeated the phrase over and over, driving the truth through his fear. He turned it into a mantra. His heart slowed, and his breathing became easier. His stomach settled. Then he started to laugh. He laughed as he heard Master Jedrowler's voice. *A mind healer told me they sometimes try to desensitize a person on their phobias by making them into outlandish characters of real life.*

An ant the size of a wolfhound. The rocks of the bridge falling, with him leaping from rock to rock, sailing the air on solid rock. He was standing on the edge of the plateau, and the height reached up and . . . tickled him. Anton laughed as slowly the panic left him.

He felt the magic and slipped into a light trance, the trance he needed for the spell.

Pulling himself up, Anton slowly stood. He looked at the falls and saw the water slipping from shimmering Lake Mead. Slowly, in exact timed steps, he approached the edge of the bridge. As he got closer, he lifted his arms, the elvish flower in his right hand. With sure lips, he started the spell of calling.

Stepping up to the platform, he finished his spell and looked into the mist. Only a slight touch of vertigo reached him as he looked at the dancing mist. He smiled and held out the flower. It was time for the spell of binding. As the spell rang out, it was answered. From deep within the mist, a crystalline voice echo tinged with a feminine touch and reached his ears. The two spells intertwined and settled over him. Slowly, he allowed himself to bind with the Spirits.

At Anton's feet laid the harness for the leap, coiled and ready to be used. He leaned forward into the abyss.

As he fell, Anton released the flower and spoke the prayer for lovers and friends. As in Jedrowler's notes, he watched the flower dissolve, becoming part of the mist. The mist streamed by, and he watched the Spirits start their dance. Their song of welcome filled his ears.

This was how it meant to be accepted by the land, by the Spirits. He needed to prove his devotion and his faith. The flower was the symbol of devotion and the leap. With no safety rope, it was the sign of faith.

The Spirits envelope Anton, and he felt the love, the caring. His vision was filled with the white of the falls, the mist. Before him was the first Spirit, the one from which all other Spirits sprang. It was mother, it was father, and he reached for him, pulling him in as her own offspring. The young human mage surrendered to the loving embrace. The experience of Jedrowler's own leap came to him, magnified by the strength of the spell that connected them.

Welcome, child. It wasn't words. It wasn't images. Calling it a feeling would have been wrong. It was part of him. He was part of them. He reached out and touched her, touched all that came through her. And understanding flooded him.

We welcome you and all that is part of you. We have waited many of your centuries since the first of your people arrived. You showed us the light, led us from the darkness.

Images flashed through Anton, images of the Spirits as the wraiths, their deeds at the hands of the one they called Legion. The horror of what they did passed through him. Feelings filled him, not the feelings of the Wraiths, but the feelings of the Spirits, the sadness for what they had done. He tried to return his own feelings to let them know it wasn't their fault, that they were not responsible. What was done was committed by creatures they are not.

It was us. We can never allow it to be thought otherwise. To blame others means we do not take responsibility for what we did. We cannot forget. For if we do, then we are doomed to repeat it, to surrender to Legion when he returns.

Anton was now the Spirits. He was now the land. Through his channels, he was part of the circle. The spells of binding that had been cast in every step of the ceremonies were now combining, bring all of them together. For one brief moment, he feared that they would become another Legion, the reincarnation of that ancient evil.

Legion was not evil, just unclean. Legion's origin was for a noble purpose. The result is what became evil.

Legion was defeated, but not destroyed. Even now, he sleeps to the north, but his slumber is disturbed. We have felt his waking touch. We do not wish to become his means of torture, his harbingers of horror. We have waited for you, for you and the other that has ascended. You are our salvation.

Anton flexed his channels, felt the power of the land flow through him, felt the way he could manipulate the physical realm. He felt the power of all within the circle, felt how he could draw on their abilities to augment his own. All this he could make as one, just as Legion had.

Legion is many who became one. Legion lost his individuality. You refused to allow that. Unity is one who is many. Unity's strengths reside in the individual. You are Unity.

Anton knew what the Spirits said was true. He was more than a channel. He was the manifestation of Unity. Even now, all members of the circle, all of the land, every Spirit, every being, came to be Unity.

Only Unity can defeat Legion. Only Unity can stop the pawns of Legion. We are one who is many.

He was Unity.

We have proven we can resist the Legion effect. We have come together to help the people, to heal the land, to fight Legion. Unity reached within himself, drew upon the magic. Swirling around him, the wind lifted him from the gorge, the mist parted, and he broke into sunlight.

The mages and citizens around the bridge gasped as he emerged. He spun and saw the queen's men riding hard toward Wintermist Bridge and the wall beyond. They were at the outskirts of Wintermist, and Unity knew they would not reach Wintermist Wall in time.

As he commanded the wind to turn him, he saw along the wall smoke curling from the fires. Men running back and forth, preparing to defend the wall.

Unity commanded the wind to carry him to the plateau of Wintermist School. As he soared through the air, he looked past the wall to the invading army. Thousands of men were closing on the wall. He could hear their battle cries.

"Not this day, servants of Legion!" His voice rang across the battlefield, and all stopped and stared. "We are Unity, and this is our land! You have destroyed enough, killed enough. Return to your accursed master, begone to the plains of hell!"

Unity was not bothered by the Ancient Magic. He was the Ancient Magic, and he used that magic. Around the warriors of Terrapin Xon, the air came alive. Heat burst in their face, and cold froze their limbs. Those not immediately affected turned and in a panic rushed about, many grabbing horses. Others with stronger leaders were mustering to carry on the attack. They had a mission.

Unity reached and pushed the ground. The maw of the land zigzagged among the enemy troops, hundreds falling to their death. Slapping his hands together, Unity rejoined the land, making the soldiers part of the land for eternity.

Unity's senses burned as he felt the enemy to the east. The people of the land were there, defending, fighting, and dying for the land. Unity brought the river up, and it washed over the banks, sweeping along the eastern side. As it receded to its natural course, black forms bobbed on the surface. The defenders stared, many dropping and thanking their god.

Anton felt the last of the energy give way. He looked across the land and saw the enemy in turmoil. Here and there, some were trying to become organized to counterstrike. He could see and sense the users of the Unseen Forces trying to comprehend.

As Unity faded, he took the Ancient Magic with him, leaving Terrapin Xon's Force Shapers defenseless. Given time, the enemy would regroup and resume the attack. But the defenders of Wintermist, the individuals of Unity, the mages, nor the Spirits of Wintermist would allow it.

With the last of his energy, Anton lifted himself from the mountainside and settled in the waiting arms of the mages and fighters on the wall of Wintermist.

"The lad did it!" Xantrawler turned to Duncan and the Lord Marshal, "He has given us what we needed. Duncan, assemble your men and take care of any of those foolish enough to think they can still conquer us. Lord Marshal, take your knights and complete your mission, rescue General Klaydon."

Both men nodded. The Lord Marshal hurried down the stairs while Duncan called his men to assemble. Turning, the weaponsmaster watched Mage Master Gardner hurrying down the parapet, toward the crowd of mages supporting Anton. "Get us a healer up here now!" the Mage Master snapped.

Xantrawler yelled to a messenger who spurred her horse toward the bridge. Only then did he look at what was on the wall. The battlement was littered with the dead, many charred by the dragon's breath. Near Duncan's ballista, fried dragon meat clung to the walls and floor. Some of the temple guards moved past him and hurried down the stairs. Other soldiers assembled along the wall to replace Duncan's men.

Xantrawler looked to the gatehouse exit and smiled as he watched his friend take the reins of the horse waiting for him. The hero of the Valley was back, and there would be new songs sung of this day, sung of Duncan Dragonslayer.

The weaponsmaster laughed.

Duncan smiled when he saw the large number of men in his company. That meant he lost only a small amount. With the battle they went through, that was a small miracle in itself. Compared to the wall, this mop-up expedition should be easy. He would not let his guard down.

As he settled in his saddle, ten mounted temple guards approached.

"By the wishes of Odium, we are placed at your command, Weaponsmaster Pentock."

Duncan bowed. "I am doubly blessed to be so honored. Blessed be Odium. With his warriors, the day shall be ours."

Duncan prepared to signal for the portcullis to be raised when he was surrounded by young lads holding polearms. He looked them over, then spoke to Joshua,

"This is dangerous, lad. It would be best if you and your command stayed behind."

Joshua looked at the weaponsmaster, his lips set in a way familiar to Duncan. "We are volunteers, sir. The last thing my father and his men did was swear their allegiance to you. His honor demanded for him to protect you, and he did. With his dying breath, he kept you safe. Will you have me disgrace my father by not following our family's oath to you?"

Duncan looked at Joshua, and no longer saw a lad. As with many, he had left childhood behind. An innocence was lost, one never to be found again. Duncan too lost his innocence many years ago in a valley of honor. He dreamed for the day when all could retain their innocence. For now, men and women like him, like Xantrawler and Sergeant Kentell, young lads like Joshua, older lads like the Lord

Marshal, and even Mage Anton would continue to sacrifice theirs so others may retain what innocence and freedom they have.

"As you wish, Wheatfield." Duncan looked at Josh's command.

"I'm sorry. There is only eight, sir."

A lone temple guard rode up to Josh. "By Odium's command, there shall be nine. As long as the Nine exists, Odium shall ride with them."

Josh softly said, "The Nine shall ride." He returned his gaze to the weaponsmaster and brought his fist over his heart. The other eight followed his lead. "By our honor, we pledge ourselves to Duncan of Pentock!"

"So say we all!"

"Heard and bound!"

Duncan knew this time there would be no future regrets.

Chapter Thirty-One

Xantrawler stepped into the courtyard and ran a weary hand over his face. The sun was behind the mage school, placing a halo around the sentinel. In the shadow, the chill of evening was settling in, but it wasn't the cold that caused him to shiver.

The courtyard was filled with injured fighters. They were not serious enough to be moved to the impromptu healer's hall set up in the lower level of the gatehouse. The Master Healer and the healers that had accompanied the queen's men were inside, trying to save lives. Out of sight of the injured men were the unmoving bodies of the defenders who had fallen. For Xantrawler, there were too many young, too many old.

This was supposed to be a posting where the old could retire and still feel useful. It was a posting where the young could learn to be soldiers, with little risk of dying before they learned their trade. Despite their age and regardless of their inexperience, these men had done well. Xantrawler was proud of each and every one of them.

Off to the side, the queen's men stood guard over captured enemy troops. Without their armor, they no longer were the ferocious invaders from the north.

The afternoon had been filled with dispatching companies of the queen's soldiers to round up prisoners. Already a number of enemy captains and mages had been brought in. The general of the queen's men took the captains for questioning. Many of the enemy mages were gibbering idiots, and the rest cowered at the sight of Mage Master Gardner and his mages.

The Lord Marshal had ridden in. He only had a few men with him. The rest had volunteered to stay with General Klaydon and assist with hunting down any stragglers. The general did send his regards to Xantrawler and promised to visit with him before they headed for the North Wall.

A short time ago, three wagons from the city arrived, and Xantrawler smelled the aroma of roasted meat emanating from one of them. From another wagon, kegs of ale were handed out, and he could see fresh loaves of bread being tossed about. He heard a feminine voice and made a mental note.

Xantrawler silently sent thanks to the ones who showed their appreciation in such fashion. What they considered a small contribution went far for the morale of the men. He would have to talk to his officers and noncoms about dropping hints to the men about patronizing certain establishments.

The clatter of hooves within the gatehouse tunnel caused Xantrawler to turn.

Duncan entered the courtyard. He was dirty, bruised, and looked exhausted. The same could be said of the rest of his men. Next to Duncan and surrounded by half of the new Nine rode a stranger, his hands bound to the pommel of his saddle. Weapons and helm had been stripped. He wore simple clothing with no insignia of rank or company. He was a bearded man, rugged face with lines and a deep tan that showed that most of his life was spent outdoors.

Duncan called a halt, dismounted, and walked up to Xantrawler. The captured enemy was led on his horse. The man held his head up, refusing to acknowledge total defeat.

Duncan saluted Xantrawler and said, “May I present Ulla Thrawt, Warlord to King Rathveil of Terrapin Xon.”

“That is quite a catch.”

"And if it wasn't for one of the mages that accompanied us, I would not know that. It seems the good warlord does not believe in learning to speak our barbarian tongue."

Xantrawler looked at the warlord. "Sorry to disappoint you, but us barbarians have won."

"You lead these fighters?"

"I am Weaponsmaster Xantrawler in command of the Wintermist Wall."

The warlord bowed his head. "My sword would be yours, Weaponsmaster. But this fighter managed to disarm me."

"Duncan is a Weaponsmaster, the best I have ever trained."

The warlord turned to Duncan and bowed. "I should have known. You are a good leader. I watched your men protect your flanks as we battled. Young though they be, they were willing to lay down their life for you. A common thug does not command that degree of loyalty. It's a pity this war must now turn into a protracted engagement. I would have welcomed the likes of you into my army."

"Warlord, I wish this war to be over now. I am too old to see so many young people die on both sides."

"Weaponsmaster, you have the wisdom of our people. You would have made a good war chief. Ah, but those days are past. Perhaps when this is all over, I will visit, and we can exchange stories."

Xantrawler said, "When peace is made, I would welcome a visit from you to our country."

"Ha, this is just one engagement. The war is not over. Your men are good, but we have a destiny foretold in the Sacred Scrolls. This land will be ours, and King Rathveil will be your ruler. You will see. He is a kind and generous ruler."

"Warlord Thrawt, I would love to continue this banter, but night is coming, and I'm sure these men would prefer to take you to the duke's keep." Xantrawler signaled a squad of men-at-arms. "So I will bid you good evening watch."

As Warlord Thrawt was led away, Duncan ordered his men to dismount and stand down. After seeing to his horse, he returned to Xantrawler.

"How bad is it out there?" Xantrawler asked.

"The land will recover. They did little damage, and I saw lots of livestock wandering the countryside. For invaders, they had better manners than some of our own people."

Xantrawler nodded. "You can brief me in the morning. Before you head to your barracks, why don't you stop at that wagon over there. I think someone would like to see you."

Duncan gave a wide smile, hugged his friend, and headed for the indicated wagon. As he approached, he heard a familiar voice admonishing the soldiers. He looked at Sasha's face in the torch light, watching how the flickering flame highlighted the red of her hair, the curve of her nose, and the splashes of freckles across her checks. He laughed as she slapped the hand of an over eager soldier.

Sasha turned toward the laughter. "Laugh churr and you will . . ." Her mouth stayed opened. She gasped, then stood straight. Smoothing her dress, she tried to hang onto her composure. "Weaponsmaster, it's good to see you back safely."

Duncan chuckled. "It's good to see you, Sasha. Would you like to take a walk?"

"Why, dear sir, what would people say?"

"Oh, go on, Sasha, I'm sure the weaponsmaster's intentions are more than honorable," a soldier called out with anonymity within the crowd. Sasha blushed. As she took Duncan's arm, a couple of soldiers started to make some good humor comments, but a look from Sasha stopped them. Their fear of their weaponsmaster paled next to their fear of Sasha.

The two walked in silence. No words were needed. They could sense each other's fear. Sasha had believed she would never see the weaponsmaster again. She looked at him and smiled. "Duncan Pentock, I don't know what I will do with you. You come to town, turn my world upside down, and change my opinion on sword swingers, then go off and try to get yourself killed."

"Part of the job."

"No," she said softly. She put her other hand on his arm and stepped closer. "What you did is not part of the job, it's part of you. You are one of the few people in this world who honestly cares. That's why you had such a hard time with the Nine. It took time, but your good sense overcame your grief."

Duncan looked in her eyes. "Well, someone knocked it back in me." He rubbed the side of his face. "I've had Underdwellers hit softer."

Sasha slapped his arm. "I swear! What am I going to do with you . . . you sword swinger!"

Duncan spun her around, then pulled her close and held her head in his hands. "Tell me your favorite flower."

Sasha let herself become lost in his eyes as her lip trembled.

"I need to know. It's the spring leap I want to do, isn't it?"

Sasha didn't say anything. She didn't dare. She last cried when her mother died. Now she felt her eyes well up. Only this time, they weren't tears of sorrow.

"Duncan." She wrapped her arms around the Weaponsmaster and held him tight. As the last rays of the sun cast a golden glow across the far end of the lake, Duncan lowered his head, and his lips met Sasha's.

Anton sat in a cushioned chair looking out the window. With his fear of heights conquered, he looked at the sight Mage Jedrowler use to spend hours admiring. He understood why the mage loved this room.

It had taken some convincing to get the Master Healer to allow him to sit here and not return to his bed. Anton needed to see that everything was safe with the Spirits. He needed this contact, needed his own eyes to see that the Spirits were safe, not just feel through his connection.

He understood the spell. For the spell to be complete, the two channels had to join as one. He was as much a part of the Spirits as they were a part of him. The land was a part of the Spirits, and the people of the circle were a part of him. In the first part, the Spirits entered them, entered him. The circle accepted the Spirits through him, their channel.

With the second phase, he and the Spirits became one. Then the land accepted the circle through him and the Spirits. With his leap of faith, he showed he was willing to accept the responsibility of this union. He felt everyone and everything in the union. The people of the circle, the deer who was taking an evening drink at a stream near the dwarvish mine, a tree that no longer drank sap, its last season now passed. He felt the maple giving up the last of their sap for maple syrup, the return of the field flowers. He was Unity.

More people would join the Union, and as they did, the bonds of Unity would strengthen. The risk of the Legion effect would recede. Each individual would add to the bond. Unity, one who was many.

Somehow, Anton thought, this is what the original Nacromages wanted. They didn't mean to create a Legion. They wanted to protect their people. It was their underestimation of the minor gods and their lack of understanding of magic that brought about their error.

That and their lack of the guiding love of the Spirits.

Anton reached for the goblet of wine the Master Healer had brought. He knew the healer had laced the drink with medicine to make him sleep, but he didn't care. It was time to rest. Tomorrow was a new day, and after he recovered, he would finish fulfilling Mage Jedrowler's dream.

As the medication started to work, his mind drifted; and for a moment, he was in the mist. A passing thought whispered in his ear. It wasn't just Jedrowler's dream, but the Spirit's desire, their wish to repay the population of Mead for the faith they had given. To protect them from the return of the wraiths.

As his eyes closed, Anton felt a warm, loving hand glide across his face. He felt the love of a mother, the pride of a father. For a moment, just as sleep took him, he saw the bearded face of his friend.

As the sun disappeared, the Spirits descended into the heart of the falls. Within the mist, they greeted each other. They shared their joy, shared the emotions they had received from the people. They allowed the energy of the positive plain of the abyss to fill them.

As they came together, they danced, and they sang. Their crystal voices filled the falls with their joy. On Wintermist Bridge, travelers paused. They heard the roar of the falls and in the background a crystal song. They left the bridge with a lighter heart. For some, the grief at the loss of a friend or a loved one eased. They felt as if they had just poured their heart out to their best friend, who in turn filled the empty place with love.

The Patriarch of the Spirits gathered his children. She let them know they had done well, that thanks to them they were safe from the threat of Legion.

Within the perpetual milky white of the falls, the Spirits turned and looked downstream. They saw the flickering shape of a human, his long beard flowed in the breeze, his mage robe fluttered, and a smile played on his face.

The leader of the Spirits sent the combined thanks to the apparition, to an old friend.

For the first time in eons, since the defeat of Legion, the Spirits of Wintermist bowed to another being.

This time it was out of love.

THE END